SECRET
LOVE 3

THE SAGA DON'T STOP

By

LaShane Moore

Starting over is not so bad:

some love is not meant to stay

MOOREHOUSE BOOKS   CALIFORNIA

MOOREHOUSE BOOKS

This is a Fiction book. It is all a product of the author's imagination, the stories that take place in the book happens in today everyday life. Any resemblance to actual events or persons living or dead is coincidental.

Warning: Adult Content. This is a story of erotic fiction and is for Adult Readers Only. The Book contains substantial sexually explicit scenes and graphic language.

ISBN#978-0-9986208-3-1

Cover Design by Darrell Frye

To all my readers that love this Secret Love Series this is for you.

In This Book!!!!!

Katrina brings the *Smarts* and the *Intelligence*.

Mike brings the steamy *Romance* and the sexy *Erotic* scenes.

Gary brings the *Crazy Secrets* and his *Unthoughtful Actions*.

Brandy brings the *Funny Juicy Secrets* and the *Juicy Drama*.

With the four characters above, plus the rest of the characters, this book will give you plenty of entertainment that will keep you on the edge of your seat. But not just that, it's also inspiring and motivating.

Recap from Secret Love 1 & 2

Gary and Katrina's relationship started when they were high school sweethearts. They were married at eighteen years of age. Both shared the same interest in Real Estate, took their courses at the same time, and were hired at the same time, but through different Real Estate companies. Together, the two were a team that made lots of money, and in no time, they bought a big house for themselves.

The two were living a picture-perfect life until early one morning when Katrina received a phone call from her baby sister because she needed somewhere to stay for a while. Not thinking twice about it, Katrina let her stay with her and her husband. A few weeks passed and that night he was still trying to get him some from his wife.

"Hey baby, can your husband get some loving tonight?" he'd asked.

Lying down in bed next to him she whispered, "Babe, I'm tired. I've been selling houses all day, and I have another client at eight in the morning."

"Please Katrina, you said the same thing the other night, and the week before, I just can't get a little bit?" he asked with his firm deep voice.

"Not tonight babe," Katrina told him.

That night just like many other nights lately, he was left up to using his hand, before he closed his eyes. Although he was becoming used to not getting intimate every night lately, he didn't want to get use to it, but with Katrina, Katrina left him no other choice. By that next morning he couldn't resist it. He sighed softly and slid in bed with her sister Brandy. He slowly began grabbing her by the hips and as he pulls her back into him, he went in deeper every time. It didn't bother him that she was asleep still, just after a few pumps is when she had awakened. She thought she was dreaming the dream of her life and it felt so real, she didn't want to awake from it. Then she thought while her eyes were still closed that her sister had let her guy friend Chris back in before leaving for work. As he continued gripping her body, he continued going in from behind. Gripping her breast when he started going faster, he kept adjusting the speed from slower than back too fast. As he pushed down in her deeper, it was a feeling she was not prepared for. The sound of her moan was his hint to keep going. Neither of the two wanted to part from each other's enjoyment, especially after making each other's toes curl, moan, and body dripping wet the way that they were.

Once Brandy's eyes had opened all the way is when they were done and seeing it wasn't her friend Chris, her eyes got big. It was Gary. Brandy didn't know how Gary could think he could just slide his dick in her, sticking it inside her while she's asleep, or just putting it in her for that matter. Brandy couldn't believe her sister's husband had no shame, but why her? She wondered to fucking have an affair with him.

"Why me Gary?" Brandy asked him.

"Brandy, I was horny and you were just lying there. I saw your body hanging half way out your covers, and I instantly became aroused. It hardened so quick from a glimpse of you is why I had too."

It had only taken a brief glance before that loyal husband wasn't so loyal anymore. She couldn't believe he'd admitted that to her. Brandy didn't know how to start, or where to start to tell him to leave her alone, and she sure as hell didn't know how to tell Katrina. She knew she couldn't call it rape due to the enjoyment she actually just had herself, waking up her body parts from not being active in a while. *A little quickie, I will keep this secret I'm not trying to have my sister lose her mind and blame me for everything all for ten minutes of sex*, she thought. Trying to ignore him since the first encounter didn't last long for her. Brandy couldn't pull herself to tell him to stop.

Three years later, Katrina found out a secret that had been withheld from her. She learned her three-year-old niece is actually her stepdaughter due to an affair her husband and her sister had four years ago.

It was at Katrina's niece's three year old Birthday Party. An hour or so into the party her niece ran past saying "Daddy, Daddy!" Katrina knew Chris was still inside. Her eyes turned around and looked and it was her husband. She just knew she heard her niece's voice saying daddy daddy. She was thinking she didn't hear what she thought she heard. Katrina was kind of curious then. She went and asked Brandy what was up with her niece calling her husband daddy. Brandy just looked at her silently. Without any hesitation she had to tell her, it was now already out, no more keeping it to a secret. Before anything could settle quickly Katrina started taking off on her sister, punching her in the face. Then Karina started kicking his ass too. Katrina was so devastated feeling like a fool she left out crying. She stopped by the store to pick up some new locks and keys went home and changed all the locks, and put him out.

After a five-year separation, Katrina decided to reunite for the sake of their own daughter, giving her husband another chance at their marriage.

This is how the beginning to the end happened

Gary received an unexpected phone call- the one he had been waiting on for years. She began by saying, "Hello, Gary. This is Katrina." Topping it off, she told him he could come back to his family. He decided he wasn't going to ever let anyone get in between his thoughts again. He wasn't trying to do anything to mess up again.

After a year of trying Katrina's love for him still wasn't the same. She contacted Mike and he came over. Gary arrived home wondering who's car was in their driveway. Gary hopped out the car. He couldn't wait to ask Katrina who's car it was. Gary entered through the garage, walked through the kitchen and into the living room. He saw Katrina standing their looking at him.

"Hey Katrina, who's car is that?" he pointed towards the drive way. He heard an unexpected voice from behind. He turned around and saw a Rasta dude with dreads. Suddenly, Gary's eyes scrunched up; his eyebrows were going inward creating a mad look.

"What the hell is this?"

"Baby, tell him," Mike sounded.

"What the hell do you mean baby?"

Katrina hesitated in answering.

"Tell me what!" Gary shouted angrily. "What is this Katrina?" Gary continued asking while pointing at Mike.

"Gary, I'm sorry. I tried, but I can't do this anymore. It's not working out. I don't want to do this anymore."

"Katrina. No! Please, don't do this," Gary shouted. A tear ran down his face, but Katrina was serious and shortly after Gary left the house. Gary had to go back to his boy Mikey's house until his money was right and to get his own again. It took time, but Gary moved out and into his own place along with meeting another woman named Asia. They dated and in less than a year, he married her.

Prologue

Paula was back on top. As the bed held her up, she was going up and down on it. It was feeling so good she looked down at it, then she looked back up at him. Paula was riding him so gentle for a long while, then shortly the moans sounded from her mouth. In seconds she was getting louder. She was feeling a sensation go through her body and then her speed picked up and his grip on her back kept them close. She felt all of him inside. She stopped and the look into his eyes was so intense. He was silent, but his actions didn't say stop.

Moments later he rolled her back over so he could get back on top of her. His stroke inside her was steady and the bed kept hitting the wall. Suddenly, he began to go faster. She then started shoving him to slow down to stop the knocking noises of the headboard hitting the wall. Gary was so into it, and he wasn't listening. Apparently, he will be the one to put their son back to sleep once he wakes up she thought to herself. He kept plunging into her going in deeper and deeper. The feeling he was feeling he couldn't control. He then released a breath; she knew at that moment that meant he was more than likely done. This night visit turned into another long, wild, crazy, unexpected but fun time as before, but she loved every bit of it. They laid there for a while, then he sleds her arm off his chest to get up. He stood to his feet. She quickly sat up looking at him.

"Babe, where you going? She asked him. "I thought maybe you would stay until the morning."

"You know I have to go home to my wife."

"You can lie to her and say you fell asleep at your boy's house after having way too many drinks."

"Man Paula, I don't want to keep jeopardizing my marriage!"

"Again with that talk huh."

"This will be our secret, how is she going to find out?" Paula then pressed her lips up against his lips and pecked them. "I want you," she whispered looking into his eyes that were already looking back at her without saying a word.

"You just had me."

"You know what I'm talking about!"

"I'm not about to go there with you tonight." He put back on his shoes and grabbed his jacket.

"Alright, Paula bye," He looked at her and said.

"No, you are not leaving."

"Yeah, I am."

"I want you to stay!"

"I told you before I came I couldn't, so don't act like I didn't tell you this already!"

"Alright, bye Paula," he said again.

"Alright bye Paula, I don't think so, I want you to stay." She kissed the side of his face, he hugged her, and then he sat back down on the bed. Paula wouldn't accept a NO from him, she knew he would give in because she knew him. He took off his shoes and sat his jacket back down.

"Paula, I hope you haven't been telling your friends and your family that we are back seeing each other, you and I both know it's just sex and our son and that's it."

Paula raised her eyebrows. "Okay," she said.

"I'm for real Paula."

"Yeah, this will be our little secret like I told you already."

"Alright, I am trusting in you."

"Yeah, please do!"

They were tired so they went and lie down underneath the covers and passed out.

Later in the night and *"Wham"* was the sound of their son crying as he woke up. She hopped up looking around, wondering why she the only one getting up, she knows Gary ass heard the same damn noise, so why isn't he getting up. Damn. No. What the fuck. It was just her in the bed by herself, *Paula was dreaming.* But it felt so real. It was just a dream. Paula had woken up from a dream thinking she were actually just making love and sleeping with Gary. She sat all the way up confused, it felt like it had actually happened for real. Damn, she was even wet down there.

That's what got her up and out the bed. She did not want to get out of her California King sized bed so early this morning got drunk last night she woke up with a hangover. Mother's duties sure did not have time to activate it was a 24-7 type of thing. She gets up to tend to her son, then went back to sleep. Once she had the time to call Gary she did. Paula dialed Gary's cell phone.

Gary was out having a bit to eat at his favorite Mexican spot. Usually he always orders to go, but this time he had time to sit. He didn't have another client for another hour, so he has time to kill. Gary's cell started buzzing it was on vibrate. He grabbed his phone from off the table and it was Paula.

"Hey, Paula what's up!"

"Hey babe," she sounded.

"What's going on?"

"Oh nothing, just had this crazy ass dream last night. That shit about us seemed so real. I woke up wet down there and everything, that was crazy!"

"Yeah, that is crazy."

"Besides that, I was just thinking about you and our great time we shared the other night and I can't wait to have some of that good loving again."

"Paula, we can't keep on doing that, I told you I don't want to keep jeopardizing my marriage!"

"I told you this will be our secret!"

"Paula I can't, when I come I just want to only chill with my son, we can chill too, just no more sex!"

"That's a problem."

"Paula, I can't!"

"But you already did, why stop now?"

He sat there with his cell stuck to his ear mad at himself for even getting involved with her ass like that. He should have known this was going to happen to deal with her ass again, but he was not prepared for it to actually happen.

"Ummm, you over there quiet so this means I'll see you tonight," she responded.

"Not tonight, tonight is not a good night."

"Ok then, tomorrow night and I'm not taking "No." It's either tonight or tomorrow night, so which one is it?"

"Tomorrow," he told her.

Paula held the phone grinning, "Okay then, I will see you tomorrow."

"Alright." he said so dryly.

Yeah, if he know better he would keep this going, our little secret won't be a secret for too much longer if he doesn't give me what I want, she thought to herself.

"Bye Gary."

"Alright." they hung up.

He didn't intend on having a drink in the middle of the day, he was only there to have lunch, but after that conversation with Paula, a drink right now was much needed. Gary waved his hand in the air as he got the server attention.

"Yes, sir do you need me to get you anything?"

"Yes please, I would like to order a drink!"

The waiter grinned at him, "Yes, of course, what drink would you like to order?"

"I need a shot of Hennessey."

"Ok, no problem sir, coming right on up."

Minutes later the server brought back his Hennessey. He sat there with his shot thinking what he about to do. After taking his shot he still didn't know. But it was already that time and he needed to get working.

Later that evening Asia began to hear Gary, as he walked in the house she was already smiling. She waited all day to see this face. "Hi baby, so how was your day today?" she asked him.

"It was a good day sweetie."

"Baby, I talked to your dad earlier and your daddy is crazy!" he laughed.

She laughed. "Well, you better get used to it babe, you're stuck with me now."

Later that night, Gary looked over looking at his wife while lying in bed as she slept. He couldn't sleep too much on his mind with Paula, his son, and Paula trying to make him have sex with her. It was just too much and still trying to act normal like nothing going on. That next morning waking up he was up staring at her.

"Baby you okay?" she asked.

"Umm, remember we met at a grocery store and then our first date was at a bar, we danced, then a week later we went out to breakfast."

"Yeah," she smiled looking into his eyes. Their conversation was interrupted as Gary's cell began to ring. He was hoping it wasn't Paula's ass calling him this morning.

Before he answered, he noticed the number wasn't hers. "Hello," he answered.

"Hey, Gary did I call too early?"

"May I ask who I'm speaking with, I don't have this number stored?"

"Oh, this is LaShawnda. It's been a long minute since we last talked," she chuckled.

"Oh yeah, how are you?" he asked.

"I'm fine, it's been a long while since we last talked. It's good to hear your voice, so how have you been?"

"I'm good, I'm married now."

"Oh, oh I'm sorry!"

"Oh no, it's fine," he told her.

"Oh, I see why you didn't remember me," she laughed.

"Oh, it's not like that. I just cleaned out my phone after I got married."

"Well, congratulations to you."

"Thanks, alright bye," Gary said.

"Oh, and it was good hearing from you again!"

"Same here, bye and have a good one." They hung up.

Before Gary could even say who he was just on the phone with, Asia asked, "Who in the hell was that!"

"That was LaShawnda, an old friend I had met at the bar."

"An old friend huh, and I hope it wasn't the same bar you took me too."

CHAPTER

1

Asia and Gary

It's Monday Evening; what a beautiful day this has been, blue skies, a cool breeze, not hot, it was still just right and now to finally kick off these shoes is what Asia couldn't wait to do, her feet were talking to her. When Asia made it home she first checked the mailbox, grabbing all the mail inside. Then, second, she walked into the house with her purse, cell phone, the mail and the junk mail in her hand. Once she got inside, the third thing she did and couldn't wait to do was kick off her heels. Then she went to the kitchen, poured herself some juice, and sat at the dining room table looking through the mail. She took a sip of her juice then sat her cup down on the table, *"nothing but bills,"* she said to herself, but then she saw Gary had mail from Laboratory Corporation. She took a deep breath; she began holding her chest; she couldn't believe it.

"What the fuck?" She mumbled as she continued looking through the mail. *Why in the hell is he receiving letters from the DNA Clinic and now child support*, she wondered. This shit didn't make things any better just three days ago he had gotten a random call from a woman. She didn't want to open his mail, even though she felt she had every right to at that moment. Instead, she called him while he was out working. Asia got her cell and dialed Gary holding the phone up to her ear as she stared at the mail in front of her.

"Hey baby," he answered.

"Gary, the DNA Clinic!"

"Huh?" he didn't know what she meant by that.

"Gary, you just received a DNA letter and a Child Support letter."

"What!" he said.

"You heard me! Do I need to open it?" she said.

Over the phone she heard silence. There was a ten-second delay in his response; then he said, "No, I'll open it when I get home."

"You'd better tell me something!"

He tried to think fast, but not fast enough for her. Asia hung up the phone without even waiting to see what he was about to say. She moved from the table to the couch.

All she could do was sit there and stay pissed off. She didn't know what to do or what to think. Sitting there on the couch with her legs crossed, as she waited for him, tears rolled down her face. He ended his day early and went straight home to his wife. He didn't want his wife's mind wondering and shit. Gary arrived home quickly.

As soon as Gary walked in, Asia eyed him. "What the fuck Gary!" She screamed. That's when the argument started.

"Let me see the mail," he told her.

"You been out making more babies or what," she started going off on him. Her head began moving from side to side as she snapped her fingers.

"Let me see," he said calmly.

"Gary, what the fuck is really going on?" she yelled.

"Baby, just calm down!" He shouted.

"How can I calm down?"

"Baby, I need you to just calm down."

"I'm calm now, talk!"

"I ran into my ex. She said she got pregnant and had our son, so I went over to spend time with him."

"GARY YOU HAD NO RIGHT BEING AT THAT WOMAN'S HOUSE!" She yelled.

"I know, I was just seeing my son."

"Huh, so what, you have another child out there?" He was startled by her question. "Please, don't tell me you been cheating on me with another woman and shit!" He was barely able to get a word out his mouth. He didn't want to make things worse by trying to keep up with her tone. Two yelling people were not going to accomplish anything. Gary continued to tell Asia about the son he had with Paula and then just told her something about why the letters came.

"Tell me what really happened when you went to her house!"

"Baby, I'm trying to."

"Now tell me. I'm listening." She was hurt that he hadn't told her before. "Gary, I'm your wife, and even before I became your wife, you were not supposed to have been keeping shit from me. We are in this together." After arguing with him, so many things were going through her mind. Her eyes got watery and she wanted to cry, not much after then the tears came rolling down her face.

"Out the blue, you see your ex, who claims her child is yours, then you go to her house to supposedly see your son, but then you don't tell me shit. Really, yeah you were fucking her, that's the only time people hide shit is when they're fucking around."

"Stop jumping to conclusion's."

"I'm not jumping to conclusions, that's what I think and that's what I know."

"Why would you think something like that?"

After she found out the age of his son, there was no need to calculate the dates back to when she had first met him. That happened before she came along, but just knowing he had been going to her house and she knew nothing about it was a problem. She knew how exes try to come back in the picture somehow. She was determined to find out if he really went over there to only see his son, or if he was cheating on her with Paula. Asia wanted to tell her family or at least her sisters and her girls, but she was too embarrassed. She didn't feel like hearing them say, "I told you not to marry him."

Later in the evening, he wanted to take her out. They needed to at least enjoy their night from all the stress from earlier. Asia didn't want to. She preferred to stay under her blanket watching TV and remain upset, but she went through with it anyway. She was just going to look at it as; at least she wasn't going to have to cook dinner for them that night. At dinner Asia just sat there with a slight attitude while picking at her food.

"Baby, stop looking like that. Let's enjoy this time."

Gary tried to cheer her up and get her mind off the bullshit, as he sat there trying to enjoy himself, but she was making it difficult to look at sitting across the table mad. Although she looks cute, even when she's mad he didn't want her to be mad. He slightly stood up leaning towards Asia, going closer to her face for a kiss. As he got closer she turned her head, she didn't want to kiss.

"I can't get no kiss baby, I'm so sorry baby, please stop being mad at me and say something," he said before he tried kissing her again. Asia was cold with this silent treatment and he didn't like it. She then let him kiss her on the lips, he noticed the smell, and it was the smell of that new perfume he just bought her.

"Oh, I see you're wearing the perfume."

"Yeah, I decided to wear it tonight."

"You like it?"

"Yeah, I love the smell," she responded.

After that kiss is what got her to talk a bit, it wasn't her normal full-fledged conversations, but at least she had a smile on her face, their table wasn't quiet, and they both were now enjoying themselves at dinner.

"Ok, now that you have got me to talk, let's talk about why you have a DNA letter and a fucking child support letter coming to the house Gary?"

"Baby!" he sounded.

"Baby," she repeated. "Baby what, you asked me to talk and this is what I want to talk about."

"Let's not do this at this restaurant," Gary said.

"Do what? We're just talking. Oh now its not do this here at this restaurant, but moments ago you were like *baby say something,* yeah ok."

"Let's just talk about something else and we can talk about that when we get home."

"Really there is nothing else to talk about but that."

Asia went back to being quiet; they sat there and ate their food in silence. Once arriving home she went and sat her purse down on the dresser, then she went straight to the shower. She turned on the shower water and out the blue, the thoughts from earlier came back up in her head and once again, she was back mad as hell. Then she locked and closed the door to the bathroom.

After showering for ten minutes, she dried off and put lotion on her body adding to the softness of her skin. Then she sprayed more perfume on, the new one that Gary had bought. Next then she stepped out the bathroom only with her towel robe on, and walked to their closet and got her sexy lace gown out the dresser drawer. Asia slipped it on and went and got in bed.

Gary leaned over kissing her on her lips then wrapped his arms around her to give her a hug. As he hugged her Gary inhale her scent. It was again the smell of that new perfume that smelled so damn good. Then he got up from off the bed and got in the shower himself. He took a quick shower, five minutes and then he was out. He too got in bed right along with her. She kissed him good night but that's all she did, she was way too mad all over again to do anything else.

"Baby, you're going to sleep on me like that?"

"Yeah, I am Gary."

"Asia, tell me you not still mad."

"No babe, I'm not mad I'm just going to bed."

Gary knew that wasn't the truth she had to be still mad or something. Although Gary was right, Asia didn't feel like playing his games tonight. She knew that he knew that she was still mad at him is why she lied about still being mad at him. He just knew he was about to have another night like the night before. Once Asia got her head all comfortable on her pillow and really closed her eyes and didn't open them, nor did she move from her position after twenty minutes, he knew she was out. So he had no choice but to go to sleep too.

Gary woke up early that morning and Asia was not there beside him. It was not like her to up and leave at the crack of dawn. He hopped out the bed looking all around the house seeing if he see her. But no, she was not there. He went straight for his cell phone to call her; he quickly dialed her cell phone pushing the numbers all fast. Asia saw that it was Gary calling, she just ignored his call and didn't answer.

"*Hey, this is Asia. Sorry you missed me, leave a message and I'll get back,*" beep.

He hung up the phone and dialed her number right back in seconds and again she did not pick up her phone for him.

"Hey, this is Asia. Sorry you missed me, leave a message and I'll get back," beep.

"Baby, I know you saw me calling, please call me back. I want to make sure everything is okay!" he left her a message that time. Then next he texted her saying that he was sorry for not being honest and telling her the truth. He knew if anything she would at least see this text message first before even listening to his voicemail.

She read his text but still didn't respond, she didn't feel like talking right then, she just wanted to think. When Asia finally made it back home she planned to go in quietly and slide back in bed she knew he still wouldn't be waiting up two hours later. As she walked in he was already, sitting waiting on the couch in the living room. The two looked at each other straight into each other's eyes, the first thing he did was walk up to her giving her a hug. They embraced each other, then he asked her what's wrong. She rested her head on his chest nodding side to side. They walked to the bedroom and crawled into bed. As they both lay in the middle of their bed, he cuddled up scooting in behind her. She really didn't feel like being bothered, so she sunk her head with a tight grip on her pillow, then they both went back to sleep.

Asia woke up still feeling sad. She wished she had her sisters near at a time like this, she wished they were still living down here and not in Arizona.

This is not what she pictured starting her first and new marriage. She only pictured her love/her husband, her two step daughter's, and kids for them in the future. Nowhere in her mind did Asia picture another woman, and other children other than his daughter's.

Now that she calmed down just a little that morning she wanted to address the situation. Now she needs to know what was all that about, but since she felt like being thoughtful, she decided to address it tonight instead, after settling down after work. But for now, she just prepared a small breakfast real quick. Asia made a pot of grits, scrambled eggs, bacon, and toast. Afterward she sat at her island in their kitchen by herself and ate. She didn't bother waking Gary up even though he did need to be up too. Once Asia was done she walked in the room, walking in Gary was waking up.

"Good morning baby, breakfast is in there," she pointed towards the kitchen.

"Good morning baby, but why did you eat without me?"

"Who said I ate without you!" she said sarcastically.

"Asia, because you're still chewing." He says as he stands there.

"Gary, you were sleeping to good."

"Is that right?" he said looking straight into her eyes.

"See you later babe, I'm gone. Go eat and you have a good day today." She told him as she kissed him.

"You too honey." He said. Then Asia began heading to the door.

"Asia." He says.

Asia turned around looking back into his eyes.

"Babe, I love you."

"Love you more," she replied.

Although she means and feels every bit of what she just said, but how dry she just said it someone else would have heard that and wouldn't believe it at all. She was just still upset with him.

Asia walked to her car and drove off playing some church music trying to set a different tone as she drive through traffic. She made it to school pretty quick it wasn't that much traffic. She walked in passing the front desk and walked straight into class.

"Hey boo!"

"Hey ladies!" she said loudly.

"Ugh. No!" Catherine, Jennifer, and Emily all said at the same time.

"No, what," Asia smiled.

"You need to walk back in here, but smile. We did not sleep with you last night." They were the only ones there so far. They were a little early, not even the instructor was there yet.

"Oh, my bad, you can see it on my face?"

"Yes, I can, is everything okay boo?"

"Yeah boo, thanks for asking, but I will be okay; hubby just pissed me off yesterday, that's all."

"Speaking of hubby, are we still going on the double date with the hubby's to that sip and paint on Thursday?"

"Ummm, maybe not. I was thinking us ladies should go to the spa."

"The spa, we can't go at night!" Emily sounded.

"I know I was thinking on Saturday," Asia responded.

"Oh, okay, that sounds like a winner. I do need a massage to my back, it has been killing me lately," Jennifer says.

"So yes, let's take the time to pamper ourselves, just us ladies, it will be fun."

"Yeah, it's been a long time since we went," Catherine said.

"Yes and were due for it."

"Which one you have in mind?"

"I was thinking we try Massage Envy this time."

"Is it reasonable or are they expensive?"

"Oh no, they're reasonable."

"Ok cool, Massage Envy it is." Saturday approached they all met up they were ready.

"We're here, and I'm excited. We're about to get a massage!" she said with excitement.

"I know right, something I need by a professional."

"Girl for real," Emily replied.

A couple of staff members came out to the waiting area for them.

"Hey, ladies how are you!"

"We're fine, thank you," the four of them said at the same time.

"So what are you ladies getting today?"

"A deep tissue massage," they sounded.

"Ok, let me take you ladies to the back."

They followed them to the massage room where they had to get undressed only leaving on their panties. Once the workers went back in there they were all ready for them. The massages started, they were feeling good and they were relaxed. For the most part, they were silent enjoying their massages. Once their hour was up the workers woke up the ladies because they all had fallen asleep and they left the room.

"Oooh, that felt so good, we straight fell asleep," Asia sounded.

"That massage was amazing as always," Catherine added.

"It sure was," Emily and Jennifer added as well.

They got dressed and then they left.

Asia hugged her girls bye, got inside her car, and left driving headed home. She had no other plans. Getting home she turned on the living room TV, walked to the kitchen to pour some juice, then walked back to the living room. Asia sat on the couch taking sips of her juice trying to find something on TV.

From every sound or noise she heard from the outside she thought it was Gary arriving home. Still bothered from the letters that came in the mail, wasn't going to let that slide that easy and forget about it, they needed to talk. She just didn't want to regret saying something at that time while she was as mad as she was. Asia wanted to talk now. Ever since she'd been home within these last couple of hours, she has been watching that clock every half hour. In the middle of the day, she's home thinking he would have been there a long time ago. No telling where he could really be right now, especially after telling her earlier he had a light day today.

As soon as Gary walked in the house, Asia was ready.

"I only loved you."

"Baby, can I at least get in the house good?"

Asia had a serious look on her face.

"How was your day; I can't even get a *how was your day* and a hug," he sat down on the chair.

"I'm not in a playing mood," she walked up on him and said.

Gary looked up at her. "Do you really have to walk up on me like that?" he smiled slightly, then put his head down.

"I'm not playing Gary, I'm really serious!"

"Me neither I'm being serious. I had a good day today. I saw some clients today, things are looking good."

"Gary!"

"Asia, I only wanted to spend time with you, my wife. You are my heart, and you are everything to me, Asia."

"Yeah, that's what you're saying, but your actions are speaking a little different."

"Asia, I don't have any thoughts of sleeping with anyone but you, now and even before we got married."

Gary had to get that all out in one breath because with the rage he saw in her eyes as he walked in, he knew she was about to start going off on him about that DNA and child support letter. Asia couldn't even get a word in, not that she tried because she didn't, she wanted to hear what he had to say and like she figured it was NOTHING.

"I had never lied to you about nothing Gary!" she yelled.

He stood there, not knowing what else to say after that, just seconds ago he'd lied to her. Asia decided to cut that conversation short, it was making her blood pressure go up. Asia knew getting Paula's number from Gary wasn't going to be possible, so she made time to search her on Facebook. It had took her two days before she found her, but once she did, she inboxed her asking her many questions after telling her who she was. Paula didn't respond right away. Paula did not even respond that day, not even the next day and yes she was pissed about it, but what could she do about it. As the days passed by she became more messed up in her head.

Here she thought she had a nice good man finally, married him, took them both off the market. Why in the hell was she waiting for another woman to respond to her on Facebook and had been waiting for some days already? This was crazy as hell. She knew it had to be more to this than what he was telling her.

It was hard for her to go to sleep and wake up like it wasn't still on her mind. After another busy day and getting home from the grocery store, Asia picked up a few things for dinner, she went straight home afterward to start dinner.

"Baby, I'm home!" he yelled out.

"I'm in the kitchen!" she yelled.

Gary walked into the kitchen, hugged and kissed her on her lips. "Baby, what's for dinner? I'm starving."

"I'm making a pot roast with red potatoes that are half way done, macaroni and cheese, cabbage, candied yams and corn bread."

"Damn baby, is all that other stuff ready? That sounds good, all of it."

"Yeah, almost," she giggled.

"Heck yeah," he said.

"By the time you shower and wind down from your day, everything will be ready."

"Alright, babe I'm about to go take a shower now."

"Alright babe," she said.

Right after Asia heard Gary get into the shower, Asia quickly went to the room and straight for his phone. Asia sat on the edge of their bed as he was taking a shower. She was checking all of his text messages on his phone. Asia was swiping through his text messages. Once he got out the shower is when she began reading them out loud. Gary had tried to clear his throat with nothing to clear it with. Asia began yelling and screaming at him.

"Hold up baby, just calm down a little, and stop yelling it wasn't even like that!"

"What you mean it wasn't even like that!"

"What you mean it wasn't even like that!" she yelled out again.

He turned back around and went back into the bathroom.

She felt humiliated; she was hurt in a matter of seconds because he had lied. Once he came out the bathroom, she was sitting in the same spot holding his phone.

He could barely look at her directly in her eyes with the look of fire in her eyes right now. If looks could do what it looks like, he would be on fire and dead right about now. He was not trying to lose another good woman. He knew he needed to think of something real quick.

"You fucked Paula!" she yelled.

"Seriously, you think I would do that?"

"You need to leave right now or I'm going too!" she yelled.

"Baby please!" he said.

"Baby please my ass, I just need to think alone," Asia said to him.

"Babe," Gary said.

"Leave!" she screamed.

"Can I eat first? I'm starving."

"I know you are, and now you're going to fix your own plate."

"Is it ready?"

"How about you go see if it's ready," she said.

Gary threw on a pair of black jeans and his brown and white button down shirt. He went to the kitchen looking at everything. It looked like it was done to him. He took the cornbread from out the oven. Gary made his plate, wrapped it in foil, and left the house calling his boy Mikey. He dialed his number as he walked to his car.

"Hey bro." He answered.

"Man, you at the house?"

"Yes I am, man is everything good?" Mikey asked.

"I don't think so, but I'm on my way, oh and call up the fellas too."

"Alright man," they hung up. Gary glanced back at the house, and then he turned back around, shook his head, then got into his car and opened the foil from his food. He sat there inside his car and ate his dinner thinking to himself why in the hell he didn't erase all those old text messages, eating his food and mad at himself for not thinking about the what if's. After he was done eating he sat his plate on his back seat, started up his car, and pulled off. Gary left to go see his boy. Once he got to Mikey's house, Marcus and Sam were already there. They were just waiting on Manny now. They all were sitting in the man cave staring at Gary wondering what he wanted all the fellas over for.

"Aye bro everything good my dude?" Marcus asked.

Gary's eyes looked down towards the carpet shaking his head. His boys were sitting there clueless. They didn't know if somebody just died, or if they had to go beat some dude's ass.

"Naw man," Gary sounded.

The doorbell sounded. "Hold up, let me get that." Mikey ran to get the door, it was Manny. Manny walked in giving Mikey some dap. "Hey bro," Mikey said.

"Hey, what's up bro? Is everything alright? I got here as quickly as I could."

"I don't know, Gary was just about to tell us." Mikey and Manny walked back to the room with the rest of the fellas. Manny gave all the fellas some dap. Then he sat down too and looked at Gary.

"Man, so tell us, what the fuck happened?" Mikey says.

Gary glanced up at his boys.

"Man, I fucked up."

"What Happened?"

"Wifey found out about an ex I hooked back up with briefly."

Marcus looked at all his boys grinning, he pointed at Gary. "Y'all hear this fool talking about briefly." Marcus laughed.

"Awwwww man, we thought we were going to have to beat some dude's ass or something, then the way you were looking, man, it looked like you were about to tell us somebody died," Mikey said.

"Man, this shit is serious, man my girl just made me get out the house."

"Like for good?" Manny asked.

"Man, I don't know. She was crying, screaming, and yelling and shit saying I need to leave and if I don't then she would."

"Man," Mikey said shaking his head from side to side.

"I can't believe this shit has happened to you again. Man, I hope she's good after she's not mad anymore, it may take her some days, I think you both will get through this," Sam told him.

"Man, thanks for that bro." Sam shook his head up and down.

"Yeah man, you can stay here until she let's you go back home," Mikey told him.

"Aww bro, I really appreciate it big time. Chevon isn't going to be tripping?"

"Naw bro, she didn't trip the last time, you good, don't worry about nothing."

"Thanks, man." Gary sounded.

"Man, let's drink." Manny sounded.

"Fasho, let me get some glasses." Mikey left the room to get some glasses with some ice for the fellas and himself. Shortly he came back to the room passing everyone a glass with some ice. Mikey had a little mini bar hooked up in his man cave. They all helped themselves to Hennessey and some had vodka. Mikey turned on the game. This is what Gary needed for sure. Later that night once the fellas left Mikey went to grab his boy a cover and a pillow. Afterward he went to go join his girl in bed. He walked into the bedroom and it looked like she was asleep.

"Hey, babe you sleep?"

Chevon's eyes opened with the sound of his voice. "Almost babe, I'm tired. I was trying to wait up for you, the fellas left?"

"Yeah, except for Gary, I told him he could spend a few nights if he needed too."

Chevon looked over at him, "What, his new wife put him out?"

"Damn." His eyes widened, his eye brows raised with his surprised expression. "How'd you know?"

"Oh she did," she chuckled.

"Shhh, babe he might hear you." He whispered.

"My bad, I didn't mean to laugh, I was just kidding."

"No, but she did."

"What did his ass do this time?"

"His wife found out about his ex-Paula by going through his phone, and something about some DNA letters came to the house, and him and this other woman have a kid."

That was a whole lot to digest right there. Chevon didn't even know how to respond to that. She was at a loss for words. Chevon rubbed her hand across her forehead. "Wow, I don't even know where to start, all of it is crazy, and I just can't believe he's in another situation like this."

"I know, me neither babe, but that's my boy, I have to look out for him."

"Yeah, no doubt, not saying you shouldn't. I like Gary, he just don't think about his actions when he does things, and the effect it can cause afterwards."

"Alright, alright babe, that's enough talk about my boy. Give me a kiss." Chevon leaned in towards his face and gave him a kiss. Then he wrapped his arms around her giving her a hug. Then they both slid down underneath the covers more and went to sleep.

The next morning Gary woke up and got dressed. He needed his daughters. Gary was headed to Katrina's house to pick up Simone, and then next he had plans to pick up Paige, if her momma doesn't be on that bullshit today. He wanted to take them both to Knott's Berry Farm for the first time. Once he made it to Katrina's house he pressed the code to the gate to enter, he drove in, and then he parked in front of her house. He got out and rung the doorbell.

Katrina and Mike both were sitting on the couch watching TV as the doorbell sounded.

"Oh babe, that's Gary," she said after looking back. She had seen him through her open window.

As she was about to get up to get the door for him, Mike told her to sit down, and that he would get it. Mike got up from off the couch and walked to the front door to open it.

"Hey, what's up Mike?"

"Hey, what's going on Gary?"

"Just about to take the kids to Knott's Berry Farm today."

"That's what's up."

Shortly Gary and Simone left out the house and went to the car; they drove off heading to pick up Paige. As he made it to Brandy's apartment he got out the car and told Simone he be right back. Gary walked up the stairs, approaching Brandy's apartment he knocked on her door. In minutes she answered opening her door.

"Hey Brandy," he spoke first.

"Hey Gary," Brandy said to him.

"I wanted to get Paige. I'm about to take her and Simone to Knott's Berry Farm."

"Oh, okay. Hold on, let me go get her." Brandy closed her door half way then she went to Paige's room. Standing in the doorway of her room Paige was lying across her bed watching TV.

"Paige, your daddy is about to take you to Knott's Berry Farm," she said.

"Oh, he is on his way," Paige asked her.

"No, he is at the front door waiting on you." Paige had a big smile on her face. She got up from off her bed and put on her socks and shoes. She was already dressed for the day she grabbed her jacket. She gave her mother a kiss and hug then she was out the front door.

"Hey daddy," Paige sounded.

"Hey, baby what were you doing?"

"Nothing, I was just in my room watching TV," she told him. "You called."

"No, I just came over."

"Oh, okay."

"Why?" he asked.

"Nothing, I was just wondering."

"Oh, but yeah I picked up your sister too."

"She is in the car?" Paige asked.

"Yes, she in the car," He nodded his head.

"Okay."

"Yeah, it's only going to be the three of us."

"Oh, Asia is not coming along?" she asked.

"No." He paused. "No, baby, not this time. It's just going to be us."

"Okay."

They made it to the car, got in, and now the three of them were now headed to Knott's. They walked around and got on almost every single ride, and some rides they got on twice. They were having so much fun. Gary had played some games and won his girls some large stuffed animals. He also bought them a souvenir cup and a Knott's Berry Farm T-shirt. Later that night they couldn't leave without getting a funnel cake. Gary had bought one for everybody; He was not about to share. After leaving the park they walked to their car and then they were headed home. Gary dropped the girls off then he went to Mikey's house. He got there and went straight to sleep. He was very tired. The next morning Chevon woke up, she walked into the other room where Gary was still sleeping.

"Gary!" she called his name. No response.

"Gary!" she said it again, but this time louder. His eyes slowly opened.

"Hey Chevon!" he said.

"Gary, we're about to start getting ready to go to church this morning, you need to come too," she chuckled.

"I know I should, alright let me get dressed."

"Okay." Then Chevon walked out the room and back to hers. Walking into the room Mikey was already turning over to face her.

"Hey, good morning baby."

"Hey babe, good morning, I was just in their waking up your boy, I told him he needs to come to church with us, and he was like ok."

Mikey chuckled.

Everyone was up now, getting ready for church. Afterward Chevon went to the kitchen to make some coffee. Then she made everyone a bagel with cream cheese, bacon, and scrambled eggs. An hour passed then the fellas went to the kitchen for their coffee and their breakfast Chevon made.

"Thanks, babe," Mikey said to Chevon.

"You're welcome babe."

"Thank you Chevon, I appreciate this."

"Oh, you're welcome."

Once they were done eating then the three of them left.

***

A week went by. Gary was still there at Mikey's and Chevon's house chilling. Chevon was wondering how long Gary was actually going to be there. To her it didn't look like he was even concerned about his wife. Later that night in bed she decided to bring it to Mikey's attention.

"Babe, a week ago it was a few nights that turned into seven. Has he at least tried to call her to see if he can go back home, so they can work things out?"

"I don't know babe, but I'll ask him in a minute."

"Well, no rush baby, you can ask him tonight or in the morning."

"Alright," Mikey said.

The next day Mikey had a talk with Gary about him trying to talk to his wife, not waiting on her to make the first call, because she was probably over at the house waiting for him to make the first call too.

So after Mikey and Gary talked, Gary dialed Asia's cell phone number. He held the phone to his ear as his eyes closed praying that this phone call goes well.

"Hello."

"Hey, baby."

"Hey."

"Baby, can I please come back home? I miss you, I don't want us to be like this at all, I need you, baby."

"Yes, you can come home, but you better come straight home."

He smiled, "I will babe." After hanging up the phone with her he went and thanked Mikey and Chevon for letting him crash there for a whole week. He then thanked Mikey for that little talk not long ago. Gary went and grabbed his stuff from out the room.

"Alright y'all, thanks again!" he shouted as he's leaving out the front door.

"Yeah, you better fly home boy!"

Gary turned around and smiled at Mikey, "Aye, she was like you better come straight home."

"Yeah, you better listen to your wife man!"

Gary chuckled. "Alright, I will holler at you tomorrow!"

"Alright my man," Mikey told him.

Mikey then closed his front door. Gary got into his car and took off going straight home to his wife.

***

Rhonda called Asia.

"Hello," Asia answered.

"Hey Asia, you still going with me to my coworker's wedding dinner party?" she asked.

"Mmmm," Asia sounded.

"Don't Mmm, I asked you months ago and you said yes."

"I'll go, but Gary's ass is not coming."

Rhonda laughed.

"For real, I'm not taking him nowhere with me."

"Okay." She laughed again. "Girl, what the hell happened?"

"I'm just not taking his ass, when is it?"

"Next week on Saturday, and no worries because I'm not taking Will's ass neither. Why, so he can be rushing me to leave because he wants to go back home, I don't think so."

"Yeah for real, so what are you wearing?"

"I'm not sure yet, but their colors are Pink and Blue."

"Oh, okay."

"I'm going to find something out my closet."

"Yeah, me too," Asia said.

Asia didn't bring up the fact she just let him come back home just days ago.

"Well alright, Rhonda I will see you next week girl."

"Alright, Asia." They hung up the line together.

Three days back home, he'd noticed her still acting a little different, but that was expected behind everything he'd done. It was three o' clock in the evening and Gary was just now realizing he had not eaten all day since his bacon, hash brown, egg, and cheese omelet, the breakfast he had to cook for himself since Asia didn't. No wonder why his stomach was now talking to him. He was surprised his client wasn't saying anything about his stomach growling. Either they really hear it or they were trying to act like they don't. It didn't matter, they were almost done anyway. Then he was about to go grab him something to eat.

Rather than going to McDonald's since it was just minutes away from the property he was just at, he kept driving. He had a taste for some fried pork chops, some yams, and collard greens. Getting to his favorite soul food restaurant he got out the car and went inside. He was planning on sitting up in there today and eat instead of getting it to go. His eyes scanned the menu board and everything was looking good by the looks of the display picture. From the ribs to the oxtails, their neck bones and steak. But he decided to just stick to what he drove there for.

After eating all of that he was good and very full. He went back to the office. He had another client in three hours. He went back to the office to kill time. He did. Two hours passed quickly, he gave himself time to get to the next house without rushing, plus arriving early way before the client looks good. Remembering that's what Katrina use to always tell him to do, get to the property way before the client to have your own tour so you can know where everything is while showing the property.

It was late in the evening by the time he made it home. Asia heard him come in, she heard the door closed. "Babe, where are you!" he sounded loudly.

"In the room!" she shouted out.

Gary went to the room right before he entered. She was coming to the entrance of the room. He held his arms open for a hug. Asia gave him a hug. He held her in his arms. He didn't want to let her go. She looked up into his eyes; he looked down into her eyes.

"Baby, I love you," Gary said in a low tone.

"Love you too," she sounded sadly.

Her heart was still broken. Gary knew he had to work on himself big time. He was not planning to lose her too.

Days before the dinner party Asia began to search her closet for something cute to wear that's pink and blue. Gary walked in.

"Where are you going?"

"Yeah, where I'm going is to a wedding dinner party with Rhonda," Asia told him.

"Oh, you don't want me going with you?"

As Gary's eyes immediately scanned the bed with the clothes thrown on the bed, "What's up with all these clothes?"

"Trying to find something for this dinner party," she said.

"Why you just telling me about it, were both invited right?"

"Yeah, but you aren't going."

"Why am I'm not going?"

"Because I'm going by myself," she said seriously.

"How are you going to uninvite me? This is crazy."

"Yeah this is crazy, but like I told you before, we're not going to be right until I hear the truth from you about you and Paula. I wasn't playing, what you thought I forgot since I haven't talked about it since you been back."

The day of the dinner party, that evening getting out the shower, Asia was getting dressed. She had put on a short dress that was hugging her hips. He watched her as she looked in the mirror at herself.

"You're not going to ask me to come, I'm still not invited?"

"No, I'll be back. Don't worry, I will not be gone long."

Before Asia was about to leave, Gary pulled her close to him giving her a hug and a kiss on her lips.

"You look very beautiful," he told her.

"Thank you."

"I love you, baby."

She nodded her head ok.

"Asia, can I at least get a I love you back?"

"I love you too Gary," she told him.

Asia's cell had rung. It was Rhonda.

"Hey lady, you already outside?" she asked.

"Yeah, I just pulled up."

"Okay, here I come right now."

She left. He was upset that she didn't want him to come along since they would show up to all different occasion's together. Rhonda hopped on the freeway. She and Asia made it there in no time. Walking inside they were both handed a drink. They walked around checking things out, then they found them a seat. A lot of people were there already, DJ playing some jams. It was only thirty minutes since Asia had been there at the wedding dinner party and he was already texting her. Looking down reading the text message it read:

"Oh, you know you're wrong Asia," reading it all she could do was chuckle.

"Boo what is so funny, you so crazy."

"Girl, Gary ass just sent me a text."

"He mad you wouldn't bring him, you know you could have bought him, I wasn't tripping, I did invite both of you." Then Rhonda laughed looking at Asia's facial expression.

"Girl please, we don't have to go every single place together, I wasn't going to bring him and you not bring Will."

"Girl you crazy," she said.

Asia shrugged her shoulders, she did not care. Rhonda had seen Morgan coming towards them smiling. Rhonda stood up to give her girl a hug.

"Hey Rhonda, thank you so much for coming out!" Morgan said smiling at her.

"Girl, you knew I wasn't going to miss this. Morgan this is my girl Asia. Asia this is my girl, Morgan."

Morgan gave Asia a big hug. "Thank you so much for coming," she smiled at Asia.

"Oh, you are so welcome, you look so beautiful."

"Awww, thank you so much."

"Hey, Morgan where would you like the desserts to go?" Morgan was interrupted by Bobby.

"Oh, Bobby you can just put it on the juice fountain table."

"Yes ma'am," Bobby sounded, then he walked off.

"Hey boo, I will be back. I need to go check on something, but you ladies enjoy," she grinned then walked away.

"Rhonda, girl thanks for bringing me with you, once again I'm having a good time," Asia told her.

"You so crazy girl, this is what we do."

"I know Gary ass still mad he couldn't come," then she laughed. The Dj kept playing back to back jams. It was time for the bride and groom to have their dance.

"Ok, can I have only Mr. and Mrs. Taylor on the floor," the Dj announced on the Mic.

"He all feeling her up," Asia said to Rhonda as they all watched the two dance in the center of the dance floor.

"You better work those hands, Daniel!" Rhonda yelled out. Asia and Rhonda began singing to the song they were dancing too.

"That's my song," Asia said, as she was singing and dancing to the song along with Rhonda from their table.

"Girl, I guess when I get home I will give Gary some."

"You so crazy girl," Rhonda laughed.

"For real, they make me miss my baby; I don't like us being upset like this."

"Okay boo," Rhonda screamed out to Morgan. Morgan and Daniel danced to three songs then everyone was able to dance on the dance floor too. After four straight songs, Asia and Rhonda went to go sit down to take a break. Minutes later, Morgan took a seat with Rhonda and Asia.

"Who is the guy at the other table giving me those looks?" Asia asked Rhonda.

Rhonda looked and glanced, and then she leaned over asking Morgan who it was. "Oh, that's Justin," Morgan responded.

"That's Justin," Rhonda told Asia.

"Yeah, he's fine, his ass better stop looking before I forget I'm married."

Rhonda laughed shaking her head.

"You not going to forget you're married Asia you a fool girl."

"Shit, Gary ass better." Asia paused stopping herself. She was about to go into detail about what Gary's ass need to get right, but then she didn't feel like her situation should be the topic of the conversation right now. "That's all I'm going to say is that he's lucky."

"Yes, he's lucky to have a beautiful wife like you," Rhonda told her.

"Aww, friend thank you."

Asia glanced over at the handsome fella just one more time and noticed his deep stare at her. He got up and began to walk towards their table. She began to tap Rhonda's leg underneath the table getting her attention. Rhonda looked at her, and Asia was just shaking her head smiling. Rhonda looked in the direction she was looking and noticed that Mr. Good Looking was walking up to their table. He walked up to their table and stopped, smiled and waved at everyone sitting at the table, then his eye's laid back on Asia.

"Hello beautiful, I'm Justin," he reached out his hand towards her.

"Hello Justin, I'm Asia." Asia shook his hand.

Justin couldn't help himself, he had to walk over to the table. "Can I have this dance?" He leaned down as he whispered to Asia.

She glanced up at him giving him a smile. "I'll dance with you on the next song."

"Thanks," he smiled.

Justin pulled a chair from the table behind them and sat it next to her. He took a seat to hold a conversation until the next song. They couldn't help the stares into each other's eyes as they talked. They didn't realize that they just talked through that next song that came on until three songs passed. They finally got up thirty minutes after the fact to dance.

"You look very beautiful," he told her as he was dancing in front of her.

"Thank you."

The smiles and the staring into each other's eyes didn't stop. They continued talking as they danced.

"Well, before you begin to think I'm available, I'm not. I am married, Justin."

"Oh, oh I'm so sorry to be flirting with you and trying to hit on you. I do apologize, you're just so beautiful. I know if you were my wife I would be with you, not elsewhere."

"Aww, that's sweet of you to say Justin, but you know I'm having a good time here tonight. My girl brought me here tonight and I'm glad she did."

"I'm glad she did too, but I'm sorry once again for trying to hit on you, I just couldn't help myself seeing you from across the room."

"Oh, no worries. I do find you attractive, but yeah I'm a married woman, at least I know I still got it," she chuckled.

"Yeah baby, you still got it, that's for damn sure," he leaned towards her and told her. They continued dancing having a good time. They danced to a few songs. Then suddenly the DJ began to talk through the playing music.

"Okay, everyone over to the cake table," The DJ announced.

Morgan and Daniel stood beside the cake table about to get ready to cut the cake.

Everyone began flashing their cameras, taking a picture of the bride and groom.

"Awww," is what everyone said as the two cut a slice of the cake and fed it to each other."

After the dinner party, Asia and Rhonda left and was headed home. Asia got home later than what she told Gary before she'd left earlier. He was there sitting on the living room couch waiting for her.

"Hey baby," she walked over to him and said.

"Hey, baby you have a good time?"

"I did, but is that sweat on your head?"

"Yeah, it's hot."

"Then why you didn't cut the air on Gary?" That was crazy he would be lazy and just sit there sweating, she thought to herself.

"I don't know, I just didn't feel like getting up I guess."

Asia went and cut the air on, then she went to the room and took off her clothes and stepped into the shower. After getting out the shower she walked into the living room naked holding her towel half way around her body, as Gary watched. She towel dried her body, then she sat her towel on the edge of the couch. Gary looked up at her and smiled. Asia started stepping backward, he stood up from the couch and began to follow her. Asia was leading him into their bedroom. In seconds he grabbed her by her waist, slid his tongue into her mouth and began kissing her. Then he picked her up, she wrapped her legs around his waist then he started running to the room with her.

"Gary, don't make me fall!" Asia screamed as she laughed at the same time.

"I'm not Asia," he said chuckling.

Just a few steps more and then they were in their room. Gary laid her down on the bed. Gary had quickly taken off his clothes and got in bed too. They made passionate love. Later in the middle of the night, he was wakened, feeling her body backed up against his with his arm still wrapped around her. Then he went back to sleep.

CHAPTER

2

Katrina and Mike is Having a Baby

Katrina woke up to a note left on the dresser on the side of the bed from Mike. She was already smiling without even reading it yet, he always left the sweetest notes, she loved her some him.

Good morning baby I cooked you breakfast. It's downstairs inside the microwave and I took Simone to school. Love you baby, will call you later, love your husband. Katrina smiled; she got up out the bed and went downstairs to warm her breakfast. He made her three pancakes, scrambled eggs and two slices of bacon. Aww, how sweet of him she said to herself as she warmed her food. After sitting down and eating her food, she realized she had nowhere to go, because of course she couldn't go anywhere according to the doctor unless it was to a doctor's appointment. She brushed her teeth, cleaned her face, put a little makeup on, and did her hair. Then she opened all her curtains and watched the sun beam inside more and more with each curtain she opened. Katrina had placed a load of clothes into the washing machine. She was looking cute while doing the laundry. After doing that, she began cleaning up all around the house. After thirty minutes, she had to take a little break to catch her breath. Five minutes later she went back to cleaning.

Karina couldn't take this staying in the house. She had to at least step out for a minute. She thought about going to pick up a few items from Wal-Mart. She thought she'd get some household things. She grabbed her keys from off her dresser and left. Once she made it up to Wal-Mart before even going in she reminded herself to only get a few things for the house and not come out with a shopping cart full of items which seemed to happen like that all the time. Walking from lane to lane she was already seeing things she wanted of course that was not household items. She had to force herself to keep on walking. Between getting items she needed and passing up items she wanted, was very hard.

Katrina's cell began to ring. Looking down at her screen, and Katrina noticed that the call was from Sharee.

"Hey lady," she answered as she continued looking at different bath towels and matching bath rugs.

"He just choked me."

"Sharee, not again," she whispered into the phone.

Sharee began crying.

"Sharee, baby girl not again."

Sharee couldn't stop crying to Katrina.

"Okay, I'm about to put this stuff down, then I will be walking out this store."

"Okay."

"Yeah, you don't need to be still going through the same shit, it's like he's just not going to change."

"I know you're right, and my cup is runneth over with him."

Katrina left the store and got into her car and took off. "Ok, I'm on my way."

"Okay, and Katrina."

"Yeah," Katrina sounded.

"Thanks." They hung up.

Once he entered the room, she got up from the chair and began walking out the room. As she walked passed him, he tugged on her arm which made her stop in her footsteps.

"Why you leaving out the room when I come up in here, what you hiding something?" he asked her.

"No, I'm not hiding anything," she said in a calm low voice with her arms crossed over each other.

"What the hell wrong with you?"

"Nothing, and oh by the way Katrina about to come over and see me," Sharee told him.

"What you tell her."

"I haven't told her anything, she just told me she was in the area and she is going to stop by."

"Hmph." He rubbed his chin as he blew out a breath looking at her.

Katrina finally arrived and when she did, Sharee seeing Katrina there she was happy. Although she was happy she was still hurting on the inside.

"Hey Katrina, let's sit outside in the back yard on the patio."

"Of course, that's a good idea, it's so beautiful outside, it's clear and the weather is just perfect."

"Oh, it is? I haven't even been outside yet."

Sharee and Katrina began walking through the house and out to the backyard. As soon as they got out back, Katrina closed the back door behind her.

"Oh yeah, it's beautiful today, clear blue skies," Sharee said as she looked into the skies. They sat down.

"You didn't have to work today?"

"No, I took today off, I have a headache."

"Since when you start taking days off, and because of a headache?" she asked.

Sharee was silent.

"I know you taking off had something to do with him."

Sharee nodded her head.

"Where are you coming from?" Sharee asked changing the subject.

"Oh girl, had some errands to run, but when you called I was inside of Wal-Mart."

"Mike still lets you run errands and you about to pop?"

"Girl, that is me. He always say baby, stay in the house, kick your feet up and relax, whatever you want just let me know and I'll take care of it."

Sharee began to chuckle. "You just can't be still huh."

"Girl, it's like exercise to me, I'm just ready for him to come out already." She laughed.

"I hear you on that and I can't wait to meet my little godson."

"I know, me too," she smirked. Then she looked into Sharee's eyes, "But what's up with RoShawn ass though girl, what is wrong with him, why does he do this?"

"I don't know, he argues, he screams, talk's down to me every once in a while he would either push me down on the bed or slap me. We go from not talking for hours, then after that he tries to act like it's nothing. He then acts regularly trying to kiss and makeup, but by that time, shit I don't want to kiss and make up, I just want him to either love me and be right or leave me alone and let me live my life. He always says he isn't letting me leave him." Tears started filling up in Sharee's eyes uncontrollably once she said *him*. Sharee was tired of putting his feeling's first, what about hers?

Katrina stood up from her chair and leaned down towards Sharee to hug her. She had both her arms wrapped around Sharee.

"Father, I come to you right now asking for peace in Sharee's home, Lord and to heel RoShawn's spirit, so he can stop the domestic violence mentally and physically Father to her in the name of Jesus. Father, I am asking for you to protect her and help her find her way out this relationship Father. Father God, whatever spirit is taking over RoShawn I ask you to release that spirit from him, Father God in the name of Jesus, Amen."

"Amen." Sharee also said along with Katrina. They slowly lifted their heads. Katrina released from her and sat back down. They stared into each other eyes.

"Dammit, girl I can't even imagine staying in an abusive relationship. You need to get out this."

I know, I have been trying, but every time I try, he just makes it hard and won't let me leave."

"Wait, hold on Katrina, let me go make us a snack real quick. My godson has to be hungry up in there." Sharee got up from the table to go inside.

Katrina chuckled. Five minutes later Sharee came back outside to the patio with a plate of mini sub sandwiches on mini Hawaiian bread.

"Sharee, it's so peaceful out here."

"I know, isn't it?"

"Yes it is; do you ever come out here by yourself to get you a peace of mind?"

"Not as often as I should, but every once in while I may come back and read a book or something, I need to start coming out here more."

"Yeah, you should. I love it."

After eating they chatted for a few more hours; Katrina almost didn't want to leave her girl there with his crazy ass when it was time for her to go.

"Thank you so much for that Katrina."

"You're welcome Sharee, I love you, you are my sister and best friend. I just want you to always know I am going to be here for you, call me whenever you need me and I will be right here."

"Thank you so much." Sharee stood up from her lounge chair to hug Katrina. Then afterward, Katrina was about to head out. Sharee walked her out front to her car. They hugged one more time and then Katrina got inside her car and left.

Driving back home Katrina was so heartbroken for her friend. She just wished for one day she was a man and not pregnant, so she could beat the dog shit out his ass.

Sharee finally walked back inside the house. RoShawn was standing in the living room just standing there. He wasn't saying anything, but the look in his eyes had her a little scared, he had all her attention for sure. She just stared back at him walking in slowly.

"So, what did you tell Katrina?"

"Nothing, we just talked."

"Just talked huh, you couldn't do that over the phone."

"Well, I wanted to have her over, what's wrong with my girl coming over?"

He changed his look as he still stared at her. "But then y'all go outside to the back like you have something to hide."

"Yeah, but just because we go outside don't mean I have something to hide."

RoShawn knew her and Katrina both was for sure up to something, he just didn't know what.

Sharee's cell began to sound. Katrina was calling.

"Hey K," she answered.

"I just wanted to tell you to stay strong, and I love you."

"Hold on K." She moved the phone away from her ear.

"Are we done?" Then she began to walk away. She placed the phone back up to her ear.

"Hello."

"Sharee, where in the hell are you going!" RoShawn yelled out.

She turned back around, rolled her eyes at him as she turned her head back around and then continued to walk towards the room. He stood there watching her.

"Is he following you?"

"No," she mumbled.

"No. Who are you saying no to, me?" he began following her to the room.

"No." She shook her head looking at him madly.

"Then why did you just say No, who are you on the phone with?"

"Why you walking up to me like you about to do something," she took a few steps back from him.

"Man, because you be thinking I'm playing games and I'm not."

"You want me to come pick you up because I can right now?" Katrina tells her on the other end of the phone.

"This is just Katrina I'm talking too."

"I'm coming back to get you." Katrina wasn't about to wait for Sharee to respond to her question, she was just about to go back anyway. It didn't take her long to go right back, she wasn't that far.

Katrina rang the doorbell. RoShawn went to go answer the front door.

"Hey Katrina," he said.

"Hey," then she walked in.

Sharee came to the living room. "Hey K," she sounded softly.

"I need you to ride with me, I need to run an errand, then I need to stop by the house, I'll bring you back."

"Alright, just let me go throw on some clothes real quick."

"Alright," Katrina said.

RoShawn went to the bedroom. "What you about to go see your other man?"

"No, I'm not going anywhere to see no man; I'm just going to ride with Katrina to run an errand than to her house."

"How you dressed it looks like you're going more than just running an errand and to Katrina's house. Where you two trying to go!" he yelled.

"Girl in a minute his ass about to make me come up in there and kick his ass myself if he doesn't stop all that screaming at you. I'll give him one more time!" she yelled out so they both could hear.

"What you supposed to be her body guard Katrina!" he yelled back out his mouth to Katrina.

"Un Hun, Yes I am," she said softly as she smiled.

RoShawn and Sharee both walked back into the living room. "Where you really taking my girl Katrina?" he asked Katrina.

"I'm not trying to go nowhere but to run an errand with her and then to her house for a little while. I'm tired of being up in this house, it's not like you take me anywhere!" Sharee blurted out to him. He didn't have much to say after that. Sharee was glad to come at him like that because he knows she is telling the truth. Sharee and Katrina both left out the house and headed to her car.

"Girl, I wish I was blessed like you to find a good man like Mike," she told Katrina softly.

"You can, he will find you. He will be God sent, wait on God to bring him to you, but you have to leave his ass first so you can accept what God has for you."

Katrina chirped her alarm to unlock the car. The two got in the car and drove off.

"Girl yes, you see the shit I have to go through with his ass."

"Yeah, but like I tell you all the time, you don't have too."

"That's why I love you, Katrina, you always know how to make me feel better, and you tell me like it is. You never sugar coat nothing and I appreciate that that's a real friend, and thanks so much for coming back getting me out this house."

"I love you too Sharee, that's what I'm here for."

Pushing through light traffic Katrina and Sharee listened to music and talked as they ran the errand, then they made it to Katrina's house. They were done with the errand fast. Sharee got out the car then reached for her cellphone from off her passenger seat. Katrina chirped her alarm, then they walked inside the house. They walked inside through the garage. Katrina took a pack of chicken out the freezer and sat it in the sink in cold water to cook later for dinner.

"Sharee, you want some wine?"

"Sure."

Katrina poured Sharee a glass of wine and then she grabbed a bottled water for herself. They sat in the living room chatting. A half hour passed and Katrina and Sharee left the house to go drop Sharee back at home. It was almost time for the girls to get out of school. She wanted to surprise them with a ride instead of them catching the bus today.

Katrina made it up there right when school let out. She pulled up right in front of the school, parked in the red zone like it was a parking spot. The girls came out after five minutes of Katrina waiting; they couldn't help but see her truck. When the girls saw her Simone and Paige both said bye to their friends and walked to the truck. Once the girls got in Katrina decided to have some girl talk with these two. She wanted to let them know what type of guys to stay away from and what type of men they should date when they got older. According to the way their conversation was going she decided to tell them about Sharee and RoShawn. She felt so bad for Sharee right now, and she couldn't in any way see her little girls going through that same shit one day. She began to also tell them about her sister and their dad; the full story. The girls were too young back then to be told the full story, but now they were old enough. She thinks they should know now and not later, and then be mad about why no one told them.

Katrina dropped off Paige at home, and then she drove home. Getting home Katrina went and sat on the couch to relax a bit before starting dinner. Simone went to her room.

After only twenty minutes of relaxing, Katrina went to the kitchen and start cutting some potatoes. Then Simone walked in. Simone looked at the cut up potatoes on the counter and the pot of cooking oil on top of the fire on the stove.

"Mom, we're having chicken and fries for dinner?"

"Yeah," Katrina said.

"Can't wait to eat," Simone responded.

"You want to cook it?"

"Me," Simone grinned.

"It's about that time anyway that you learn how to cook."

"Ok sure."

"Alright I'll tell you what to do, but you will do everything yourself."

"Ok," she smiles.

"Ok, first you must wash your hands," she told Simone. Simone washed her hands.

"Now, normally before you begin cooking you must make sure the kitchen is all the way clean before you start cooking, but since it's already clean you don't have to worry about that part."

"Ok."

"Starting with the chicken you need to clean it in cold water, then put it in a bowl, sprinkle some seasoning on it; black pepper, seasoned salt, and garlic salt."

"Ok," Simone sounded as she did the steps seasoning all the pieces of chicken.

"Ok, now put a little mustard on it and rub it all over it."

Simone followed all the steps as they were given.

"Ok, now put some flour into a zip lock bag and throw in a few pieces at a time and shake the bag until you get flour on every single piece. You want the flour to cover every piece really good."

Simone was doing a great job so far listening to every step.

"Ok, now check your oil to make sure it's hot by sprinkling in a few drops of the flour that's already on your fingers and once you see it sizzling in the pot you can put your chicken inside."

"Ok," Simone said. Once the oil was hot enough Simone began putting her chicken inside the pot. Simone placed her first pieces into the pot and watched them cook.

"Simone, you don't have to watch it cook, just make sure you check on it in about ten minutes to flip them over if it's brown at the bottom."

"Ok," she sounded. Simone went and checked on it after ten minutes and flipped it. When it was done she took them out and added more to the pot, then started on the fries in another pot.

Mike walked inside from out the garage.

"Babe, you got it smelling good. I can smell it all the way from the garage," he said loudly, but then he looked towards the stove and it was Simone.

"Wait. What, Simone frying the chicken?" he's looked surprised.

"Yep, it's me" she grinned, "See, I got you smelling it from the garage!" she smiled.

"Yeah, you do." Katrina was sitting down at the kitchen table smiling.

"Yeah, I told her she going to learn how to cook."

"That's right, yep it's that time."

Simone was focused on her chicken. She then turned over a few pieces of chicken that needed to be turned over. Mike was happy to see her doing her thing in the kitchen.

"I can't wait to see how it taste's," Simone said.

"It looks bomb, go ahead and try one."

Simone grabbed a piece of chicken from out the bowl, she bit into it. She smiled. "It's good mom."

Katrina grabbed a wing from out the bowl to taste her daughter's first time cooking.

"This is very good Simone," she said after taking two bites.

"Thank you, mom," Simone said.

"So, what can I cook tomorrow?"

Katrina grinned. "Someone likes cooking now I see."

"Yeah, now I can cook for y'all."

"Aww, how sweet," Katrina said.

"But mom, for real, what can I cook tomorrow?"

Katrina thought about it. "Oh, you can make tacos!" she blurted.

After they were all done eating Katrina cleaned the counter and wiped down the stove.

"Oh, mom I could have done that."

"Yeah, don't worry that's the least I could do, you just cooked us some food."

The next morning Sharee was on Katrina's mind, so she called her.

"Hey lady," Sharee answered.

"Hey lady, what you doing nothing?" she asked.

"Nothing," she told her.

"Come over here."

"Alright," Sharee said. They hung up.

"RoShawn, I'll be back, about to go to Katrina's for a little while. Do you need anything while I'm out?"

"Bring me back a beer and a pack of Newports."

"Alright," Sharee said. Sharee grabbed her car keys and left the house and headed to Katrina's house. On the way to Katrina's she decided to buy her a double shot from the store. A lot was on her mind and she needed something to ease it. After leaving out the store she went back to the car and drank her drink before she started back up the car. Afterward she started up her car and pulled back slowly and left the store. Now feeling slightly better she was almost near Katrina's. Although the liquor made her feel slightly better, her heart and her appearance looked like shit. Sharee knew Katrina was going to have a lot to say and she was ready for it.

"Hey lady, I'm here." Katrina buzzed her in, then she drove through the gate. Sharee drove in and parked in front of Katrina's place. Katrina already had her front door open for her. As she walked inside, Katrina was already walking up to her smiling. Katrina hugged Sharee. This is when Katrina smelled alcohol on her.

"What, you been drinking?"

"Peach Amsterdam," Sharee said.

"Why, you don't even drink hard liquor."

"I know, but this nigga got me fucked up, I had to calm myself down from hurting his ass in his sleep."

"Damn boo, it's still morning."

"It's noon somewhere, right."

Sharee started to cry. She just wanted him to leave already; she didn't want this relationship anymore.

"So what's going on?"

"We got into it, and while we were getting into it his sister called and he started telling her shit. Then later that day she had nerves to call me. I know they know him and the shit he does, or maybe they don't, but one of them should know he ain't wrapped too tight, but they still go along with whatever he does like it is okay and shit."

"Well, you already knew that that's his family, they're going to take his side whether he's wrong or not."

"Yeah, that bitch got nerves, calling me and she doesn't even have a man, and the bitch doesn't have any edges."

Katrina laughed.

"Bitch for real."

"Wait, wait hold up, what that bitch edges got to do with anything?" Katrina kept laughing.

"Girl, that bitch bet not ring my phone again."

"Yeah, because I would have said something right then my mouth is to fly, I would have come right back at her like BITCH."

44

"Girl, you already know I wanted to, and if Mr. Asshole wasn't sitting right in my fucking face I would have."

"Oh, and his ass was right there too?"

"Yep," Sharee responded.

"Huh, his ass probably told his sister to say that shit."

"Girl, ain't no telling with his ass."

"That's crazy as hell."

"Yeah, for real, now you see the shit I be going through. I just want his ass to leave."

"So you have been telling him that over and over again, so now what are you going to do?"

"The only thing I can think of right now is to take his set of keys to the house tonight while he is asleep so that way when he leaves to go somewhere tomorrow, I will make sure to walk him to the door and lock the door behind him, so he wouldn't have to use his keys, then leave the house for a few days so his ass can be locked out."

"Okay, but then when he calls you, all you're going to do is answer it."

"No, I'm not, not this time. I'm just tired, I'm throwing in the towel, I'm done."

"Damn, that's right Sharee, you serious this time huh?"

"Yeah, I am. He is only going to keep on disrespecting me as long as I keep staying with him. I don't care if I tell him not to until he is blue in the face, as long as I'm here with him, I really don't see any change in him at all."

"That's right."

"Yeah K, I have to do this, this time."

"Well you know you can always stay here for a few days."

"Thanks, but no thank you, I will have to go where he won't have any idea."

"Where is that?"

Sharee stood there in thought. "I was thinking about checking myself into a hotel across town in somebody else name."

"That just might work."

Sharee stayed for a little while longer.

After a while, Sharee checked the time on her phone. "Alright lady, I think I'm going to head home now."

"You sure," Katrina asked her.

"Yeah, I'm sure."

Sharee and Katrina hugged each other.

"Alright K, I will call you later."

"Alright lady, you be careful."

"I will, love you and thank you, Katrina."

"Love you too Sharee, and if you need us we will be right here please do not hesitate."

"Alright," Sharee said.

Sharee turned back around and continued walking to her car. As she was leaving Mike was coming. Mike came home with some flowers for Katrina. As soon as he walked in he gave them to her.

"Thank you, baby," they kissed.

"Anything for my queen," they kissed again.

Katrina went to go put her flowers in a vase then she grabbed her card to read. She loved his little notes he wrote to her, it read:

Baby, just because you're home doesn't mean that your roses supposed to stop. I appreciate you, I love you, and I can't wait to meet our little blessing. Love your husband.

Katrina stood there grinning, he always had a smile on her face, it didn't take much and he sure loved doing it. She went to go cuddle up on the couch and watch TV. She went to sleep half way through the movie they were watching. Later Katrina woke up with her sister in law on her mind. She thought to give her a buzz. Katrina dialed her sis in law.

"Hello," Michelle answered after the second ring.

"Hey sis," Katrina says.

"Hey sissy," Michelle said happily.

"What are you doing sis?"

"At work about to leave in a minute," she said.

"Oh, I thought you were off already is why I called."

"Girl, I'm sitting here trying to figure out who in the hell sent me flowers."

"Somebody sent you flowers?"

"Yeah, some long stemmed roses."

"Long-stemmed roses," she repeated.

"I wondered who sent them, they are beautiful. They came inside a long gold box."

As Katrina listened, it sounded just like her brother and what he does for her she wondered, did Mike send those to her? "Look at the card and see whose name is on it," Katrina told her.

"I looked for it already when I first opened the box, but I didn't see a little white card."

"That's strange."

"Right, I thought the same thing too."

"Yeah, sis has a secret admirer."

"Right," she chuckled still wondering who it could be. Once they got off the phone she couldn't wait to ask Mike had he sent those to his sister. Just as she was about to yell out Mike's name Simone walked in the room.

"Hey mom," Simone said.

"Hey, baby how long have you been here?"

"Oh, I been here for a long time now, when I got home you were asleep on the couch."

"Even when I woke up you were so quiet upstairs I didn't even know you were here."

"Yeah, I was up there doing my homework, now I'm about to go study for my test tomorrow."

"Oh, okay."

Simone turned around and went back to her room to finish her homework so she could study for her test. Instead of yelling like she was about to do minutes ago, she got up and walked to him.

"Babe," Katrina sounded.

"Yeah," Mike responded.

"I have a question for you." Katrina walked closer to him to ask her question, no need for Simone to hear too she thought.

"What's up babe?" he asked.

"Baby, you sent flowers to your sister?"

"Why you say that?"

"She said somebody sent her a box of red stemmed roses today at her job and she didn't know who sent them." He looked at her like how did you know. Mike couldn't hold a straight face for long, then he chuckled.

"Well, that's good. I wanted her to feel special and I didn't want her to know her brother sent her some roses. She's been hard on herself lately and saying she is lonely. She wishes she could find her a good man and I wanted her to cheer up. I figured that would help."

"Well, I suppose it did because when I just talked to her, she sounded cheerful."

"Well that's good, that's all I wanted."

"See, that's why I love you, you're just so sweet and very special," Katrina leaned into him and kissed him on his lips. "Love you, babe," she told him.

"Love you too."

Mike stuck his tongue up inside Katrina's mouth moving his tongue all around as they tongue kissed. Minutes later Mike began kissing her all on her neck. Her head fell back and she let him do what he enjoys.

Later in the night, Sharee was calling.

"Hey lady," Katrina answered.

"I just did it," she whispered."

"Ok, I'm going to pray that everything works out for you, love you boo and good night."

"Goodnight Katrina." The two hung up.

Her phone began ringing. She thought it was Sharee calling right back, but it was her mother. "Hey Mom," she answered.

"Hey, Katrina!"

"What you doing?"

"In the bed trying to go to sleep, I'm tired."

"Oh baby, I'm sorry. Did I wake Mike to? Tell him I'm sorry, I didn't mean to."

"Naw, he good, you know Mike is a hard sleeper."

"Oh baby I'm sorry, I will call you back in the morning."

"Goodnight mom."

"Goodnight baby."

The next morning Deborah called back just like she said she would.

"Hello," Katrina answered.

"Good morning baby."

"What you doing mom?"

"Nothing, being lazy. I was thinking about coming over there today to get in your pool."

"Oh, ok you can. Come on, I'm not getting in today, but you can."

"What y'all over there doing?"

"I'm not doing anything. Mike just left."

"Simone not there?" her mother asked her.

"No, Gary came and picked her up yesterday."

"Oh, he did?"

"Yeah, he said he was taking his kids to Knott's Berry Farm yesterday."

"That Gary stays taking them girls to Knott's Berry Farm, I feel like they go every weekend."

Katrina chuckled. "Mom, it's not every weekend, he takes them every month. Mom, you know he buys season passes, that's why they go so much."

"Oh, okay I was sure wondering."

"Yeah, he gets those every year for them."

"Oh okay, I guess that's smart."

"Yeah," Katrina said.

"Well, are you going to church tomorrow?"

"Yeah, Mike and I will be there."

"Oh yeah, Simone probably going to still be with her daddy huh," Deborah said.

"Yeah, I'm quite sure he wanted the girls to stay the whole weekend."

"Oh ok, well I think I'm going to be heading your way soon, to get up in that pool."

"Yeah, come on, it's hot enough today."

"Yeah, I know, it's so hot it's making me think twice about going outdoors."

"True, but you already said you coming, now I want to see you."

"Alright, I'll be there shortly."

"Alright mom, see you when you get here."

"Ok baby." Katrina and her mother hung up the phone.

The next morning Katrina and Mike woke up late. They both woke up at ten o' clock. "Baby, what time is it?" he asked.

"It's ten."

"Alright, babe you get in first, then wake me up."

"Okay babe," she showered first. Getting out the shower she grabbed her big towel, dried off and wrapped it around her, and then stepping out the shower already dried, she woke up Mike so he could take a shower. She took off her towel to rub lotion on. On the way to the shower, Mike stopped behind and put both his hands up against her stomach. He began talking to his son through her stomach. He knew his son could hear him talk to him. The baby started moving inside her.

"Baby, you saw that!" Mike began looking even closer at her stomach as he watched his son move.

"Yeah, baby I can feel him."

Mike began shaking her stomach very lightly. This time on the side he saw his son move too. Again his son moved, again and again. Mike was shocked and enjoyed it. Every time was the first time for him, that didn't change.

"Go get in the shower babe." She brushed him off making him go get in the shower before they were late to church. She knew he wasn't about to have the time to iron his clothes, so she ironed both of their clothes for church, so when he got out the shower his clothes would already be ready and laid across the bed. Getting out the shower he got dressed. They were out the door by ten thirty. They didn't want to be late to church. Mike rushed there safely. They made it right on time. They got them good seats right in front next to her mother right before the choir came out. Luckily, she saved seats for them because as always it was a packed house. The choir began to sing. The choir sang four songs before the preacher got up to read the words for the day.

"Now, turn to the person next to you and repeat after me," the preacher said on the microphone.

"Neighbor!" the preacher shouted out.

"Neighbor!" all the members and everyone sitting out in the audience had repeated it throughout the sanctuary. No one was quiet.

"Say, neighbor, *I want you to know that I'm not perfect. I've made some mistakes, I have some failures, but I'm still blessed!*" The preacher shouted out.

Then the church repeated, *"I want you to know that I'm not perfect. I've made some mistakes, I have some failures, but I'm still blessed."*

"Look at your neighbor and say, God is on my side!" The preacher shouted out.

Everyone in the church looked at their neighbor and repeated, *"God is on my side!"*

The preacher kept preaching. Service was good and after church, they went home. Katrina dialed Gary's cell.

"Hey Katrina," he answered.

"What time you bringing Simone back, you know it is school tomorrow?"

"Oh, I know. I was going to leave here at six o' clock."

"Oh okay," then they hung up.

Simone made it back home. Simone walked in with her set of keys. "Mom, I'm home!"

"We up here," Katrina sounded loud.

Simone jogged upstairs. Then Simone went to her mother's and Mike's room. "Hey mom, hey Mike!" she hugged them both.

"What did you bring me?" Mike asked her.

She handed him a key chain with his name on it.

"Aw! Look at my baby thinking about me."

"You had fun?" Katrina asked.

"Yeah, it was funny seeing my dad really scared of rides, he was all screaming."

"I thought he doesn't mess with the rides like that."

"Yeah, when we goes he only gets on some, but Asia made him get on all the rides. She likes the same rides Paige and I like."

"Oh, he took her this time?"

"Yeah, she came with us."

"Where is my gift?" "Mike gets a key chain, where's mine?"

"Oh, I left it downstairs."

"Downstairs, ooooh, you are cold Simone," she chuckled.

Mike had to laugh too. Simone ran back down the stairs to get the funnel cake from off the living room table. She went back upstairs and handed it to her mom.

"Here mom," Simone smiled.

Katrina looked back and smiled when she noticed she had a funnel cake.

"That's right, my baby brought me back the funnel cake!"

"See, I thought about both of y'all, and I had them to put on extra powdered sugar!"

"Thank you, baby," Katrina told her.

"Thanks, Simone," Mike sounded.

"Are you hungry? It's some dinner downstairs inside the oven for you if you want it, Simone."

"No, I'm not hungry. I'll eat it tomorrow when I get out of school."

"You want to watch a movie in here with us?"

"Yeah sure, just let me take a shower real quick, so I don't have to later or I can just take one in the morning."

"No, go take it right now."

Simone went to go take a shower. While she was in the shower, Katrina and Mike were both eating the funnel cake. Once Simone got out, Mike put the movie on. The three were all laid back on the bed watching the movie. After the movie was over Mike and Simone wanted to watch another movie. Katrina looked at the time, it was past ten.

"Maybe we shouldn't, it's past ten," Katrina sounded.

"Alright, alright," he dragged the words out, "I guess we'll save it for tomorrow," Mike said.

It was getting late. They decided to just watch the other movie the next day, and then they all went to bed.

The next day Mike left for work, Simone was gone to school. After two hours of lying down, she wanted to get up and do something, anything. She was bored, nothing to clean because the house was already clean. By twelve o' clock she was bored out of her mind. She decided to go to the mall. Katrina made it to the mall, did some window shopping, walking through the whole mall. After three hours spent at the mall, her feet were starting to hurt a little. *That's enough exercise for me today* she said to her herself. She left the mall to head back home. As soon as she entered she couldn't wait to sit down and take her sandals off, her feet were hurting even more now. They were hurting so bad she couldn't walk on them at all.

Katrina's feet were really swollen badly. She waited until Mike got home to soak them. As soon as she heard him in the house she yelled his name.

"Mike, come here!" she yelled. "Baby come look at my feet!"

He went upstairs to see what was going on. "Damn babe, how long have they been swollen like that?"

"Like for the last hour."

He went and got their foot spa bucket out the hallway closet, and put some bubble bath and hot water in there; he brought it close to her and placed both her feet inside the bucket to bring her swelling down.

"Babe, you have to stay off your feet and relax. Simone and I can get whatever it is you want or need."

"Okay baby," she said.

Katrina didn't like the sound of that, even though he was right she didn't like feeling helpless.

"I can tell by that look on your face you don't like that, but baby, you don't have that much longer," he rubbed her stomach smiling.

Katrina was having it harder as her stomach got bigger. She was still expanding, which it was crazy that she was. She was already really big, all she could do was rub her hand around her big round stomach to ease the pain.

Mike helped her up the stairs. He propped up five pillows so she could lean back and get comfortable. Then he pulled back the covers on the bed and made Katrina lay down. As she got on the bed he began to pull the covers over her.

"Babe, you alright!" he wondered.

"My stomach just has pain." Katrina told him.

Mike moved the cover over a little, then he lifted up Katrina's shirt to rub her stomach for her some more. Afterwards he began to caress her sensitive nipples. Her breast were so filled with milk she was in pain. After making her feel just a little better for the moment he then pulled her shirt back down over her round pregnant belly. She kissed him. He pulled the cover up over her all the way.

"Thank you baby!" she told him.

"No problem, just let me know when they hurt and I'll take care of it, I got you."

She chuckled. "Okay babe."

"Oh, so have you thought about who's going to be the godparents?" he asked her.

"Oh, Sharee wants to be and I already told her yeah."

"Oh, Shante didn't want too?"

"I know she is going to want to be too, I haven't even brought it to her attention yet."

"Well, do people have two godparents?"

"I'm not really sure, I guess so, he could I guess."

"Well, if you had to pick only one, who would you have in mind?"

"Maybe Shante, but you know if I pick Shante, then Sharee might feel like something," Katrina told him.

"Oh yeah, you may be right. So yeah, you will have to have both of them, or I was thinking Andrea for the godmother since she has been buying him all types of things already, and lately she's been bugging me about it."

Katrina asked Mike to ask his boy Jared to be the godfather and Mike did, along with asking his longtime friend Andrea of over 20 years to be his sons' godmother. That went well, they both said yes. Mike Jr. will have three godmothers and one godfather.

She had an appointment that day for an ultrasound and to check on the baby. She listened to the heartbeat, they checked the weight of the baby and everything seemed fine.

They hadn't been able to make love in the past four months, it's been stressful for him to have to wait, but she wanted to wait until after she had the baby.

That morning Katrina was up early, she had a hard time sleeping, but while awake, her husband was still asleep. Katrina eased herself slowly out the bed so he didn't wake. She went and cooked breakfast for them both. Katrina didn't go back to the bedroom until she was done in the kitchen. When she was finally done is when she went back and got in bed, but she stayed up watching TV. That morning when he woke up, she was already awake.

"Hey, good morning babe. What are you doing already awake?" he asked.

"Oh, I couldn't sleep."

"You cooked?" he asked her from the smell of the aroma.

"Yes babe, I made you some eggs, grits with cheese, two slices of toast, turkey bacon, and sausages."

"Umm baby, sounds good. Well let me get out this bed then since you just can't stay off your feet!" he grinned.

"Oh, and I made some French toast."

"We still have powdered sugar?"

"Yeah," she said.

"That's what's up!"

He leaned in giving her a kiss on the lips, then they hugged each other. He got out the bed and walked to the bathroom. Katrina got out the bed as well and was headed for the kitchen to warm their food. After taking a piss and washing his hands, he grabbed his face towel and wiped his face. He then brushed his teeth and walked out the bedroom.

Mike joined Katrina for breakfast in the kitchen that she had cooked an hour ago. As Mike entered the kitchen he shook his head from side to side looking at his pregnant wife still moving around like she wasn't pregnant. He sat down at the dining room table; she brought over both their plates to the dining room table.

"Here baby," she said to him as she passed him his plate.

Katrina began to feel some discomfort in her stomach.

"What's wrong?" he asked looking very concerned at how she was holding her lower stomach.

"Babe, I'm having contractions."

He looked and became quiet. "How do you know?"

"Because it's been a continuous pain that keeps coming, and has been for twenty minutes now," she told him.

"Oh wow, why you just telling me?"

"Babe, I wanted to make sure that's what it was first, before saying anything."

"Un," she sounded deep. "There it goes again," she sounded.

"What do you want me to do?" Mike asked nervously.

"Baby, call my doctor!" she kept breathing slowly. "Mike what time is it?"

"It's six twenty-three."

"Okay, tell him I've been contracting for over twenty minutes now and its six minutes apart!"

After Mike talked to her doctor he told them to come to the hospital and he would meet them there. Katrina's bag was packed already. Mike grabbed her things. Katrina went and got Simone and the three left the house. As

Mike pulled out the driveway he glanced back at the backseat and told Simone to call her grandmother to tell her they were headed to the hospital.

Once they made it to the hospital the waiting room was filled with a lot of expecting couple's families sitting there waiting. By the look of everyone that was there, it looked like they had been there overnight, because it was packed.

The nurses wheeled Katrina into the exam room and laid her onto the table. Going in the nurse got him some scrubs to put on. Katrina was given a private room and Simone was able to stay and watch her baby brother be born.

Katrina was ready to give birth. Mike stood by her side holding her hand the whole time, helping her breathe calmly. Within minutes Katrina's Doctor came inside. Also, her parents, her sister, and her niece Paige came walking in all at the same time.

The nurse kept coming in her room to monitor how often her contractions were coming. After some hours had passed, it was almost about that time. The nurse had noticed how close they were starting to come.

Katrina began to feel her stomach tighten, the pains of the contractions were coming every two minutes now.

"Aaaauuuuggghhh!!!!!" she screamed, the pain had her screaming, she didn't care who heard her. It kept coming, harder and harder, her screaming noises wouldn't stop. Mike was still holding her hand over filled with joy about to see his first child be born. Her girls then walked in, Shante and Sharee.

"Girl, we could hear you from down the hall," they laughed.

"Glad y'all made it," she says as she breathes fast.

"Calm down," her nurse told her.

"Baby, just breathe," Mike said.

"But I can feel him coming!"

"I know, just breathe and push Katrina!"

"Katrina, I need you to just breathe slowly sweet heart!"

She tried to breathe slowly, but she kept breathing fast.

"Baby, please calm down," he told her. The way she was breathing fast and screaming he knew his son was coming really soon. Her eyes widened.

"Baby, he's coming, I can feel him coming!"

After six hours of labor and their baby was finally born. Mike was the happiest father and Katrina couldn't be happier right now. Afterward she was sent to the recovery room, and then she was going to go back to her room. The nurse took her baby to weigh him and clean him all up while she went to the recovery room.

Mike and Simone left the room to grab some food for everybody. They drove across the street to KFC to get the twenty dollar family pack. Getting back to the hospital he saw his sister Michelle and his mother walking towards the front desk.

"Michelle! Mom!" he yelled. The two of them turned around and then they both smiled.

"Did she have the baby already?" Michelle asked with a surprised look on her face.

"Yeah, she just had him not too long along."

"Awww, we tried making it here as fast as we could!"

"Oh, no worries, she's in recovery right now. They said they will bring her back in two hours and that was forty minutes ago."

"Awww, I want to see my nephew!"

"Awww, congratulation son. I can't wait to meet my grandbaby, finally, my first grandbaby!"

"I know, right, but yeah, y'all will see him in a minute. The nurse went to go clean him up and weigh him she said."

"Awww brother, I'm so anxious, I can't wait to meet my nephew." The four walked to Katrina's room. Entering the room he introduced his mother to baby Mike's godparents and her sister. They both met Katrina's parents. They were all waiting around the room chilling, talking with everyone. Mike pulled some plates out the bag so they could make their plates. He made a plate for Katrina and put hers to the side with a napkin over it. They all ate and right after they were done eating more of Katina's family showed up, and Andrea showed up. As she woke up in the recovery room, her eyes were barely opening, all she could see was the nurse walking in getting ready to take her back to her room. Then she looked to the right side of her and saw the other nurse pushing the infant bed with her son. Katrina couldn't wait to hold her baby, she couldn't stop smiling.

Mike saw his wife first as she barely entered. He quickly got everyone to follow him over to the other side of her room, so she would be surprised.

Once Katrina looked all the way around the room all she could do was smile. Everyone was there to help her welcome her new baby boy.

There were so many family and friends; they were all bunched up standing there with balloons and gifts. She was so happy to see everyone.

"Aww you guys, thank you!" she said loudly to everyone.

Katrina came in the room with her baby in her arms. Everyone was excited to see their new baby; both their parents were excited to see their new grandbaby. He was sleep. Once she put him down Mike passed her plate of food, she then ate.

"Babe, you have a lot of gifts, you want to open them now?"

Katrina couldn't stop smiling. "I mine as well."

Katrina thought this was so nice and thoughtful to come bring gifts and balloons up to the hospital, she was not expecting this at all. Katrina sat up in her bed as Mike passed her one gift at a time; she was opening up gift after gift. She had short sleeve onesies, more clothes, and another car seat.

Two days later, once released from the hospital, Mike was the one who stayed up at night for that late night feeding and put their son to sleep so his wife could get some real sleep. Waking up that next morning Katrina went and checked on Mike Jr. He was still asleep. Then she went and opened all the blinds downstairs, the morning heat was already beaming inside. She hurried herself to the kitchen quietly. She wanted to prepare them some breakfast along with his lunch. She couldn't wait to get back to her wifely duties. No more waiting on her hand and foot now that the baby here.

A Week Later

Their son had his first doctor's appointment, it was on a Saturday. The appointment went great. After leaving the appointment they went back home. It's the weekend and with no plans, but to enjoy their baby. The moment they walked in the house, Katrina went upstairs to change into something comfortable. Without asking if Mike was hungry she was about to go to the kitchen.

"Babe, you going downstairs?" he asked.

"Yeah babe, I'm about to go make some sandwiches."

"What kind?" Mike asked her.

"I was thinking turkey or tuna!"

"I want turkey."

"Alright, Turkey it is!"

Katrina went down to the kitchen to make lunch. Smoked honey turkey was his favorite lunch meat besides tuna. Katrina pulled opened the pantry to grab the wheat bread, sat it on the island, then went to the refrigerator. Opening the refrigerator she pulled out the mayo, mustard, lettuce, sliced cheese, American and Swiss. He always had to have both with his spoiled self and of course the smoked honey turkey. She loved him, and as she stood in the kitchen preparing lunch all she could think about was *starting over was not so bad: new baby, new house, new husband, new blended family, and new neighbors.*

The next morning after feeding Mike Jr. her door bell rung. Katrina wondered who it was. It's wasn't Mike she knew, coming back plus no one had called from the gate. Katrina sat Mike Jr. in his seat, snapped his strap, and then went for the door. Looking through the peephole it was a delivery guy holding a long gold box. She shook her head then opened her door.

"Yes, good morning."

"Hello, good morning ma'am. I have a delivery for Katrina."

"That's me."

The delivery man then passed Katrina her box.

"Thank you," she took her box.

"Have a good day ma'am."

"You too," she told him.

Katrina closed her front door and went back to the living room. She sat on the couch and opened her box. It was long stemmed red roses from no other than her husband. No one else sent her flowers once a week. Reaching for the white card in between the roses, there was a note. He was always saying something sweet. It read:

Baby, this is just because you are special. I appreciate you and I love you and I can't wait to come home to you and our little blessing. Love your husband.

Katrina stared at the card grinning. Minutes later after staring at her sweet little card she went to go put her roses in a vase.

Later that evening, once Mike made it home, Katrina left to run a few errands and to go get some things from the grocery store. She also made a stop to get something special for her husband. Once Katrina made it to the first store she called her husband.

"Hey baby," he answered.

"Hey, I'm at the store. What kind of snacks you want?"

"Anything you get is fine baby."

"Ok." They hung up and Katrina continued shopping. Leaving the store she stopped by the jewelry store to get something nice for Mike. She walked in and saw a nice gold Rolex chain. She picked that one, there was no need to look at anything else. She paid for it then she left. On the way back home she called her husband.

"Hey, baby."

"Hey, babe I'm on my way back home now."

"Oh, okay," he replied.

"How about a blinker next time asshole!" she blurted out.

Mike giggled.

"Who you laughing at, me?" Katrina asked.

"Yeah, you and your road range!"

She chuckled. "No, it's not even that. I'm not even speeding babe, it's just this asshole just cut in front of me without even signaling his blinker to get over, like damn, don't wait until the last minute."

"Well, babe let me let you drive, call me when you make it home so I can come get the bags."

"I will have your mother picked up the baby yet?" she asked.

"No, not yet, what time do you think you'll be home?"

"In a little bit."

"Oh, okay, well, call me in a minute."

"Ok babe."

"Love you."

"Love you too." Then they hung up. Shortly she made it home, pulled into the drive way, and then called Mike.

"Babe, you here" he answered.

"Yeah, babe I'm here in the garage."

"Alright, here I come."

Katrina got out the car before he made it to the garage. She put his gift inside her purse. He came and began to get the bags from out the car and Katrina went inside. When she thought he was done she called out his name.

"Yeah babe," he replied.

"Come here, I'm in the room!"

Mike went upstairs to go see what she wanted. When he entered the room she had her hand behind her back smiling. She looked into his eyes. "I have a surprise for you."

"What for?" he smiled thinking what was she's up to.

"Babe, I just wanted to surprise you with something this time. You know you're always surprising me with something, or just always doing something so sweet and special, I just wanted to show my appreciation." She pulled her arm from behind her back and handed him a jewelry box. He reached for it, then looked at her as he continued smiling. Then he opened his box. It was a gold chain.

"Aw, baby this is really nice. I appreciate this but you know as your man, and as your husband, I'm just doing my job!"

"I know and I love you and I appreciate you," they hugged and kissed.

Shortly after Mike's mother came to pick up her grandson. Mike and Katrina were finally kid free. Simone had been gone since yesterday to her sister's house. The two thought on this beautiful Saturday how could they not Bar-B-Q. He called up his brother to see what plans he and Shante had for the day. Once they said nothing he invited them over and then he took out some meat out the deep freezer that was inside the garage. After everything thawed, Mike went and got the grill ready. Mike went out to the backyard to check on the grill, he was about to get ready to start grilling the meat. Mike whipped out all his seasonings, seasoned the meat, and then threw it on the grill.

Once Charles and Shante arrived Mike showed them the meat that was on the grill.

"Aye, bro if I would have known you were doing all this I would've at least brought over some dessert, or had Shante whip up a side dish or something!"

Mike chuckled, as he smiled. "Man, come on, you know you don't have to bring shit!"

"Man, we wouldn't have minded."

"I know, now when I ask you, then okay, but now we had all this shit in the deep freezer." Mike looked at Katrina. "Yeah, she'll come home with like ten deodorants, all types of food and snacks!"

Shante smiled and then looked at Katrina.

"Girl, I be coupon shopping, so I'm always buying up all kinds of stuff," they laughed.

"Babe, we are about to go to the grocery store. Do you need anything?"

Mike thought about it quickly, "No babe!"

"Babe, do we need more ice?" she asked him.

"No."

"How about more sauce?" she asked.

"No, I think we have enough."

"Alright, babe then we'll be back."

"Alright," she sounded. Katrina and Shante left for the store. The fellas continued their conversation. Mike stood up as he continued talking with his brother. He opened the grill to fork the ribs, then he flipped them over and turned over the chicken and the hamburger patties. Then he closed the grill and sat back down.

"So bro, soon I'm going to be going to Detroit to check on the business out there."

Mike was stunned, this was news to Mike's ears what Charles was telling him right now. He didn't know that their Uncle was thinking about opening up another restaurant. "No shit, that's what's up!"

Mike started the beans and the water for the macaroni and cheese. Twenty minutes later the ladies made it back. Returning, Katrina kissed her husband and Shante went over and kissed Charles on the lips.

"You guys missed us?" Katrina asked as she smiled.

"Yes babe, you know we did for the whole twenty minutes y'all were gone," he laughed.

"Yeah, we were going to put out an APB on y'all, we thought somebody kidnapped y'all for a minute," Charles added to the conversation as he laughed along with his brother.

Twenty minutes later Mike added a little barbecue sauce and brown sugar to the beans. Then he added the macaroni noodles to the pot, then went back outside to the back.

Hours later the food was almost ready. "Babe, can you start getting the plates ready?" Mike asked Katrina.

"Of course babe," she replied.

Katrina began getting the plates ready, everything was looking good as always and they were ready to eat. Katrina had pulled the macaroni and cheese and the beans out the oven. The oven wasn't on but it kept them both warm.

"Ummm, this looks bomb," Shante smiled.

"Girl, it is, Mike ass know he is getting down."

"Aye boo, you want me to get anything?"

"Oh yeah, look inside the pantry and grab the napkins, ketchup, hot sauce, mustard and the loaf of bread."

"Ok." Shante sounded. Shante had wanted to help do something. Katrina started putting the beans, and macaroni and cheese onto all their plates. Just as she was done with the fourth plate Mike came in through the door with the tray of ribs. Following behind him was Charles bringing in the tray that had the hamburgers, links, and chicken on it. Then Katrina added meat to everybody's plate, they were all ready to grub. Katrina picked up Mike's and her plate from off the counter and Shante grabbed Charles's and her plate and took them outside.

They enjoyed their Saturday. Later that night Katrina ironed their clothes so she wouldn't have to do it in the morning, just in case they woke up late. She didn't want them to have to rush for church. They showered and went to sleep. The next day after church Mike started dinner and Katrina took a nap. Their baby was brought back home.

Mike left with his son. He wanted his wife to get a good nap with no disturbance. Getting back she was still asleep and sleeping well. He kept quiet, she was sleeping too well. The food was still cooking in the crock pot.

He went and sat on the bed with the TV turned down low. A half hour later she began to roll over. He looked down at her and she looked up at him.

"How was your nap?"

"It was good, thanks, babe."

"You're welcome, you needed that, you were snoring."

"No I wasn't!" she grinned.

"Yes you were," he smiled.

"Well if I was, that's how tired I was."

"I know babe," he chuckled.

Shortly after Mike went and finished dinner: oxtails, black eyed peas, macaroni and cheese, and greens. Katrina was glad Mike had already taken care of dinner. Then she prepared a salad.

"This is good baby."

"Thank you," he replied.

After they were done eating Katrina began to get Mike's and Simone's things ready to iron for tomorrow for work and school for them. After she was done she hung their clothes on hangers. Then she went to go check on the baby. He was still asleep. She saw he needed a diaper change, but she didn't want to wake him. She gently changed his diaper without waking him up. Afterward it was lights out, they all went to sleep.

The next morning everyone woke up dragging around the house, this how it was every Monday morning. Katrina didn't really have to get up when they did, but she was always a big help to the both of them every morning. Katrina was home with the baby. She had a whole agenda between the baby, the house duties and finding houses for her clients. Working from home wasn't that bad. Around noon she called Mike, he was like her best friend too, she loved talking to her hubby throughout the day. She grabbed her phone from off the table and dialed his cell. "Hey baby," he answered.

"Hey babe, how is your day going so far?"

"It's going good, how about yours babe?"

"It's been busy; I haven't been bored, that's for sure."

"That's right," he sounded. They talked a bit, and then they got off the phone. Later that evening Mike pulled up, he made it home from shopping. After work he stopped by the mall to get his two favorite ladies some shoes. Mike got out the car with bags in his hand. "Hey Simone!" he said.

"Hey dad!" she replied back.

"Hey, where's your mom?"

"She's up in there!" she pointed towards the house.

"Oh, okay."

As he was passing Simone as she was sitting out on the porch talking to her friends she looked down at the bags. Yeah, he spoiled them both. He loved them both dearly, she knew she had something.

"Oh, did you get something for me?"

He looked back at her and smiled. "I did actually!"

"Thank you, Thank you!" she smiled.

"I'll be right back," she laughed to her friends, and then she quickly went inside. He gave his ladies their gifts. He kissed and hugged Katrina. "Baby, I'm cooking dinner tonight," he told her.

"Ok," she sounded as she smiled. Simone went back outside to the porch showing off her new shoes to her friends. Katrina was playing around with the baby as Mike was in the kitchen preparing this dinner he wanted to cook. Simone came back inside an hour later, showered, and got ready for dinner.

Dinner was nothing fancy, but it was very good: meatloaf, mash potatoes, string beans, and cornbread. After dinner, they went to the room and watched TV. Once the baby went to sleep they took off their clothes, the looks they gave each other, watching each other undress brought an emotion over them, they took a shower together. Getting out the shower and drying off he picked her up and carried her to the bed. He gently laid her down. She was looking beautiful as always. "I love you, baby!"

"I love you more babe," she responded back. He began kissing all over her naked body. As they waited, the feel of his lips against her body made her feel like doing something tonight. Then his strong big hands began to slide up against her body as she rubbed his biceps down to his erection. The touch was gentle to the two, it almost made them say forget these doctor's orders of waiting. The moans sounded meant it felt good. The two couldn't wait until after six weeks has passed.

He kissed her lips gently and softly as his hand trailed from her nipples down pass her stomach, to the side of her hips, then to the inside of her thighs. He rubbed her insides sliding it in up and down making her moan. He made it wet enough to easily slide in how he wanted to. As he slids his wet fingers from her, he sucked his fingers.

He looked up at her. "Did that hurt?"

"No."

"So you didn't feel any discomfort?"

She shook her head from side to side "No!" she responded.

"Technically we have waited the whole time, we only have one more week to wait, it shouldn't hurt if we go a week early."

Katrina started chuckling. "Ok," she said.

He smiled. It didn't take much to convince her. She must have wanted it just as much as he did.

"But when I go in, if you feel any pain at all, tell me and I will pull out."

"Ok."

He rolled his tongue in circles around her nipples. Shortly after he slowly licked her breast, the one he was holding, he put it into his mouth. She moaned as he sucked it. His warm breath warmed her body. Then he switched over to her other breast doing the same. Suddenly he rose up a little to stick it in. As he was about to slide inside, she tightened her muscles in her groin, but then she stopped. She didn't want to hurt anything down there, they both stared into each other's eyes. He went in very slowly, as soon as the tip went in he smiled, and then sounded a moan. He kept going in slowly. As he was inside they were still looking into each other's eyes. He leaned down towards her face and they kissed with their tongues inside each other's mouth.

Tonight he was planning on making up for all the months they had missed. It felt so damn good. He was afraid to go in deep. So he stopped once it was in half way. It was hard not to go all the way in, but he was going to at least try. In between the moans, it was silence, he loved hearing that sound they heard when he was going in and out of her. He wasn't trying to change to any other positions like he normally would. He stayed at the same position with him on top and at the same rhythm and speed. They moaned until they both exploded, then they just laid be side each other until they both fell asleep which didn't take them long at all.

While Katrina takes a break from her Real Estate job, which Mike doesn't see it as a break if she still looks for houses for different clients while being at home with their newborn son Mike Jr.; she planned to start back having her jewelry parties. She likes to keep the money coming in somehow. Once the baby went to sleep she had time to go through all her jewelry boxes to see what all she had left. She was thankful to have enough for at least her first party she was going to plan soon. She received a text. It was Mike saying, babe, *I'm about to go to the gym and I'm going to slide to the house afterward*. After putting away the boxes she went and prepared lunch.

Mike wasn't there, he went to go work out at the gym. Once he got to the gym his mind was only focused on lifting weights. He trips out on the ladies who he catches that be trying to make eye contact with him. He pays them no mind and stay's in his own zone and bounce. When Mike made it home Katrina had lunch ready for him.

Katrina could hear her husband coming up the stairs. "Hey babe!" she sounded loud.

"Hey baby!" he walked in giving her a kiss.

"Babe, I made you lunch!"

"Thanks, babe."

"You're welcome."

Mike went and took a shower. After he took a shower he came out the bathroom and noticed Katrina had gone downstairs. He threw on some sweats and a t-shirt, then he went downstairs. Going into the kitchen Katrina was in their making their plates. He sat at the table. Bringing over their plates they sat, ate, and talked.

"So when does junior have his next doctor's appointment?"

"On Monday," Katrina said.

"Next week?"

"Yes, it's at eight," she responded.

"Alright, I'm going with you!"

"Okay."

They were sitting there enjoying their lunch she made.

"So babe, what do you think about me having a jewelry party, I haven't done it in years, but it will give me something else to do while I'm at home and I'll make some extra cash doing it?"

Mike shrugged his shoulders, "I say do it, babe!"

"Yeah," she said.

Mike glanced up at her, "Yeah baby if that's what you want to do, yeah I say do it!" he nodded his head.

"Alright," she responded.

"Aye babe, how is your friend doing?" he asked.

"Which one babe?" she says.

"Sharee," Mike sounded.

Katrina took a moment to answer. She looked down, then she looked up at him. "You know what, I'm not even sure, it's been a few weeks since I talked to her. Last time I was over there he was acting very shitty to her, but then that was the same day she called me crying saying he choked her," she said looking up at him.

Mike sat there and shook his head from side to side. He didn't like hearing shit like that, a man putting his hands on a woman. "You know how I feel about that. She don't have no brother's or nobody that can go over there and beat his ass at least one good time for her?"

"No, but to be honest I'm not even sure any of her family know what's been going on, she doesn't like her family knowing her personal business," she said.

"In my opinion, I think they should have known about this one because somebody would have helped her by now!"

"Yes, that's true baby!"

"Shit, I should take my ass over there and beat his ass myself!" he said hitting the palm of his hand.

"Yes I would love to see that, but his ass probably wouldn't want to fight you!"

Mike was sitting there at the table angry at Katrina's friend boyfriend for putting his hands on her. He was just sitting there in thought not saying a word. Then in minutes, they both got up from the table to go and watch TV in the living room. They decided to watch Netflix instead of cable. He sat up while she lay on the couch wrapped under his arms.

That evening, him asking about Sharee earlier she couldn't help to wonder what was going on over there and why hadn't she talked to her in a few weeks. She had to call her. Katrina dialed Sharee's number on her cell.

"Hey lady, I was just checking in on you, wondering why I haven't talked to my friend in weeks!"

"I'm fine K, just been really busy, sorry for not calling," Sharee told her.

"Oh no, it's good, I'm just glad to hear you are okay, even Mike was like how is your friend Sharee!"

"Thank you for checking in on me and tell Mike I said thanks for caring and asking about me," she said smiling.

"Oh, no problem, love you, lady," Katrina said to her.

"Love you too, y'all enjoy y'all night," Sharee said softly.

"Oh Sharee, so it's no more RoShawn?" she asks her.

"He never left, and when he found his keys missing he made me make him an extra set."

"Oh Lord Girl, well I'm about to take my butt to sleep, Mike Jr. just went to sleep I'm right behind him," she laughed softly.

Sharee laughed. "Girl I hear you, well goodnight."

"Goodnight." Katrina and Sharee hung up.

Mike walked back into the room drinking a water bottle. He glanced at Katrina "She's alright babe?" he asked looking at her.

"Yeah, and she said thank you for asking about her and she said RoShawn never left, he once he noticed his house keys missing he made her go make him a new set."

He shook his head.

"Babe, I'm about to get to bed while the baby is sleep, just in case he wakes up in the middle of the night, I can hear him," she said walking towards the dresser.

"Alright, and if you don't I will. One of us will hear his crying," he said.

"Yes, that's true."

Katrina took off her clothes and changed into her pajamas. Katrina kissed her hubby, then got into bed quietly. Later in the night, the baby woke up crying he needed to be changed. She just learned that cry. Katrina changed him, then patted him back to sleep. Once he went back to sleep, she slipped back into bed. Katrina had scooted close to Mike wrapping her arm around him. He slightly turned over facing her "He okay?" Mike whispered.

"Yeah, he just needed a diaper change, but he already went back to sleep," she said softly.

"Oh ok, love you," he whispered.

"Love you too," she said softly. He turned back over and she closed her eyes and went back to sleep immediately. Katrina woke up at six thirty, everyone was still asleep. She got up and checked on the baby, he was sleeping so peacefully, so she laid back down, closed her eyes, and went back to sleep too. Thirty minutes later Katrina found herself up again, this time she thought she was up for good. She began pushing Mike's arm to wake him up. The first push didn't do anything, he was still sound asleep, so she began shaking him until he woke up. Once she saw him open his eyes is when she stopped.

"Babe, it's seven," she sounded.

"Alright, please wake me up at seven forty-five," he whispered. He was still tired.

"Alright," she said.

Katrina got up, she wasn't tired anymore. She woke up Simone, then made her way downstairs making her some coffee. She wasn't hungry, but she made an egg and cheese omelet for Mike and prepared a bottle for the baby for when he woke up. After she was done cooking she washed the dishes she had just used. Simone left to go meet up with her friends for school. Then Katrina went and sat on the couch watching the news. At seven forty-five Katrina went back upstairs to wake up Mike. Mike got up, showered, got dressed, ate his omelet, then he left out the door.

Mike and his brother met up at one of their restaurants for a lunch meeting. They needed to discuss some things and the goals for the business this year. A few months ago things weren't going the way they were supposed to have been, starting the New Year and still wasn't, which brought them right now to come up with a different solution.

Charlie walked in smiling looking at Mike. "Nephew!" he shouted.

"Hey, what's up Unc!"

"How is daddy life treating you man?" his uncle asked him.

"Man, it's wonderful, Lil man just getting so big, he's a happy baby. Man, that's my Lil man."

"That's right, congratulations once again on your baby boy, I need to stop by the house soon and see Lil man."

"Yeah, the wife and I took him to his doctor's appointment a few days ago, and he had all the ladies in the waiting area all over him."

"Awww shit, my Lil nephew is a playa playa!" Charles said.

"Hey Charles," Charlie said.

"What's up Unc?" he smiled.

"Man, I can't call it," then Charlie took a seat.

The three discussed some issues the family business was having. They came up with a few solutions. All three gave their input and jotted notes onto their notepads. The meeting only lasted an hour. Meeting went great.

Mike called Katrina. "Hey," she answered.

"Babe, we're going out on a date later!"

"Oh, okay, a double date or just us?"

"Just us," he said.

It didn't matter to her either way because whether they were by themselves or on a double date they always had fun, no matter what the two always enjoyed each other's company.

Mike made it home, took a quick shower, and got dressed. They were getting ready to go out. They were going to leave the baby with her mother; they knew she was going to be happy to see her grandkids, especially baby Mike. Katrina loved seeing her mother's happy face just as she was when Simone was a baby, this was like Deja vu.

She missed their going out having fun days since she had gotten to be big and couldn't do anything. Oh boy was she happy those days were gone. After they were done getting dressed and getting the diaper bag together, the four were ready to go. The four left the house and were headed to Deborah's house to drop off the kids. Arriving there Mike parked his car in the driveway, then helped to get the baby out the car and he, Simone, and Katrina walked to the front door and Katrina rang the doorbell.

(Ding Dong) Mike had to ring the doorbell too.

Katrina turned her head to Mike and smiled. "Babe, momma is going to get you," she laughed. "You know you got to give her time to make it to the door!"

"Just in case she didn't hear the first one, hearing it back to back, I know she will hear that," he grinned. She began chuckling.

78

"Hey y'all," Deborah finally answered.

"Hey mom," Katrina said.

"Hey baby, now who rung that doorbell twice?" she smiled.

Katrina and Mike both looked at each other and they both pointed to each other and laughed.

"Hey Mom," Mike told her.

"Hey son," She smiled.

"Hey granny," Simone told her.

"Hey my Simone," she hugged her smiling.

"Thank you guys for bringing my grandbabies over here."

"Oh no mom, thank you for having them over while we go out."

They both walked the kids inside. Mike and Katrina both gave her mother and the kids a kiss.

"Alright bye, you guys."

"Bye, have fun!" Deborah and Simone told them. They went and got back into the car and now were headed to the forum. They couldn't wait to see Kevin Hart live on stage.

Getting there they were enjoying themselves as always, they couldn't stop laughing. They had been laughing since the moment he came out on stage.

An hour later, Katrina quickly went to the restroom to call her mother. Katrina held the phone tightly to her ear as she waited for her mother to pick up.

"Yes Katrina," she answered.

"Hey mom, I was just calling checking on the kids, how is my baby?"

"Girl bye!" she laughed, "The kids are good, you know every time we're together we have fun, I'm over here enjoying my grandkids, but you go on and enjoy yourself, bye."

Katrina chuckled. "Ok mom, bye," she chuckled again then they hung up. Katrina left the restroom and went back inside. That night leaving out the forum it was drizzling. "Babe, I don't want to get my hair wet at all!"

"Alright, I'll be back. I'm about to get the car and pull up right in front. I'll be back!"

"Okay," she sounded. Just minutes later her cell rang. She didn't bother looking to see who it was, she knew it wasn't anyone but Mike saying he was out in the front. She walked out the forum with her jacket pulled over her head, there was Mike right out front just like she suspected. Katina quickly rushed to the car, she got close to the car and he opened her door for her from inside the car and she quickly got in and they drove off. He already had the heater on. It was already warm in no time and they went and grabbed the kids from her mother's house. Then they went straight home. Everybody was asleep in the car, including Katrina. He cracked his side of the window down to get that night air to keep him awake, he didn't want to let it down too much and get the kids sick. They made it home. He woke up Katrina and Simone, then he carried the baby in leaving his car seat inside the car. He made sure everyone got in their beds, then he went to sleep too.

The next morning, Katrina and the baby went up to her job, she was missing her office and the clients, she let the staff meet Mike Jr. She was looking refreshed, from sleeping in this morning after being out late last night. They didn't stay long they were there for an hour. The visit was great. Afterward they left and went home. Returning home, she didn't feel like doing anything, just relaxing and that's it and that's all.

"Ma, me, Nicole, Antoinette, Tony, Jovan and Lester about to catch the bus to the movies," Simone told her. It was the weekend and she wanted to hang out.

"Oh lord, did you just say catch the bus?"

Simone laughed, "Yeah mom!"

"You sure you want to catch the bus? Mike can drop you guys off."

"Oh, it's fine, we have other friends that are going to catch the bus too."

"Oh, ok."

Gary called Simone's cell to talk to her.

"Hey, baby girl!"

"Hey Daddy," Simone said.

"What you doing?"

"Getting dressed," she responded.

He looked down at his watch as he held the phone to his ear.

"Where you going?" he asked her.

"Going on a movie date," she said.

"On a movie date, with whom?" he asked.

"Nicole, Antoinette, Jovan, Tony, and Lester," Simone responded.

"Who is Jovan, Tony, and Lester?"

"Friends from school dad," she dragged her voice.

"Your mom knows?"

"Yes, she's dropping us off, well actually, Mike is!"

"Oh, he is huh, where is she?"

"Downstairs with Mike," she told him.

"Alright, baby I'll call you back."

Simone hung up the phone with her dad. She knew her dad was upset about her going on this movie date with her guy friends from school by how he ended their conversation, their conversation was too short.

"Mom!" she yelled downstairs.

"Yeah!" she yelled back in response.

"My dad is about to call you about who I'm going to the movies with!" she yelled out. Simone wanted her mother to already be aware.

"Okay," she replied back yelling from downstairs from the living room. In seconds her cell rung, it was Gary.

"Hey Gary," she answered.

"Katrina, why you letting our daughter go out on dates? she shouldn't be worrying about dating right now!"

"It's just friends from school," Katrina told him.

"Yeah, that's how it starts. Don't let her go with no boys Katrina!"

"I'm not about to not let her go out on her movie date with her friends!"

When Gary noticed she wasn't going to listen, he just got off the phone with her.

Katrina looked at Mike.

"What, Gary mad she going out?"

"Yeah, he has nerves," Katrina said sounding irritated.

"What he say?"

"He doesn't want her going out with no boys and she shouldn't be thinking about dating right now," she said as she leaned back against the couch.

"But those are her friends!"

"I know, they are all really close friends!"

"We can trust Simone, she's smart, and she knows better and until she shows us different, then that's when things will change," Mike said.

Two hours later, Simone, her friends, and Mike had left the house. He had dropped them off at the movies.

The next morning waking up lying in each other's arms, she began to think about her day and what she needed to do. She thought she'd get out of bed now, she lifted up, but then he pulled her back down. She laughed. "Babe!" she sounded grinning.

"No, don't get up yet, your body was keeping me warm!"

Katrina's eyes glanced at the window and noticed the gray clouds. "Babe, what's the weather supposed to be like today?"

"You know what, I'm not sure, haven't looked at the news!"

"The news doesn't know neither," Katrina said.

Mike laughed. "Babe you just refuse to watch the news huh," he smiled.

"Well, I'm not going to say I refuse to watch the news, it's just they not always accurate, and they only show bad stuff, what about all the good stuff that happens around the world?"

"It's supposed to be seventy-two degrees!" he said.

"How you know?"

"I just looked at the weather app on my phone," he said.

"Oh," she shook her head.

"Now and days don't nobody know how to dress when they step outdoors!"

"That's how people be getting sick," he responded.

"Yeah, and I don't have no time to get sick, I have stuff to do every single day and ain't trying to make nobody in this house sick neither!"

"Yeah, you heard Simone cough this morning?"

"Yeah, I heard. I was going to say something, but I didn't because yesterday before she left I told her to put on her jacket, but she didn't talk about it's hot, and I was thinking like what about when you come back home it will be cold, but no, she didn't want to take any jacket, I said okay. Now look."

"See, kids think we don't know!"

"Right, Like shit we been there and done that," Katrina said.

"Right," Mike chuckled.

They had a chill Sunday. The next morning Mike woke himself up, got dressed and was ready to start his day. Mike kissing Katrina's lips is how she woke up, then Mike left. The baby was asleep. Katrina brought him downstairs with her to the family room while she watched TV downstairs.

Katrina reached for the remote, she thought she heard the doorbell; she turned the TV down to see if she'd hear it again.

"Ding. Dong." Katrina doorbell had rung again. She wondered which neighbor was at her door. Katrina reached closer to her door and noticed it was Gary." Katrina opened her front door.

"How did you get in the gate?" she said with an attitude. Yeah, she had one, she was unhappy of the visit without a call first and just popping up at her door like this.

"Someone was coming, so I parked on the side and just walked in here."

"Oh."

Though Katrina had an attitude, she was sure looking good. Her new baby added some more curves on her, she was already hot and beautiful with curves, but damn she was even curvier and he was liking what he saw right now. He almost wanted to ask her for a hug right then.

"You are looking good Katrina!"

Katrina wasn't in the mood for him gazing into her eyes, him checking out her body, she saw his eyes wondering her frame, nor was she in the mood to hear his compliments this morning. She needed him to get to the point of why he was there.

"What's up?" she says.

Gary licked his lips. "Yeah, I sure missed that," his eyes glanced down at her body from her breast down to her front center as he did a head nod.

"Gary, what the hell man, if you don't stop with that shit, what do you want?"

"Sorry, I can't help myself," he says.

"Well, you better!"

Gary smiled. "Alright, sorry about that and also sorry if I made you a little upset yesterday."

She shook her head.

"Sorry for all that shit in our marriage I caused too," this wasn't Gary's first time apologizing, he's been apologizing for years now, over and over again. He couldn't help it.

"Like I said time and time again, we were better than that. We were different, you were all that I knew, you were all that I needed, you was who I did everything first with. We were best friends, our bond was like no other and you fucked all that up!"

"I know, I was so fucking stupid!"

"Yeah, you were," she paused. She raised an eye brow, "I didn't deserve that!"

"No, you didn't and I'm so sorry," he said as he shook his head.

"But then when I sensed something wasn't right, I confronted my sister and she denied anything was going on between y'all, you even lied to me too, the lies you two came up with were crazy!"

"I'm sorry Katrina!"

"Gary, fuck your sorry man, that shit happened, but it should have never happened. I was pissed, it was you that fucked up our marriage, you both played me, my husband and my best friend, my sister, my blood. I was ashamed in front of my family. MAN, you embarrassed me in front of my family, our family, our daughter, that shit hurt bad man!" she said sadly.

He stepped a foot out trying to reach for a hug from her. She stepped back, she didn't need any hug. She kept talking, he had her fired up.

"That shit was crazy. I couldn't believe you would hurt my heart and our marriage like that, just because a few nights a week I'd come home too tired trying to bring in extra money for our household. I did that for us, and the way you thanked me for stepping up, having your back like a wife is supposed to, is have an affair on me, ARE YOU FUCKING SERIOUS!"

"And then, you put me out and we separated, but years later you called me up to reunite, you know that was the happiest day of my life."

"Yeah, I did, I thought after all that time maybe we could put our marriage back together, but it was hard, week after week, and month after month all I could think about was you fucking my sister and I realized my heart and my love for you just wasn't there anymore, and I realized you didn't deserve me anymore. I'm sorry it took almost a whole year for me to realize that when I did."

"I was so lost without you," he tells her.

"All that matters now is that I'm married to a great man, I have my new family, we good over here."

Gary turned around and left. She closed her front door, Katrina's morning was going well until he popped up at her house and now thinking about Gary ass and their argument was the last thing she wanted to be thinking about this morning. She lay back on the couch and pulled her cover back over her.

Once the baby woke up she got him dressed, then Katrina and Mike Jr. went to go pay her grandmother a visit.

"Hi, Katrina you brought my baby to see me!"

"Yeah, granny we had to chill with you today."

CHAPTER

3

Charles and Shante

Sleeping next to him still hadn't got old for her nor him, they both enjoyed sleeping right next to each other, cuddled up every night with his arms wrapped around her underneath her covers.

Just like any other night, she was waiting for him to get off work. Instead of TV tonight at least until Charles gets there she decided to get some school work done early. She sat at her dining room table on her lap top doing work for one of her online classes. Once getting there she opened the door up for him. He walked in giving Shante a kiss on her lips.

"How was your day babe?"

"It was good, better now that I'm off and home with you; how was yours?"

"It was good, you know my days are always good," she chuckled.

"Babe, you cooked? I smell greens."

"Yes, babe I cooked some hot water cornbread, greens, rice and neck bones."

"Un Un Un, damn babe, you hooked it up!"

"Yes, I hooked it up."

He walked to the kitchen and looked inside all the pans. "I can't wait to eat," he said.

"What you going to wait for, I can make your plate now if you want babe," she said.

"Oh, no baby I'm about to hop in the shower first!"

"Okay, babe."

As Charles got in the shower, she continued doing her work on the computer trying to hurry and finish. Charles went and took him a long hot shower; he needed that, it was what he had been waiting for, relaxation. He stood in that shower and just let that hot water run on him for a long time, then ten minutes passed, he washed up with soap. After he was done he turned off the shower, got out the shower, and dried off with his towel. He walked into the bedroom with his towel wrapped around his waist area; he grabbed some pajama pants and a T-Shirt out the drawer and put them on. Shante had barely just finished her work also at the same time. She heard his footsteps walking around the room. She pressed send to send her assignment to her teacher, and then she closed her lap top.

She stood up from the table and walked to the kitchen to make their plates. He took a seat on the couch grabbing the remote control from off the table to find a good movie for them to watch.

"Ooh babe, there are a lot of good movies that are about to come on tonight."

"Oh yeah babe," she said.

Minutes later Shante came walking into the living room holding both of their plates. The two sat next to each other eating their dinner. Afterward she took their plates to the sink and quickly sat back next to him, now that they were done eating they were able to cuddle up on the couch enjoying themselves, they wouldn't have it any other way.

He glanced down at her as his hands are wrapped around her feeling the warmth of her skin, thinking about when they first met up until now. He was thinking of when he met her when was the last time he felt the feeling he's feeling right now. As he thought, he couldn't exactly remember. She felt him looking at her. Her eyes turned to him without turning her head. She slightly smiled.

"Baby, is everything okay?"

"Yeah, I love you."

She smiled bigger.

"I love you," he said again.

"I love you too," she said softly.

"You're smart, you're beautiful, and I'm glad your mines."

"Awww babe, how sweet, I'm glad I'm yours too."

He pulled down her pajama pants, she had the comfy and warm ones on. He'd began to pull them all the way off including her panties. As he spread her legs, he begins to lay down in between, lowering his head. Reaching her center he began flickering only the tip of his tongue on her lips down there. Only minutes into it, and she began moving her hips upward as she sounded a moan. She scooted down more on the couch, getting more comfortable. After tasting her they made love.

That next day Shante went into work tired from staying up late with Charles. She walked in dragging; after she made her a cup of coffee she was good. She got her some energy, just enough to get her going. Shante made phone calls, filed paper work, and scheduled appointments for the attorney. Shante's coworkers just made it in.

"Hey, Ms. Shante!"

"Hey ladies, y'all coming in late today I see," she said as she glanced at her laptop that was sitting right in front of her on her desk, looking at the time it's eleven thirty.

"Yeah, your boss scheduled us to come in late today," they whispered.

"Why?" she whispered back.

They both shrugged their shoulders, "We don't know," they both sounded at the same time. "So why are you whispering?" Rebecca asked.

"Be quiet," she grins. "I was whispering because of y'all were, and I'm tripping' because he's not even in here."

"Where is he? I saw his car out there?" Candice asks.

"He just walked through the parking lot to get the mail," she told them.

"Oh, okay," they said regularly.

"Hey Shante, what are you doing tonight?"

"Not sure, why, what's up?" she asked.

"It's my husband's and my eighteenth year anniversary and were having a little party at the house. I would love for you to come!" she said in an excited voice.

"Oh sure, wow, eighteen years, what's the secret?" Shante asks.

"Love, great conversation and understanding," she said.

"That's right, that's awesome, eighteen years," she said smiling.

"Yeah, we married in ninety-eight and have three little girls." Rebecca handed Shante an invitation for her anniversary party later.

"Thank you," She said glancing down at her invitation.

"Alright Shante, I hope to see you tonight girl," she said walking out her office.

"Alright lady," she said smiling.

Rebecca and Candice walked to their offices.

Hours later Shante took a second from work to make a quick call to her man. She called Charles. He answered his phone quickly.

"Hello, Beautiful!"

"Hey handsome, how is work going?" she said with a smile.

"Going okay, it's just been a busy day running around checking on the stores and stuff," he said.

"Okay," she smiled holding the phone.

"How about you?" he asked.

"Same here babe, just been busy, have loads of papers I have to go through that are on my desk," she said leaning back in her chair.

"Okay, Okay, have you ate lunch already?"

"No, I haven't yet," she replied.

"Well, I'm not too far from your job; I can stop and get you something!"

"You sure you don't have too," she says in her soft sweet voice.

"No baby, I don't mind it," he said.

"Oh, ok then, that's fine," she says.

"Okay, I will be there in twenty minutes," he told her.

"Okay babe, you're so sweet," she said smiling.

"Baby, you want Flame Broiler?"

"Yes please, can you get me a teriyaki chicken and beef bowl with brown rice?" she asked in one breath.

"You want the vegetables too right, that they put in there?"

"Oh yes, of course." They continued talking the whole way of him driving there, all the way until it was time to order the food. After ordering is when he told her he would see her in a minute.

"I love you, baby."

"I Love you too."

They hung up their cell phone. When he made it to her work, he took the food inside with him and went to her office. Seeing him walk in put a big smile on her face like always.

"Thanks, babe," she said smiling.

"No problem," he sat the food down. They were sitting at her desk about to eat lunch together.

"Usually Candice and I, or Rebecca and I, always take lunch together, but they came in not long ago," she said grinning.

"Oh, okay, no need to explain," he told her.

"Oh, I know babe, I was just telling you," she said.

"Oh," was his response as he grabbed the food out the bag.

"Well, as long as I beat Mr. Attorney to the punch is all that matters!" Shante shook her head and grinned. "Babe," Shante sounded.

Charles turned his lip up and looked towards the ceiling.

"Babe, I told you he has not tried to hit on me!"

"But he buys you lunch too often and that's the first sign," he whispered.

Shante laughs. "Babe, two times," she laughed more.

"Yeah, I find out that Mr. Attorney man tries to hit on my woman, he's going to get a beat down," he grins with his serious look in his eyes.

"Yeah, then you're going to be clickity-clack right to jail and you know I can't have that, I'm not going to have the money to bail you out," she chuckle.

"Yeah, okay," he nodded.

"Then a six-foot dude named Don is going to be asking to braid your hair for a cigarette," she said laughing.

"Shut up," he chuckles.

"Yeah, and you don't even have enough hair to grip for the braid."

"You're crazy," he tells her as they both sat there laughing. They were talking and laughing. He always cracks some type of jokes.

It didn't take them long to finish their lunch that they enjoyed. They leaned back in their chairs. He stretched his legs out, he is good and full now.

He wishes once he leaves them he could just go to the house and take him a nap, but that wasn't happening.

Shante's coworkers walked passed. "Hey, you guys!"

Shante and Charles both turned their heads at the same time.

Her co-workers waved at her and Charles. "Hey!" they said back as Shante and Charles waved back at them both.

"Oh, we see he brought you lunch."

"Yeah, he did," she smiled. Then they both walked off.

"If they don't stop it, of course, he brought me lunch like you see the empty bowls, bags, and stuff," she smiled.

"Oooh, moody," Charles said.

"Man, be quiet."

"Babe, the one in that white dress gave me an invitation earlier."

"To what?" he asked.

"To her and her husband's eighteenth-year anniversary party tonight at their house," she told him.

"You going? I'll go with you?"

"Maybe we can stop by for a little while, I guess."

"Yeah, it might be fun."

"Wow, eighteen years huh!" Charles sounded.

"Right, that's what I said too," Shante added as she looked deeply into his eyes. "I can't wait until I can say that I've been with you for eighteen years!"

"I know, me too," he paused. "Alright baby, I guess it's about that time for me to raise up out of here," he told her. He stood up, then walked around to her desk. "Give me some shuga."

"Shuga, you ain't sixty."

"Ok, a kiss."

"That's better." She chuckled. They kissed and hugged, then he left.

Later, once Shante left work, she relaxed for two hours, then she began to look for something for her to wear to this party. After looking through her clothes hanging up in her closet, she found a royal blue fitted dress. She ran her some bath water. Then she sat in the bath and took her a bath. She received a message alert. It was Charles saying he would be there in ten minutes. Afterward she got out and got dress.

Ten minutes later, Ding Dong, sounded it was her doorbell Charles was at her door. She didn't know why he rang the doorbell instead of just coming in with his key. Shante walked to the front door to let him in.

Charles made it there already dressed and ready to go with her to her coworker's anniversary party.

"Hey babe," they kissed.

"Why didn't you use your key?" she asked.

"I don't know," Charles said checking her out. "You about ready?" he asked her.

"Just about, give me five more minutes."

"No rush babe, I'm waiting on you."

"Okay."

Twenty minutes later they left her house. They made it to the party. They walked down the walk way leading to the backyard and the caterers' were preparing they noticed the food. And they noticed that they were going to be serving prime ribs, shrimp and baked potatoes. They were not expecting prime ribs, but they couldn't wait to eat it. Since they were about to have prime ribs meant they paid a lot for this.

Shante and Charles got to the backyard. Rebecca was smiling; she was happy that her coworker made it. Rebecca came and hugged them both.

"Shante, I'm so glad you both came!"

"Oh, no problem," she smiled.

"So what do you think?" Rebecca began pointing around the backyard.

"I love all the decorations, everything looks really nice and elegant back here," she smiled.

"Thank you. Girl, my sisters and I did all the decorating last night. After decorating the chairs they ended up spending the night and we woke early this morning and made all the center pieces early this morning before I went to work."

"Wow, y'all did all this?" she says with much excitement.

"Yes," she nodded.

"Damn girl, y'all did one hell of a job. I thought you paid some professionals to do it." Shante looked all around, she was so impressed by the fact that they done all of it themselves. A nice bouquet of flowers was set as center pieces on everybody's table. "Everything really looks amazing Rebecca," she nodded her head.

"Girl yes, we did everything. As you can see the only thing we didn't do was cook. Anthony wanted Prime Rib so we found a caterer who did it."

"That's right, well Happy Anniversary lady," Shante passed her a bag with an anniversary gift inside.

"Aw, thank you guys so much," Rebecca smiles at them both for her gift. Alright, you guys, find y'all a table, they're about to start serving the food in a minute.

"Ok," Shante says.

Rebecca went back to walking around hugging and talking to her guest and family. Shante and Charles found them a table. As they walked towards the table, Shante and Charles both were looking around at the family. They were between Rebecca's and her husband's families put together. They almost had a whole backyard full. They found them a table that was right next to the outdoor heater, then they sat down in the chair.

It was no secret that Anthony brought in more of the income. Rebecca always talked about his trucking company, and all the money he makes. Shante was happy for them. As long as she'd known her coworker the only thing she didn't know that was the length of years that they were married. Rebecca had always talked about how happily married she was at work. She had even talked about how she and her husband had struggled years back, but to see how they were doing so good now, she was just happy for them. They were an inspiration to Shante, that's what Shante felt being there. Shante's mind drifted. It made her picture her future with Charles. Once her attention came back, Shante looked at Charles.

"Babe, I love you."

"Babe, I love you," he repeated, trying to say it like her. She smiled and so did he.

The party taking place in their backyard wasn't so bad now she thought since they're heater's back there. She thought she was going to be freezing to death, but Rebecca had four outside heaters. They even pulled their table and chairs closer to the heater. They were able to feel the warm breeze blowing which was good. That's where they planned to eat and danced right in that same spot. Drinks were being passed out, and they were both handed a drink.

"Thank you so much," Shante told the waiter as she was handed two drinks. After taking her first sip, suddenly Shante smiled and waved as she sees Candice and a teenage girl approaching her.

"This must be the beautiful princess you talk about at work," Shante smiled and gives the young girl a hug.

"Yes!" Candice says as she turns to look at her daughter. "Callie, meet my coworker Shante and her boyfriend Charles."

"Hello Shante and Charles, it's nice to meet you!" she smiles.

"Look at you looking just like your mother's twin with the same color dark eyes and long dark hair."

Callie smiled. She shivered and then leaned on her mother. Shante noticed Candice's daughter was shivering. "Are you cold sweetie?" Shante asked looking at Callie. "That's why we're standing right here by this lamp heater," she chuckled.

Callie grinned. "I know, we're about to go stand next to one too after we go back to the car right quick to get her jacket."

"Yes, a jacket is for sure needed out here," Shante says. Then Candice and her daughter walked off.

"She's married too?" Charles asked.

Shante shook her head no. "She never really told me why she's not with her daughter's father. One day at work when she was telling us something about her daughter's father I believe, I was like so, you guys together? she was like no, then just changed the subject and started talking about something else. I never asked again."

"Oh, but she seems cool and she has a nice and respectful daughter," he said.

"Yeah, she has always been cool and very nice and sweet since we met and she's never changed up."

"That's right," Charles mumbled.

"So, how you feeling babe?" he asks Shante.

"Feeling good," she says as she takes sips of her drink. He took a sip of his drink then sat his cup back down.

The waiters began walking around serving everyone their plates. Shante and Charles were handed their plates along with a refill of their drinks. They began to eat.

"This food is really good babe!"

"I know it is," he sounded while he was eating.

After they were done eating they leaned back in their chairs looking at some of her family already out there dancing. They smiled.

"Babe, you ready to go out there and dance?"

"Sure, why not babe," Charles told her.

Charles stood up from his chair, Shante stood up as well. He pulled her chair back some and the two went out there on the dance floor in the middle of the backyard and began dancing too, with music playing from their live DJ. After a few drinks in their system, they partied for hours. They danced for hours until their feet said sit down. Those hours out there dancing went by so fast. Once that alcohol was in their systems, it warmed them up a bit. They went back to their table, it was eleven twenty already. Shante noticed Rebecca was still smiling, she was just happy all day, her smile never went away.

Candice walked over to Shante and Charles, they could tell she had been drinking too much. Shante and Charles both looked at each other real quick as they both raised their eye brows. Candice just started talking. Candice was saying things that weren't making any sense, then she began to say, "*I want a little baby.*"

"Huh," Shante sounded.

"I want a little baby," she says again, then she grinned. After she walked off Shante went and gave a heads up to Rebecca. "Hey, Rebecca I think Candice had too much to drink."

Rebecca turned around to look Candice's way. "Oh yeah, she sure did," she looked at her from a distance. "Yeah, I'm not going to let her drive like that."

"If you want, later Charles and I can drop her and her daughter off!"

"No worries I can get Anthony to take her."

"You sure?" Shante replied.

"Oh yeah, I'm sure he wouldn't mind."

"Oh, ok." Then Shante walked back over to Charles.

"What did she say?"

"I told her we could drop her and her daughter off once we get ready to leave, but she said she was going to have her husband drop them off."

"Oh, ok."

Rebecca walked over to Candice. She saw her staggering, so she began to walk faster towards her. She got up on her and grabbed her arm. "Hey, Candice, you okay girl?"

"I want a little baby," she smiles.

"What, girl you had too much to drink, let me sit you down."

"Okay," Candice says. Rebecca sat her down back at her table next to her daughter. Her daughter was embarrassed.

"Callie, don't let your mom get up."

"Okay," she says.

"Baby, I'm going to have my husband drop you guys off at home shortly."

"Okay."

"Yeah, I can't have my friend drive home drunk."

"Thank you, Mrs. Rebecca."

"Oh, no problem sweetie," she whispered leaning towards her.

Shante and Charles stayed until midnight. They didn't mean to stay that long since they had to work in the morning, but they lost track of time.

Shante and Charles were getting ready to go when Rebecca walked over to them noticing they were getting their things to leave.

"Shante and Charles, I want to thank you both for coming and helping us celebrate our anniversary."

"Yes, thank you guys so much for helping us celebrate, it was a pleasure having you both at our home," Anthony butted in.

"Oh, thank you for having us, I appreciate the invite," Shante said as she hugged Rebecca and hugged her husband Anthony.

"Yeah, I had a lot of fun," Charles added as he hugged Rebecca and shook Anthony's hand.

Shante and Charles left, they had fun. When the two were not working they enjoyed themselves together. They had fun doing everything they could together. Charles drove Shante back home, then he drove to his house. Getting home he couldn't go straight to sleep he had been so used to lying up under Shante. Shante and Charles were deeply connected to each other's heart.

That night getting back home Anthony walked in, "Please don't have me drop off any more drunk friends, good night!" he told her.

"Babe, I'm sorry," she chuckled. "Good night to you too, what baby, she gave you a hard time on the way to her house?"

"I don't want to talk about it. Good night!"

The next morning Shante had to catch herself. She had rolled over and was getting ready to awake Charles until she realized he didn't sleep there last night, she chuckled at the thought of how he was on her mind all the time. She got up and went to work.

After Charles day ended he called Shante. Then Charles went over to see her. It didn't take Charles long at all to get to her house. He knocked on her door.

She answered.

He entered.

"Hey, Shante baby, I missed you."

"I missed you too," she laughed.

He smiled.

The two sure knew how to make the other person smile all for no reason, just being in each other's presence did that.

He grabbed both her hands and kissed the back side of them, then he pulled her close to him and kissed her soft lips and they released. They then looked into each other's eyes in silence. Seconds later he asked if she was ready to now take their relationship to the next level. They had been dating for almost three years. Butterflies immediately started going through her stomach, she was nervous and excited.

This day was definitely the day to make their relationship move onto marriage. He was ready and so was she. Before meeting and getting together with Shante he had been single, but sleeping around with different women was not his style. Since the first day they met she had made his heart feel like something. He was glad to have been introduced to her, but then again he knew his brother Mike knew his type and what he liked.

In her seductive voice, she told him *yes* she was ready. He spun her around, he was excited.

She had really been enjoying him, with his kindness, his sweetness and how he always thought of her before himself; his politeness, and how he'd opened up doors for her everywhere they went, for her he was such a gentleman and she liked everything about him. Making her feel special and loved was something he had no problems doing. Her boyfriend before him was not as good as him, and she wasn't all mouthy like his last lady, Shante was humble and very sweet.

After he put her down on her feet they kissed on the lips again. Before she could say let's make love he was already all over her, attacking her in a good way with his dick. He raised her dress. Her smile grew bigger as both his arms were wrapped around her. He missed her like he hadn't seen her in weeks. Her dress in front was very low, the way it was designed it caused her breast to show a lot and then with her push up bra underneath, didn't make it any better, but better for him anyway. It was easy for him to lean his head down against her breast as his dick slid all the way up inside her, nice and slow, as Shante's hands were pressed down firmly into his back holding on.

"Oh baby," she whispered. That felt real good she thought.

"Ahhhh," he moaned. He kept kissing her passionately while inside her. She was very moist down there and he felt it trying to slip out, but he kept on going until it went all the way back in and it did. He began going in faster, he stayed in that same position for a while. He felt that sensation going through his body but he didn't want to cum yet, so they switched positions. He turned her over and slid it back in from behind as he had one leg on the couch and the other leg on the floor. He went in. He kept going in and out, in and out, not all the way out, both positions felt too good. She was so warm on the inside.

The thought of him taking her to the room because it wasn't that much room on the couch didn't cross his mind. He was about to make it work like they were. After another ten minutes they switched positions again and she got on top of him. His hands gripped her butt. He began grinding her up and down into him as she rode him with the sensation she felt that was starting to go through her body. She couldn't control herself. She began bouncing up and down on it moaning louder. Then she lowered her face to his and licked his lips. She lifted her head up, then did it again bouncing up and down on it squeezing her pussy lips closed as he was hard inside her, then released slowly as she bounced up. He jerked as he felt her lips tighten on his shit. He sounded a moan and held her firmer. He opened his eyes and stared up at her, he was about to cum. As he began to cum so did she. They both cuming at the same time. Her stare was deep into his eyes before her eyes begin closing. She began going faster and faster. He began to grip her even more firmly, the moans were coming continuously, then after they stopped they just laid there, they couldn't move.

They both had cum at the same time. They paused, then the two blew out a breath. They were both out of breath, so they closed their eyes and went straight to sleep. They woke up in the middle of the night and got in the bed, waking up together is what they enjoyed. They showered and got dressed.

"Hey beautiful," he leaned forward to her to give her a kiss on her lips.

"Thanks, baby, so do you. You look very handsome as always." He grinned showing all his teeth.

"Thank you," he told her. They were getting ready to go out to breakfast with his friends and their ladies. They were ready, locked up, and then went out through the front door. He held her hand all the way to his car, he opened her door to let her in, then he went around to his side and got in. They left the house.

Meeting up with Chris's friends was going to be fun, they had also invited them to church with them as well. They all had planned to eat breakfast first then head to church.

Once they arrived, his friends had just pulled up too. They all walked in at the same time and as they walked in the waitress was already walking them to a table, and there was not a wait to sit at all. They ordered they chatted, they ate, they chatted some more just having a wonderful Sunday morning so far. Afterward they left heading to church. Charles and Shante had followed behind his friends. After service Charles drove back to Shante's house. They had no other plans for this Sunday.

Getting back to the house they went to the bedroom to change into something more comfortable. They started back all over again, they couldn't get enough of each other.

Charles kissing her was letting her know he wanted some of her, and she was ready to give him just what he wanted.

"You ready, you want some more of this?"

He gazed into her eyes. "Yes, I stay ready for you baby."

She chuckled.

She slightly bent over touching the bed, he got behind her sliding his hands down her side, gripping her thighs, as his body got all up on her closely, he slid it in at the same time.

"Mmmm," were the sounds she made as he went in. He moved it in slowly in a full circle, Shante was still moving up forward and backward with her hips as he was still moving in a full circle from behind.

"Let's move more on the bed," he wanted to get all the way on the bed.

"Okay," she said softly. He picked her up and scooted her up on the bed more.

He squeezed her body tight up against his, as he scooted her more on the bed, he stopped once they had reached the center of the bed. Her eyes closed shut as she continued to receive all of him. Continuously feeling each thrust deeply made the moaning get louder each time. He kept going in and out, slowly to faster, softly to harder, she was feeling every single sexual sensation she was supposed to feel and it felt really good. They switched position to her being on top now. After a while he could feel her hips lift up from him, he had her routine down, he knew she was about to start bouncing up and down on it. He knew what came with that, her squeezing her pussy lips on his shit. Just as he thought it, she was definitely doing her thing. After that one position, they switched it to another position again up until the moment they both had cum at the same time. After they were done they lay down and cuddled up, he was tired. They didn't know what it was that had come over them, but they both had been extra freaky these last couple of days. In fact, he loved it and so did she.

"Babe, you all out of breath; breathing all hard," she laughed.

"Yeah, I was putting in work right now."

"I'm sorry for making you do all the work."

"Oh, no worries babe," he told her.

"I enjoyed you like before, it's good every time." They both had given all their energy, they were still trying to catch their breath.

"Thanks, babe I can't wait to make you my wife one day, I want to show you how I can be everything you need!"

"I will and I'd like that you have been showing me that since we met."

"Yeah, I admire Mike's and Katrina's relationship, how they really care about each other and do everything together, it's like I want that too."

"Yeah, we do that already."

"Yeah, I know baby, I guess what I mean's I can't wait until we are able to live with each other."

"Yeah, making us official, I'd like that," he sounded.

"Sooo, what are we eating tonight?"

"You pick, what do you have a taste for?"

"You want pizza?"

"Yeah, I haven't had pizza in a while, yeah that sounds good."

"Alright, cool." Shante dialed Dominoes and ordered a large pizza and a box of wings."

Once the pizza got there they ate and called it a night. They went to sleep in her bed wrapped in each other's arms.

The next morning driving in her car just leaving Starbucks from getting her a Caramel Frappe with extra caramel, she was now headed to work.

Shante's cell started ringing. Katrina was calling Shante. Her cell was hooked up to the blue tooth in her car is why Katrina's voice started sounding through the speakers.

"Good morning lady!"

"Hey, Hey Diva, how are you doing this morning?" she asked.

"Fine girl, just dropped Simone off at school."

"Oh yeah, so how is my princess?"

"Girl, she's fine, but she's mad at me for not taking her driving yesterday after church."

"Driving?"

"Yes, girl bumped that the fact she had a serious attitude, I'm like what."

"What, she's trying to learn how to drive!"

"Yes, but she's not about to learn in my Benz, nor my truck!"

Shante laughed.

"Girl, I'd rather pay for her to go to driving school."

"What you say, Katrina, she not hitting shit today," Shante laughed again.

Katrina chuckled. "Girl, who you telling shit no days," Katrina said.

"Okay, *right*," Shante said.

"Girl," Katrina said.

"Girl, she is growing into a young adult."

"Shit, she already looking like one right now," Katrina added.

"Girl, I was saying the same thing the last time I saw her."

"I know right, where does the time go?" Katrina said.

"Soon your baby girl will be in college."

"Girl, don't say that, that just means we're getting old."

"No, we're getting young," Shante chuckled.

"Girl, how was your weekend by the way?"

"It was fun and interesting."

"Hmmm, interesting, why interesting?"

"Charles and I spent all Saturday and all Sunday together, just at the house enjoying ourselves and having different conversations about all types of stuff. Then yesterday morning we went to breakfast with his friends and then his friends had invited us to church with them. It was us, with his two boys and their ladies. I actually had fun."

"Ah shit, what happened? I know you don't do no double dating with ladies you don't know," Katrina chuckled.

"I know right, but it was cool, we were all enjoying ourselves."

"So, you and my brother in law, so what's he like? I mean, I don't mean to be all in y'all business, but a sista wants to know?"

"Oh girl, I'm not tripping, I don't know where to begin!"

"Oooh, like that," Katrina says.

"Yes, girl!"

"That's right," Katrina said.

"It's like, I can't sleep without thinking about him, I almost feel like my heart skips a beat when we're together."

"Aw!" Katrina sounded.

"I can't even remember the last time a man made me feel the way he does."

"Awww Shante, I'm happy you feel how you feel about him, love is so beautiful, especially when it's right."

"Yes, girl," Shante said.

"Yeah, my brother in law is a sweetheart."

"Yes, he is," Shante added.

"Do I hear wedding bells for you too any time soon?"

"Well, we have talked about it, but it's just been a talk."

"Why you say it like that?"

"Because he just brought that up for the first time this weekend, but that's all we did was just talk about it, we didn't say like when or nothing."

"Oh, okay, at least that's on you guy's mind so that is a good thing."

"Yeah, you are right. Well lady I'm going to let you go, I just made it to work. I will call you later."

"Ok." They hung up the call. Shante got out her car, sounded her alarm, and went inside work. After her eight hours, she'd put in today she was headed home. After arriving home she couldn't wait to get inside. Not long after Charles had arrived at Shante's house.

"Hey babe, I'm home, you home!" he yelled out. He walked in with the key she gave him.

"Yeah, I am!" she shouted out. She walked downstairs to him. They kissed and hugged.

"What would you like to eat for dinner? I was about to get ready and start dinner?"

"I kind of wanted some tacos, did you see the ground turkey I sat inside the refrigerator?"

"Yeah, I saw it, I wasn't sure if you wanted spaghetti, enchiladas or tacos."

"Oh, I didn't think about enchiladas, that does sound good."

"You want that?"

"Do we have everything for it?" she asked him.

"Let me check," Charles checked the pantry.

"Yes, babe we do have everything."

"Okay then, I guess enchiladas it is," she said.

"Okay, sounds good to me, I will start cooking them now."

"Babe, how things going up at the restaurant?" she asked.

"Things going good. I have one lazy worker and I have one that's been coming in late every single day for the past two weeks. I told him it's been getting out of hand, he needs to come to work on time. Every time he says he will, he really don't."

"So what do you think the problem is?"

"I don't know, he hasn't really said, but all he says is Charles my man, I promise I will try and be on time."

"He's a good worker, but it's like him being late causes the others that are scheduled to leave to have to stay later, and sometimes they be having things to do. Aye babe, you don't want tacos instead, or if you really want the enchiladas then I'll make them?"

"Babe, go ahead and make tacos and I can make the enchiladas tomorrow, no worries babe."

"You sure baby?" he asked.

"Yeah, I'm sure babe."

"Okay."

"Okay, so back to what I was saying, yeah he needs to come on time. Yeah, I'm going to talk to him one more time and then after that, I don't know."

The next morning they left out at the same time.

Charles dialed Shante's cell, then he slipped his phone back into his pocket so he could talk to her through his earpiece. The phone had rung a few times. "Hello!" she answered after the third ring.

"What you doing babe?"

"At home," she said.

"I'll be there too, shortly."

Charles said bye to the employees, and waved bye to the customers that were inside the restaurant waiting for their orders. He walked to his car and got inside.

"Alright, babe I'm just leaving out the parking lot of the restaurant as we speak."

Shante laughed, "Okay, babe."

Charles talked to her the whole time while he was driving there. Thirty minutes passed and Shante heard Charles come in with the sound of his keys. They hung up the phone. "Is that my honey!" she yelled.

"Yes!" he yelled. Charles came in. The first thing he did was set his keys on the living room table and went straight to the kitchen.

"Hey babe," she smiled.

"Hey lovely," he hugged her.

"How was your day babe?"

"Baby, my day was good, long and busy."

"Yeah, and mines was just long, but good."

"That's right."

"I'm going to be hiring at the restaurant. One of my employees told me today that he has another job, yeah the same young man we were talking about last night, yeah and that he will do what he can to still come in until I hire someone."

"Oh wow, guess that explains why he has been late."

"Yeah, but that still didn't give him the right to be late, it's like once you commit yourself to two jobs you have to commit yourself to be on time to both too."

"That is so true, and you would think he would have done that. You have anyone in mind?"

"No, not yet. I'm going to put a now hiring sign up in the window tomorrow."

Charles walked back into the living room, grabbed the remote control from off the table, then sat on the couch. Charles flipped through the channels; he ended up on the news channel. After Shante put the meat in the pan over the fire, she prepared the salad, then she went and sat next to Charles on the couch. After a while, just as she was too comfortable, it was time to check on the meat. While she was already in the kitchen she started cooking the beans and the rice. Afterward she went back into the living room. Shortly, Shante got up and checked on the meat, stirred it, and went and sat back down. Shortly after she returned back to the kitchen and the meat was done. She rolled them up, then placed them inside the oven. Forty minutes later the food was done. Once dinner was finally ready Shante reached up and grabbed two plates from out her cabinet to make their plates.

"Babe, do you want your beer?" she yelled from the kitchen.

"Yes babe, thank you," he responded.

After making their plates she walked back into the living room with his plate in one hand and his beer in her other hand. Charles had found them a movie to watch.

"Here's your dinner babe," she passes him his plate and his beer. His eyes laid on his food, his concentration was strong as he got his plate from Shante.

The two ate and watched a movie. After they finished eating he began touching on her back as he kissed her.

"Babe, that was so delicious."

"Thanks, babe."

After the movie they went and took a shower. Inside the shower, he rubbed her breast with her soapy wash cloth wiping them clean, then her body. Getting out he dried off and went and grabbed his sweats out the drawer and threw them on. Shante dried off and put on one of his long white T-Shirts. "Baby, let me give you a massage!"

"Okay," he replied. This is what he needed. Charles had laid across the bed on his stomach. Shante sat on top of him and gave him a massage. After she was done he felt so relaxed, he felt like going straight to sleep. His eyes were closed.

"Ummm," they moaned.

Charles had received a text message alert. He grabbed his phone which was on the bed next to him. He looked at the screen of his phone, it was his brother Mike. He opened the text to read it.

Aye bro, I'm planning a party for Katrina. I want it to be the biggest surprise birthday party, she's turning thirty-six. It's going to be at the Western Hotel in Long Beach. Make sure you and Shante save the date and tell Shante it's a SURPRISE!! Lol.

"What!" she chuckled. "I know how to keep a secret, I won't tell her," she grinned.

I wonder why he isn't having it at the Sheraton Hotel; we have a cousin that works there unless the date he wants is already booked, he mumbled.

"Yeah, that's probably what it is," she said.

Charles sent his brother back a text: *Alright, fasho, we will be there.* Then he pressed send.

CHAPTER
4

Katrina's Family Reunion

Katrina and Mike have almost been married for a year now. During their marriage so far everything has been perfect, no arguments and no yelling, things truly have been wonderful for them two. Waking up to their newborn three months ago has been their biggest blessing staring into their baby's eyes. It was hard to believe that three months have gone by so fast, their little man has gotten so big and Katrina couldn't wait to show him off to her whole family in a few weeks at the Family Reunion.

Lately, all Mike keeps hearing his wife complain about is getting her pregnancy weight off. He doesn't like hearing her put her own self down.

Baby, you just had a baby, stop putting yourself down, you look damn good, your body looks better than some people out there that haven't had a baby at all, is what he would tell her. Although she didn't feel it herself, he kept telling her how beautiful she is, he loved complimenting his wife.

Katrina couldn't wait to get back to her old self. Katrina started back eating healthy.

"What you hooking up in there babe," Mike looked back and said.

"Oh, some baked fish, brown rice and some green beans."

"Oh, ok!" he said loudly.

After the food was done, the both of them sat at the kitchen table and began having lunch together.

"I'm so glad you were willing to come back after a year of not talking to me, and when you came back while I was going through my situation with Gary and the divorce, I just want to thank you again for staying babe, that was the hardest thing I went through."

"I told you I was here for you when I said that I meant it for real."

"Yep, you did tell me that and I thank you."

"I love you."

"I love you too," he told her.

He bit down on his fish. She was eating her food too, taking sips of the sweet tea she had made, as they still carried on their conversation. After they were done eating and chatting, Katrina went and grabbed her keys and her purse.

"Alright babe, I will be back, I'm going to the gym."

"Alright baby I'll see you when you get back," he kissed her. Katrina was determined. She had a routine of exercising on the regularly; she was determined to get this fat off her body.

Brandy called the house phone to talk to her sister, but Katrina wasn't there. While Mike had her on the line he thought he should ask her what she is doing later tonight.

"Nothing," she responded to him.

Mike asked Brandy to let Simone and his son come over there while they step out for a minute.

"Oh, okay no problem," she replied.

"We are only going to be gone for about three hours."

"They don't have to leave, I'm not tripping, bring my niece and nephew over here, they can spend the night."

"Yeah," he sounded.

"Yeah, I'm not doing anything else."

"Okay, cool thanks, Brandy."

"You're welcome, anytime." They hung up the phone.

Mike went and packed his son an overnight bag for his Aunt's house.

When Katrina and the kids walked in the house, Mike was sitting in the living room with two bags sitting next to him on the couch.

"Hey dad," Simone said smiling.

"Hey baby girl," he said. Then Simone went upstairs looking down at her cell phone in her hand.

"What's that baby," she asked him as she grins looking at the bags next to him.

"Clothes, snacks and formula," he told her.

"What for?" she smiled.

"I have something planned for us later tonight."

She smiled, "We going by ourselves, or are we taking the kids?"

"We're going by ourselves, your sister is going to watch them."

"My sister, when you talk to her?"

"She called early asking for you, then I asked her what was she doing later, and she said nothing, I only asked her because I was trying to give your mother a break."

"Oh lord, she could barely watch herself," she chuckled.

"Leave that girl alone."

"Is she picking them up?"

"No, we're going to drop them off to her."

"Simone, go pack you an overnight bag for your Aunt's house, you and your brother are going over there tonight and spend the night!" she yelled upstairs.

"Okay mom!"

Simone went upstairs to her room and packed her an overnight bag.

"Babe, do I need to do anything?" she asked him.

"Nope, I packed our bags too."

"Our bags?" she chuckled. "You got it all planned out huh," she smiles.

"Well, you know" he grinned. They then left the house and the kids were dropped off. As Mike and Katrina made it there, Katrina began looking around and twisting around in the passenger seat, this area frightened her.

"Babe, where are you taking me?" she wondered.

He laughed. "Why you say that?"

"It looks scary, it's dark as hell, and I don't see anything but trees."

"Just wait babe, you will see something in a minute."

They continued driving up the hill. Once they made it up the hill they parked their car, got their bags out, and closed the doors.

"Babe," she sounded as she looked at him.

He laughed again; it was funny to him the way she was freaking out how the place looked all scary. This was her first time here, and their first time together; he'd been there once before many years ago. Then they had to walk up some steep stairs.

"Babe, why didn't you tell me we were going walking, I should have brought my tennis shoes instead of wearing heels."

"Take your shoes off, I bought your sandals."

They stopped at the fourth step and Katrina took off her heels and put on her sandals that her husband brought with them. Once they made it up to the top they saw the office where you check in and then they saw the different cabins. Katrina looked at him and smiled.

"What?" he said to her as he had a grin on his face.

"I love you, babe," she told him.

"I love you more babe," he said to her.

They walked straight to the check in desk and checked in. After checking in they given Katrina and Mike some towels and then they were escorted to their own private cabin. As they were walking to their cabin they saw other couples there at their cabins too. When they made it to their cabin, it was set up so nice for them. It had candles surrounding their Jacuzzi and rose petals all around it as well.

"Oh, okay, the Jacuzzi is outside how nice. This is nice babe, with the candles and the rose petals."

"You like it?" he asks.

"I love it, I love the view."

"This is all for you baby."

"Baby, you are the best husband in the world."

He smiled.

"Awww babe, I wish I would have known we were getting in the Jacuzzi so I could have brought my bikini."

"Oh, you don't need a bikini."

"Oh," she paused.

He smiled.

"Okay," she sounded. She began admiring the view and the different cabins. Before arriving there that night Mike had paid extra over the phone for their cabin for a better view, candles, and those rose petals, he knew she was going to love it. The view was just so beautiful they were able to see all the lights of LA from San Dimas, it was so pretty.

He pulled her close to him and kissed her lips softly, then he kissed them again and again, and then they began tongue kissing each other. After they kissed a romantic passionate long kiss she thanked him for bringing her there. Then he began taking the things he had brought for them out the bag. He had whip cream, strawberries, a bottle of wine, and a bottle of

Hennessey. He also brought his radio. After pouring their drinks and cutting their music on they were ready for the Jacuzzi. He unzipped his pants and pulled off his pants and boxers. She pulled off her dress, unsnapped her bra and sat it down on the chair that was there. He took off his shirt, and then she took off her panties. The two stepped into the Jacuzzi naked. Getting inside they were drinking their drinks and eating strawberries with whip cream. They talked, sang to the music playing, just having a romantic evening, feeding each other strawberries.

After about thirty minutes there he grabbed her by her hips and lifted her up with his hands; she wrapped her legs around his waist. He took his hand and stuck his penis inside of her. He began moving back and forth in side her. Their breathing was heavy, the deeper he was going the more the moaning sounded. After while he began kissing her neck, she leaned her head back, she felt very good and relaxed. She began tightening up her vagina, made him go deeper up in it faster. After they were done they couldn't do anything but laugh at each other on how they got busy so fast and they just got there. They went back to enjoying themselves. They started taking pictures of each other from her phone. They only had the cabin for three hours. Later that night after getting back home they went to sleep.

The next morning waking up she had cooked the two of them breakfast. Mike woke up, used the bathroom, cleaned his face, and brushed his teeth. Then he walked in the kitchen with Katrina.

"Good morning baby."

"Good morning."

He eased up behind her hugging her from behind.

"Babe, I enjoyed myself at that place last night, I liked that, we're going to have to do that again someday."

"We will."

Once breakfast was ready they sat at the table to eat.

"Babe, I'm excited to start back having my jewelry parties again, to give myself something to do."

"You should be babe."

"Thanks, babe," she grins looking into his eyes.

"Yeah, you should probably do it next week; since you still have all that jewelry left."

"Yeah I know, that's what I was just thinking."

"Well, there you go then."

"I'm going to call up the girls a little later and let them all know."

After they were done eating they got dressed. They left to head to her sister's house to go and pick up the kids. Half way there Katrina called Brandy.

"Hello," she answered.

"Hey sis, we on our way to pick up the kids," Katrina says.

"Okay, they're right here eating breakfast right now."

"Okay, tell them I will be there in a minute."

"Okay, sis."

"Okay bye."

"Bye." They hung up. Not long after they made it to Brandy's apartment.

"Babe, I will be right back," she told Mike.

Katrina jogged up the stairs. Katrina knocked on her door. Brandy opened her front door for her and she walked in giving Brandy a kiss on her cheek and a hug. "Thanks sis for watching the kids for us last night."

"Oh, girl it's nothing, anytime."

"Thank you," Katrina smiled.

"Y'all had fun last night?"

"Yes, we actually did. The view was really nice, and we really enjoyed ourselves."

"Where did y'all go?"

"Some place in the city of San Dimas, it was dark as heck down there. That shit looked scary at first, but then when we went up this hill we saw the cabins and stuff, it was really nice."

"You didn't take any pictures?"

"Umm, not many, I just took a few."

Katrina went in her purse for her phone to show her sister some of the pictures she did take from last night.

"Oh okay, how beautiful Katrina," Brandy told her as they both looked at the pictures together.

"That's right," Brandy says as she continued looking through the pictures. Once Katrina saw her get to a certain picture she knew that next picture was one she couldn't see, "THAT'S IT!" Katrina said fast.

Brandy looked at her as she still held her phone.

Katrina smiles. "You can't see the other pictures."

"Ooooh, you nasty," Brandy smiled.

Katrina smiled. "Yeah, I told him we're going to have to do that again."

"Okay, right. Yeah, it looks like y'all had a ball."

Katrina got the diaper bag from off the couch, gave her sister another kiss and hug, then she got the kids and left. Once they made it home Katrina laid back on the couch relaxing. Later that afternoon Katrina had called up the girls and told them she was about to start back having her jewelry parties again. They were happy that she was because it had been a while since she last gave one.

The next day Katrina had made up some invitations and sent them out. She was excited to be doing this again, she couldn't even think of why she stopped in the first place. Once Mike got home she couldn't wait to talk to him. He walked right in and went straight to the bathroom. Coming out the bathroom he joined her on the bed. He leaned towards her giving her a kiss.

"How was your day babe?"

"It was good."

"So babe, I think I want to host a party every month instead of every three months like before."

"Go for it babe."

"Ok babe," she says.

Mike never told her NO about anything, he would always tell her to go for it. Besides, her jewelry parties, she was about to start doing again, she was also working from home with her coworkers' assistance. She was always getting new clients and she planned on finding a house for all of them. Being on maternity leave she couldn't help herself, she had to.

"I had a good day. I have eight new clients and all of them are looking to buy. One of them wants me to find her a foreclosure."

"That's good babe."

"I know right, and I plan on finding all of them a house."

"So you and Jackie are working out I see."

"Yeah, working from home isn't so bad for now, but at least we're able to split the commission."

"But see baby, that's why you're always winning because you don't stop and you're loyal to your clients and to what you do."

"Awww, thank you, baby," she smiled.

"Aye, babe you going to the gym?" he asked.

"I'm tired babe and I was going to go a little later."

"Oh, okay, because I was going to go with you." Mike was used to her going every day around this time, he wanted to hit the gym with her.

"Let me take at least a two-hour nap then we can go work out."

"Oh, okay."

"You mind waiting until I wake up?"

"Oh, no babe, I don't mind."

Katrina set her alarm clock and slept for two hours, once her alarm woke her up they left. She and Mike went to the gym and worked out together for two hours. They both had a good workout. They both left the gym tired, out of breath and sweaty, and both their shirts were damp leaving out the gym.

Driving home they chatted discussing the plans for this weekend.

"Babe, your mom going to watch the baby Saturday?" she asked.

"I haven't asked her yet, but I'm sure she will."

"I see you're excited about this fishing trip," she smiled.

"Yeah, it's been a minute."

Suddenly Mike saw this gray car in his rear view mirror changing in and out of the lanes, driving really fast. The person driving the car could be in a rush to get somewhere or intoxicated, he wasn't trying to find out either. Mike pulled his car over quickly on the side of the road to let that car passed them by. Once that car passed is when Mike proceeded back to driving. Not long after they made it home safely.

Once the weekend came Katrina's mother picked up her grandson. Mike, Katrina, and Simone drove out to Murrieta Hot Springs to go fishing. It's been a while since he last went fishing but they had a lot of fun. Mike caught two really big fish and that second fish is what did it to his fishing pole. The next morning Katrina went out to the store, she wanted to surprise Mike with another fishing pole.

Katrina's cell rung while she was looking at the different poles, she grabbed her phone from out her purse, it was Michelle.

"Hey sis," she answered.

"Hey, what you doing lady?" she asked her.

"At the store buying your brother a fishing pole, going to surprise him with it, and he doesn't know I'm buying it."

"What happened to the one he had or he just wants another one?"

"Girl, we went fishing yesterday and he broke his pole on the last big fish he caught," she chuckled.

"Oh wow, how many fish did he catch?"

"Two."

"Oh, okay."

"Hey, are you coming to the house later for the jewelry party?"

"Yeah, actually that's what I was calling you for, I wanted to see if you needed me to bring anything?"

"Oh no, sis you don't have to bring anything."

"Oh, ok."

"K."

"See you at four."

"Yes, at four."

"Ok, see you then," they hung up. Katrina continued looking at the poles. After finding one like the one he had she walked up to the counter to pay for it. After paying she left and went home. Once home she took her shower first because she knew if she started organizing and setting things up now, she would to be late getting dress.

Katrina was getting ready to host another jewelry party. She came downstairs dressed. Simone saw Katrina about to start setting up all the jewelry.

"Mom, would you like some help?"

"Oh sure baby girl, you know I'm not going to turn down some help."

Simone walked over to the box and began pulling out the blue jewelry boxes out the box and taking off the tops and placing them behind the box. They began placing all the necklaces in one section, all the bracelets in another section, all the rings in another, and then it was the mirrors. Katrina had four mirrors which they placed a mirror at each corner of the long display table she decorated. Katrina couldn't wait to see them all, she couldn't wait to show off all her new pieces of jewelry she had. After Simone helped her mother she went in her mom's room with her baby brother to watch TV, while he was asleep. Katrina had all the jewelry set up really nice. She had all the food and snacks set up on the table all pretty, she was ready.

All Katrina's guest were told to arrive at 4 pm and yes it turned four and all her guest were there on time. As Katrina's guests were all coming in she greeted them as they entered her home with a hug. Everyone came in going to the table with the appetizers and making their plates and pouring themselves some wine. They already knew just what to do coming in, then afterward they began taking their seats in the family room, the area where she always hosted her jewelry parties. She started off by thanking everyone for their attendance, then she jumped right into telling them about the different types of jewelry she had as she pointed to each piece while they were eating. Everyone was enjoying the pieces she had, they were old to her but new to them. After eating they were trying the different jewelry on, looking in the mirrors, everyone there was buying all of the pieces she had that evening. Mike got home. Katrina was in the middle of her jewelry party, but she stepped away to greet, kiss and hug her husband.

"Hey babe," she smiled.

"Hey babe, how is the party going so far?"

"It's going well as always, all the ladies I invited to the party showed, there were a few new ladies that came. The neighbor Stephanie from eight houses down brought them, they all been buying stuff, everyone is enjoying themselves, it's going good babe," she smiled.

"That's right babe."

"Your sister is here too," she told him.

"Oh yeah, she is, I forgot you did tell me she was coming."

"You want me to bring y'all anything from out the kitchen or do you need any help with anything?"

"Oh no babe I got it, I have some food over there on the table," she pointed.

"Oh, what did you make?"

"I made turkey enchiladas, sweet corn, and Spanish rice."

"Damn babe, heck yeah I want some, you hooked it up today. I thought you said you were making finger foods."

"I was going too, but then I ended up making that," she pointed to the food.

"Yeah, it's bomb and very cheesy," she told him.

"I already know it's cheesy, you're a cheese lover."

Katrina chuckled. Katrina walked over to the table and made her husband a plate. Mike stepped in the family room, he didn't want to be rude.

"Hey ladies, hey sis!" he waved his hand up.

"Hey Mike, hey brother," they all spoke back to him with a pleasant smile. Katrina walked over to him handing him his plate. He looked down at his plate.

"Mmmm," he sounded, he looked back up to her.

"Thanks, babe, let me get out your hair and let you get back to your party.

"Alright babe," she responded. She was walking back to go join the ladies. Mike was about to go eat in the room. Katrina looked back and noticed him heading upstairs to the room. She smiled because she left the fishing pole lying on the bed. He is not going to be expecting to see another pole.

Less than two minutes Mike came back to the family room and stuck his head in.

"Thanks, babe," he smiled.

"You are welcome babe," she was smiling back at him. Then he went back upstairs to his food.

After the jewelry party was over they were both in the mood for some sex. He helped her clean up everything and he took down the tables and put all them back into the garage. The kids were asleep. Simone was in her room and baby Mike was in their bed. They decided that they were going to sleep on the floor that night in the living room. Katrina went back into the kitchen and washed all the dishes and cleaned up the kitchen while Mike was finishing up the family room. She then turned off the kitchen lights and walked back into the living room with Mike. Katrina saw him coming out the bathroom like he had taken a shower already.

"I see you couldn't wait for me."

"For what?" he asked.

"To get in the shower."

"Oh sorry, babe."

"Un huh," she smiled.

Katrina went and got into the shower.

It was for sure time for some mommy and daddy time. Katrina went to go check on both of the kids again quietly as Mike got two covers from the hallway closet; he made them a pallet on the living room floor. Katrina walked back into the living room.

"Baby, come and lay down."

She smile,. "Here I come daddy," she said seductively.

She walked over to him, he grabbed onto her hand. Katrina had kneeled down and laid down on the floor on her back. He spread her legs open as he lay down in between lowering his head in between her legs and began flickering the tip of his tongue on her lips. Only minutes into it and she began moving her hips upward as she sounded a moan.

TWO WEEKS LATER

This is the day that the Johnson Family's three day Reunion starts. The excitement begins to meet the family they still don't know or seeing family that she hadn't seen since she was a kid, some she hadn't seen since the last reunion two years ago. For Katrina, she's not a Garrett anymore, she was coming to her family reunion re-married and with a new baby. She's a Jackson now.

Getting to the hotel for the banquet was exciting, about to see all the family and meeting family she didn't know. As soon as Katrina, Mike, Simone and the baby entered it was nothing but smiles. They entered giving hugs and saying hi, and walking inside the Banquet it was all smiles. It was so amazing seeing all her family again.

Katrina could tell already which families were there; the Sawyers family. "The Robinson side of the family is out here representing from St. Louis," she mumbled to Mike. The Sawyers were thick, but Robinsons were really thick, it was a wonderful moment seeing all the family there.

"Baby, you have a very large family."

"I know, we have the Johnsons, the Sawyers and the Robinsons."

Everyone was all walking around talking, hugging each other, and taking pictures with everyone.

Katrina saw her mom, she Mike and Simone walked over giving her a hug and a kiss.

"Katrina baby, you saw Brandy yet?"

"No Ma, we barely got here ourselves."

"She's late!" Deborah walked off shaking her head with a small smirk on her face.

Everyone was smiling when they saw Katrina's and Mike's three-month-old baby.

As Katrina was hugging different family members and saying hi, she introduced Mike. Mike was being shown so much love he was overly welcomed and very comfortable around everyone. Baby Mike was being passed around. He was so energetic and happy, he was being good. After twenty minutes of walking around the room, seeing and hugging everyone, they went to go stand in line to make their plates. Mike went and found them a table way on the other side of the room. He sat down with Mike Jr's. car seat, diaper bag, and Katrina's purse. Minutes later Katrina's cousin Rachel had brought him back the baby.

"He went to sleep on you I see."

"Yes, right on my breast," she chuckled.

"This little fella," Mike looked down at his son. Mike held his son in his arms as he was still sitting at the table.

Katrina had put all types of food onto her and Mike's plate, Simone made her own plate. Katrina came back to the table, passed him his plate, then sat her plate down too.

"Oh, he fell asleep," Katrina whispered.

"Yeah, she said he fell asleep lying on her breast."

"Aw, my pooh was tired," Katrina reached for him and sat him down in his car seat. Mike's eyes were staring at his food, everything looked delicious on his plate.

"Un Un Un," was all he could say as he shook his head and smiled. They all were in different conversations at their table as they ate.

"Babe that was way too much food you put on my plate, I'm stuffed, I can't even move."

"I see you ate it all though," she laughed.

He laughed, "Of course, I had too, everything was good."

Katrina, Juanita, and Vionna went to go get something out the car.

"So cousin, I have to ask, I didn't want to ask you around the family, but mom told me about that shit with Brandy and Gary."

"Girl yes, isn't that some shit!"

"Girl yes, I still can't believe that shit. I was like no way would she do that shit to her sister."

"Yes cousin, they both played me lying and shit. When I tried to confront the situation they denied it, but then when I found out it was at Paige's birthday party, family there and shit. I was so pissed, I was so embarrassed, I could have killed they asses, *and ooh* I was mad."

"Girl yes, you're better than me cousin. I'm sorry, I would still be beating her ass," Juanita told her.

Katrina smiled, then she chuckled. "Yes, I was kicking her ass for a long time after it happened, shit every time I saw her I just started beating her ass. Yeah, we're alright now, but let me tell you, it took me a long as time to get over it. I'm good though, I'm married to a really good man that would not even dare do that shit to me at all."

"That's good. I'm so glad that God is blessing you and Mike," Vionna told her.

Lights begin to shine their way through the windows of the Benz pulling in, Katrina noticed her sister and Paige. "Look who's pulling in now!" she said loudly. Katrina stood there shaking her head, *"Look at my sister trying to be like me with her Benz,"* she mumbled.

They looked in the direction Katrina's eyes were looking in.

"Who is that?" Juanita and Vionna both asked her at the same time.

"Oh wow, look at that car!"

"Huh," Katrina mumbled. Another one of their cousins had walked up. Jerome gave them all a kiss and a hug.

Jerome pointed, "Isn't that Brandy?"

Katrina turned around and watched her sister getting out a Benz. Brandy closed her trunk, sounded her alarm and began walking towards the hotel. The first people she saw were her sister and her three cousins Jerome, Vionna and Juanita whom she had not seen in a while. Brandy's head leaned back as she had the biggest smile, she couldn't believe who she was seeing.

"Hey, what's going on y'all, why y'all outside and not inside!" she yelled in her excited voice as she was smiling happily to see her family. Brandy looked down and tapped Paige smiling.

"Paige, there goes your Auntie K, and your cousins Jerome, Vionna and your cousin Juanita from St. Luis." Paige ran through the parking lot and ran up to her Auntie giving her a hug first, and then she gave her cousins a hug too.

"Auntie K, where is Simone," she's up there she pointed towards the hotel. "Baby, when you go through the front door the stairs are right there, we're right on the second floor. As soon as you get to the second floor you will see all the family."

"Okay," Paige went inside.

Brandy finally made it to them. "Hey sis, hey cousins!" she shouted smiling.

"Hey cousin," Jerome, Vionna, and Juanita says as they all hugged her.

"So sister, who you leech off of to get that?" Katrina asked her.

"What?" Brandy smiled.

"Who did you leech off of to get that? You sure as hell didn't buy that on your own with no job!"

"Katrina, why are you doing this here," Brandy said.

Katrina didn't care about putting her sister's business on blast, she wasn't holding anything back. She planned to keep putting her on blast whenever she felt like it, Katrina not going to stop until her sister gets it right. She just wanted to see her sister doing better and wanting better for herself. Their cousins that were standing there with them listening were still stunned from hearing what Katrina had told them about Brandy before she walked up. The first thought they had as they stood there with their raised eye brows was that a fight was about to go down any moment now. Since Brandy didn't say much back, their cousins Vionna and Juanita started putting their two cents in too, telling her to have her own independence, she doesn't need a man to do for her, and that she needs to get out there and handle her own responsibilities.

Brandy looked down and closed her eyes and shook her head from side to side. Brandy wasn't surprised that she became the topic of discussion. She wished they'd leave her alone with these questions and mind their own damn business. Listening to the shit they had to say she found herself defending herself against their statements, she made sure she watched the words she said and how she said them. "I feel like I'm being attacked right now, I just got here," she smiled.

"Oh no cousin, don't take it like that, we don't mean it like that, we just wanted to shoot you some advice from cousin to cousin," they told Brandy. They had to stop her right there, she was thinking they were coming for her.

Brandy was about to get all in her feelings and start going off on these Bitches family or not. But she had to first think about it after releasing a deep breath and coming to the realization that they weren't worth her breath; going off on them in front of the hotel, making a scene. Although they were asking for it, she decided not to give it to them, she would behave, she didn't come to start any problems. After all that she just ignored them and excused herself from them and walked off. However, what they were saying was right.

"Y'all stall Brandy out," Jerome smiled.

"I'm cool, I'm not tripping," she smiled. "I'm going inside, its cold out here," Brandy turned around walking towards the hotel.

"Brandy, wait up!" he felt bad and caught up to her, they both went inside to mingle with their other family members.

Brandy went in seeing so many of her family she hadn't seen in years and some she never met and so did Jerome. They were both talking away to everyone. More family was still forming a line to begin making their plates. Katrina and her cousins made it back inside. Her cousins went and made them another plate, Katrina walked to her table to go get Mike.

"Come on babe," she pulled him along with her to walk him around to introduce him to everyone he hadn't met yet.

He smiled.

"It's time you meet the whole family and this isn't even everyone," as he looked around, it was so many of her family he'd thought that was everyone. Her family is so large.

After mostly everyone got their plates and had already started eating, Katrina's uncle, her mother's brother and his rock band stood up on the stage and performed their songs. Her Uncle and his band had everyone grooving and singing from their chairs. They sang eight different songs. What an awesome performance as always. After the performance family members began to walk around to continue to meet and talk to other family members.

Katrina walked around, she saw her cousin and smiled.

"Hey Cousin Marie," Katrina looked at her cousin Shannon.

"Hey Katrina," Marie and Shannon said.

Katrina hugged them both.

"What are you feeding this boy?"

"Everything," Marie said. "Yeah, he would eat the whole house if I'd let him."

Katrina laughed. "My God Shannon, you are so big!" Katrina began touching his arm. She shook her head from side to side. Shannon began flexing.

"Don't be flexing your muscle on your big cousin," she smiles.

Shannon chuckled.

"How much do you bench?"

"Three-eighty," he said smiling.

"Dang, that's a lot."

Katrina gave him and her Aunt another hug, then she continued walking around talking to family.

That night getting home, Mike and Katrina both showered together. After they showered they began watching the news. Watching the forecast Katrina worried about the family picnic tomorrow. If it rains like it says she doesn't see the picnic happening. The two watched a movie until they went to sleep.

That Saturday morning, the second day of their family reunion the sky was dark grey and gloomy, it looked like it just may rain earlier than what the forecast said. After checking the forecast is what confirmed that they would catch a storm today in the late evening. Reading the text message she just received she sighed and shook her head. "What's up babe?" Mike asked.

"My uncle just sent out what looks like a group text saying *no rain, no storm is going to stop and put a damper on their reunion.*" Katrina got up from the bed. "Do you want an English muffin with sausage, egg, and cheese?" Mike nodded. Katrina turned around and walked to Simone's room and asked her the same. Although she knew what her answer was going to be, Katrina asked her anyway.

"Yes mom," Simone replied back as she smiled.

Katrina went down to the kitchen to make breakfast for them. Breakfast didn't take Katrina long at all. "Come eat!" they heard Katrina's voice and they came downstairs. After they were done eating Katrina poured them some orange juice.

"Thanks, babe that was good."

"You're welcome babe."

"Thanks, mom," Simone sounded.

"You are welcome sweetie."

Mike grabbed the baby and took him back upstairs with him. Simone followed, then went to her room. Afterward Katrina had washed the dishes in the sink. Once she was done she turned off the kitchen light and went upstairs. They began to all get ready for the picnic; they had changed their whole entire attire. In less than two hours they were ready, Simone and the baby were too, then they left the house. Leaving the house and looking at the weather Katrina shook her head. She began imagining how today was about to turn out. Once they became half way driving there Katrina was so close to telling Mike to just turn around it was already drizzling, she knows no family is going to want to stay up there if it began raining harder. They all had to meet up at the park at two that afternoon. The more they drove, the rain was picking up. Getting to the park just like her Uncle said there is no rain that's going to stop them, and by the looks of it, he sure was right. Once there, it was so much family there.

They got out the car with their umbrellas, beanies, and jackets, then they walked quickly to the cabana. Katrina, Mike, and Simone began hearing their names being shouted out. Once they got over there with their family they began hugging all the family. Walking past the food table it had everything, plus it was more meat on the grill. Katrina looked at all the food and totally forgot about her diet, she wanted some of everything. They were forming a line.

"I'm about to go stand in line, I see it's about to get long."

"I guess I'll go stand in line with you, so you don't have to make all three plates by yourself."

"Aw, how thoughtful baby," she chuckled.

He laughed.

After making the plates they sat and began eating. Simone sat down to eat. Mike bit down into his barbecue chicken, then his attention directed to the parking lot where a group of Katrina's younger cousins were all crowded up against her cousin's black Yukon.

"What's going on over there?" he asked her.

"Where?" she asked.

"Over there in the parking lot."

Katrina looked. "Oh, they probably over there smoking or about to smoke, that's the smoking marijuana crew," she said.

"Oh, okay." He went back to eating his food.

Simone ate all her food and then started playing a card game of *Speed* with her cousins. Once the game started the other cousins started crowding around them.

"Aye Mike, are you done eating?"

"Yeah," he said.

"Let's go play some ball."

"Alright, for sure," Mike stood up. "I'll be back babe."

"Go have some fun," she smiled. Although she wasn't sure how it was going to be fun as hard as it was raining. Mike left walking with some of Katrina's family to the basketball court on the other side of the park. That looked like it was just six minutes away. Katrina got up and walked over to her Aunt.

"Hey Auntie," Katrina kissed her cheek and hugged her.

"Hey Katrina!" her Aunt sounded.

"How you been Auntie?"

"I have been great, just working you know that's all I do."

"I already know and you know that's all I do too," they laughed.

"So how is the new hubby?"

"The new hubby is great Auntie," Katrina smiled.

"Yeah, I heard." Her Aunt gave her that look straight into her eyes. Then they both shook their heads.

"Yeah, when I heard that I couldn't believe it, I'm sorry she did that to you baby."

"It's fine Auntie, I was hurt, stopped talking to her for some years, but we talk now."

Her Aunt sat there looking at her and nodded her head.

"I have a wonderful husband now, I'm just blessed God put us together."

"I know that's right baby."

"But what's so crazy is that Gary was wonderful and everything I dreamed of up until that happened."

"I know that's crazy baby, he was your high school sweetheart, you guys had been together forever."

"I know, but I can't think about the past anymore. So, Auntie to change subjects I see you have a new man," Katrina's eyes glanced with a smile at the man her Aunt brought with her to the family reunion, then looked back at her Aunt.

"Yeah, he's a nice guy, were just dating right now."

"That's right Auntie."

"Hey, cousin!" from different cousins' voices is all you heard that day.

They were sure they were the only family there. Two hours into the reunion it was raining cats and dogs. The rain never let up, it just rained harder and harder and everyone was still having a good time enjoying every minute. Everyone acted like it wasn't raining, family was just happy to be seeing each other and spending time.

Bre, Katrina's cousin had called over all the kids. They all came running over from the swings and the slides. Bre was about to put on some music.

"Ok, who wants to battle!" she said loudly.

"I do, I do," is all you could hear from all their little voices. Bre put on the music and they all started dancing. Everyone turned their eyes to the kids and watched them all dance. The kids were showing the adults how they get down. They knew those different dances to well and all of them were on beat. After all that dancing, the family took pictures and some ate again. Most were sitting around catching up with family. Hours later the discussion was who was going back to the hotel? Who was going to the casino? Who's going to stay home to watch the kids? *Of course, that question was for the*

Cali family. Once they figured all that out they began to help pack up all the stuff they had out there.

After everyone parted ways from the park, groups of family members went all in their own directions, some went from the park back to the hotel, some went from the park to their house, and then the rest went from the park to the casino. The ones who ended up at the casino went to the nightclub that was there at the casino.

The next morning which was Sunday morning was the last day of their reunion; everyone was meeting up at church services that were starting at eleven. It was a full house at church that morning and the service was great as always. After church everyone had to meet up at Great Aunt Lucy's house for the family gathering.

Right after church and arriving at Aunt Lucy's house it was so much food made and set out, she and Aunt Inez hooked it up. All the family was there having a good time. They even had a cake there for Katrina. After everyone ate the food is when they sang the happy birthday song to her. Her birthday is next week but all the family wouldn't be there is why they did it early. The reunion was coming down to an end. It turned out to be so much fun even with the bad weather conditions. Before some family left they quickly talked about where and when is the next family reunion. They voted for Texas. No one was in a rush to leave. They knew they were not going to see their out of state family for another two years.

A WEEK LATER

Mike and Simone fixed Katina breakfast that morning, it was her birthday. "Happy Birthday to you, Happy Birthday to you, Happy Birthday dear mom, Happy Birthday to you," were the sounds of Mike's and Simone's voices that awakened her at seven in the morning. Although he had work and she had school was their reason for being up that early, she on the other hand, had no reason besides the fact it's her birthday. She was still on a maternity leave. It was cute them singing Happy Birthday to her. She woke up smiling seeing her hubby, Simone, and Mike Jr. They got her out of bed and brought her to the kitchen where they all ate.

They hooked her up some pancakes, waffles, bacon, eggs, sausage, hash brown, milk, orange juice, and tiny muffins. At breakfast, he handed her a gift. She opened her gift and it was a necklace from Mike and Simone. "Aw, thank you, you two." Katrina stood from her seat and walked around the table and kissed and hugged them both. That's not all he had for her, the other gift was her surprise birthday party that's going down tonight.

It was his baby's birthday and he couldn't wait to see the look on her face, his baby is 36, although she could still pass for 25 or 27 years old. He knew this party was about to be epic, especially with her crazy uncle being there.

That night as she and her girl entered the room to the hotel, everyone starts shouting out surprise. Katrina had a very surprised look on her face because she thought she was about to walk into a women's conference to support her, but after seeing her husband, her family and friends she knew then this was for her. She couldn't help her smiles after seeing family and friends, she knew this was something her husband had put together.

Everyone began singing the *Happy Birthday* song to her, they were sounding like the mass chorus no one was off key they sounded really good. Her smile grew bigger and it brought tears to her eyes for the love she was feeling. Once the song ended Katrina walked up to her husband and kissed and hugged him.

"You did it again baby," she says smiling looking into his eyes.

"You're my baby," he told her.

Katrina then walked around and thanked everyone one by one as well; she kissed everyone on their cheeks and thanked them for being there for her birthday celebration. Katrina began laughing and talking to everyone walking around as she was hugging everyone. Everyone there all knew about this surprise party but her and she found it funny and loving that everyone kept it a secret from her to make it that much more special to turn out like this.

Everyone was mingling, enjoying themselves and having a good time. The food was brought out to everyone at their table after a while. Katrina's Uncle, the pastor stood up from his table and got everyone's attention for prayer, the room silenced immediately. He prayed over the food for everyone, saying a quick prayer. Afterward everyone began eating. Later on in the celebration a full-size cake with thirty-six candles already lit was brought out to her. Katrina began laughing when she saw it because it had so many candles on it; everyone began laughing too along with her. Once her cake got right in front of her she closed her eyes and said a quick wish, then she blew out all her candles and everyone applauded and shouted Happy Birthday to her again.

Mike enjoyed seeing his wife happy he knew she would love this surprise party, he was happy everything turned out as planned. The only thing that was forgotten was a photographer, but everyone had their cameras and everyone took pictures with their cell phones.

Deborah had the knife and cut up the cake into pieces and placed a piece on the small cake plates, everyone took a plate and began eating their cake. Once Mike and Katrina finished their cake they set their plates down on the table and went onto the small dance floor. Heading to the dance floor she looked at him still smiling.

"Aw baby, you pulled this off!"

"All for you," he said smiling.

"Thank you so much baby, you are truly the best!"

"You are too, are you enjoying yourself?"

"Of course baby, you always throw me the best birthday celebrations."

"Thank you."

"You're welcome honey." They hugged and kissed.

They stood there on the dance floor and began dancing together with their arms still wrapped around each other. Mike and Katrina's dancing made more of their family and friends come out to the dance floor and dance too. After an hour of dancing, everyone began taking pictures with their cell phones with each other. Then they went back to dancing.

The next morning Katrina had sent out a group text to everyone that was at the party last night, asking if they all could send her all the pictures they took from their phones at her party last night. Mike and Katrina wanted to get all the photos they could from last night to make a photo book out of it.

"Yes," were the replies she had received from everyone who had took pictures.

Shortly she began receiving pictures from everyone. "Babe look," she told him. Mike's eyes narrowed down at her cell phone looking at all the photos that were coming in.

Her Birthday and their Anniversary were so close together, they actually could have had celebrated them together, but Katrina liked having them separate.

Just three weeks later

It was their anniversary, Mike was so anxious to get home to set up their candle light dinner; he wasn't expecting her home for another three hours. Three hours later when Katrina made it home she walked in looking surprised. She had no idea of what Mike had planned for them. He was so special and very romantic, he never disappointed her. He had rose petals at the walk way trailing her to the dining room table. The house smelled so good from the food he had cooked, the light was deemed, and soft music was playing. He felt good about everything he'd did so far tonight, just because of the big smile he had put on her face so far.

He handed her some flowers and two gift boxes. She smiled at her flowers and then she opened her first gift box. It was a Diamond Necklace inside the box. Then she had opened the second box, it was a diamond tennis bracelet.

"Aw baby, thank you so much. This is so beautiful I love it, babe."

"You're welcome baby, Happy Anniversary," they kissed.

"Let me go put these in water," Katrina went to the kitchen and put her flowers in a vase and then she quietly opened the cabinet where she hid his gift. She went to go join her hubby at the dining table. Coming out the kitchen she began walking towards him with the gift she had for him behind her back.

"What do you have behind your back?" he asked her smiling.

"Close your eyes," she said seductively. He closed his eyes, she walked closer to him. She snapped a gold Rolex watch onto his wrist. His eyes opened and looked down, he smiled.

"Thanks, baby," he said.

"You are welcome babe," then they both sat and ate dinner.

The next morning they were still celebrating their anniversary. He cooked her breakfast.

"Babe, you are the best."

"So are you," he told her.

"Thank you, babe," she said.

"You are welcome babe, and also I wanted to take you out to the movies."

"Ok."

They began to get dressed.

As they were getting ready to leave out the door Mike noticed she wasn't going to bring a jacket. "Babe you should bring a jacket."

"Why babe, it's hot outside?"

"When I watched the news this morning, it said it will rain tomorrow."

"Babe, tomorrow not today," she laughed.

"I know, but I can smell the rain coming."

The three left and went to the movies. Simone missed out, she wasn't there. They arrived at the show thirty minutes early. They had paid and walked inside the theatre. They walked over to the concession stand. Mike paid for them two slices of Pizza each, nachos, candy, and two drinks. They didn't eat lunch. He handed over the money and they got their food and snacks. Then they were headed to theatre 7. He walked in ahead of her to open the door for her. Going inside Mike quickly spotted some seats. They found them some good seats, then sat back in the seats just in time. He leaned over to Katrina and whispered I love you in her ear. Katrina told him she loved him too.

After the movie was over they were glad they saw it, it was a great movie. Driving back home from the movie theatre, Katrina had just noticed the lightning in the sky. "Babe, you see that?"

"Yep, and I told you I smelled rain coming," he chuckled.

"I know it just might tonight instead of tomorrow, this California weather for sure, one day it's hot then the next day it's pouring down raining," she laughed.

The sky was looking gray.

"Well, remember earlier I tried to tell you to wear a jacket."

"Yeah, you did say that huh. It sure does look like we're going to get more than rain."

"More than rain?" he looked at her.

"Yeah, like storming and thunder since its lightning which was crazy."

Mike looked into the sky, "I know, it sure does."

Later that night before they could even make it home it had started to drizzle. Mike turned on their windshield wipers.

"Damn!" she said sadly.

He looked over at her. "What babe?"

"It is raining!" she responded. She did not want her hair ruined.

He laughed. "The rain is not going to hurt you!"

CHAPTER

5

Asia and Gary

Gary left to go get a haircut and lined up.

Thirty minutes later Asia's phone rang. She looked at the number, she had a feeling it was Paula calling.

"Hello."

"Asia."

"Hello, may I ask who is calling me?" Asia asked.

"Hello, this is Paula."

"Hello, thanks for returning the call from the message I left you."

"No worries."

"So, what is this going on, when Gary went to your house?" Asia asked her.

"Yeah, as soon as he walked in he couldn't help but keep his eyes on me, even when I mentioned to him that our son was asleep already. That didn't make him leave, that actually made him get more comfortable on the couch."

"But knowing he's married like he mentioned to you, why in the hell did you come on to him?"

"Well, to be honest, he came on to me first, then I did, unfortunately, you are married to a man that doesn't know how to keep his dick in his pants."

Asia pulled the phone away from her ear and looked at her phone crazy thinking to herself, is this bitch crazy? Asia was feeling insulted. But then she kept listening, thinking this woman sure has a lot to say right now. Asia decided to keep her cool, for now, to get as much information as she can from this woman.

"So tell me, Paula, how did this happen?"

"It all happened so unexpectedly. One minute we were on the couch talking, laughing and having a drink, the next minute our tongues were down each other's throats, and his hands all over my cleavage."

Hearing all of this straight from Paula's mouth Asia felt like her heart just dropped. She couldn't imagine that he would do something like this to her. But then again, Gary had done this to his ex-wife. But why her though, she thought to herself.

"So what he did that every time he came over there?" Asia wanted to know every single detail.

"Pretty much, and not once when we were enjoying our time together did he mention our son, or even you for that matter."

"Huh, is that right!"

"He didn't bring him up and I didn't either, I was pretty much just going with the flow of things. The only one time he went into the room to check on our son is when he was leaving."

It was obvious to Asia that Paula was telling the truth, it sounded just like Gary.

"Yeah, so this son that just popped up out of nowhere."

"Yeah, my son: Me and Gary's son, shit you saying that shit as if I'm lying or something, talking about just popped up out of nowhere what the fuck!" Paula just snapped.

"Didn't mean it like that, I didn't say you were lying about it, didn't mean to offend you, but how do you know this child is even Gary's child?"

"I can send you a picture of him right now," Paula said arrogantly.

"Yeah please," Asia told her.

Paula went through her gallery to find a most recent picture of her son, then she texted the picture to Asia.

"Alright, I just sent it now."

"Okay."

"Did you get it?"

"Umm not yet, oh wait, it just came through now."

Asia opened the text and looked at the little boy she kind of noticed that the boy had some facial features as her husband like the eyes, and his lips. Seeing him, yeah he does look like he could be Gary's child, for sure.

"Yeah, he does look like him," Asia told Paula.

"Hmp," Paula sounded a noise shaking her head from side to side.

"Well, Paula I will let you go, thanks for returning my call and sending that picture. That confirms everything I need to know."

"Alright," she sounded.

"Bye."

"Bye."

After hanging up the phone with Paula she had to take a deep breath. The way Asia was feeling right now, like they both had her fucked up. Asia was about to beat his ass, than hers. Period point blank, Asia was giving zero fucks right now.

Paula made it her business to tell Asia she was having sex with Gary when he was coming over to see their son.

Gary came back from the Barber Shop. He walked back inside the house as she was there sitting on the couch. He comes in looking all innocent and shit with his fresh haircut like he hadn't done anything. Gary went and sat next to her holding a conversation. In their conversation she kept throwing in subliminals to see if he was going to mention anything, but he never did and she was getting so annoyed by his statements. She couldn't hold her tongue anymore.

"Gary, what the fuck!" Asia yelled out as she hits his chest with a hard punch.

"Dang baby, what happened now!" he yells as he holds his chest.

"Paula called me today telling me that you two had sex when you were going over there to see your son."

He got up and walked away.

She ran up behind him and tugged on his shoulder to stop him.

"Gary, is she telling me the truth right now?" she asked looking into his eyes.

He didn't want to respond to her, he was afraid to turn his head the other way. Her stare was something vicious.

"Huh, talking about you told her I don't know why you texting me, what you trying to make my girl mad," she mimiced what he just said a few nights ago, how he sounded when he told her that bold face lie.

"Baby, Paula is lying!"

"No baby, you're lying!" she told him.

Asia began hitting on him and pulling on his shirt.

"So you believe her over your husband Asia?"

"Gary, I don't want to believe any of it, but the fact she's calling me out the blue with the shit, I have a major problem with it."

"How in the fuck did she even get your number?"

"That's not important, that doesn't even matter, what fucking matters is what you did, and you thought I wasn't going to find out."

"But I told you what I only went over there for, was to see my son," he said.

"No, you didn't, you didn't tell me shit until that letter came in the mail. The day you found out when you saw her ass at the fucking mall, that's the same day I should have found out. Then you fucked up when you started entertaining her, if you would have just only gone there, only for what you said you went there for, then we wouldn't be here today arguing and fighting about this shit now, and yeah, I saw the little boy. She sent me a picture of his ass too."

"What!"

"Yeah, I saw him," Asia went to her text messages and brought up the picture."

"Ain't this some shit," he sounded.

"See!" she said.

He stood there looking at Asia's phone at his son, mad as fuck at Paula's fucking ass.

"Have you ever seen me entertain the next motherfucker?"

"No." He shook his head.

"I know and you not." Asia was screaming from the top of her lungs, she was so mad at everything.

"Asia, calm down."

"Calm down, how in the hell can you tell me to calm down after finding out some shit that my husband is out there doing behind my back. I can't calm down I'm too mad right now. This shit is not cool Gary, it's not cool at all! What's her address?"

Gary became paranoid, he wondered if she knew he was lying to her about sleeping with Paula. Because the way this never ending argument is going, he almost feels he might as well tell her.

"Baby, I fucked up, I shouldn't have lied, I should have been honest, and I should have never done what I did. I have everything here, I don't know what's wrong with me, and I am so sorry. This shit will never ever happen again."

"Mann, what's her address?"

"Her address," he repeated.

"Yes, Gary her fucking address I said!"

Gary just gave her Paula's address, he felt like what more could go wrong. Asia wrote it down and put it inside her purse.

"What, you're going to go over to her house or something?"

"Don't worry about what I'm going to do; I might want to go take her a thank you gift for fucking up our marriage already."

"Oh."

"Oh, my ass she didn't do this shit by herself, both of y'all motherfuckers are to blame!"

The two went to sleep without saying much to each other at all. In the middle of the night, Asia woke up, she had Paula on her mind. Lying in bed for an hour not being able to fall back to sleep she figured she get her ass up and pay this Paula a visit. Asia left out the house with no jacket. The night was crisp and cold, it felt like ice so she went back inside to grab her jacket. Then she left out the house again. Asia put her address in her GPS and it led her straight to Paula's home. Getting their Lord knows all she wanted to do was knock on her door and fuck this bitch up so bad. Asia just decided to fuck her car up. At least she hopes it's her car, shit it's in her driveway. Afterward, Asia left and went back home and went to sleep like it was nothing. He woke up to his newspaper sitting right beside his coffee, and his breakfast which it had surprised him due to how mad she still were before them going to sleep.

"Thank you babe!" he yelled.

"Oh, you see your breakfast?"

"Yeah, thanks, sweetie."

"Oh, no problem," was her only words she responded, no baby or no coming to him to give him a hug afterward at all. She was still mad.

"What are you doing?" he yelled out.

"Back here putting some clothes inside the washing machine!" she yelled back.

Once she started the washing machine she walked back into the kitchen.

"Hey, baby!"

She gave him a head nod. He didn't like this and didn't want his wife walking around the house with her face all frowned feeling like something.

Gary didn't want to have any issues with Asia. He thought about driving over to Paula's house to have a talk with her, but then he got to thinking this is why he's in trouble now for going over to Paula's house. Instead, Gary walked outside to the front. He called Paula and begged Paula to stop calling him and texting him.

"This is what you're calling me for, I'm glad you called, I was just about to call your ass?" Paula said.

He lowered his voice down a notch, "No Paula, ain't shit going down with us anymore!"

"Boy please, I'm not thinking about your ass."

"I'll just send you a check once a month and I'll come by every other week to see my son. But let me call you only," he told Paula.

"Well, why you're sending checks, make sure to send enough to get my car painted."

"Your car painted, I'm not about to help you with your car."

"Yes the fuck you are, coming over here fucking up my shit, I don't have any enemies, so I know it's you and your bitch or probably just your ass!"

"What the fuck are you talking about Paula?"

"I went outside this morning to FUCKIN BITCH keyed deeply into my car door!"

"Man, I still don't know what you are talking about, me nor did my lady do that shit!" Gary hung up the phone with her, and then put his phone on silent mode in case she tried to call him back once he goes back inside the house. Gary went back inside.

Once Paula saw that she was pissed. She called the police to file a police report. Paula didn't know who did this to her car.

"Ma'am, do you have any enemies?" the officer asked.

She thought to herself, no but then the call with Asia made her think she probably did this and the more she thought she knew she did this. After dealing with the police she then called her insurance company although she already knew who did that shit.

"No officer I don't," she told him.

A week later Paula's car was sent to the body shop to be fixed and repainted. She came back even harder. She threw another tone of paint making it two-toned, it was tight and looked good.

Gary couldn't even lie anymore, he'd already hurt her enough, and Gary had to tell her the truth.

"Yeah, what she's saying is what happened, I'm sorry."

She stared into his eyes in silence.

"Hit me. Slap me right here," he pointed to the right side of his face. She didn't bulge. He urged her to hit him. She didn't because that wasn't going to make her feel any better.

"Man, you got this woman calling our home telling me some shit my husband done, are you serious, shouldn't no other woman be calling me telling me shit about you period!" she said with a raised voice.

She was leaving him in silence. It was quite awkward to have a comeback after that lie.

"So what, your feelings came back for her?" she asked in a calm tone.

"No," he responded.

"Then how did you end up in bed with her and then you came up with this big ole lie about it."

"It was just sex Asia sweetie, I promise, I only went over to her house to see my son because she asked me to come see him, but then when I got there he was asleep. Then before I knew she began saying she needed us to talk about him, but yet she kept offering me drink after drink; one thing led to another, than to us having sex. Babe, she took advantage of me, it's like she had more control over me, baby."

"I know you don't think I'm some type of fool, if you think I'm going to believe that you let her get you drunk, take you in her room, fuck you, and not at any point you were able to stop the situation!"

"I fucked up Asia!"

Her eyes kept a deep stare in his eyes. She began thinking maybe she didn't marry the right one after all.

He knew she was pissed, by the look of fire in her eyes right now. If looks could do what it looks, he would be on fire and dead right about now. He was not trying to lose another good woman.

Although it has been almost six years since he got a divorce from Katrina, he was not at all trying to get one from Asia. He understood her anger, he definitely wanted to make things better.

"Baby, I fucked up, I did, but I'm going to do everything in my power to prove to you from this day forward there will be no more fuck ups."

"What do you plan to do to gain my trust back Gary, because as of right now, it's all lost."

He stood up close to her and hugged her.

"Babe, I don't even want to say, actions always speaks louder than words, I just want to show you with my actions. I love you," he told her.

"Prove it!" she responded.

"Ok."

He took his left hand gripped her chin to give a kiss to her lips.

"I'm sorry," he said. She continued just to stare at him.

Asia was very hurt after finding out the truth about what her husband really did, but she still loves him, even though a thought of leaving did cross her mind.

Asia knew she couldn't watch Gary's every move; she wasn't going to be able to function if she thought about what the hell he was doing when she was out working.

Gary had to prove to his wife Asia that nothing was still going on with his son's mother. He knew, either way, she was still not going to believe him, but he knew trying would be worth it.

That night at dinner it was silence between them. Watching her eat as he ate was like he wasn't even sitting across from her, he had to say something. "Asia."

Asia looked up at him and nodded her head.

"I promise, I thought I was only going to see my son."

She made a grunt sound.

"Baby, you are my wife, you really think I would mess things up with you on purpose? I'm not trying to move backward."

She sat there looking at him as she was in thought. Thirty minutes later after she was done eating dinner she got up from the table and showered. Once she had gotten out the shower he was in the kitchen washing all the dirty dishes from dinner. She brushed her hair back and pinned it up, then she got in bed and watched TV. An hour later he walked into the room holding two glasses of wine for them both. He passed her a drink, then he walked around the bed and sat next to her.

"Baby, I fucked up, I did, but I'm going to do everything in my power to prove to you from this day forward there will be no more fuck ups."

"Gary, how many times are you going to say that? Don't tell me that shit no more, just do it."

He leaned closer to her trying to hug her as he asked *what he should do.*

She took a sip of her wine then looked at him crazy.

"I'm not about to tell you how to be a husband, you already know just what I want, and what I'm not taking being your wife."

"Asia baby," Gary said.

"No, you better figure it out."

"Alright then, I will show you, actions always speak louder than words. I just want to show you through my actions," he told her. "I love you," he told her again.

"Like I said, stop telling me the same thing just prove it," she responded.

"Ok," he said. He took his left hand and gripped her chin again to give her another kiss on her lips. "I'm sorry!" he said.

She continued just staring at him as he kissed her again. She then leaned back as she continued taking small sips of her wine. Looking at the TV, but in thought, she couldn't believe he had her doing shit she doesn't normally do, which was staying after this. She wasn't even mad, she was just more hurt than anything. She looked over at him and he was already looking at her, all she could do was turn her attention back to the TV. That night was so emotional for the both of them.

Going to sleep she felt like an emotional wreck. Waking up the next morning to him already up in the kitchen cooking breakfast, she straightened their bed, brushed her teeth, got dressed and did her makeup. Coming out the bathroom he was already back in the room with breakfast. "Hey baby, here's your breakfast," he handed her plate.

"Thanks, babe," she smiled.

The two sat on the bed, ate, and watched TV. After they were done he took their plates to the kitchen and just sat them on the sink.

Minutes later Asia heard her line clicking; In the middle of her business call; she looked down at her phone and noticed the call was from a blocked number. She wondered who it was, so she answered. "Hello, this is Asia speaking."

"Asia this is Paula."

"How can I help you PAULA!" She looked up at Gary making sure he heard the name she'd just said as she sat there with the phone held to her ear.

"Tell him to stop calling me, tell him if he wants some pussy he better fuck you now."

"Excuse Me Bitch!"

Then Paula hung up her phone. Paula felt like fucking with Asia since Asia wants to come over to her house and fuck up her car and shit.

Getting off the phone with the woman, she couldn't even finish her business call. She told them she has an emergency and that she would have to dial them back. Getting off the phone completely she looked at Gary. "Gary, you promised me things were going to be better. You told me to stop jumping to conclusions and not to worry, but how can I not worry when she keeps calling telling me shit."

Paula was keeping her distance from Gary. She knew he was going to start shit with her for telling his wife the shit she had been telling her lately. He calls her phone daily, back to back, and leaves nasty messages on her phone, that she's still not answering or responding to. Gary was pissed that Paula would cause drama in his new marriage. He wished he would have never been fucking her when he did those few times.

Asia was so stressed out behind all this nonsense behind Paula, she just went to the store to buy her a drink. She needed something stronger than the wine she had in the refrigerator. He left the house right after her. He needed and wanted to cheer his wife up badly. He bought her some flowers and went back home. Once Asia got back from the store and walked in and saw Gary with the flowers she asked what those were for.

"What's those flowers for?" she asked him again.

"For you babe," he told her.

"Gary, ain't no damn flowers about to cheer me up. You have to do better than some fucking flowers!" she told him.

He got mad and threw the flowers in the trash. Mintues later she asked where were her flowers.

"I threw them in the trash."

"Why did you throw away my flowers Gary!" she yelled.

"Well babe, you were talking like you didn't want them, saying I needed to do better than some fucking flowers," he told her.

Asia was mad at Gary for throwing away her flowers and she was mad about the call she got from Paula. She stood there giving him the look and silent treatment. He went and got her flowers out the trash can and gave them to her. She took them from him and went to put them in a vase.

"I'm sorry for throwing away your flowers and everything else you're still upset about."

"Gary, sorry is just not enough for me, it's not."

Listening to the tone of her voice he just didn't know what else to say and do.

"Baby, I'm so fucking sorry and I love you. I just don't know what else to say to make you feel at least a little better about the situation."

"How about you leave me alone for right now, it's like the more you talk about it, the more you apologize and the more I get mad. I'm like so tired of hearing Paula's name in this house."

"Alright babe," he sighed.

It bothered him that his wife didn't want him saying anything to him right now. Shit, he hated the silent treatment shit. But this is what she wants so he knew he just has to deal with it until she's ready to talk. Getting her store opened is all she needed to be thinking about right now. It was a lot to it and she just wanted to be focused and for her business to be successful.

Asia was feeling like she was coming down with something, she wasn't feeling well. She began to feel like she had to throw up. But nothing would come up when she tried to make it. The next day Asia interviewed a few ladies. After interviewing she had to make a decision and so after going over their applications she hired only four ladies. The next day she called the ladies who she thought would be a great fit for her store. Out the blue again she was right back feeling like she has to throw up. She went to the bathroom hovering over the toilet, but minutes later the feeling went away. She stood back up and was getting ready to leave out the bathroom, but suddenly the feeling came right back. She began to feel something trying to come up. She spun back around and threw up inside the toilet. After throwing up Asia felt her forehead, her cheeks, and underneath her chin. She wasn't hot, she felt normal. She stood still thinking she hadn't been coughing, what kind of sickness has her throwing up, Asia didn't know. So she went to the store and picked her up a home pregnancy test so she could rule that out before actually going to the doctor. After taking the test Asia just found out she's pregnant.

She first told Gary the news, and then she decided to share it with her family. Asia called her parent's house to tell them her news. Her sister answered. "Hey sister," her sister said.

"Hey, what y'all doing?" Asia asked.

"Nothing," her sister replied.

"Tell mom and dad I'm pregnant," Asia says so plainly.

"What sister, you're pregnant!" Myisha said with excitement.

"Yeah, I just took a test."

"I'm excited for you!"

"Thanks."

"As soon as they get back I will tell them."

"Alright." Then Asia hung up. Shortly after that call, Asia's dad called Gary's cell. "Babe, this is your dad calling," he told her as he was looking down at his ringing cell phone.

"Hello," Gary answered.

"Hey son, congratulations!" he said.

Gary paused looking at Asia's face. "Hey dad, man thank you, we appreciate that," Gary looked at Asia and shrugged his shoulders.

He kept going on and on, talking about all types of things. It had Gary and Asia shocked that her dad talked to him that long tonight. Before tonight he had never been on the phone with him that long. It seems like now that he got his daughter pregnant his connection with him is now stronger. This was the first time her dad called directly to Gary phone to talk to him instead of calling Asia's phone to talk to him.

Thirty minutes passed. "*I know I have talked your ear off tonight.* Well, I have one last thing I want to say, son," he said.

"What's that?"

"Son, please just make sure you take care of my daughter!"

"I will dad," he said in response. The second Gary and Asia's dad got off the phone, Asia's phone sounded. *Daddy* popped up on her screen. "Hey daddy!" she answered.

"Hey, baby Congratulations!"

"Thank you, daddy," she told him.

"How are you feeling, and what's been going on out there?"

"I'm feeling okay, and what's been going on out here," she repeated. Gary looked at Asia. "Nothing has been going on daddy, beside the fact I'll be opening up my clothing store very soon."

"I'm so proud of you baby, I really am. You are doing very good, look at you, you're about to open up your own clothing store and you got you a good loving husband over there. What more can you ask God for," he told her.

"Thank you, daddy," she said again.

"Baby, your mother wants to say something."

"Okay."

"Hey Asia, congratulations baby. If you need me, call me!" she says.

"Hey mom, thank you so much, and I will," Asia chuckled.

Asia hung up her cell and looked at Gary.

"Don't worry I won't tell my parents that you cheated on their daughter since we've been married," she said moving from by him.

CHAPTER

6

Brandy and Her Lovers

Thursday morning waking up and stepping out the bed and looking in the mirror Brandy remembered to text her hair stylist to see if she could do her hair today. Brandy text her. Brandy walked to her kitchen and made her a cup of coffee and a bagel with cream cheese. That's all she wanted, but she toasted an extra bagel and made three slices of bacon and scrambled eggs for Paige so when she woke up it would be breakfast sitting on the stove for her.

Brandy heard a noise. She looked down at her cell phone, it was vibrating. She had received a text from her stylist Kaye telling her she could do her hair at twelve thirty. Brandy text her back saying *ok, thank you and see you then*. She continued cooking. Once Brandy finished cooking is when Paige came walking into the kitchen. "Hey, good morning baby, I just made you breakfast."

"What is it?"

"Bagel, eggs, and bacon," Brandy said.

"Thanks, mom!"

"You're welcome, and the cream cheese is inside the refrigerator on the door!"

"Okay," Paige responded.

"I'm about to go to the shop and get my hair done, do you want to come or do you want to stay here?"

"I'll stay," Paige said.

"Alright," Brandy said, then walked to the living room and watched TV.

Two hours passed, Brandy grabbed her purse from out the room and threw on her hat that was on her dresser. Brandy left to get her hair done. Getting to the shop Brandy took off her hat and sat down in the chair. While getting her hair done Kaye mentioned to Brandy she does eye lashes now. Brandy never tried the eye lash extensions so she thought she'd try it to see how she liked it. After getting her hair washed, blow dried, and pressed, she did Brandy's eye lashes. Afterward, Brandy rubbed her hair and looked in the mirror at her eye lashes "I love it, Kaye," she smiles.

"Thank you, Brandy," she smiled back at Brandy. Brandy stood up and gave Kaye a hug. "Hey Brandy, before you go do you want to smoke?"

"Hell yeah," Brandy smiled.

"Alright, for sure, I already have one rolled up."

"Okay," Brandy told her.

Brandy followed Kaye. They were going to her car. As they walked out to the parking lot they were getting closer to an all-black charger on black rims. It was obvious Kaye had a brand new car once she chirped the car sounding the alarm. "Hey, Kaye this you?" Brandy pointed out her finger at the car.

"Yeah, I just bought it a few weeks ago."

"I like it. My sister's homegirl just bought an all-black Camaro with the black tint and black rims looking just like yours."

"Oh for real, that's right."

They got inside the car and chatted while they were smoking. By the time they both reached their level of highness Kaye put the blunt out. "Here

Brandy, you can take the rest for later." Kaye passed Brandy the rest of the blunt.

"Oh wow, thanks, Kaye."

"Oh, no worries, I have more."

They got out the car. Kaye walked back into her salon and Brandy walked to her car and left. After leaving there she went back home. She thought she was so cute she couldn't stop looking in the mirror. She thought to herself, she is to fly to stay in the house tonight, she needed to go out. A few hours after being home Brandy called her cousin Porsche; she held the phone to her ear until she answered. After a few rings, she finally answered.

"Hey, Hey cousin," she answered.

"Hey Ms. Porsche," Brandy said.

"Hey Brandy!"

Brandy asks her if she wants to go out tonight. Porsche said hell yeah. Brandy laughs through the phone.

"But wait, my hair not done."

"I just got mines done earlier."

"So what, are we going to be up in there with your shit all fly and mine's not?"

"Well, when we go out tonight I hope I can find me a man," Brandy told her.

"Girl, your ass is crazy, you trying to get wifed up?" "I'm trying to have fun."

"Ha-ha," Brandy laughed.

"For real Brandy, you can't go to the club expecting to find your husband there because trust me, after you find him in the club, that's where he's going to stay."

"Ok, cousin I get it."

As bad as she wanted to see her future with a husband, she decided to just have the mindset of just going out tonight and having a good time.

"I guess I'll get up and start straightening my hair."

"Okay cousin," Brandy chuckles.

"Whatever. I wish my shit was already done too."

"Cousin, call me when you're almost done."

"Bye!" Porsche sounded.

Brandy went to the bathroom and turned the knob to the bath tub, she ran her some bath water. While her water was running she looked for a dress to wear. Looking through her closet at every hanger she stopped at her burgundy dress with the back out. She decided that was the one she was going to wear since she had not worn it yet and been having it for a while. Brandy pulled her dress out the closet and laid it on her bed. Then she went and got into the bath. Brandy sat in the tub for about ten minutes relaxing before she began scrubbing her body. After she was done scrubbing her body she reached for her towel that was sitting on the toilet and began drying herself as she was still standing up, still inside the bath tub as her water was slowly draining out.

Brandy stepped out the bath tub wrapping her towel around her body. She went to get her lotion from underneath her sink in the cabinet. She put on lotion, then she smoked her piece of blunt she had from earlier. Brandy put on her burgundy dress and brushed her teeth so she wouldn't have that blunt smell on her breath. Then she took off her head scarf, combed her hair down, put on her heels, and took a quick glance in the mirror to look at herself to make sure she was on point. She looked at herself from the front, she was good. Then she turned her body around to make sure everything was looking just right. The first thing she noticed was the lining of her panties, due to the thin material of her dress she was able to see it too good, so she took off her panties and put them back in her drawer. She grabbed her purse, cell and keys, then walked to her kitchen. Brandy reached for her bottle of Tequila on top of her refrigerator. She kept it in the brown paper bag it was in, but then she placed that bag into a plastic bag, then she left her house.

Brandy drove to the gas station; she needed two cups and some ice. Brandy pulled into the gas station and parked. She cut off her ignition and opened her driver side door, then she instantly had a text message alert come through on her cell as soon as she was about to get out the car. She looked down and saw it was from Porsche. The text message read, *"What's your status?"* Brandy texted her back letting her know that she was at the gas station grabbing two cups and some ice and then she would be on her way. Porsche had texted back saying *Okay.*

Brandy got back in the car and was now headed Porsche's way. Brandy had another text message alert going off again. She looked down while still keeping her eyes on the road. It was Jordan and the text read: *Girl, Chris is up here.* Brandy texted her back saying *I'm on my way now.*

Once Brandy got on Porsche's Street she called her cell to tell her to come outside. Minutes later Porsche and her boyfriend came outside and walked to her car.

"Oh, Porsche, if I would have known that your dude was coming I would have gotten an extra cup, my bad."

"Oh no, that's fine we can share."

"You sure?" Brandy asked.

"Girl yes," Porsche noticed Brandy's red cloudy eyes. "You smoked?"

"Yeah," Brandy smiled.

"How you going to smoke without me?" Porsche asked her.

"Shut up, you said the other day you stopped; you told me you were going to stop smoking for a while."

"Yeah, but I started back."

"Well my bad, I didn't know you started back cousin," she chuckled.

Brandy poured their drink before starting up the car. She passed her cousin her cup. "Wait a minute, somebody's looking different by the eyes," Porsche says as Brandy smiled. "You have contacts on?"

"No," Brandy took a few sips drinking her drink straight. "I have on eye lashes."

"Oh, okay, you cute cousin. Girl, I can't wear that shit, my eyes are too sensitive."

"Well let's see how these go, this is my first time wearing them."

"I like it, Brandy," Porsche kept staring at her lashes.

"Thank you, I like them too."

Brandy turned her ignition and started up her car and drove off. On the way driving to the club they were singing to the music that was playing from Brandy's radio getting themselves ready for the club. After arriving at the club they got in line about to pay, Brandy seen Jordan and Misty from outside sitting in their spot. Brandy began waving and blowing kisses to her girls. The three walked in heading straight to their girls first to give them a hug.

"Girl, Chris ass is in the back."

"Oh yeah," Brandy said and looked at her cousin.

"Let's go back there and surprise his ass," Porsche said.

Brandy and Porsche both walked to the back. Once they got to the back they walked straight to Chris, he was sitting out there talking with his cousin and some girl. Brandy gave his cousin a hug then she hugged Chris.

"Oh, your hands are cold," Chris told her.

"I know they are, it's cold out here."

Brandy then looked at the woman that's sitting next to Chris; the woman looked back at her too.

"Hi, how are you," Brandy spoke to her.

"I'm fine, you the most real one here!"

"Oh, thank you," Brandy responded even though she really didn't know what she really meant by that, but she guesses it didn't mean anything bad since she didn't know her from a can of paint.

Brandy then looked back at Chris.

"So, what's up?"

"What's up?"

She looked at him thinking he was going to give her a conversation other than saying what's up. Once she saw he was acting a little funny she walked away.

"Ok well, I'll be back," she told Chris. Then Brandy and Porsche went back inside and went straight to the bar. It only took a few minutes before the waitress got to them.

Brandy looked back at Porsche asking her what she's getting.

"Oh, the same thing we always get, and oh, it's my treat, drinks on me tonight."

"Oh thanks, cousin," she smiles.

Brandy told the waitress two Adios Motherfucker's. After their drinks were made, Porsche was about to pay, but then asked for another one for her boyfriend. As the two turned around to leave the bar Lamar was standing right behind them. It's been a minute since Porsche seen him after their last argument.

"Hi Porsche," Lamar spoke.

"Hello, Lamar."

After Porsche spoke back to Lamar she and Brandy kept walking past him and walked back over to their table with their girls Jordan and Misty. Once they finished their drinks they went out on the dance floor and danced the whole night. They didn't stop until they turned the light on. They had a lot of fun. Leaving the club that night they were still pumped up. Brandy drove her cousin Porsche and her boyfriend back off at Porsche's house then she drove home.

Brandy tried thinking of other things but it wasn't helping because Chris kept popping up in her head. It wasn't even a sexual thing, she missed her friend, her man, her finance; the man she would have been already married to by now. She began thinking how things would have turned out if she would have never done what she did, or if she would have never gone to her sister's house. She blamed Gary for all this, only if he would have never slid in her bed that morning having sex with her everyone wouldn't have been going through all the craziness.

A week later out the blue Brandy received a text message from her friend Marcus, she had not heard from him in a while.

"Hey, you going out tonight or what?" he texted her. "Yeah, I am," she responded back to him.

Brandy and her cousin went out to the club, and her girl Misty was going to meet them up there. They had so much fun last week they had to go back. Once she made it to the club he was already there, he spotted her first and walked over to her.

"Hey Brandy!"

"Hey Marcus," she smiled seductively at him.

"You want a drink?"

"Yes, you know I do."

"What you want? I'll buy it."

168

"A Martini," she said.

"Okay, no Adios, tonight?"

She chuckled, "I'm switching it up tonight."

"Oh, ok," he said to her.

They walked up to the bar and he ordered them both drinks; beer for him, and a Martini for her. After the bartender passed him both drinks minutes later, he handed her, her drink. After taking sips of her drink and it got all up in her system she danced with him the whole night. Brandy's girl Misty was taking pictures of them dancing out there on the dance floor. Misty didn't dance much that night like she would normally, but she stayed drinking her drink slowly, she still had fun. The morning, once the club was over Marcus, followed behind her in his car to her house. As soon as they both made it there they took off their shoes to get comfortable.

"Whew!" she sounded as soon as her heels came off. She couldn't wait to take off her heels after dancing in them all night.

"You think you can give me a face towel and a big towel?"

She did as he asked and went and got him a face towel and a big towel out the hallway closet.

"Here you go."

"Thanks, babe."

"You're welcome."

"Could we take a shower together?"

After all night clubbing, she didn't see why not. He unzipped his jeans and took them off and sat his jeans on the floor. He pulled off his shirt and sat it right on top of his jeans. Brandy took off her dress and put it inside her closet on top of her hamper. She got in the shower with him. After getting out the shower he walked into her room by her bed and he lay down on the floor. When she came out, the second she noticed him on the floor and not in the bed, she laughed.

"Why are you on the floor?" she asked staring into Marcus' eyes.

"Come here," he whispered seductively.

She walked up to him as he watched her every move. He raised his hands up to her telling her to sit on his face.

Brandy stood over him slowly taking off her gown which she didn't even know why she'd just put it on in the first place, slowly squatted down right in front of his face. Their gaze became stronger into the eyes of each other. He lifted his head up more towards her vagina sticking his tongue out, she spread her lips open with her fingers as he slid his tongue in between. Immediately she closed her eyes to the good feel of what she was feeling. After sucking and slurping it for as long as he did, it felt like her legs were about to give out on her, they were starting to hurt. "You okay?" he asked her.

"My legs are beginning to hurt a little," she told him.

"Well, just relax," he told her. She then sat all her weight on his chest. She was about ready to get up in the bed now. He wanted to stay on the floor because he didn't need her telling him not to fast because of the bed keep hitting the wall like last time, so he wanted to stay right there on the floor. They ended up staying right there on the floor and then they had sex all that morning.

When the two were ready to go to sleep is when they finally made it to the bed, they cuddled up under each other and went to sleep.

The next morning getting dressed, they hugged and then he left. Later that day Marcus called Brandy after he made it home.

"Hey, you made it?" she answered.

"Yeah, and I enjoyed myself with you last night, this morning," he smiled as he held the phone talking to her.

"I enjoyed you too last night Marcus, and this morning," she told him as she smiled too, holding her ear to the phone.

Once the two hung up their phones Brandy hopped on Facebook for the first time that day and the first thing she saw was herself being tagged in Misty's pictures from the club last night. *"Oh, my God,"* she mumbled to herself. She was not trying to see herself on Facebook as the first thing she saw, and Brandy quickly deleted them off her page. She immediately called her girl to see why in the hell did she tag her in that post, she didn't want everybody seeing the picture with her all up on Marcus like that.

"Oh, my bad boo, I should have told you first that I was going to tag you in the pictures I took last night, I'm sorry," she said back to Brandy.

"No worries, I already deleted them, man, you're going to get me caught," she chuckled.

"I'm sorry, my bad."

"No, it's cool, just let me know next time beforehand, so I can tell you no or yeah."

"Alright, no problem," Misty said.

That night Brandy wanted to gas up so she didn't have to in the morning. She got in her car and drove to the gas station. Brandy went inside, paid for her gas, and walked around the inside. She was thinking of getting something to snack on at the gas station, then she left out the store and as she was pumping her gas a guy in a diesel truck was trying to get her attention. He honked, she waved, then he parked and got out his truck and walked over to her car. The two introduced each other by shaking each other's hand and telling each other their names. He winked his eye she noticed as he said his name, then she smiled. Then they started up a conversation, they talked, laughed, and the both of them were flirting with each other.

They were having a good conversation, shortly after as their conversation was coming to an end he asked her the next time he's in Cali could he come see her. She told him yes if the price was right. She got straight to the point of what she wanted, she already had a pretty good idea about what he wanted.

"Sounds good Beautiful," he told her.

Before they parted they exchanged numbers.

The next day Brandy received mail. Looking through her mail it was a letter from Terrell. She stared at it, and then she opened it. She pulled the letter from out the envelope and opened it, it read: *Though we've been apart for a year I still think about our last date in San Bernardino. You had such a great time and so did I. I thought you were going to give us another try, but I haven't heard from you since. I still think about you all the time and the thought of you still brings joy and life to my soul every time with smiles and hopes that you will still give our love another try. Love Terrell.*

Brandy grinned. She ended up calling his number he left on the envelope. Looks like he got a new number. She dialed his number. He was grateful to see she read the letter and called his phone. They talked and by the end of their conversation she had told him she would give him another chance, but she wants to take things slow. He was fine with that. He planned to make sure nothing gets in between them this time. She let him come over.

Brandy called up Jordan.

"Girl, come ride with me to the sex shop?"

Jordan laughed.

"Girl, you laughing but I'm serious."

"Brandy, what you about to get from the sex shop?"

"Girl, some shit Terrell and I can use in the bedroom, you know, to spice up the sex a bit since it's been a while with him."

"Did I just hear you correctly? So you're back talking to Terrell Brandy, the same person you said you were not fucking with anymore?"

"Mmmm yes," she sounded.

"Mmmm, okay," Jordan said.

"So, are you going to come?"

"Yeah, I'll go with you."

"Okay cool, love you, friend."

"Love you more Brandy."

Brandy picked her up and getting there to the sex shop they saw so many different toys. Like with all this stuff, what do you even need the man for is what she was wondering to herself? After purchasing a few things they left and once Brandy returned home Terrell was there waiting for her. He walked up to her staring into her eyes, then he stopped and began staring deeper into her eyes more and up closer. He grabbed her chin and pulled her mouth to his sliding his tongue into her mouth. They both began kissing so passionately it had felt like an *I miss you kiss or an I still want to be with you type of kiss*. She was feeling the same, but this time she planned to take things slower. They went inside and headed for the bedroom. After the door closed shut his boxers began to come off slowly. Terrell began caressing her breast. Next Terrell took off his boxer shorts all the way. She reached for his balls, and began massaging them, then minutes later she moved up his penis, gently massaging it in a stroking hand position motion and they used the toys she had. They had a wonderful night.

Days later Vincent was back in California and he wanted to see Brandy, so he called her up.

"Hey, what you doing?" Vincent asked Brandy.

"At work," although she wishes she wasn't, but her homegirl hooked her up with it, and it's under the table, but she doesn't see herself doing this shit that much longer, she's tired of wiping ass and shit.

"What time you get off?" he asked.

"I'm off at ten o' clock. Why? What are you up too, are you out here?" she asked.

"Yeah, I've been down here since last night."

"Oh, okay."

"I want you to come see me; I have a gift for you."

"Aw, thank you, Vincent, how sweet of you. Ok well, I'm off at ten."

Perfect he thought, he couldn't wait to see her.

"How has your day been?"

"Long and exhausting, when I get off actually I want to go straight to sleep, but I had my daughter record Empire. Since I'm at work."

"Ok, that's what's up. I want to watch that too."

"Ok."

He needed her, he wanted to sex her so badly. She knew just what he wanted, even though she was tired. She just wanted to shower and see her pillow, but he's been coming through for her since she met him, so she couldn't let him down. Brandy got off, went home, and showered. Terrell was lying there watching TV. Once Brandy got out the shower she got herself together.

"Babe, you're just getting in, where you going now?" Terrell asked her as he looked at the time on his phone.

"Umm, I'm about to go meet up with my girls to go shopping," she was lying.

"This late, at eleven o' cloc?" he said as he looked into her eyes. She didn't know that he knew she was lying.

"Yeah, this late," she sounded.

"Um." he replied.

Brandy kissed him then left to see Vincent. On the way driving there she had to remind herself to try her best not to get all caught up in the moment with feelings when she sees him, knowing this is just a quick fuck and Terrell is back in the picture, but the way he fucks her, how could she not. It was going to be very hard and she knows it. It was nothing new, this was something she had to remind herself every single time she dealt with him and to tell herself that this was just a friendly good fuck.

Brandy arrived at the hotel room, she knocked on the door. "Come in!" he shouted from inside.

Brandy slowly opened the door as she entered his hotel room, he came up behind her and wrapped his arms around her waist. He was behind the door and he was so happy to see her, but he was happier she came. He began kissing all over the back of her neck, then he turned her around kissing her on her lips. He slid his tongue between her lips slowly as their tongues began to roll around each other's.

They kissed all the way to the bed. She scooted back on the bed, he crawled over her at the same time she was scooting back, in-between her legs is where he started, right in her center. A slight moan she made caused him to go in deeper with his tongue, after about twenty minutes or so he crawled up to her face, tongue kissing her as he lay right on top of her. Shortly after Brandy wrapped her legs around him, he was as hard as a rock, she could feel it through his pants. They both slid their clothes off fast, he put on his condom. Vincent stuck it in.

"Can you feel my dick baby?"

"Yes, I can feel it," she moaned. "It feels good."

"This dick feel good baby!" he asked her.

"Yeah, real good," she moaned. Her moaning made him go faster, then he began going in harder and even deeper, minutes later he changed the paste to a slower motion.

Shortly the position was changed to getting both her legs and raising them up in the air. He opened them widely, she was so wet as he slides it in and out of her.

He brought her legs down as he continued going in, all the way, harder and harder, deeper and deeper, hearing her moans with each thrust he made. Once her moans became louder he knew she was about to come soon, but so was he. Her moans were still sounding, and now so were his. She gripped the sheets and the bed as she was able to feel herself about to come. He began going faster, moving back and forth at a steady fast paste, her moans got even louder, then she began moving up and down faster trying to go at his pace.

They both felt a burst of cum warm them down there and then they both just laid there. After a while, she went and took her a quick shower, cleaned herself up, got out then dressed. He wanted her to stay the night with him, but she couldn't and he already knew why which is why she wasn't going to go at first because she already knew he was going to pull this again. Brandy got all her bags with the gifts he had for her. An hour later she returned home, but she left her bags in her trunk.

Walking into her apartment Terrell wondered if she really was just with that guy. "Where you coming from?" he asked Brandy.

Brandy stopped in her tracks looking at him with a crazy look.

"Brandy where you coming from? don't tell me no lie neither, and don't tell me you're seeing another dude neither," he said.

"What lie, I don't have time to lie Terrell, and what dude? Don't come at me like that, I just walked in the house!"

"I'm coming from shopping like I told you, I was with Misty and Jordan, is that okay with you!"

Terrell tried catching her in a lie. "See, look at my phone, you will see messages from my girls about us going to the mall!" Brandy was a step ahead of him, she erased the calls, the text messages on her way home and then had her lie straight saying she just came from the mall with her girls.

"Where are your bags? Why didn't you bring them in and are you sure you just didn't meet up with a man?"

Terrell accused Brandy of talking to someone else after reading her text messages while she was in the shower a few hours ago when she made it home from work, how could he not. She played dumb like she didn't know what he was talking about until he started telling her in detail what Vincent was saying in her text messages that he'd read. She listened and then she thought, did he read my text messages?

"You went through my cell phone!"

"Yeah, I did, when you were inside the shower."

"Man, don't go through my phone, that's my phone!"

"See, I knew you been lying all along, you playing me."

"Huh, don't go there buddy!"

"What you mean don't go there, I'm going there!"

"Oh, just like you were playing me with your bitch!"

"What!"

"Yeah, that's what I thought!"

"Brandy, how long are we going to be going through this back and forth shit, fuck them let's just worry about us!"

"Yeah, fuck them," Brandy replied.

Their gaze into each other's eyes was so strong and intimate, he pulled her closer. He began caressing her body as they kissed each other on the lips. He then sucked her top lip, sucking it just a little into his mouth. The kiss turned into a tongue kiss with their tongues in and out their partially closed mouths. He grabbed her by the back of her head and began kissing her a little roughly. He then turned her around and raised up her dress, she had no panties on like normal. He quickly unzipped and pulled down his pants and boxers. They got up on the bed and he slid his penis inside her from behind. Brandy reached her right hand behind her grabbing to hold on to his waist as he was going in her deeply still from behind. During sex, while he's still on top he began kissing her earlobes with his mouth using the tip of his tongue. After sex Brandy and Terrell went to sleep. The next day she went to work, work was work and nothing was special about it. Once she got off she went to the grocery store to buy a can of olives. She was about to make enchiladas, rice, beans, corn on the cob, and a salad. Getting back home Brandy began to prepare dinner. Terrell was in the room lying down.

Later that night. "Mom, I'm home!" Paige came in and said.

Brandy peeked her head from out the kitchen. "You must have smelled the dinner from wherever you're coming from!"

"Mom, I was just down the way at my friend Catherine's house!"

"Oh, ok!"

"Is dinner ready mom?"

"Almost, but won't you come help do something since you're back."

"Yes, mother, here I come!"

"Mother," Brandy repeated mocking her.

Paige started laughing, then she washed her hands, "Mom, what you need me to do?"

"Well, everything is basically done, get the garlic bread and put three slices in the oven."

Paige went into the freezer, but it was only one slice left. "Mom, it's not enough, it's only one left."

"Damn, I wish I would have known that before going to the grocery store. Well I'm not about to go back, so just get three slices of bread and just put butter on it and throw it in the oven."

"Alright," Paige responded back.

None of these guys knew they were getting played. Lord knows she didn't want to be doing this again, but what she wasn't about to do is struggle with her daughter, rent, and bills. Cheating was something that came naturally back in the days, in her younger days it was nothing.

Terrell wasn't doing much of anything and he had no hustle. Brandy needed money and was not about to tell him how to get it.

The next morning Brandy's cell went off. It was Charlie calling her. "Hey daddy!" she answered.

"Hey Baby, what are you doing?"

"Nothing, just lying down naked in the A/C," she told him.

"You are?"

She chuckled, "No, I'm just kidding."

"Oh, I was going to say," he paused, "So you're not doing anything?"

"No, not right now!"

"What do you have on?"

"Just a shirt," she said softly.

"A shirt," he said.

"Yeah," she said seductively.

"Wow, how about what's under that shirt."

"Oh daddy, I don't have on anything underneath."

"Can you come over? I need your company."

"You don't have to work today?"

"No, not today."

"Okay daddy, I'll be over there shortly, let me slip some pants on."

"Ok sweetie," then they both hung up their line.

Brandy's voice alone excited him; he couldn't wait until she gets there. Shortly after Brandy left to go see Charlie, her cell was already ringing it was Charlie. "Hey, sweetie, did you leave already?"

"Yeah, I did Charlie."

"Oh ok, sweetie I will see you when you get here." Brandy was quiet.

"Okay sweetie," they hung up. Once she finally pulled up in front of his home, she got out to walk to his front door. Approaching his door she rung his doorbell. Charlie opened up his front door for her with a smile, they both hugged upon her walking in, then immediately a conversation started.

"You're looking beautiful sweetie."

"Thank you," she said.

"Would you like something to drink?"

"Oh yes, sure. What kind do you have?" she asked because every week he was always buying new bottles of wine.

"I have Merlot, Chardonnay, and Stella Rosa Platinum."

"I will try the Stella Rosa Platinum. I haven't tried the platinum one before."

"Ok, coming right up."

Charlie grabbed two wine glasses from the cabinet and poured them both some wine. They both took a seat on the couch, sipping their wine as their conversation continued. As the wine got into her system she was becoming very touchy, rubbing on his leg. Minutes later they walked from the living room to the bedroom. He was ready to rub his hands all over her body. It didn't take them long before they were ready to move on to the next point. Brandy was more just about her money. Charlie was a great friend, but she loved their money relationship more. It was business for her and pleasure for him.

"So, how do you want it this morning, I'm here to do whatever it is you want me too."

Rubbing on her was a pleasure to him. He started with her breast; he began to rub all over them. He took off her bra and began sucking on her nipples as he gave them a gentle massage. He sucked them for a long while as he kept massaging. Then he lifted his head to look at her.

"You taste amazing," he said in a low tone.

"Thank you," she told him back. Then he switched to her other breast. He began to suck on her nipples as he gave that one a gentle massage too. Then they had sex. After they were done, it only took seconds, and he was laid out across the bed. Brandy tired him out, he fell straight to sleep. Brandy grabbed her belongings while he lay across the bed sleep, which didn't make her any difference, as long as he remembered to make her deposit today. As she began to walk out the door she just decided to wake his ass up so he wouldn't forget to go the bank today.

"Charlie," she shoved him lightly, he was snoring.

"Charlie!" she said louder with another shove. This time he woke up. He couldn't believe how she just put his ass to sleep.

When he woke up and realized she was getting ready to go, Charlie didn't want her to go. From the vibration of her purse, her phone was ringing. She unzipped her purse and took it out her purse. It was Terrell, he began calling her, but she couldn't answer it right then, so she sent him to voicemail. Brandy made it obvious to Charlie that he wasn't the only one she was seeing, he had no idea of who this other guy was, but it didn't bother him, she spent the time he needed and wanted with him. Not that Charlie needed to know, she just thought it's about that time she let his ass know now, so he could stop asking to come over to her house.

"Charlie, I need to let you know something, please don't get upset with me when I tell you!"

"What is it, sweetie?"

"You are not the only one I'm seeing!"

"Oh baby, whoever he is, don't have anything to do with me."

"So you not mad?"

"Oh no, because whenever I want to see you, you always come over," he said.

Their conversation continued. Charlie got up from the bed and he held his hands wrapped around her back as he looked down at her. "I already put the money in your account."

"Thank you," she said softly. They embraced each other tighter with their hug before she left.

"I did it before you even made it here," Charlie had already deposited what she needed into her account prior to her getting there. Now it didn't matter to her that he went back to sleep, now he can go back to sleep for all she cares since he had already deposited what she needed into her account prior to her getting there anyway. She then left and he closed his front door behind her. Then she heard him open it back up. She looked back.

"Oh, I just want to watch you leave," he told her. She smiled and shook her head, then turned around and kept walking. Brandy walked out to her car, chirping her alarm, and then she opened her car, got in closing the door behind her and started up her Benz.

She pulled the seat belt strap over and across her chest, then snapped it lock, then she pulled out his driveway. She looked over at him, he was waving bye; pulling back out his driveway she was waving back bye to him.

If it wasn't for Charlie spoiling her she wouldn't be still dealing with him, he would have never gotten a taste or a feel of her body that he can't seem to keep his eyes and hands off of.

Going home she always had to make up some type of lie of where she'd been to Terrell. Bills needed to be paid and he sure as hell didn't have anything on it. She chilled the rest of the day with him.

The next morning Charlie sent her a text, he wanted to take her out to breakfast. Once Terrell left the house she went and showered. She was now ready for breakfast. She picked up her cell phone and keys off the dresser and left. Brandy drove to Charlie's house. She dialed his phone. After a few rings, he answered, "Hey sweetie!" he answers.

"Hey, I'm outside are you ready?"

"Almost, come inside for a minute!"

"Okay," Brandy got out her car and went inside. He was ready in five minutes. He walked in front of her to lead the way, to be a gentleman he opened the front door. The two left his house in his car. Brandy's cell rung, it was Katrina.

"Hey sis," she answered.

"What you doing?"

"Nothing," she responded.

"I was going to tell you to come over and keep me and your nephew company."

"Awww, what's my nephew doing?"

"Nothing, over here looking at me talking to you," Katrina told Brandy.

"Alright, give me a few hours!"

"Okay," Katrina sounded, then they hung up. Brandy doesn't acknowledge when she's with him or that he's been the one taking care of her. She was tired of everyone being in her business judging her. After breakfast, she went to her sister's house and spent time with her and her nephew. Afterward, she drove back home.

It had been a few days since she last checked the mail and that was the first thing she did when she got out the car. Brandy got the mail out the mail box and it was Paige's progress report. Paige's grades had dropped tremendously. She went from all As to all Ds and Fs. Brandy was pissed at her, she went straight to Paige's room. Brandy barged into Paige's room. Paige was lying on her bed on her cell phone looking at her Facebook.

"What the hell Paige!!" Brandy yelled at her holding up her progress report.

"Well, I had missing assignments, but I already turned them in. But by the time I turned them in the grades were already in, but my report card grades will be different!"

"They better be Paige!" Brandy walked out her room.

Vincent was back in town, and after handling his business, he met up with Brandy again. When she saw him all she saw was his white teeth. He couldn't stop smiling once he saw her. His eyes were checking out her body.

"How you been?"

"I've been good."

"Just good?" he smiled.

"Well, I been great," she smiles.

He smiled, "Now that's more like it."

"How you been?" she asked him.

"Just been driving on the road, that's all mainly. You want me to pour you a drink?"

"Yeah, that's fine," she was hoping he had some drink there. He poured their drink into a plastic clear cup. He passed her, her cup. They began drinking and from that moment on they continued talking. They had a lot to talk about. They talked for a long time. He even showed her pictures of him driving in the snow. Then their conversation continued, there was no pause button on their conversation until Vincent's cell began to ring. He didn't want to interrupt their conversation, so he quickly dismissed the call, but then his cell rung right back. It was his wife again he looked at Brandy.

"Let me step outside for a minute, I have to take this call."

"Okay," she replied. He stepped out the front door of the hotel. He didn't think she could hear him, but she was able to hear him. She couldn't believe what she was hearing. The conversation with his wife was starting to annoy him so he got off the phone. After his call, he stepped back inside.

"Why did you go outside, you know I heard everything you said!"

"You did?"

"Yeah, I did!"

"Brandy, I'm so sorry!"

"Who was that?" she asked she wanted to see if he was about to lie after she just said she heard everything.

"Brandy, that was my wife," has voice stopped and quickly looked up at her.

"Your wife," she sounded as her arms crossed her chest, she shook her head.

"Yeah," he sounded.

"Why you never told me you were married?" She didn't care, but she wondered why he never told her. She knew he had to have somebody, she knew how this trucking driving shit works. They always had a woman in every state. Somebody different to lay up with in the bed when they touch down to whatever state they're in.

"You know what, I don't know why I ain't never told you, I guess I didn't think it was important!"

"Wow, you didn't think that was important, wow okay, so Vincent why are you cheating on your wife with me?"

"Well, she doesn't do anything, I haven't had any sexual pleasure in like three months going on four months now!"

"Why?" she asked him.

"She says she doesn't want to!"

"Why?" Brandy asked him again.

"She says because of her hormones and that she doesn't feel the urge to want to, so she doesn't."

"Well, that's not fair to you."

"Shit, that's what I said."

"Well Vincent, I'm sorry for what you're going through, but yeah, your wife know she's wrong, she has to please some type of way, that's crazy!"

"Yeah, and I just want some affection, that's all."

"How long has she not been giving you some affection?"

"Since the beginning," Vincent said.

"If you've been so unhappy, and she not giving you what you need, then why do you stay married to her?"

"You're right, I don't know, because I'm close to telling her if she's not going to give me what I want and need then give me a divorce!"

Suddenly he and Brandy became extra cuddly with each other. The drink had them feeling good. He began to brush his hands over her breast. Making her nipple hard, every time he brushed over it, it was getting harder. She went and sat on the bed and laid back. He climbed on top of her and started kissing her. Then he took both their clothes off and they started having sex. After they were done she just wanted to sleep.

"You not leaving Brandy, are you?"

"No, I'm going to stay." She figured she'll tell Terrell she fell asleep at Jordan's house. She didn't want to prior to coming earlier, but right now she felt different and didn't feel like driving. They went to sleep.

The next morning she left the hotel early. She wanted to get home to make sure Paige went to school on time. After dropping her off early her cell rings. "Hey boo," is how Brandy answered.

"Hey boo, how was your night last night? You know I want to know all the details too? Because I was calling you and it went straight to voicemail, I was like yeah she with somebody."

Brandy started telling Jordan all the details about last night. Jordan was sitting on the other end of that phone feeling like she was watching a reality TV show, but listening to it. She loves hearing her juicy stories.

Brandy paused, "You heard me?"

"Girl, I hear you, this is getting juicy, you can write a book," Jordan says.

"Your ass is crazy," Brandy chuckled.

"So girl, his phone rings and he's like I have to take this call, I'm like oh, no problem, but then he quickly answered it going outside on the porch. I was trying to figure out why in the hell did he go outside, but he didn't realize that both of the front windows were wide open, so I could hear him talking."

"Ooh, what was he saying?"

"Girl, he was saying baby this and baby that and I love you."

"I thought the call was maybe his boss or something calling is why he went outside, but hell no, it was another woman."

"Shut up, wow!"

"At this point, I couldn't wait for him to come back inside so I could question his ass."

"So then what happened?"

"So when he came back inside I questioned him about it."

"Girl, then his ass said that was his wife calling!"

"His wife," Jordan sounded surprised.

"Yes, girl his wife!"

"What!"

"Exactly, my same thought," she said.

"You knew he was married?"

"I knew nothing about any other woman; I mean, I'm not stupid, I knew he had somebody," she says.

"So then what you say?"

"*Why are you cheating on your wife with me, what she's not enough?*"

He was like, *well she doesn't do anything, and I haven't had any sexual pleasure in like three months going on four months now.*"

"Why?" Jordan asked.

Brandy laughed, "Girl you know we think alike because I asked his ass the same shit!"

"He was like; *she doesn't feel the urge to want to because of her hormones so she doesn't.*"

"Oh no, his wife know she got to give her husband some. That's why he dipping and dabbing in yours. See girl, write a book, I'll be your number one supporter!"

Brandy laughed, "Girl, I can't with you this morning," she laughs again.

188

CHAPTER

7

Brandy went back to her Ex

Terrell came over. He rang the doorbell. Brandy answered. After walking in he came and hung up his jacket in the closet, closed the door, and headed straight for the couch, took off his work boots, and began telling her about his new job he'd just started today as he was massaging his feet. Brandy just sat there and watched him.

"So first day of work must have kicked your butt today, you coming over taking off your boots, and then you start massaging your own feet."

He talked and she listened to him talk about his day. She was happy for him finally finding him a job.

"So Brandy, how would you feel or where would it put your mind if I told you I love you, you are the only woman I want to ever love even through all the shit you have done to me, and that I want us to stop playing, make us official again, and let me come back for good. I thought I could stop during that long time we weren't together, but it was hard. I couldn't stop loving you, sometimes I think maybe because I haven't talked to anyone other than you, I just don't want to."

Brandy sat there wondering how he goes to that from a conversation he's having with her about his first day at work and his feet. She sat there looking puzzled.

"Like how do you really feel about me, about us, like what do you want us to do?"

Brandy began to open her mouth to respond, but just as she was about too, he says *wait!*

"Even though I've been back and we're taking things slow, I don't feel like we're really working towards us getting back stronger how we use to be, and we need that right now. I want to wake up to you every morning I want to go to sleep with you every night. No more of, I'll call you tomorrow or tonight. No, I want to be already here and not having to go."

As Brandy listens to him *I love you too, I want us back how we were,* is what crossed her mind.

"You're right, we should, I agree."

"Let's try those different toys tonight."

"What!"

"Those toys you bought."

"Nah, let's do without the toys," she says.

"Okay."

Brandy left the living room and ran him some hot bath water. She was about to give him what he needed tonight, all of her and her full attention. She turned off her cell and tossed it inside her purse. While he went to take a bath in the water she just made for him she went to the kitchen to make them some dinner because a man coming home from work dinner should be ready. Brandy wanted to do this right if she is about to do this with him and that's the plan. Brandy is in the kitchen cooking steak, broccoli, mash potatoes, and corn bread. Terrell returns back to the room before she did, she was still in their cooking dinner. An hour later she returns to the room and when she walked in Terrell's hand was underneath the covers and the cover was moving up and down. Brandy done came in and caught Terrell fondling himself. She put her balled fist on her hip as she stopped in her footsteps and parted her legs apart and shook her head.

"You couldn't wait for me," she smiles.

"What baby?"

"I see where your hand is, and I see the covers moving up and down!"

"My leg was itching?" he smiled.

"I'll be done shortly in the kitchen."

Brandy went back to the kitchen to finish up in the kitchen. After the food was done, she prepared three plates. She sat Paige's plate in the microwave for when she gets home and then she took her plate and Terrell's plate in the room. They sat there watching TV and eating their dinner. What they were watching had them so deep in it, it was good. Once the movie was over he was ready to eat her. He grabbed at it. Then he leaned back and looked deeply into her eyes. "You want me to lick?" he asked her as his eyes glanced down there. He smiled.

"You know I want you to lick," she said softly.

"Tell me how you want me to lick."

"What kind of question is that?" she asked as she looked at him funny.

"Yeah, tell me how you want me to lick it, you know I like when you be detailed about shit, you know that shit turns me on."

"I want you to lay me down slowly and spread my legs wide open as your head go down in between my legs feeling the wetness of your tongue lick all around it over and over and over and over again, as it slowly goes inside me gently and slowly as deep as it can go," she said seductively.

"Damn baby, you want it that deep?"

"Yes, I sure do, and then I just want you to lick it, suck it, and eat it until you get tired!"

"Damn, like that!"

"Yep, you asked!"

"I sure did huh," he smiled.

"Lean back."

Brandy slowly leaned back right beside him. He pulled down and took off her shorts. He looked into her eyes as he spread her legs wide open. He put his head down in-between her and he began licking her center just the way she wanted, wet and deep. After twenty minutes of licking and sucking her pussy, she was still silent leaning back, no moans no sounds. He looked up at her, when she looked up she was looking down at him watching him suck on her pussy.

"Why you looking at me?" she asked with a smile.

"Because you haven't said anything, I wanted to know how it feels to you."

"It feels good Terrell."

He then put his face back down and went back to sucking her pussy. She was so sweet he couldn't get enough.

Terrell was sucking on her pussy for so long she got tired first, but she didn't say anything. After he was done she wanted sex, she had enough of the four play already. Brandy climbed on top of him, then she sat up on him and began bouncing on it up and down, he held her with his eyes closed. The more she heard his moans the more she kept bouncing. After a while, Terrell flipped her around so he could be on top. Every time he went deep in it, she moaned. When he came up he moved in a full circle up in her. She felt his dick drowning in it and she loved it.

He put it on her good, but so did she, they had put it on each other. Terrell was hot, he got up and went and sat by the fan. They were exhausted then they went to sleep. When she woke up she just wanted to make love to

192

him again. She woke him up, she wanted sex. They had sex then they cuddled back up and went back to sleep.

She was happy for things to be back serious now with her and Terrell once again, but dealing with Charlie on the side, and Vincent, when he's in town all of that now, has to come to an end. Waking up for the second time that morning it was now six thirty in the morning. Brandy glanced at the clock on the dresser and wow, it was almost time for Paige to go to school. Paige's ass needed to get up, she didn't want her to be late to her first period class. Brandy got up and woke her up.

"Paige, get up, it's time for school!"

"Alright, I'm going to get up in a few minutes!"

"No baby, you have to get up now!" Brandy was not leaving out her room until she got herself up and out that bed. Moments later Paige turned over slowly with one eye open.

"Mom, I'm about to get up now."

"Okay, get yourself up then!"

"Alright!" then that's when Paige got up." Paige got ready, then she left."

Brandy is now left to think how and when she's going to tell Charlie and Vincent she can't deal with them *anymore.* She sent them both a text, the same text that is. Vincent said alright he understood, but Charlie on the other hand obviously thinks she is joking and not taking her seriously. Brandy didn't know how to end this arrangement they had going on, the extra help she's receiving from Charlie will soon be missed and she doesn't want to let that go at all. Damn, but she has too, and right now. Since Terrell is working now she should be good.

Charlie called her. "So you just recently told me about another man and now today you're trying to leave me for him. Come on, no way!"

"Charlie, we can still stay in contact."

"Does he take care of you like I do?"

After him saying that Brandy didn't even want to talk no more. "Bye Charlie," she hung up the phone.

The next morning her cell phone rung, but she was asleep and her phone kept ringing so Terrell answered it.

"Hello!"

"Hello, can I speak to Brandy."

"Brandy, who in the FUCK is this guy on the phone!" Terrell yelled out.

"I think I may have the wrong number," Charlie said.

"Naw, you asked for Brandy, who is this?"

"This is Charlie."

He pushed her side until she woke up."

"Babe, what?" she asked.

"Who is Charlie?"

"What!" she thought she was hearing things, she began thinking he was talking in her dreams until he asked the question again.

"Here!" he passed her, her phone.

Brandy looked at him, then she looked at her phone, then she looked back at him.

"Here!" he said louder.

Brandy hesitated in taking it from him.

"I don't want to talk."

"He called for you; he wants to talk to you," Brandy took the phone from out his hand and hung up her phone.

Terrell wanted to know who he was. After Terrell found out what had been going on with Charlie. All hell broke loose.

"Brandy, what the FUCK is up with you, you think that shit was okay! How would you feel if I go off and do the same shit back to you just to have some extra money in my pockets and just to be able to get the extra shit you can't help provide!"

"You did."

"Oh, so what is this your way of paying me back?" he stood there mad as hell at her, then he headed for the front door.

"Honestly, it wasn't even a real relationship, we actually had a deal that he knew about for him to make deposits to my account and I pleasure him when he wants some."

Terrell got mad, turned around, and walked off.

"Don't walk off, I'm trying to explain!" she yelled.

She followed behind him. They both ended up on the porch yelling and arguing at each other.

"*I just can't sleep around this motherfucker!*" was the sound of a yelling voice coming from their next door neighbor.

Brandy looked back, then she looked back at Terrell, then they just continued going back and forth.

"*How much longer are you going to be out here yelling?*"

"*If you have problems, go back to your fucking house and close your windows!*"

"*I'm tired of bitches!*"

"*Girl, you better go in that house and close your door.*"

"*Bitch, you can't tell me to go in the house.*"

"*Bitch, you can't tell me to stop yelling!*"

Brandy's neighbor got mad and slammed her door closed. Then once Brandy was done yelling at Terrell, she went inside and slammed her door too.

Brandy and Terrell continued their talk as their voices calmed all the way down. "I'm sorry, I should have said something. I should have stopped it when we started back talking."

"Yeah, but instead you kept entertaining his ass to get money!"

"Well, I said I'm sorry, I shouldn't have been entertaining him at all."

"How am I supposed to know you won't still fuck with him again, or do this shit with someone else again."

"Because I'm telling you, that's why!" she told him.

"Brandy, I don't believe the shit you have to say to me right now."

"Well, I don't know what else you want me to say."

"So this just means you lied to me about so much shit, this whole time you've been fucking with the both of us!"

"Come on now, this is not a tit for tat, but you did me the same way with your ex and I forgave you."

He looked at her locking his jaws tight, he was pissed at her. Then he left.

"Where you going!" she yelled out.

"I will be back."

Although Brandy didn't want to break his little old heart, she had no choice; this all must come to an end now. While Terrell was gone Brandy called Charlie; she held the phone up to her ear.

"Hey beautiful," he answered. "Sorry about that, was that your daughter's father tripping on me for calling your phone yesterday?" he asked. Brandy didn't even answer his question.

"Hey Charlie," she sighed.

"What are you doing, you about to come over and see me?"

"No Charlie, not anymore."

"Why?"

"I'm sorry, we just can't talk anymore, my ex and I are back together, that was actually him who answered my phone when you called yesterday!"

"What, when did this happen, yesterday?"

"Months ago!" she said.

"What do you mean months ago?"

"Yeah, I kind of mentioned that to you, I just didn't tell you any names."

"How are you going to end our relationship and what we had going on?"

"Actually Charlie, it wasn't a relationship, it was a deal, a deal you knew about. You make deposits in to my account and I pleasure you when you want it, that was the deal. It's just that you started thinking it was more than what it actually was!"

"Damn Brandy!"

"I'm sorry Charlie."

"Well, I'm not going to stop seeing you because he wants you, shit I want and need you to Brandy!"

"Charlie stop it, and stop calling my phone because you don't know what type of man you're dealing with, his ass is crazy, he might try and hurt you if you don't stop!"

"Hurt me, what you mean he might try and hurt me, if he comes near me I'm calling the police on him."

"The police," she responded.

"Yeah, I will, so he better stay away."

Once Terrell came back after he cooled off Brandy told Terrell just what Charlie was saying. "Tell his old ass to stop calling your phone, before I kill his ass!"

Brandy dialed Charlie. "Hey sweetie!" he answers.

"Charlie, my boyfriend said you need to stop calling my phone before he has to kill your ass!" she wanted to warn him. Terrell was serious. Brandy made sure she told Charlie what Terrell had said so he would know just how serious he is.

"Brandy, I'm not cool with his threats and shit, but baby I want to see you." Brandy hung up on him.

One thing for sure Brandy knew Terrell would himself or at least have someone do something to hurt him bad. Charlie didn't get the picture either did he listen to Brandy when she told him she can't see him anymore because he kept calling her phone as if she didn't tell him anything. After the third day in a row, she finally answered him. "Charlie, what do you want? I told you I can't see you anymore," is how she answered his call.

"Brandy sweetie, don't do this to me, I want to see you right now!"

"Charlie, please stop calling my phone, I don't want to see you get hurt!"

"Oh, oh so what, you care about him?"

"Bye Charlie, I have to go, just don't call my phone anymore," then she hung up with him without giving him a chance to say bye back.

Two days later Terrell tires were flattened. Seeing his tires, all four for that matter, he knew it was somebody he knew. He wondered who in the hell would be that bold to come to their apartment building and straight flatten all four of his tires. He was really pissed. Brandy helped him call around to some tire shops trying to find the size he needed to fit his car. After calling around, about the seventh shop had his tires. She drove him there to pick them up.

Later in the day Brandy received a text saying I hope you have four new tires handy.

"Oh my God, Charlie did this," she said to herself as she read the text message. Then she thought to herself, wait a minute, how does he even know where I stay, I never told him and he never came over, I always went to him. Brandy then dialed his number.

198

"Charlie, you did that?"

"What, you think I was going to be okay with you ending our relationship like that for him, and then you let him make threats to hurt me."

"I'm sorry, but you should have just accepted the breakup, even though it wasn't a relationship it was a deal. You come to where I live, and how in the hell you know where I live in the first place, you've been following me?"

"It doesn't matter anymore!"

"It does matter!" she yelled.

Terrell walked in from outside from jacking up his car.

"Brandy, who is that you yelling at, don't tell me it's that motherfucker again!"

She nodded her head saying yes.

"He the one that done that to your car!" she lipped talked to him.

Terrell began shouting talking madness to Charlie. "Tell him when I see him I'm going to kill his ass!" Terrell was shouting out.

"Charlie you shouldn't have come over here and you shouldn't have flattened my dude tires!"

Charlie could hear everything Terrell was saying in the background.

"Brandy, you need to tell him he better stop threatening me!"

"Charlie, why did you even come up over here and do what you did!"

"No, he doesn't understand, it was me and you Brandy, how you think I was supposed to take this?"

"Not the way you did Charlie."

Brandy couldn't believe he thought his response was about to be excusable for what he had done, no matter what he's feeling still gave him no right to do what he had done to Terrell's car. That wasn't about to justify his actions.

"I'm going to fuck you up!" Terrell kept yelling loudly.

"Put him on the phone, why he yelling all that in the background!" Charlie says as he asked to speak to Terrell.

"I don't think you want that!" she told Charlie.

"What?" Terrell asked her.

"He told me to put you on the phone!"

"Give it here," he said.

Brandy just held the phone looking at him.

"Give me the phone Brandy, let me talk to that motherfucker!"

Brandy hesitated as she stared into his eyes, then she passed him the phone with a sigh. Brandy couldn't hear what Charlie was saying on the other end of that phone, but from the replies from Terrell she figured it out. Brandy sat there and listened to them both go back and forth, not once did she think to stop the arguing. Terrell was standing there yelling at Charlie's old ass over the phone about him sleeping with her. Then after a while, they hung up. Terrell went to the room and in seconds he comes back out with his jacket on and with Brandy's keys in his hand. "Come on!" he said angrily.

"Where we going?" she says with a worried look on her face.

"We are going to Charlie's House!"

She sat there shaking her head from side to side, she didn't want to go.

"You're coming to so let's go!" he yells.

Brandy slowly rose up from off the couch grabbing her jacket and putting on her shoes. They walked down the steps to the car, got in, and Brandy took off. Terrell couldn't believe all this shit was happening all because of her ass. Terrell was so angry he was really mad at this Charlie situation, but even madder at Brandy, he couldn't even say anything to her their whole ride there. Brandy was just the driver, she didn't say one word to him, and she was not trying to make him madder than what he already was. They pulled up in front of Charlie's house. Terrell pointed, "Is that his car in the drive way?"

"Yeah," she responded.

Terrell got out the car quietly and he ran up to the car and quickly stabbed all four tires with his pocket knife. After he stabbed the last tire he picked up one of Charlie's Brick that was in his yard and busted his side window. After he did that he ran to the car, hopped in and Brandy took off.

Charlie heard the sound of glass shattering, he went outside to see what had happened and walking outside he didn't hear any commotion or see anyone outside. He didn't know where the shattered noise actually came from, so he went back inside. The next morning leaving out for work is when Charlie noticed all the glass on the ground on his driver side. Looking up seeing his window busted, his eyes then scanned his car and that's when he noticed all his tires were on flat. Charlie called the police, then he called his job to let them know he would be late and told them he had car troubles. It took the police a long time to arrive at his home. Getting there they knocked on his door so they could question him and do a report.

"So sir, do you know who did this to your vehicle?" the officer asked him.

"No, but I have an idea of who it could be officer."

"Who do you think may have done this sir?"

"A guy by the name of Terrell."

"Terrell what, do you have the last name?"

"No officer, I don't have the last name for him."

"Why do you think it's him?"

"Well officer, I was just recently dating a woman who he is dating right now, and he became upset when he found out about me."

"Well sir, the most we can do is investigate the situation."

Charlie gave the officer both their names and their address. The officers then drove over to Brandy's Apartment to speak with her and Terrell. Arriving at her apartment the officer got out his car, walked up to Brandy's door, then he knocked.

"Who is it!" was how Brandy answered.

"Detective Armstrong," the detective said.

Terrell looked at her. "What the fuck, why is there a detective at the door?"

"I don't know," she whispered. Brandy walked to the door nervously, and then she opened the front door.

"Good morning detective, how can I help you?"

"Is there a Terrell here as well?"

"I'm right here, what's going on detective?" Terrell sounded from the couch.

"Well I'm sorry to bother the two of you this morning, but I'm doing an investigation. It was reported that you too may have something to do with the flatten tires and busted out car window that belongs to Charlie Henderson yesterday evening at about ten o'clock pm."

"No detective," Brandy responded first then Terrell replied the same.

As Detective Armstrong was listening to Terrell he also quickly used his peripheral vision to look back at Brandy to see if either of their expressions were going to alert that they could have been lying, but no, there was no different expression that showed anything. Since they both denied the incident, he couldn't do anything without any witnesses actually seeing them doing it.

A few weeks went by and the two still were having many arguments about Charlie. Brandy was tired of the silent treatment from all the back and forth arguing, she wanted to think of something they could do or something she could do for them to make things better and right. Brandy was happier he didn't leave her behind this.

The next day Brandy thought of making him a nice healthy breakfast. Lying on the side of him she looked over at him. "Baby, you want Pancakes or French Toast?"

"French Toast," he said.

"Scrambled eggs or Boiled eggs?"

"Scrambled, he responded again."

"Bacon or Sausage?" she asked.

"Damn babe, can you just go in there and cook the breakfast without asking me what I want!"

"Well damn, I'm just asking so I can cook you just what you want or do you just want some cereal then?"

"Babe, I'm just saying I'm tired, it's too earlier for all these questions plus I'm still pissed at you Brandy!"

"I'm just saying too and I don't know how many times I have to say sorry!"

"You know what Brandy, please stop talking to me right now," he told her. They both appeared to be upset.

"Look Terrell, I'm so sorry once again, that will never happen again. I do love you."

"I love you too."

Brandy went to the kitchen and made the two of them some breakfast. She also made him some hash brown and grits with cheese inside too. After eating breakfast Terrell looked at Brandy. "Brandy, I do not plan to be mad all day, so please don't say nothing to piss me off."

"I don't want to be mad nor argue either. I just want to have a chill day today." The two depended on each other to have a non-arguing day. They stayed on the couch all day, they didn't move from that couch. They kept finding good movies such as funny comedies to watch on TV. Brandy began to realize her daughter had been gone since this morning and hadn't come back home to check in nor had she called all day.

Brandy called her sister.

"Hello," Katrina answers.

"Hey Katrina, is Paige over there?"

"No."

"Oh, okay."

"Is everything okay?"

"Well, I've been calling her cell and it's been going straight to voicemail. It's getting late and her ass still not home yet!"

"Oh wow, no I haven't heard from Paige in a few days."

"Let me go ask Simone has she talked to her tonight."

"Okay."

Katrina got up from out her bed to go ask Simone had she heard from her sister tonight. Simone was lying in her bed asleep. Katrina shoved her, waking her up.

"Hey mom," she said.

"Hey, baby did you talk to your sister tonight?"

"I talked to her earlier, not tonight just earlier."

"Oh, so you wouldn't know where she would be at right now?"

"No."

Katrina placed the phone back to her ear, "Brandy, Simone said she has not talked to Paige tonight, she just talked to her earlier."

"Alright, thanks, K I'm going to call you back."

Brandy sat in thought; she was feeling a headache coming. She is pissed off that Paige is out this late. She didn't have any of her friends' numbers that she could have called. She continued thinking if she should go and hop in her car and about where would she look.

Now Simone couldn't go back to sleep after being waken up behind her sister, she wondered if her sister was okay. The question about her sister made her wake up all the way. She sat up and got out her bed following her mother to her room.

"Mom, is Paige okay?"

Katrina turned around to look at Simone.

"I hope so baby, Brandy hasn't heard from her and her phone is going straight to voicemail." Simone walked out of her mother's room back to her room, grabbed her cell from her night stand, and sat down on her bed. Simone dialed her sister's cell and it went straight to her voicemail on her too. Simone then dialed their dad's number. Gary's cell phone started ringing. Gary was in the bathroom on the toilet. He heard it.

"Baby, can you please see who that is for me!" he yelled out to Asia. Asia looked at the screen of his cellphone and it was Simone.

"Babe, it's Simone, I hope everything's okay for her to be calling so late!" she said quickly right as she was about to answer it. "Hello, Simone," Asia answers.

"Hey Asia," Simone spoke.

"Hey, baby girl."

"Is my dad there?"

"Yeah, is everything okay?"

"Can't nobody get a hold of Paige, my Auntie, been trying to get a hold of her, I tried and it's just going straight to voicemail."

"Oh wow, that's not good, it's late."

"I know and we're worried, plus she's never done this before."

"Let me take the phone to your dad, he's in the bathroom."

"Okay, thank you."

Asia walked the phone to the bathroom and gave the phone to Gary. "Hello."

"Daddy, can't nobody get a hold of Paige."

"Damn," he paused, "You already tried calling her cell?"

"Yeah, but it's going to voicemail."

"Alright, I'm about to see what's going on."

"Ok daddy."

Simone and Gary got off the phone and Gary dialed Paige's cell, he got her voicemail too, so he dialed Brandy's cell.

Brandy quickly answered her phone, she didn't even look at the number to see who was calling her phone right now. She was hoping it was Paige. "Hello," she answered.

"Hey Brandy, you still haven't heard from her yet?"

"No, not yet."

"I'm on my way over there."

"Alright," Brandy said to him.

They hung up. "Babe, I will be back, I'm about to see if I can find Paige."

He walked up to her and kissed her then Gary left. He drove over to Brandy's neighborhood. Gary began driving around with both his hands on the steering wheel looking down every street seeing if he saw his daughter. Gary had turned corner after corner trying to find her. Gary prays that his daughter is okay, but when he sees her he can't wait to have a talk with her, because this shit right here is not cool at all.

Paige made it home, walked in like shit was okay. "Paige, do you know what time it is? Where have you been, and why in the hell you didn't call me to let me know something?"

Paige's eyes narrowed the carpet, she knew her mom too well, anything she says right now, no matter what it is, is going to make her yell louder. "Paige, you better look at me while I'm talking to you, so where have you been?"

"I was out with my friends."

"This late?" Brandy asked her.

"Yeah, we went out to our other friend's party."

"You went to a party without asking me if it's okay."

"Well, I'm sixteen, I didn't think I had to ask."

"I don't care if you're sixteen you still have to ask!"

Paige blew out a light breath and tilted her head down looking at the floor.

Brandy stood up and put one of her hands on her hip, "Look at me while I'm talking to you Paige!"

Paige's eyes were back at her mother.

"Okay, you're on punishment so go to your room!"

Paige stormed out the living room to her bedroom and quickly shut her door.

"Don't slam my door!" Brandy yelled out.

Brandy quickly went to Paige's room, twisted her door knob, and pushed it opened. She took away her cell phone for slamming her door the way she just did since that was the one thing she mostly cared about. Brandy's cell rung, it was her mother.

"Yes, mom."

"Have you heard from Paige yet?"

"Yeah, her ass just walked in the door not long ago."

"Thank you, Jesus. Brandy, did she say where she had been?"

"She's talking about she was out with friends."

"This late?" her mother said.

"That's what I told her, so I put her on punishment and sent her to her room. Her ass got the nerves to storm to her room stomping her feet and then slammed her door, so I went in there took her phone and went off on her."

"Oh, I know Paige didn't slam her door."

"Yes she did, I don't know if it's these new kids she's hanging with or what."

"I don't know, but she knows better, I'm going to stop by there tomorrow afternoon and have a talk with her."

"Alright," Brandy said.

"Alright, baby well you get you some sleep alright."

"Alright mom I will, but I have to call Gary real quick because he's out there driving around looking for her, but I love you and you too."

"Alright, baby love you too."

Brandy and her mother got off the phone. She dialed Gary. Gary's cell started going off. He looked down, it was Brandy. "Hey Brandy, you talk to her?"

"Yeah, her ass just walked in right now."

"I will be there in a second."

"Alright," she said.

Gary was now headed to her house. He was glad she was home, but he needed to talk to her so this shit doesn't happen again. Gary got there and knocked on her door.

"It's open!" Brandy yells out. Gary walked inside and Brandy was there sitting on the couch.

"Hey," she said so dryly.

"What's wrong, where is Paige!!"

"She is in her room. Yes, please talk to your daughter because I put her on punishment for coming in late. She had the nerves to get an attitude, storm to her room and slam her door." Gary shook his head, this wasn't like her and he doesn't want behavior like this to start.

"Paige!!" he called her name loudly.

"Yeah," she responded back from her room.

"Come here!!"

Paige came to the voice of her father.

"So Paige, what's going on baby? You know what you pulled tonight, going to some party without asking your mom, and making sure she was okay with you going is not cool at all. There are so many sick people out in those streets and you had us all worried that you were not safe."

"I was fine dad."

"But that's not the point Paige, you had me driving around the neighborhood looking for you too, your sister called me worried, so I was out there trying to find you."

"I'm sorry, I didn't mean to make you all worry. I really didn't think mom was coming home, she is always gone, being with that person and this person for money and getting gifts and cars from these men. I'm always home by myself anyway so I figured what I did didn't matter anyway, isn't this how we got this apartment because of you anyway? She took you from my Aunt Katrina."

"What the fuck and where in the hell you get that information from? I'm grown and you need to watch your mouth little girl!!" Paige looked at her mother and then back at her dad, "But dad, next time I will ask mom if I can go to a party." Paige knows she just made her punishment worse, but she was just telling the truth.

Brandy looked at Gary, she couldn't believe what their daughter just said to them. "Gary, you hear this shit, this is your fault," she looked at Paige. "And Paige, I didn't take him from your Auntie, he came on to me, so if you're going to say something make sure you say it right!!"

"Paige, what you just said was not respectful, honey you know better than to talk like that, you never talked like this before and you're not going to start. You have to treat your mother with some respect, no matter what, and come in at a decent time and let your mother know where you are going period!!"

"Yes, daddy."

"Paige, we just want to know where you are so if something was to ever happen at least we will know where to find you!"

"Alright daddy," Paige said.

"Now come here and give me a hug," Paige walked up to her dad and gave him a kiss and a hug. "Alright, good night you guys," Gary left and went back home.

He made it back, "Hey babe how'd the talk go with Paige?" Asia asked.

"Things went alright."

"I'm glad she is okay and made it back safe."

"Yeah, but her mother needs to watch what she does around her."

"Oh, she does things around her?"

"I don't know so much about right now since she's back in a relationship with her ex, but I know before her ass was with this dude and that dude."

"Yeah, because the kids see all that shit, like where you think they're getting their behavior from, kids will mimic what they see."

"Yeah, you could tell just by what she was saying and as a kid, she saw her mother."

"It's like even when she didn't think she knew or was watching she was," Asia shook her head.

"Yep, she sure was," Gary replied as he told Asia what his daughter was saying.

"Oh wow, I just can't believe it. It's so hard to believe she actually said all that shit."

"Yeah, she did."

"Wow!"

"What did Brandy say?"

"Is not about what she said her face was like she wanted to hurt her. But then she started putting me in it involving me saying it was my fault because I came on to her. One conversation lead to another conversation then that one was leading to another, it was crazy."

"Damn."

"Yeah, after that I just left. I didn't want to hear anymore of that."

"I hear you on that."

"Yeah, everybody arguing, we are not going to get nowhere like that."

"For real, we'll you did the right thing," Asia told him.

"Thanks, babe."

"Now let's get some sleep." They kissed and cuddled underneath the cover and went to sleep.

The next day Deborah went to Brandy's to have a talk with her granddaughter Paige. When Deborah got there she could hear Brandy yelling at Paige. She knocked on her door. Brandy went to let her in. Brandy and her mother chatted first before she went to Paige's room. Brandy was hoping that her mother could talk some sense into Paige's head.

Deborah went into the room with her granddaughter. "Baby, it's not safe hanging out late, do you want to get hurt out there in those streets?"

"No grandma."

"Okay well, you need to listen to your mom."

"Yes ma'am," Paige sounded.

Later in the week, Jordan called Brandy. "Hey lady!" she answered.

"Hey boo, you want to go out this weekend?"

"Yeah, where to our spot?" Brandy asked.

"Hell yeah," she responded back.

Jordan picked Brandy up. "Hey girl," Jordan said as Brandy was getting in her car.

"Hey!"

"You ok," she laughed.

"Girl."

"So what, is there still more drama going on with Charlie?"

"That's over now, but it seems like it's not because Terrell keeps on bringing it up and when he does he keeps arguing about it. I apologized over and over, but he isn't trying to hear any apology. One day he's cool, then the next day or two he's back on that same shit. Then my daughter has been working my last nerve lately."

That Saturday night they arrived at the Savoy fifteen minutes to eleven, it was already very packed in the parking lot. Jordan barely found a park space in the parking lot. She cut off the engine and they both pulled down the visor checking their makeup and hair. Once they were ready they both got out the car.

After getting inside Jordan saw the guy who was trying to talk to her two weeks ago when they were last there. She stared at him, but she noticed how he must not have remembered her because he didn't even bother to walk her way.

Brandy leaned over to Jordan and whispered to her.

"Girl, isn't that homeboy that tried to holler at you a few weeks ago?"

"Girl yes," Brandy said.

"Who is the girl he's dancing all close up on?"

"Must be his woman," Brandy said as she looked at them from across the club.

He was slowly dancing closely on this Hispanic woman.

"Come with me to the car, I need a cigarette, I left my pack inside your car."

Brandy and Jordan walked outside to the car.

"Girl, since when did you start smoking cigarettes?" "I told you, the people in my household got me stressing and shit."

"Dang Brandy, girl don't have them stressing you out and shit!"

" I know right, that's why when you was like do you want to go out, I said hell yeah, I needed to get out the damn house for a few hours."

"Yeah, for real," Brandy said.

Jordan's phone was in the palm of her hand, she scrolled the numbers until it stopped at Reggie's name. "Hold up Brandy, let me make a call real quick."

"Ok, for sure." Brandy stood there just smoking on her cigarette. Jordan stepped away from her homegirl to dial Reggie. Jordan dialed Reggie. He answered after the second ring.

"Hello," he answered.

"Hey, baby what are you doing?"

"I was asleep."

"Oh yeah, you were?"

"Yeah," he sounded.

"Oh, I was wondering if you wanted any company?"

"Jordan, you want to come over?"

"Yes."

"Ok, come on."

"Ok, I will call you when I'm close."

"Ok."

The two hung up the phone. Then Jordan and Brandy walked back inside the club. They both walked back in dancing to the song that was playing as they entered.

An hour later leaving the club she dropped Brandy off, then she drove to see Reggie. When she made it there she called him to tell him to come open up the gate. He came down seconds later to let her in, they both walked to his apartment. Jordan walked in behind him giving him a hug, wrapping her arms around his neck. As he hugged her he rubbed her butt.

"Why you don't have on any panties?" he asked her as he took a seat on the couch.

"Because I didn't want to put any on," she told him. She then took a seat too on the other couch.

"Make love to me," is what came out his mouth next. She thought to herself, love, but I don't love you anymore, I just want to sex you because I'm horny and have no one to have sex with right now. Reggie saying those words reminded her at that very moment she shouldn't be getting back involved with this man. Suddenly she pushed the words out of her head and kept her focus on what and why she went over there in the early morning for. Reggie stood back up.

"Would you like something to drink?"

"Yes, what do you have?"

"Water, Juice."

"I'll take water."

"You sure water, I have Ciroc too?"

"Ok, I'll take Ciroc."

"You want it straight or mixed with juice?"

"Mixed, you know I don't like taking nothing straight."

He went to the kitchen and made them both a drink, then they both walked to his room. They sat on his bed side by side talking and taking sips of their drink. Their eyes locked in on each other. He missed her was her only thought, and she missed him was his. Soon after his hands rubbed her skin, moving from her calves up to her thighs.

Reggie caressing her skin felt so damn good. After finishing up her drink she sat her glass on his little dresser next to his bed, then she began to get more up on his bed. He didn't even finish all his drink, and he sat his glass down too and laid back. Once he saw her getting more comfortable she leaned back on him. He began to find them a movie to watch on cable. As he's scrolling looking for a movie to watch he ended up stopping on "Addicted".

"Have you seen this movie before?" he asked her.

"No, I haven't," she sounded.

"Oh, ok me neither, but I have heard that this movie is good and it's by Tyler Perry."

"Oh, ok, cool."

Reggie and Jordan had cuddled up with each other watching the movie together.

Once the movie went off she began pulling her dress off and laid it down on the bed. Then she unsnapped her gold chain and laid it down on the edge of his bed. He turned off the TV. "Hey, you need this light?" he asked her.

"No."

He turned off the bathroom light and got in bed grabbing her close to him. Jordan was very horny as he slid inside her. She became wet fast, it didn't take her long at all, moving inside her back and forth with the grip of his hand pressed against her butt. They had sex all morning for hours. It was five in the morning when they fell asleep. At eight thirty that morning Jordan slid out the bed quietly trying not to wake him, she had to use the bathroom. Going to the restroom, sitting on the toilet, she glanced down and noticed a small cardboard that read *choker* on it. It sure as hell wasn't his, that clearly belonged to a woman he's dealing with right now. Now coming out the bathroom to wash her hands she now noticed a black styling comb that also belonged to a woman as well, clearly the same woman. She was disappointed to think all the sweet nothings and their conversation that they had meant something, it hurt like hell to see he was just full of shit once again. Jordan told herself she was not going to make a scene about it since he is really not hers anymore; she walked back towards the bed.

Jordan climbed back in bed next to him and he wrapped his arms and legs back around her body, she went back to sleep. Jordan woke up again and looked at her phone to see the time and now it was ten o'clock, she shook him a little letting him know she had to leave. He didn't budge; he continued holding her tight around her waist.

"Reggie, I have to go."

No response from him, she knew he heard her because once she said she had to go he just held her tighter like he didn't want her to get out the bed.

Again she said, "Reggie I have to go, I have to be at work at eleven!"

That last time he slowly moved his arm from around her. Then she was able to get from underneath him and get dressed, afterward she left.

CHAPTER
8

The Christening

Katrina wanted to get the baby Christened. Katrina contacted their pastor to schedule a Christening. Then they invited all four godparents and their immediate family to join them in christening their son. That weekend Katrina and Mike went shopping for a christening outfit for their son, they were planning a christening for him next Sunday. Walking around the store looking through clothes, Katrina ended up seeing a 2-piece pants and jacket.

"Ooh babe, we have to get this, this is too cute!"

"Ok, let's get it!"

"Ok."

Katrina and Mike bought him a cute little white suit. Katrina found her and Simone an all-white dress and Mike got him an all-white pants and jacket suit too, to match his son's suit. Waiting for next week Sunday that week passed quickly. Sunday arrived in no time. Mike Jr. is getting christened today. Katrina woke up early smiling and excited for this Sunday morning her baby is getting christened today. Katrina slid out of bed while Mike, Simone, and the baby were still asleep. She walked downstairs to see what she was about to prepare for breakfast. Katrina started cooking the dinner first for later after church. Afterward, she started on the breakfast. The smell of bacon is what woke Mike up. He then went downstairs.

"Good morning babe!"

"Good morning babe," they kissed.

"Baby, you talked to your moms, pops and you homegirls to remind them?"

"I didn't even have to remind them but I did talk to them last night, they are all so excited about the christening ceremony," she told him.

"Oh okay that's right!" he smiles.

"You excited babe?" she asked him.

"Yeah, I'm excited too, my man is getting christened!" then Mike looked over at the counter at all the things she had cooked.

Katrina noticed him looking at the food she had cooked, "Oh babe all that stuff is for the dinner were going to have for after church, I just told everyone to come over here for dinner after the christening," she said.

"When did you cook all this, this morning, because I went to bed way after you last night?"

She chuckled, "Yeah, when I got up this morning I started cooking the dinner for later and then when I was done I started breakfast."

"Oh okay, I was about to say I know this wasn't here last night."

"Waaa-Waaa," was the sounds coming from Mike Jr.

"Look who is up!" she smiled. Katrina left out the kitchen to get the baby. Going into Mike Jr.'s room he was laying on his back in his crib. He stopped crying as he looked at her as she walked in. Katrina picked him up smiling. "Good morning baby, you ready to get christened today?"

Mike Jr. made some cooing noises. She walked him in the kitchen.

"Stinka!" Katrina says with excitement to her baby smiling right in his face.

"Stinks, you ready to eat eat?"

Mike walked up to them and looked in his son's eyes. "Are you excited about getting christened today too Lil man?" he smiles.

Katrina passed Mike their son so she could make the three of their plates, Mike went and got the car seat so Katrina could feed him in it. Mike called down Simone so she could come down and eat. Afterward, they sat and ate. "So babe, do you need me to do anything before I go hop in the shower?" he asked.

"Ummm," Katrina sounded.

"Tell me now because as soon as I'm done eating I'm about to hop in the shower unless there is something you need me to do first," he laughed.

"Why you laugh babe?"

"Because I know you'll tell me at the last minute."

"No I won't!" she chuckled.

"Either you can fold the clothes or clean the bathrooms."

"How about I fold the clothes," Mike said.

"Okay, that works for me."

After they were done eating Mike went to the living room to fold the clothes she put there last night. Katrina grabbed Mike Jr. from the car seat and walked with him to his room, she was about to change him. After changing his diaper she laid him back down so she could clean both bathrooms. Katrina started with the upstairs bathroom first, then their bathroom. Coming out the bathroom and walking through their bedroom she glanced at the clock over on the dresser.

"Babe, it's nine thirty-five!" she yelled out.

"Okay babe!" he yelled from the living room. Katrina walked downstairs to now clean the downstairs bathroom.

"Babe, we have thirty minutes to leave to get there a little early!"

"Alright babe, are you already done?" he asks.

"Just with the upstairs, I'm about to do this bathroom then I'm getting in the shower."

"Cool, me too, so what time do we have to be there?"

"The pastor said by ten forty-five at the latest."

The four left out the house at ten thirty. "Oooh, it's chilly out here this morning!"

"I know, and the sun is shining."

"I know, I'm glad I bought my jacket."

"Momma, you're always cold, even when it's hot," Simone sounded.

"Shhh girl," she chuckled.

"I'm just speaking the truth and you know it's true," Simone laughed.

Although Katrina wanted them to leave at ten, she knew that wasn't going to happen. Mike drove the truck, they were already running late. "Baby, you think you're going to get us there in twenty minutes?"

He looked over at her, "I don't know babe, I will try without us getting a ticket."

"No, we don't need any tickets babe," she chuckled. Katrina gets on her cell phone, she wanted to make a video real quick then post it on Facebook. She pressed record and began recording herself.

"Good morning Facebook, happy Sunday. Today is a very special Sunday for my family and I, my baby is going to get christened today," she smiles. Katrina turns her phone to Mike Jr. Katrina looked back at him.

"Stinka, say good morning Facebook," she chuckled at the way baby Mike is looking, then she turns the camera back on her.

"Okay Facebook, we're running late, but were headed to the church now, you all have a blessed Sunday," then Katrina pressed stop. She uploaded to her timeline on Facebook and posted it, then she got off her phone. She turns towards Mike.

"Babe, you think Mike is going to behave in church during his christening?"

"I hope so."

"I guess we'll see."

Getting to church service it had barely started ten minutes ago. They went to the church office to check in for christening. Everyone had met at the church for his christening both of their parents, their sisters, his brothers, and other family members from both sides, but Katrina had them all meet in the sanctuary.

The deacon asked to hold him. She passed him her baby. Katrina, Simone, and Mike stood beside him as he talked to baby Mike.

"Are you ready for your christening?" the deacon asked the baby. "Are you ready?" he said again smiling at the baby. The baby was smiling back at the deacon.

The godparents all had arrived and went to the office too. They were all in there together. The deacon had everyone sign some papers on behalf of baby Mike. Then the deacon led them all into the sanctuary as they stood at the altar. As soon as Deborah saw her grandchild she had to smile. The family was called up. They all joined them as well. Deborah stood close to Katrina, she tapped her leg. Katrina turned her head looking at her mother smiling, "Aw Katrina, my grandbaby looks so handsome in his little satin suit."

"Thanks, Mom."

"Look at him, he's so precious!" Mike's mom said.

"Thank you mom," Katrina says to her mother in law.

Everyone stood there commenting too, on how precious and handsome he looks, everyone was smiling at him. Right before the preacher began to talk, Katrina kind of noticed how Andrea was looking at her husband. Katrina was beginning to feel like something, she did not want to feel that way up in the church about how Andrea is looking at her husband. Katrina took a deep breath. She was not trying to show out in the house of the Lord in front of the pastor and everyone in the church. As soon as Andrea saw Katrina looking at her she tried to play it off with a smile then eased her eyes off him. Katrina smirked back at her but couldn't wait to talk to her once the Christening was over. The pastor came down. Katrina held her baby standing in the center as everyone stood surrounding her. The pastor read from the Bible. Baby Mike was doing very well during the ceremony. The pastor asked for Baby Mike, as he held him in his left arm he held the microphone in his right hand, and then he prayed over him. After the prayer, everyone began clapping, shouting hallelujah, and taking pictures. The pastor passed baby Mike to his daddy.

"Babe, Mike did really well," she whispered into his ear.

"I know, I'm glad he did," he smiled looking at his son.

Afterward, Katrina asked Andrea to sit by her. Andrea followed her to where she's sitting.

"Hey Andrea, what was all that about?" then she smiled.

"Oh what," she smiled back.

"The way you were looking and smiling at Mike during the Christening."

"Oh, it was nothing."

"Oh, ok because when I saw you I was starting to feel some type of way."

"Oh no, I'm sorry, I didn't mean anything by it," Andrea responded.

"Oh, ok, well Andrea girl, you was about to have me cut up in the church."

Andrea chuckled. Katrina began chuckling with her. Mike's mother looked noticing Katrina talking to Andrea, she wondered if she's talking to her about the way she was just staring at Mike during the christening. Although Katrina felt at first that wasn't really the place and time to bring that up, she was feeling some type of way about it, and she couldn't hold it in. She had to say something, she was not about to be feeling uncomfortable at her home church and at her baby's Christening.

After the church service was over everyone left out the sanctuary and went to the multipurpose room. Shante and Sharee, her homegirls and baby Mike's godmothers made it to him first.

"Let me see my baby."

"Okay," Katrina smiled. She passed him to Shante first.

"Look Katrina, he's smiling," Shante said grinning.

Katrina looked and smiled, "Yeah, I see his half of a smile, I see it."

Shante held him for a while talking and playing with him, then she passed him to Sharee. Sharee began playing and talking with her god baby telling him how handsome he is and how well he did in church today. Shortly afterward Jared walked up to, Mike's boy and the godfather. "Hey god son!" he says to Mike Jr. Then suddenly one of the members of the church came over and grabbed his fingers. "Hey little fella," she smiled talking to baby Mike. "Little fella, you got christened today."

Baby Mike made a sound.

"Yes you did handsome."

She looked at Katrina and Mike, "You both have a handsome little man and he's such a good baby."

"Thank you," they both smiled.

Katrina's mother walked over to them, she stood on the side of Mrs. McKinley, she reached for her grandson's hand. "Hey, handsome, hey granny's baby, you got christened today, aw!" Deborah couldn't stop smiling. Another church member came over to congratulate Katrina and Mike.

"Hey handsome, hey," Sister Duffy sounded.

Baby Mike start smiling, his smile made hers broaden. Sister Duffy looked at baby Mike then up at Katrina and then up at Mike.

"He is y'all's twin!"

"Thank you, Sister Duffy."

"He looks just like the both of you."

Baby Mike began yawning. His other god mommy Andrea walked up smiling. Katrina smiled back.

"Awww, my baby getting tired, aww he's yawning."

"Andrea, you want to hold him?" Katrina asked her.

"Of course I want to hold my god son."

Katrina passed him on to Andrea, everyone was surrounding him talking and laughing. Katrina had excused herself. She walked from Andrea to go mingle with other members of the church. Mike's mom stopped her.

"Katrina, I saw you talking to Andrea," she smiled.

"Yeah, I had a little chat with her."

"Is everything okay, for a minute it looked like you were telling her off?"

"Yeah now, but not at first, I just had to clear something up."

"What happened?"

"I didn't like how she was looking and smiling at Mike."

"Yeah, I saw that too."

"Oh, you saw that too? Yeah, I didn't like that, she was looking like she wanted him right then in the church or something."

"That girl been liking him for years, but he never gave her a chance."

"Liking him!" was all Katrina heard.

"Liking him!" she repeated again.

"Yeah, when they were younger she used to buy him clothes and give him money, she always had a crush on him."

"Oh, really he never brought that up in conversation, not even when he made her the godmother."

"Oh no baby, he never dated her or anything, baby trust me, you have nothing to worry about with her, I promise."

Instead of mingling, she decided to go back over there. She and her mother in-law walked over there. They all started taking pictures, after the picture taking then they all left the church.

Everyone was headed to Mike's and Katrina's house. Not even five minutes on the road and Katrina was already thinking about the food.

"I can't wait to we get home baby, I'm ready to eat!"

"Me too, so who's all coming?" he asks.

"Well, everybody that came to the christening. I invited some people from the church, I left your mother in charge to tell y'all family, then I posted it on Facebook to my family, most of them replied saying they coming. There were only a couple said they couldn't make it because they had to work."

"Hope we don't run out of food, I think if you assign somebody to make the plates we will be good."

"I know, that's what we should do."

They made it home and Katrina had to quickly go put the food in the oven. More family was arriving and more of Mike's family was also showing up. Everyone stood around talking as the food was warming up. Katrina's uncle and Mike's uncle had started a game of pool in their dining room.

Mike's mother stood and said a prayer over her grandson. Afterward, the pastor said a prayer again over baby Mike, and then he blessed the food. Afterward, it was time to eat. Katrina had asked both Michelles to make plates, her Aunt, and her sister in law. They told her sure they would. There were many conversations going on all around the house, laughter and pool going on, they were having a good time. A half an hour passed and it was now the time to form a line, the food was all warmed and ready. Both Michelles were ready to start making plates. Everyone began to eat, they were having a great time celebrating a special day for their son. After dinner, they talked and took more pictures. A few hours had passed, then everyone was starting to leave. After everyone left Katrina had wanted to finally bring up Andrea.

"Hey, baby I had a talk with Andrea earlier!"

"Oh ok, that's cool, about what?"

"You didn't pay any attention to the way she was looking at you during the Christening, shit, it made me feel some type of way, so afterwards I had a few words. We cleared it up, but now the question I have for you is why you never told me she always liked you and that she used to buy you clothes and give you money?"

"She told you that!"

"Why you never told me?"

"But did she tell you that!" he asked.

"Why does that matter, is it true or not?"

"Baby, it's true but we were young, I never did anything with her. She stopped coming on to me over fifteen years ago, really we only just good friends really!"

"Alright babe," Katrina says. After Katrina and Mike cleared that up she guesses she's okay. They went upstairs to watch a movie. Afterward, they were both tired and were ready for bed.

"Good night babe!"

"Good night," he replied back still thinking who had told her. He kissed her.

CHAPTER
9

Asia Sister's Came To Visit

Asia was standing there rubbing her pregnant stomach, for her first baby this is supposed to be a happy moment and not a moment of hurt and pain that she's going through right now. Although it's been like two months ago now, she couldn't help but to still think about it.

Gary noticed her rubbing her stomach.

"What my baby doing up in there?"

"Moving around," she sounded.

"I see you have that vest on, you looking good in it even though you didn't like it at first."

"It's cute, I just said it wasn't a real faux fur vest, but after adding my little accessories to it, it's cute." Asia had not worn her white and brown bangles in years glad she never threw them away or gave them away, but they looked cute with her tan vest he bought her.

"What's going on with that look on your face?"

"Nothing," she sounded, but then she just looked at him. Even though he tells her to stop thinking about it, she tried not to, but she can't help but think and wonder, and when she does the anger is there and the tears come rolling down her face.

"Paula is nothing to worry about anymore!"

Asia stared at him, she didn't say a word. *If he says my name one more time, I'm about to slap the shit out of him*, she thought to herself. She knew if she responded back to his comment she just might slap his ass. She took a breath and didn't comment.

Asia didn't feel too good, she turned to Gary. "Something is not right!" she told him. He looked at her. Asia was holding her forehead and standing still.

"Babe, what is wrong?"

"I don't know, but I feel like I'm about to pass out right now!"

A week away from turning five months and out of nowhere she began having this intense pain in her lower stomach, she also started feeling light headed like she was about to pass out. She tried drinking water, eating a sandwich, and rubbing her lower stomach, but it wasn't working. The pain was getting stronger and stronger. She yelled for Gary to come here.

"Yes, babe is everything okay!!"

"No, my eyes are becoming very blurry I can barely see anything. I'm still feeling a lot of discomfort in my lower stomach."

"Why?"

"I don't know, but this shit hurts like hell."

She sat on the edge of the chair with her legs open rubbing her stomach. He kneeled down on the floor right in front of her rubbing her stomach looking up at her.

Asia told Gary she needed to go to the hospital. Gary panicked, he got up from off the floor and went and grabbed the car keys. She stood up from off the chair and grabbed her purse and then he grabbed her hand, locked the front door, and led her to the car. He ran around the car and hopped in and they took off to the hospital. Driving there felt like it was taking forever to get there even though he was driving fast as hell to, but the pain was getting stronger and stronger by the minute. They were nervous, they didn't know what was going on.

"Are you okay?" he glanced over and asked her.

She nodded her head yes, but he clearly could see she wasn't doing okay with all the noises and facial expressions she was making sitting in the passenger seat. "Baby we're almost there," he said.

"Okay," she nodded her head fast up and down.

Once getting to the hospital he pulled up in front of the emergency room doors, hopped out the car and quickly ran inside to get help. Then he immediately came right back out with two nurses, one who came out running with a wheel chair. They got her out the car and wheeled her into ER. Gary parked the car on the side of the hospital, he didn't have the time to try and find a parking space. He quickly ran up to the hospital through the double doors, and asked the nurse if he could go back there. He was instructed to wait in the waiting area until the doctor or nurse came to get him. He couldn't even sit down; he just wanted to stand until he knew what's going on with his wife and their baby. Asia lost the baby. An hour later of waiting is when they came out and told him that she miscarried their baby. Asia was placed in a room. That's when she was told she had miscarried a boy. After hearing that Asia just wanted her husband. Her nurse went back out to the waiting room to get her husband for her. Once Gary walked into her room, looking into his wife's eyes all he could do was cry.

"Baby, I lost our baby."

Gary sat down beside her to hug her in silence. He continued to shed some tears. It was hard trying to comfort each other.

"Gary, it was a boy."

He turned around and looked back at her. "I know babe," he told her.

He leaned to her as tears ran down his face and gave her a hug. "I'm sorry baby."

"I'm sorry to babe."

Later that night driving home in silence was sad. The two were just wiping their tears all the way home. Getting home Asia called her sisters crying, she wanted to tell them that she just lost her baby.

"Hello sis, why are you crying?" Octavia answered.

Asia didn't say anything. She was just crying holding the phone to her ear.

"Stop crying sis, what's going on?"

"Sister, I just lost my baby!"

"No, sister you did, I am so sorry to hear that!!" Octavia said with many expressions and so sadly. Myisha heard Octavia and immediately began crying too. "Octavia put the phone on speaker," Myisha told her and Octavia did. "Sister, I am so sorry to hear that oh my god!"

Asia was crying harder. "Sister, stop crying!" Myisha told her.

"I can't, this is just so hard to deal with."

"I know sis, I can't even imagine what you're going through right now." She talked to her sisters a little while longer, then she hung up from them both. All she wanted to do was drown her head in her pillow and cry for the rest of the night.

The next morning Octavia and Myisha couldn't go on to starting their day without calling to check on their sister. Octavia dialed Asia's phone.

"Hey sis, good morning," Asia answered.

"Hey sis, we wanted to make sure you're ok." Then Octavia pressed the speaker button. "Hey sis," Myisha shouted.

"Hey Sis," Asia spoke calmly.

"Sis, don't sound so sad, you're going to make me cry," Octavia said.

"I'm trying but no, I'm not okay at all."

"We know, we love you sis, and it will take time, just pray sis."

"Thank you and I love y'all more. Yeah, I've have been praying and talking to God since before it happened."

"Look at it like this sis; things happen for a reason, maybe God said not yet."

"Or maybe because I was stressing a lot."

"Stressing, about what sis?"

Asia hesitated; she just hopes to tell her sisters about Paula goes well.

"So apparently Gary has another child by someone named Paula and when he was going over to her house to see this child they were having sex."

"Wait, wait, wait, back the hell up!"

"Okay, to what part?"

"Girl everything," Octavia told her.

Asia waited a moment for her sisters to say something, they were in such shock from what she is saying.

"You're not talking about his daughters?"

"Nope, he supposedly has a whole son with this woman named Paula!"

"Wait, where did he come from?"

"Girl, he said one day he saw them in the mall and she stopped him and said hi, and she was like you're a father, and then pointed to the little boy."

"Asia, are you fucking serious sis?" they whispered.

"Girl yes, but the crazy part is that he never even told me any of that until one night I came home checking the mail and found a DNA letter and a child support letter in the mail box, so for a long fucking time he was going over to this woman's house and didn't tell me shit."

"Aw, now that's fucked up!"

"Yes, it was."

"Naw Gary!"

"Yes he did, now he's telling me not to believe her and not to listen to her lies. Sometimes I feel like I don't know what I'm going to do."

"Asia, when I get paid in two weeks Octavia and I are flying down there to see you."

"Alright, are y'all coming for real?"

"Yep," Myisha said.

"Alright, cool, can't wait to see y'all, I miss y'all sis!"

"We miss you too."

"Ok, love you guys."

"Love you more, and sis, we are so sorry about everything you are going through and sorrier about our little nephew."

"Thank you Myisha!"

"Alright bye," Myisha sounded.

"Alright bye," Asia said back.

They hung up.

A week passed and Asia's sisters called her to check on her. Myisha dialed her.

"Hey sis!" she answers.

"Hey Asia, how are you doing out there?" she asked.

"Good," Asia responded.

"You and Gary cool?"

"Yeah, we good," is all Asia could say even though she had thought about leaving his ass at one point.

"So what, you found out that stuff you were telling us wasn't true?"

"Girls you know what, I'm not even worried about that, I'm fine, just excited that I'll be opening my boutique in a week from today. I'm so super excited!"

"We're excited for you, sis!"

"Yeah, my dreams of opening up my own store are finally here!"

"I know right!"

"When y'all coming?"

"Tomorrow morning we're going to fly out there!"

"Alright, I can't wait!"

"We will call you when we touch down at the airport."

"Alright, and I'll be on my way once y'all call."

"Alright," they both said.

The next morning Myisha and Octavia touched down at the airport. Octavia dialed Katrina. "Hey sis we're here," Octavia said in her excited voice.

"Yay, I'm so happy and can't wait to see y'all."

"Us neither, Sis I wanted to tell you that you don't have to come and get us, girl the Uber is so real up here at this airport."

Asia laughed. "You sure sis, I can leave the house right now."

"Naw for real, we can take one, it's like over twenty Ubers up here," Octavia chuckled.

"Alright, sis I will see y'all in a minute."

"Alright," Octavia sounded excited.

Asia sisters had come down to visit her. Arriving in Asia's and Gary's place they rang the doorbell. Their sister answered the door quickly, she was excited to see her sisters.

"Hey sisters!" Asia shouted.

They smiled and shouted *Hey* back.

The three walked straight to the couch to sit down, the three were talking.

"Hey Sis, where is Gary?"

"Fuck Him!"

She almost choked up.

"What, wait a minute, did I miss something here, what the hell I thought everything was cool now?"

"Yeah, I thought you said he cleared everything up and said he wasn't fucking the woman."

"Girl, Gary's ass is lying, but shit now it's something else I just found out!"

"Shut up!"

"Yes, damn shame huh."

Both sisters nodded their head to her answer.

Asia told her sisters she wanted to take them out to eat and for drinks and talk to them about what's been going on. They both looked at her with their questioning eyes, they wanted to know what was going on now, but they decided to wait until they got to the restaurant they were going to, so then they just said *okay*.

Asia began driving her sisters to Maestro's, surprisingly to them Asia didn't once mention a little bit of what she wanted to talk about in the car driving to the restaurant.

After ordering their food and drinks she was now ready to talk to them about what's been going on, she sighed. They noticed the look on their sister's face, it wasn't a good look at all.

"Asia, what's going on sis, did we miss something about him when we met him?"

She hesitated, and then she began talking.

"I guess I did too, him telling me he's been cheating on me."

"What!"

"Yeah," she says as she nods her head up and down looking deeply into her sisters' eyes.

"He's cheating right now Asia?"

"He has since we've been married, but he says he's not anymore."

"Wow, I thought Gary was so different."

"I guess he didn't change until we said I do."

"Girl now, his ass probably been like that, it's just that he just now showing his true self."

"Yeah, the person who he really is," she mumbled as she blew out a deep breath.

"Un Un sister," Octavia said.

"Or probably because his last marriage was to his childhood friend and he'd only been with her since childhood up until about twenty-seven years old, so after they divorced he probably felt like he had to fuck with that woman and that woman to see what's out there."

"Sister, stop over thinking this, you don't need this and don't make any excuses for him. This is not cool, you probably should leave him."

"This is all crazy, maybe things can be worked out!"

"Or maybe they can't, he will continue to do it, if you stay."

Asia saw their frustration during their conversation. The conversation was very intense, they were both very mad at him for all that's been going on and how she is getting done. Asia had told her sisters the story in pieces, and how she wanted to tell them, what she hasn't told them and she doesn't think she will is that with Gary's ex-wife he had an affair with her sister, they think both his daughters are by the same woman.

"I prayed about it and I will continue to pray about it, I know God didn't bring me this far to get married just to end up divorced, this is him testing our faith and our loyalty as a new married couple."

"I guess Asia, you may be right or we can go beat the chick's ass, that will make me feel better," Octavia told her.

"No, leave her alone and please don't mention anything to Gary!"

Asia hopes her sisters could understand her, even though she's pissed and hurt she just does not want to up and leave her marriage.

"Yeah, I hope so," Asia sounded.

"So what's going on with the store?" Asia's sisters changed the subject.

"I'll be open in a week from today, I'm so super excited"

"I'm excited for you sis!"

"Yeah, my dreams of opening up my own store are finally here," Asia was too excited.

Although the subject was changed that didn't stop them from asking her was she sure she didn't want them to beat this woman's ass for her. No matter how many times they both asked her did she want them to confront him and then beat this chick's ass, Asia's response was still *No*. As embarrassing as it was coming from her New Husband she didn't want any more BS added to what was already going on. They couldn't even imagine their sister still staying with this fool, their sister deserved better, well luckily it was still early means she has the whole rest of the day and evening to hopefully change her sister minds. Getting back to the house, Asia told her sisters not to mention anything they talked about at Maestro's. Instead of responding with a yes or ok, they both just looked at her.

Now that they were back at the house Asia and her sisters had more drinks and they listened to music. As Asia was listening it was almost sounding like every song was fucking talking to her, Asia was disappointed in herself. Octavia and Myisha did what they could do to try and cheer up their sister, telling her not to blame herself, it wasn't her fault that she didn't know. The next day of her sisters being down in Cali they became their sister's private investigators, they wanted to see if he was out there still doing some shady shit their sister doesn't know about. They were willing to do this for their big sister because they needed her to stop the stressing and crying, being a new wife this is something she just should not be going through.

Asia's phone started to ring, it was her mother. "Hello, mother."

"Hey, baby."

"Hey."

"What are you doing?"

"Nothing," Asia said.

"What are your sisters doing?"

"They're not here," she said.

"Where are they at?"

"Doing something I told them not too."

"Oh lord, what's going on?"

"They out spying on Gary," she told her.

"Spying on Gary, why are they spying on him, what is he doing?" she asked while taking sips of her coffee.

"They said they just want to make sure that when he leaves the house he isn't going to another woman's house."

"Well, is he going to another woman's house?" her mother asked her.

"No, but they wanted to make sure for themselves."

"I wonder whose idea it was ,Octavia's or Myisha's?"

"It was Octavia's!"

I figured that's your sister," she chuckled.

"Your daughters!" they both laughed together. Asia hated lying, it's like once you tell one lie then another lie always follows, then after that lie then another one comes out of nowhere to hold up the last lie. Asia almost told her mother too much, but the conversation ended well.

That Saturday was worse because they had a whole lot to say to his ass, to their mother and father and the fact Asia doesn't want them saying anything is a problem. They love their sister and have always respected her decision, but this one right here, they want to say something, and when they came back home they couldn't stand the fact he's walking around the house pretending to be a way he wasn't. He didn't even know they already knew the deal with him and what he has been doing. Later when he left the house again they pretended to leave and hang out, but they left to follow him one last time. It was in the late afternoon.

Asia couldn't stop from being mad at herself and for not catching it before it happened. She went and laid down on her bed to stare at the TV, the TV was watching her basically. Later Myisha and Octavia returned back to the house, Asia was in the kitchen about to pour her a drink.

"Look at you sis, about to have a drink by yourself, pour us one!"

Asia poured them a drink too, she was trying to wait for them to drink with them at first, but they took too long. After passing them their drinks they told their sister they didn't catch him doing anything out the ordinary.

They took a sip of their drink.

"Oh, this is good sis!"

That's the new drink I bought, it is called Stella Rose. I had bought that and Rossi Burgundy, they are both good.

"Oh, Stella Rose, oh yeah, we had this before. It's good, but not this one, the Platinum kind."

"Oh, okay, my first time buying it and tasting it, I like this!" The three took sips of their wine as they talked and listened to music.

Once Gary made it home Asia sat her drink down and went to go kiss and hug her hubby, they both went to the room for a second. Gary was the only male with a house full of women, so he called up two of his guy friends to kick it over at their house. Once Gary's boys came over is when he and his boys joined his wife and sisters in the living room.

"Okay, okay, I see brother in-law, you kick it with us once your boys come over."

He laughed.

The conversation they were having was changed once the men joined them. The six of them were having a good time chilling. Asia was so happy to have her sisters there and she felt like she wasn't in this by herself. It hurt they were out following him around in the streets earlier for the reason they were, but more so they have her back, and right now that's what matters.

That Sunday morning Gary woke up and cooked breakfast for everybody. After breakfast, Katrina began looking over all the orders, she wanted to make sure she ordered everything that's on the list. Gary and her sisters were doing nothing, they were all sitting around the house not doing much. "Hey, babe let's all get out the house and do something!"

"What do you want to do?"

"I don't know, something," she told him.

"They went out on an outing."

Things seemed okay while they were out, but her sisters were not being fooled. "I'm saying something to his ass by tonight," Octavia mumbled to Myisha.

"What, you can't, Asia will be pissed at us," she whispered back.

"Well, I'll be damned if we leave here next week to go back home and our sister is out here feeling some type of way because of his ass."

"I really don't think we should get in their business like that, asking him questions and shit."

"Well, I don't think I can hold it in any longer!"

"Asia told us in confidence and we told her that we were going to keep quiet."

Octavia looked at her with a blank look on her face. Myisha looked her in her eyes. "Are you still going to say something?"

Octavia nodded her head yes.

"Alright," she sighed, Myisha just left it at that.

"But I'll give it a few more days."

"Okay," Myisha says.

The four stopped by the nail shop. Asia's sisters wanted to get a full set. Asia decided while she's there she might as well get her nails and her toes painted pink, pink is her favorite color, so Asia asked for a manicure and a pedicure. She didn't like getting the nails, she'd like rocking her own nails which were very short just the way she liked them.

"Babe, you should let them do your feet!"

"My feet," he repeated.

"Why you say it like that?" she chuckled, "Yeah, your feet, men get their feet done all the time."

"No, I'm cool," he told her.

"Excuse me, can you have somebody give my husband a pedicure please," she told the lady who was doing her nails.

"What?" Gary couldn't believe his wife would still tell them too after he just said no, he didn't want too.

"Babe, come sit down in that chair," she pointed.

Gary sighed. Then he sat down in the chair. Once they started on his feet he couldn't keep from looking down watching them doing his feet, and once they began massaging his feet, Asia noticed how that smile grew on his face, all she could do was smile and turn her head.

Leaving the nail shop two hours later, Asia had to throw it in his face. "So babe, I see you were enjoying your foot massage," she smiled.

"What you talking about," he smiled. "Yeah, I did that shit did feel bomb as fuck!"

"See!"

Days later Myisha noticed that look her sister was giving her, she had that feeling she was about to say something now. Myisha shook her head at her sister telling her no don't say anything yet; She put her finger to her lip and said. *"Shhh not yet."*

"Why!" Octavia lipped.

"Just not yet," she whispered.

Later when they were by themselves is when Octavia asked Myisha why she told her not to say anything yet. Myisha didn't have an answer for her other than Asia told us not to say anything. That wasn't good enough for her. "I will give it two more days, but after that, I'm asking so sis on Friday please don't try and stop me. Remember we leave on Monday, I have to ask way before we leave."

"Ok," Myisha said.

After their outing, they went and grabbed something to eat, by the time they all returned back to the house they were all tired and just wanted to relax. Once Asia went to her bathroom inside her room to shower that was when her sister took advantage of her time to ask Gary what the hell his fucking problem was.

"Gary, can I ask you a question?" Octavia said, her voice sounded upset.

"Yeah sure," Gary told her.

"Why do you have my sister out here losing babies behind her stressing and shit behind you, Gary you know that's not cool at all, you're foul!"

Myisha held her breath, she was tempted to add in her two cents, but Octavia had it. The sound in her voice confirmed to him she knew just what she's stating. He thought this shit was crazy, he understood they were her sisters and all, but he wasn't feeling them knowing his personal business and what he is and is not doing. Gary didn't have to confess to anything because they knew something already if not all of what he has done. This was crazy as hell. How can he go sit at the bar like this and pretend to have a good time when he's not, he's too mad for the bar right now.

Gary didn't want to go now, he was very upset that they knew what was going on, and they came at him like that. They wanted to get out the house for an hour to celebrate, he wanted to stay.

Asia began to get ready and her sisters went to go take showers to get ready too.

"Babe, you're not about to get ready, so we can go to the bar?" she asked him.

"Babe, I don't feel like going, we've been out all day, we just got home and you already want to leave again!"

"But babe, we talked about this earlier and you said yeah."

"I know babe, I changed my mind now."

Asia stood there looking at him with her big round pretty brown eyes he loves staring into, "Babe, you sure you don't want to go to the bar?" she asked smiling.

"Like I said babe, I'm going to stay at the house, I can have a drink with you here later."

She turned around with hurt in her face and finished getting ready. Once her sisters were ready she grabbed her keys and her purse. Asia and her sisters were headed to the Bar & Grill to have a drink to celebrate the opening of her store tomorrow. They were gone for only five minutes before

Gary decided to go he realized he really should have went with them too. He hurried and grabbed his keys and left too. Suddenly Gary showed up just like she expected him to. He had ordered him a drink from the waiter just in time for them all to toast to her boutique. They all had only one drink. Gary's eyes kept slightly looking over at his sister in laws, he sat there listening to them talk and he was just there showing support. Leaving there they drove home following each other. Pulling up in front of the house he pulled to the side so Asia could pull up in the driveway first, then he pulled in behind her. Going inside the house she followed him upstairs and went to bed. They went to bed early, they had a big day tomorrow. That was their first time in a long time going to sleep at eight on a Saturday night.

Asia was up, it was still dark, looking at the time it was only in the middle of the night, she was so excited she couldn't sleep. That morning waking up the sun had not even risen and she was already ready to open her boutique.

Gary woke up from the noise she was making, "Baby, you got everything you need to make this day a success?" Gary asked her.

"Yes babe," she said with a smile.

"Babe, you don't want to lay back down, you got like four hours to go?"

"I'm too anxious!"

"Babe, it's five o' clock," he said as he looked at the clock with one eye open and one eye closed. She eventually laid back down and went to sleep. Once Asia woke up three hours later, she woke up her sisters. They got up and began helping her getting things ready.

"Gary, are you almost ready?" Asia asked him.

"Yeah, I just have to put on my tie."

"Okay!" she yelled.

They headed out early, it was the opening of her store and everything was running on schedule. Gary, her sisters, and her staff: Mellissa, Yolanda, Star, Pamela, and Jadah were getting the last bit of things together.

"We have twenty more minutes before we open," she said softly smiling. Everyone was standing next to the counter waiting to open. Asia's cell started going off. It was her mom calling her. Asia looked down at her phone, "This is mom calling!" Asia answered.

"Hey mom," Asia answered.

"Hey, baby!"

"You opened yet?"

"No, not yet we have twenty more minutes."

"You excited baby?"

"Yes, I am, too excited!"

"I know you are," she said. "I'm so happy for you baby."

"Thank you so much, mom."

"Where is Myisha and Tay Tay?"

"They're right here."

"Hey mom, good morning!" they shouted.

"She heard y'all," Asia told them. Their talk was short, Asia was about to get ready to open soon.

It was exactly ten o' clock, it was time to unlock the door. They were officially open. Mellissa stood out in front of the door with flyers to pass out to people walking through the mall. People were slowly coming in and every thirty minutes Asia's staff had a different customer to help, and by noon they had a customer to help every five minutes.

Gary stayed helping her out on her first day. "Wow, babe customers are liking your store babe!" Gary says.

"I know," she smiled.

***

The next day even more people came through her store. They were so busy that day the day flew right on by. Her first two days were a success. That evening getting home Gary couldn't wait to ask her about her day.

"So, how did your second day go?"

"It was very good, it stayed busy all day."

"I'm not surprised because yesterday there were so many people coming in, not just looking neither, but they were all buying your clothes."

"I know," she smiles.

That Tuesday morning Myisha and Octavia were awakened by Myisha's alarm she had set last night on her cell phone. Knocks sounded at Asia's and Gary's bedroom door; it was Myisha in the hallway knocking on their bedroom door.

"Yeah," Asia sounded from her bed.

"Hey sis, our plane leaves at nine ten," It was the time that they headed out and flew back to Arizona.

"Okay," she sounded. Asia began moving Gary's arm.

Her movement woke him, "Babe, where are you going?" they were clung together with his arm wrapped around her.

"I'm about to make breakfast."

"Do you have to do that now babe?" he was warm in this position, he didn't want her to move.

"Babe, their plane leaves at nine and I'm going to need you to drop them off for me at the airport."

"Okay."

Asia got out of bed and grabbed her robe. She had no bra on and no panties on. She stepped out the room and went downstairs. She went to go start breakfast. Asia was making breakfast for everybody, she wanted to make her sister's favorites: French toast, eggs with cheese, bacon and hash brown. She wanted them to eat a good breakfast before they left. After eating Gary went to get his jacket and keys and she walked up to them smiling, "Remember, don't tell anyone, keep your mouths closed," she whispered to them as she hugged them both.

"Yes sister," they told her.

"Thank you guys for coming down I enjoyed our sister time and thank you so much for helping me at the store," she said in her regular voice that time.

"We enjoyed ourselves too sister, we had fun spending time with you and our brother in law, and sister, congratulations again on your store," Octavia told her.

"Thank you, Tay Tay!" Asia hugged her and then stepped back.

"For real sis, that's a big accomplishment, you inspire me all the time sis, I'm proud of you."

"Awww," Asia almost wanted to cry from what her sister had just said. Asia walked up to Myisha and hugged her tightly. The three left the house and were headed for the airport.

"Gary, you have to work today?" Myisha asked.

"Yeah," he said.

"How is that going?"

"What," he looked at her.

"The Real Estate Market, is people buying houses right now?"

"Yeah, it's alright, some are, yeah."

"Oh, okay."

"Awww, we missed your daughters we didn't get the chance to see them."

"Yeah, I didn't pick them up this week. I knew I was going to be too busy with Asia opening the Boutique, had to make sure that was a success for her."

"Indeed it was."

"Yeah, I'm glad y'all came down and helped us out, that was good looking for real."

"We're glad we came too, her store is about to make so much money I can see it."

Gary's conversation with Octavia and Myisha on the way to the airport was short, between their short conversations the three were mostly silent. Knowing how talkative he was they already knew he was still, upset his body language showed it. They looked at each other and raised their eye brows at each other and kept quiet. They both were thinking the same thing. Gary didn't have to fight through that much traffic at the airport this morning thankfully. Getting to the airport he stepped out the car and grabbed their suitcases from out the trunk for them.

"Gary, you're not mad at us are you, about the other night?" Octavia asked him. "You know it is all love, we just have to protect our sister," Myisha added. Gary looked them straight in their eyes, he looked at Octavia's eyes, than to Myisha's eyes, he stepped towards them, shook his head as he gave them their suitcases. Gary knew he had to stop being mad at them because if that was his brother Simmie he would have said something too on his behalf.

They actually like him besides what he did. They knew his intentions were not to cheat on their sister and make her lose the baby. They knew he just got himself caught up in a situation that he really could have prevented.

Gary gave Octavia a hug, then he stepped to Myisha and gave her a hug next. He walked away from them waving bye, then he got back inside his car and left.

After Gary returned home and showered for work he went up to Asia closely before him leaving. He began rubbing his fingers through her long black curls, then he placed his fingers on the tip of her chin. They stared into each other's eyes asking her does she have plans to leave him. Asia has been had her mind made up, she was going to work things out and hold onto her marriage. She just wanted him to prove her wrong, letting her know she's making the right decision to stay.

"No," she responded.

"Ok, thank you, I love you!" he told her.

"Why you ask me that?" she wondered.

"I just wanted to know."

"Oh, okay."

"I plan to keep proving to you babe, that this will never happen again, and that all my focus is on us and our marriage."

"I know babe, and you are doing a good job so far, I believe we will be okay as long as you keep at it."

He didn't want to say the real reason; he didn't want her sisters to get mad at him for saying something. He wrapped his arms around her giving her a tight hug and a kiss on her lips.

"Alright, babe I'm out."

"Ok babe, you have a good day at work."

In three hours Myisha and Octavia made it back home. Myisha and Octavia hated they had to keep their mouths closed about the whole thing. Asia knew just how her parents were, more so her dad, soon as he heard what happened he would be quick to drive down there with his gun and make this man leave from out of his own house then pressure her into getting a divorce and wouldn't stop until she gave in.

The next day at work, Asia called and asked Gary if he could buy lunch, but then bring it up to her store. She didn't have any time to stop from what she was doing today, the time wasn't going to allow. Gary arrived. "Things are looking good, I see you added an extra table!"

"Yeah, I ordered it. It just came in today actually, in fact, I ordered it from the same place where you ordered our desk at the house."

The next day that evening Asia came home to an almost empty laundry basket, "Babe!" she said.

"Yeah babe," he answered.

"You washed all the clothes?"

"Yeah babe, I washed the clothes and I cooked dinner already." Asia smiled, she was surprised. "I wanted you to come home and just relax and kick your feet up or something, you've been on your beautiful little feet all day."

"Thank you, baby," she sees he appreciates what she does for him and around the house. *Look at him trying to take a load off me, how sweet.*

Asia called out to Arizona to see what her sisters are doing, she misses them already.

"Hey sis," Octavia answered.

"Hey, sis, I miss y'all already."

"What you doing Asia?"

"Nothing," she said.

"How about y'all," Asia asked.

"Dad and mom up in their room sleep. I'm over here watching TV and scrolling through Facebook and Myisha just left for the mall with her friend.

"Oh ok, so what happened when you told mom and dad, what did they say?"

"About what," Octavia said.

"About the baby," Asia said.

"I thought you said not to say anything."

"You can tell them about that, I don't want them surprised when in a few months they are going to be expecting me to be expecting."

"Oh, okay, they're sleep right now, but I'll tell them when they wake up."

"Okay."

"Alright, well talk to you later!"

"Alright, later," Asia said back.

"Later," they hung up.

Three long hours since she made that call to her parent's house, her daddy just got the message because he is now calling. *Daddy* popped up on her phone. Asia had taken a deep breath before she answered.

"Hey daddy," Asia said.

"Hey, baby so what happened with the baby?"

"Daddy I miscarried."

"I'm so sorry sweetheart!"

"No, it's fine dad."

CHAPTER
10

Sharee

Sharee woke up and looked over at RoShawn, "RoShawn why do you keep disrespecting me?"

"Don't wake up with that shit!"

"How can I not wake up when we went to sleep last night, that's what you were on RoShawn!"

"I respect you when I want to respect you."

"You can get out of my bed too!"

"Sorry baby, you know I didn't mean that."

"Yeah, you did!"

Sharee got mad and got up, "Where you going, come get back in bed!"

"I'm about to go clean up and wash clothes." She began cleaning up since she was too tired to do it last night; she also began putting their dirty laundry into the washing machine. She felt something hard as she was placing RoShawn's black pants inside, she went in his back pocket to get it out and it was a Comfort Inn Hotel key. She stared at the card, and then Sharee slipped it into her pocket. Sharee was pissed, she went to the kitchen and then she went straight to the room with a knife.

"Sharee, what are you about to do with that knife?"

"I'm about to stab your ass because you're playing games with me!" RoShawn got up and tried taking it from her, but then she accidentally stabbed him with it in the process.

"Damn Sharee, what the fuck did you do!" he looked down at the blood on his shirt. Then he snatched the knife from out her hand. "Fuck man, I gotta drive myself to the hospital," he left. Then so did Sharee too. Shortly after he dialed her and told her to come back home, he needed her to put a bandage on him because he was getting blood all in his car. Sharee met him back at the house and she cleaned him up and put a bandage on him like he wanted. Sharee dialed Katrina's cell phone. Once Katrina answered she told her she needed to come over and talk to her.

"Sharee, are you okay?" she asked.

"No, I'm not okay Katrina!"

Katrina told her to come on over, then she told Sharee the code to get inside the gate. They continued to talk. As Katrina was talking Sharee held the phone to her ear listening as she went and took out her makeup from out her makeup box underneath her bathroom sink. RoShawn walked into the room as she was almost done applying her makeup.

"Why in the hell you in here on the phone with the door closed, who in the fuck on the phone Sharee!" He said loud and deep voiced.

"Hold on," she whispered. She slid her phone down on her lap.

"Who was that?" he blurted out loudly.

"You loud like you don't trust me, how about I don't trust you!" she took the hotel key from out her pocket and threw it at him. "I'm not the one that can't be trusted."

RoShawn was walking fast towards her charging at her, "Who was that on the phone," he said angrily all in her face with his hand around her neck.

252

"It was Katrina!" by her saying was made him think she hung up on her, but her girl was still on the phone. She wanted her to hear his crazy ass.

"Where you going?" he asked.

"Going to Katrina's," Sharee told him.

"Oh, you'll put on makeup and shit when you leave to go see her, but with me, you just look like plain Jane."

"Why do you do this, always starting unnecessary arguments RoShawn? I'm so sick of you arguing at me, especially while I'm on the phone with my girl, do you know how humiliating that is!"

"Man, who cares what she thinks."

"What about how I feel though?" she told him.

"Come here," Sharee put her phone down and walked to him. RoShawn pulled her close, as she got closer he hugged her.

"You know I be having my outburst and shit, I need anger management," he chuckled holding his chest.

"Yeah, which you need to calm that down," she told him.

"I will."

Sharee looked him in the eyes. "It's like we good one week, then the next week or two we up in here having war, I'm tired of that, I can't do that!"

"Babe, I'm sorry."

Sharee really had nothing else to say because there he goes acting normal like nothing never happened which was crazy. Sharee just wanted him to treat her right, one thing she knew is that she did not at all deserve this treatment. Then he walked out the room. Sharee went to her phone, looked down at it, and saw Katrina is still on the phone.

"Hello."

"Girl, un un," Katrina sounded.

"See what I keep going through!"

"Sharee, fuck him, you don't have to keep taking that shit from him, you need to leave his ass!"

"What happened with Sharee?" is what Sharee could hear from the other end of Katrina's phone, Mike being concerned for her as always.

"Honey, Sharee over there getting attacked by RoShawn's ass," Katrina told Mike.

"Attacked," he replied.

"He keeps starting unnecessary ass arguments with her for no reason, like that shit gets old."

"Is everything okay with her though?"

"I'm not even sure, but Sharee is about to come over here and talk to me."

"Yeah, tell her to come over here."

"I just want to get out this relationship; I should not be in a relationship that I'm scared to be in," Sharee mumbled.

"Just hurry up and get over here girl!"

"I will," they hung up.

"Sharee!" he yelled from the living room.

"Yeah," she sounded, then she went to the living room to see what he wanted.

"Hey, I'm going to the hospital, this shit is hurting bad and the blood is coming through the bandage."

"Alright," they said, then he left out the house.

Sharee put some different clothes on, she combed and brushed then sleeked her hair back into a pony tail. Then she left. She was headed for Katrina's.

Katrina's cell rung, it was her mother.

"Hey mom," Katrina answered.

"Hey Katrina, I was calling to tell you I baked a couple of cakes last night."

"Please tell me one of them is a Carmel?"

"Yes, that's why I called you."

"Oh yeah, I will be over there to get me some," Katrina said.

"I baked it for you actually."

Katrina smiled, "Thanks, mom!"

"You're welcome baby!"

"Mom, hold on, real quick," Katrina's line was beeping. Someone was calling her, she clicked over to answer her other line and it was Sharee, they began talking. Katrina was still on the line with her mother while talking to Sharee.

"Hey lady," Katrina said.

"What you doing?"

"On the phone talking to my mother," Katrina said.

"Oh, tell mommy I said hello."

"Alright I will, but where you at?"

"I'm here, I was calling because I'm at your gate, but I forgot the code."

"It's 5419," she laughed.

She clicked back over to her other line and told her mother that it was Sharee and that she just got there, and that she's going to have to call her back because something happened to her and her boyfriend.

"Ok, call me back to tell me what happened."

"Okay, I will." They hung up the phone.

Sharee was over to visit Katrina. The redness in Sharee's eyes standing at the door says she's been crying already. Katrina looked into her eyes and slowly shook her head. Sharee walked right on in. Katrina had closed her door behind her. Sharee came in crying. Katrina looked back at Mike then she turned around approaching Sharee.

"Aww Sharee, what's wrong?" she says as she was immediately walking up to her girl to comfort her.

"Girl, I'm sorry to keep bothering you with my bullshit," she says as she cries.

"Don't say that, I am not tripping, you're my girl."

"Thanks, girl."

"You already know."

Sharee cried on Katrina's shoulder, Katrina knew with this cry RoShawn did something to her besides arguing. "Sharee, this shit is not healthy for you, you need to really get out this relationship with him. I know you love him because you're still there with him and you keep taking his shit, but I'm your girl and I don't care if I have to tell you over and over again. I'm not going to stop until you change your situation, clearly he's not. It's like your allowing his actions by staying with him, it's not worth it for you to keep hurting like this. I want to see you happy, I haven't seen you be your normal self in a while. I don't like to see you crying and hurting like this," she says as she's talking to her softly, rubbing her back. Sharee kept crying. Katrina stood there hugging her until she felt like talking.

"I feel so stupid for keep allowing him to treat me this way, I don't deserve what he is doing to me, and I am a good woman!"

"Yes you are, I don't know why he keeps doing this to you," Katrina said as she hugged her. She felt bad for her friend. She didn't like to see her going through it like this.

"Me neither, I deserve better!"

"Girl, I was feeling the same way when I separated from Gary years ago, but I prayed and asked God for strength, you'll be okay."

"I'm not strong like you!"

"What, I know because you're stronger than me," she told her.

"I want to leave, but I can't."

"You can and if you don't you will regret it."

"Everything he would ask me to do, I would do it, I mean everything, with no if's, and's, buts, I did it, and for him to keep treating me this way, it is fucked up and I'm tired."

Sharee's phone began ringing. She looked, it was RoShawn. She turned the ringer down, then threw it back in her purse.

"That's him?" Katrina asked.

"Yes, it is!"

"That's right, don't answer it, let his ass sit over there and think about what he is doing to you."

"I don't want to talk to him right now. So back to what we were talking about, we are not married like y'all, but I'm a damn good woman to his ass, shit I do all the wifely duties."

"He knows it too is why he doesn't want to let you go."

"But why cheat and treat me so fucked up the way he does?"

"You caught him cheating on you?" Katrina asked.

"I found a hotel key in his pocket from the Comfort Inn."

"What did he say about the hotel key?"

"He's talking about *the key is not his*, I know his ass was lying."

"Then why was it in his pocket, he's not going to be having nobody else's hotel key in his pocket."

"So I asked him this morning why does he keep disrespecting me, and you know this motherfucker had nerves to say I respect you when I want to respect you, while he's lying in my bed."

"Are you serious?"

"I told his ass to get out my bed."

"Then he called himself trying to explain and say sorry."

"Shit, what's wrong with him it's too late for that!"

"Exactly, that's why I didn't even let him finish, I just flashed out. I stormed to the kitchen and got the biggest knife out the drawer I tried to stab his ass."

Katrina's eyes got big. "Sharee!"

"What."

"You didn't!" Katrina's eyes widened even more.

"Yes I did, but then while he was trying to snatch it from out my hand he caused me to stab him for real," she shook her head.

"Where is RoShawn right now?"

"He drove himself to the hospital."

"Do you think he's going to say you did it?"

"I don't know because he was mad as fuck that I stabbed him."

"He left first, I wasn't about to stay at the house, so I left, but then shortly after he called me back to the house and had me put a bandage on it for him. He was leaking too much blood and it was dripping all on his seat and that's when I called you."

"Damn Sharee!"

RoShawn kept calling and tears were falling down her face. She didn't feel like talking to him right now. After his tenth time calling her phone she finally answered.

"Yes RoShawn!" she answered.

"Sharee, what are you doing?"

"I was on the phone trying to pay a bill."

"Well, you've been gone for a long time, you know I'm in pain."

"Not really, but RoShawn I'm on my way now."

"Alright." They both hung up.

"He got you lying, you know that's all bad girl when you can't even tell your man the truth."

"I know."

Sharee felt no need to tell him where she really was. If she would have told him she was really at Katrina's house, then he would have known they were over there talking about him. She didn't feel like adding to her stress. Sharee left Katrina's and went home. When she left there, she was feeling a little better.

Getting home they both did a lot of looking at each other. He felt she needed a massage to unwind. He began massaging her back. She sat there wishing he would just stop and leave, she didn't need any damn massage, what she wanted was for his ass to get his shit and get the fuck up out her house.

The next day Shante called Katrina to see how Sharee was doing. Katrina told her what was going on, and then Katrina called Sharee.

"Hey lady," she answered.

"Hey, Boo!"

"What's going on?"

"I wanted you to meet up with Shante and me in two hours."

"Ok."

"We're meeting at Starbucks to get coffee and talk!"

"Ok."

They arrived at the same time and as soon as they sat down Sharee sparked up a conversation.

"What's wrong with me?" Sharee asked.

"No, there's nothing wrong with you, it's him who has the problem!"

Sharee buried her face into the palm of her hands. Katrina and Shante both hugged her telling her to wait on God and that things will get better. After the crying and wiping tears, Sharee was a little settled.

"How have you been Shante, I haven't talked to you in a week," Sharee asked.

"Girl, I just been busy between work and planning the wedding," Shante said.

"How is that going?"

"Girl, it's a lot, but I'm excited!"

"As you should be," Sharee says as she was still wiping her face.

"We're so sorry you have been going through this," Shante told her.

"Thanks, ladies, but you don't have to apologize for him being the asshole that he is to me."

The three held hands and then Katrina led the prayer as their eyes closed. They had to say a prayer for Sharee.

After the prayer their eyes slowly opened, Sharee lifted her head, her gaze looked into Katrina's eyes and told her thank you for that prayer. Katrina and Shante both saw the hurt in their friend's eyes, but after that prayer, they knew she was going to be okay.

"I wish I could tell him it's over."

"You can."

Sharee was quiet; she listened, but didn't sound a sound.

"You deserve a Godly man or something, someone who's going to love you, treats you with some respect and adore you."

"I know I do," Sharee sounded.

Katrina and Shante wasn't holding anything back, words were just rolling off their tongues. They were not giving Sharee enough time to think, they felt every time she thinks too long, she always find reason on why she should stay with RoShawn, but she shouldn't because the longer she stays, the more he takes advantage of her.

"Well just know boo, we have your back and we are here for you Sharee," Katrina told her.

Later in the evening when she made it home, there goes RoShawn again with the look in his eyes. She knew any minute now he's about to start up some mess with her for no reason. She stopped in her footsteps and all she could do was stand there and stare him straight in his eyes.

"What you going to do, stab me again, yeah you better think twice if you try and try that shit again Sharee."

"I can't do this anymore I'm tired of how you have been treating me!"

"Now you tired, so what, you want to break up with me now, why now, you never said anything like this before!" he shouted.

"I have, you just weren't listening."

"Yeah right, what, your girls told you to do this!" he shouted loudly.

"My girls!" she shouted, "No my heart!" she shouted.

Suddenly she started going off on him, it came out of nowhere, built up frustration she's been holding back for a very long time. RoShawn was looking at Sharee like he didn't even know who she was. RoShawn was taken by surprise by her hostile tone of voice; it took him so much by surprise he couldn't even respond right away as normal. He looked at her staring at her mouth and eyes.

"You want a better man, you think you can find somebody better than me? Well, that's not going to happen because ain't nobody going to want your ass. Watch, you're going to find yourself fucking for money because ain't nobody going to want you as their woman for real!" he shouted.

She couldn't believe all of what he had said. She has had it up to here, she wasn't listening to him anymore. It was like it's been on the tip of her tongue for a long time and she couldn't hold it back any longer. She turned around and walked away crying.

"I'm sorry Sharee I will change and start treating you better," he said like he meant what he was saying right now. But now for her it's too late, he should have been doing it then and the things he was saying wasn't cool.

"Sharee, I treated you that way and said those things because I thought you were going to leave me."

"Well thank you for this lesson."

"What you mean a lesson?"

"I know in your right mind you didn't think I would stay after saying all that, I know I did before, but I just knew you were going to change, I really love you, but it's too late," she spoke calmly.

"Baby, please don't say that."

"Bye RoShawn!"

"I'm not going anywhere!"

Sharee sat in her chair in the room and called Katrina. "Hello," Katrina answered.

"Katrina, I need you and Mike over here right now, this motherfucker is not trying to leave!" she yelled.

"Okay, here we come right now." Sharee hung up her line from Katrina and she walked to her living room and sat on the couch, he followed her to the living room and sat on the couch too. She got up and sat on the love seat, she didn't want to sit next to him, she began staring at RoShawn madly.

"Sharee, do I really have to go?" RoShawn asked her as he shed tears down his face. His tear drops didn't mean a thing to her. Sharee's heart didn't feel any sympathy for his pain he'd caused.

Katrina went and told Simone they would be right back and for her to watch her little brother. Katrina rushed over to Mike.

"Baby come go with me to Sharee's house," she said. Talking fast and moving faster grabbing her purse and shoes. Mike didn't know what they were rushing for, but it had to be something serious.

"Baby, what's going on?"

"Oh, I'll tell you in the car."

They both ran out the house, Mike closed the door behind him, Katrina ran and got in her car. Mike hopped in the passenger seat and she quickly pulled off before he could close the door all the way. He immediately put on his seat belt.

"Baby, Katrina put on your seat belt!"

Katrina began telling him as she's pushing through traffic, luckily they didn't see any police, yet she hopes not too as she drives to her girl's house. Once he found out what was going on he really didn't want to get in the middle of her and her boyfriend and what they have going on because he didn't want to go over there, talk shit to him, or beat his ass then she ends up back with him. But what he only planned to do was make sure he doesn't put his hands on her.

"Why has she been with him so long if he is an abuser?"

"But he wasn't always like that; when she first got with him he was straight, over time he changed up on her."

When Katrina and Mike got out the car RoShawn heard their car doors close, he looked out the window.

"Oh, okay, Sharee I see you called your back up, oh, okay!"

"RoShawn, I just want you out!"

Sharee went and opened her front door for them.

He walked up to her trying to hug her. She stepped back saying Bye again. RoShawn just got a few of his things and left. After him leaving the house, she had a smile of relief, not that she was happy for breaking up with him, because she did love him, but smiled because now she feels her pain is gone. Sharee plans to work on herself to get Sharee back to her normal self is necessary.

"You feel relief?"

"Yes, I do and I really appreciate you both coming over."

"Girl anytime, I'm just glad you finally did it."

"K, I'm glad I did it too!"

"Me too Sharee, you didn't need that in your life, I'm glad you ended that relationship," Mike added.

"Shit, things with us been over, I been feeling this way for a long while, he just wouldn't leave always thinking I wasn't serious. I had to show his ass how serious I was this time. I just couldn't take it anymore."

"You good boo?"

"Yeah, I am."

"Alright boo, well we're going to take off." Sharee gave both Katrina and Mike a hug bye.

After Katrina and Mike left Sharee walked to her bedroom and took off all the sheets and cover from off her bed and placed them inside her washing machine to wash it all. As the bedding was washing she went to the kitchen and put her some food in the oven, poured a glass of wine and sat alone. Although she didn't like the lonely part, Sharee was glad he was gone; she was now free of hurt and pain. She has now promised herself to not let another man hurt her again. After her laundry was all done she made up her bed, then it was time for bed to wake up early for work in the morning.

The next morning Sharee went into work smiling, feeling good and looking good. She barely got there and her cell was already ringing. Before looking at her cell she already knew it was probably one of her girls. Looking down at her screen it was Katrina.

"Hello!" Sharee answers.

"Hey lady, I know you're at work, but I was just calling to check on you, you were on my mind."

"I'm fine, thanks, girl!"

"Well, you don't sound fine, I hope you not at work feeling sad and shit, fuck him, he is not worth the energy in your thought."

"I know."

"I know the break up is fresh, and the way to get over that real quick is to go and fuck somebody else, go get you some new dick."

Sharee chuckled. "Katrina. Girl, you are crazy," she chuckled again.

"No, but for real, to get over that real quick you need to go fuck somebody else."

"I did. Didn't know years down the line we would be married and with a son, but you see how God works."

"That's what I was thinking too, I don't even go out, what am I supposed to do, go fuck some random person."

"Not saying that, but you need to get out, go have some fun and go live a little!" Katrina smiled. "Naw. I'm just talking, but just take this time to worry about you!"

"Yeah, that's what I was going to do, and that's what I stopped doing being with him is why I had to end it. Yeah, I'm about to take a break from men and relationships right now."

"Yeah, I feel you girl."

The next morning before going to work Sharee made her a pot of coffee Going into work she felt good, she even wore her hair down, something she had not done in a very long time. She figured she wouldn't think about yesterday and go forward from today.

Sharee's cell rung like every morning about this time, this was how close her and her girls were. Call each other every morning just to say good morning and have a good day.

It was Shante calling her. "Hello," Sharee says with a lot of excitement.

"Hey lady, you sound happy!"

"I am, I just got to work, I feel good now that he's gone."

"Good for you, I'm happy that you're happy."

"Thank you!"

"Hey, I was wondering when you get off work later, if you're not doing anything, if you want to come over, have a few drinks, play some cards and eat."

"Yeah, absolutely," Sharee said.

"Ok, cool, I called Katrina too and she's coming by too."

"Ok cool, I will see you later, when I get off I'll be right on over."

"Sounds good to me," Shante replied.

"Awesome," Sharee and Shante hung up.

Later that evening and getting off work Sharee called Shante.

"Hey Sharee," Shante answers her phone.

"Hey lady I'm just getting off work, I'm about to go change then I'll be right on over."

"Alright cool, see you in a minute."

Sharee wanted to stop by her house to change clothes. Getting home from work that evening as Sharee was pulling up to her house RoShawn was there sitting on her porch.

"Oh that's what you do, you just pop up over my house without calling?"

"I came to get some more of my stuff Sharee."

"You not coming up in here!" she yelled out her window from inside her car.

"Yes, I am."

"I just got off work and don't feel like being bothered with you, you better come on the weekend, like on Saturday morning and I would advise you to get all your shit this time."

"Sharee, let me get my shit, while I'm already here!"

"RoShawn, I'm not playing you're not coming up in here!"

Sharee got out her car and was walking right pass him, walking towards her front door.

"Oh, so you just not going to let me in, are you serious!"

"I wasn't playing; no I'm not letting you in!"

RoShawn left. Then Sharee went inside her house. Sharee changed her clothes and left, she was headed over to Shante's house. Getting there she knocked on her front door, as soon as she walked in the smell hit her nose. "Girl, it smells bomb in here, what did you cook?"

"Charles and I made lemon pepper chicken wings, fries, salad, and garlic toast."

"Umm, lemon pepper chicken, my favorite!"

"Right," Katrina chuckled.

"Girl, mines too!" Shante replied.

"That's why I came over here tonight. I came for her lemon pepper!" Katrina smiled. Shante turned her head and quickly looked at Katrina.

"Ain't that about something, you came for my chicken but not for me, for us!" she grinned.

Katrina was silent sitting there smiling, then she spoke, "Yeah, I came for y'all too," she chuckled.

Sharee sat down and told them who was at her house when she pulled up. Just saying his name got them started. All you heard throughout the living room was chatter about RoShawn, everyone was having something to say, that's his bad because he sure lost a good one. The night was fun hanging with the ladies.

The next day in the evening Katrina called Sharee. "Hey lady, I was just checking on you, how are you, how was your day?"

"Hey, lady thank you so much for asking, I'm alright but I just heard some terrible news about my Uncle."

"What happened?"

"He might have to get his legs cut off soon."

"Why?"

"He went to the hospital, and they found the gain green on his toe and it's spreading up his leg."

"Damn, for real, your Momma just told you."

"No, he just called and told me."

"Damn Sharee, I'm so sorry to hear that shit!"

"Then it's like knowing this, he's still smoking cigarettes every day, like *come* on uncle."

"So what if he stops smoking cigarettes today that will stop him from getting his legs cut off or something."

"I mean, but damn K he smokes literally a whole pack in one day and its twenty cigarettes in a pack and this is everyday."

"Damn, I'm still tripping on how he might have to get both his legs cut off though."

"He called not too long ago saying is my niece going to take care of me once my legs get cut off."

"What you say?"

"I told him I will do what I can, I'm just not wiping no ass, I'm sorry I can't clean nobody's shit!"

Katrina chuckled, "That's what Brandy does right now and her ass complains about it every single day. But being that it's your Uncle and not a stranger it may be different."

"Mmmm, I don't know!"

"Awww Uncle," Katrina sounded.

"I'm so mad about it because I don't want my Uncle to have to get his legs cut off."

"Man, I know, and isn't he diabetic too?"

"Yes girl, and that's what I'm saying, and the smoking a pack a day is contributing to his sickness."

"Yeah, cancer is nothing to play with and getting yourself checked out frequently is what you have to do because I use to stay on Gary's ass. Even though we were married and we didn't have anything of course, but I use to always tell him Baby go to the doctor and check out your health. That's how one day he ended up finding out about his cancer before it actually formed into Cancer all the way and was able to have surgery before it turned fully into it."

"Man, that is so true because a lot of men just don't get themselves checked out, it's always the women!"

"Yep," she sounded.

Saturday came and Sharee called RoShawn.

"Hello," he answered.

"What time are you coming to get your shit, it's already seven, I thought I told you to come this morning," were the only words she had for him.

"I will be there soon."

"What's soon RoShawn, I'm trying to start my day!"

"If you're not here before I plan to leave I can sit your shit outside in the front for you."

"No, I will be there, shit I was sleep, I can be there in two hours," he told her.

"I will sit all your stuff out in the front if you're not here in two hours; I'm not playing games with you today!"

"Sharee man, don't put my shit outside, you going to make me have to fuck you up if you do!"

"Well, do you want me to call the police then, so they can be of some assistance to me to make sure you don't try crazy shit?"

"No, you don't have to call the law, man just don't put my stuff outside please, I'm about to get up now and throw some clothes on, I will be there in a minute."

The two hung up. Sharee was still trying to deal with the situation still days later of him getting all his shit from out her house.

That Friday was pay day. Sharee and her coworkers couldn't wait to the check man got there with them checks. They sat around the job and talked about their raise was on there.

"I know I want to see if they put that raise on there!" is all Sharee kept saying.

"Talking about a fifty cent raise, I been here for six years, I should be getting more is all I'm saying," Sharee said to her coworker.

The three were planning to go out that night later after work, once the checks came. Something Sharee didn't do. She needed this, going out with her single co-workers. Checks came in right before they got off work. After work they went home, showered, and got dressed. They were picking Sharee up. Her coworkers Jennifer and Catherine called her once they pulled up to her house. "Hello," she answers.

"Hey Sharee, we're outside," Catherine said.

"Okay, here I come now."

Sharee grabbed her red purse and left out her door. "Hey girls," Sharee smiles as she gets into the car. Her voice got louder once she got inside and closed the car door. She was happy to be getting out the house tonight.

"Hey lady," Jennifer looked back and smiled at her.

"Yesss, we about to have some fun tonight!" Sharee said loudly.

"Yesss," Catherine shouts out. They pulled off. Driving there they talked the whole way. They made it to the club as Jennifer brought her car to a stop. They were surprised to have found a good parking spot.

Sharee and her coworkers walked and got in line. They stood in a long line to get inside; they couldn't wait to make it to the bar. As the three stood in line Sharee's phone began vibrating through her purse, she went in and reached for her phone out her purse. She looked down at her screen; she had no idea why he was even calling her phone. She didn't answer it. She shook her head and tossed it back down in her purse.

"Who is that?" Catherine and Jennifer both asked, then they both laughed.

Sharee took her phone back from out her purse, turned her phone around and showed Catherine and Jennifer. It was RoShawn, then she put her phone back in her purse. Moments later she heard a "ding" sound sounding from her purse, it was a text message she had received. After opening her text it was a message from RoShawn she reads from her mouth: *"Why are you showing them your phone?"*

The three of them turned around and looked around so fast.

"Ya'll see him?" Sharee asked.

"No," they said as they both continued scanning the parking lot.

Sharee didn't stop looking and scanning the parking lot quickly and slowly at the same time and didn't see him, then she began to scan all the black trucks to see if it was one that looks like his. Shortly she ended up seeing his truck to the far left side of the parking lot, she ended up texting him back to see what he wanted, since he had already seen her not answer his call.

After two texts back and forth with him, she didn't plan on letting him get to her at all; it was her night to have fun with her girls from work. Ever since he's been gone from the house, she has stayed on his mind.

Sharee and both her coworkers paid ten dollars to get in the club, the three walked to the bar and these handsome gentlemen they met walking to the bar just that quick offered to pay for all their drinks. They let them. Drinks were ordered, then they thanked them and found them a table to sit at.

"Jennifer, what's up with your girl missing work the other day?" Sharee asked.

"Right, with all the planning and buying all that food for our gathering," Catherine added.

"She was like I'm going to make sure this gathering turns out awesome," Jennifer said. Yeah, the registration department can't mess with the payroll department," she laughed.

"Yeah, I remember when she said that we were in the break room," Jennifer said.

"Yeah I know," Sharee replied.

"So why didn't she come?" Sharee looked at Jennifer. "I know it was a work thing, but damn, she was bringing the fried chicken, that was like the main dish," she chuckled.

"Girl, for real," Jennifer said. "I guess the dick was more important than coming to work that day," Jennifer said.

"Girl, she's a mess," Sharee said.

The three laughed and kept drinking their drinks.

Sharee's song had come on. She hopped off the chair, put her glass down, and pulled her coworkers out on the dance floor. She began dancing, singing to the song, and waving her hands up in the air.

"Ayeeee!" Catherine cheered her on pumping her up even more, not that she needed it. Then her co-workers began dancing too. After four songs dancing by themselves, the three began dancing from guy to guy. Shaking their asses, twirling around as the guys held their hands in the air. They were all smiling the whole time on the dance floor, they were just having fun, and so were the men they were dancing with. That early morning getting back to the house Sharee went inside and pulled off her shoes real quick. They were talking to her saying *Bitch take me off*.

That Saturday she slept in the bed all day, she didn't wake up until five that afternoon. The next morning she visited a different church that was a little closer to her house. After church service, Sharee had noticed an old time friend she used to work with.

"Hey Stephanie," Sharee shouted out smiling.

"Hey Sharee," then Sharee and Stephanie hugged each other. They're friends and haven't seen each other in years. They both still looked the same. "It is so good to see you!"

"It is so good to see you too," Sharee said. "You're looking cute, I am so loving the highlights, you went to the shop?" Sharee began rubbing Stephanie's long straight hair.

"Actually I did it myself yesterday."

"Girl, I didn't do anything on Saturday, my coworkers and I went out Friday night and I woke up yesterday morning with a hangover and stayed my butt in the bed and slept all day," she leaned towards her and whispered.

"You're so crazy, I woke up with one too, but it was not that bad," she whispered back, then they laughed.

"Did you use foils?"

"Yes girl, I took out the sections that I needed, I put the foil on my hair, I applied the bleach on top then I folded the foil in half."

"That's right; you did a good job Steph."

"I have been going to the shop and getting it done, but going every month was getting expensive so this time I decided to do it myself, I'm like I can do this myself."

"Okay, right, save wherever you can, especially if you can do it yourself."

"Hey, give me your number Sharee, we have to hang out and do lunch!"

"I know right!" the two exchanged numbers.

The next day at work Sharee couldn't wait to see her girls too let them know how much of a good time she had with them on Friday. She approached Catherine's cubicle first. "Good morning Cat!"

"Hey, good morning Sharee," she smiles at her, then they hugged. "Girl, we had way too much fun on Friday," Catherine smiled.

"I know right, we must go out again soon," Sharee said.

"Yes, we needed that, I'm down, you just let me know when and I'm down," Catherine replied.

"Okay, sounds like a plan to me," she smiled. "Alright lady, I'll see you at break."

"Okay," Catherine replied.

"Alright," Sharee said, then she walked on and walked past Jennifer's cubicle.

"Hey chica," Sharee sounded to Jennifer.

"Hey Sharee," Jennifer replied. They quickly hugged. "See you at break lady!"

"Okay girl," then Sharee went straight to her cubicle.

They all are working in another department today. At the break the three hooked up, "Hey what are you ladies doing later?" Sharee asked them.

"Later when, " Jennifer says.

"Like later after work," Sharee sounded.

"I hope this concerns some type of food," Catherine said.

Sharee chuckled. "Yes, it does. I wanted to know if after work y'all want to go out for food and drinks?"

Out of nowhere, the drizzle came, rushing to get inside the restaurant they didn't want to get their hair wet. The waiter walked them to a table, there was no wait. They pulled out their chairs to sit. They scanned the menu that they were just given. Minutes after Catherine waved down the waiter so they could order. They ordered their food and talked as they waited. It didn't take too long before their food made it to their table. As they began to eat they began wondering if the drizzle was going to stop or would it pick up heavier. Sharee was mad that her pressed hair was about to look like shit and she'd just gotten it done days ago. After dinner, about to leave the restaurant and noticed the drizzle picked up, it was raining a little bit harder.

"Oh wow, it's coming down," Catherine and Sharee looking at the rain coming down through the window.

"I know and I don't have a jacket or umbrella," Jennifer said. They walked fast to the car and left driving out the parking lot.

The next day Sharee had met someone. He was kind to her and then he asked her for her number, and then he gave her his too. He made sure he called her that same night. They talked for hours, and he made sure by the end of their conversation he asked her out. Two days later Sharee went out on a date for the first time since her break up. As the two were driving through this crazy traffic he received a text message, he looked down and it was RoShawn.

"Are you guys still out on your date?"

"Yeah, we went to that restaurant you told me to take her too." HE HAD TEXT BACK.

"I know, I saw you, now where you headed too?"

"Let me see now." He texted back.

Bobby looked over at Sharee, then he glanced back on the road, "So now what Ms. Lady, what would you like to do next?"

"Well, since it's starting to rain I guess I'll call it a night and go home."

"You want to go home already?"

"Yeah, I had a good time so far, but I'll go home now."

As he listened to her talk he was texting RoShawn back at the same time.

"Man she wants to go home." He texted him.

"Naw man, not yet, man try and take her out to one more place."

Bobby sat his cell phone down on his lap and took a deep breath. He glanced over at Sharee smiling, "You sure Sharee because I don't want to end it right now."

She turned her head looking at him. Then he repeated himself. She wasn't trying to be mean, so she told him they could go for coffee. Afterward he took her home. He pulled up to her house slowly.

"Do you need me to walk you to the door?"

"Oh no, I'm fine you don't have too."

They said bye, then she closed his door and then was headed to her front door. As soon as she entered her home, she heard a deep voice say, "It's been thirty days and twenty-one hours since we broke up, baby I miss you and I'm sorry, do you think you can forgive me and take me back?" Sharee turned her head around quickly to see who it was.

"Oh my god, what the fuck," she blurted nervously. Sharee's heart was racing even more once she saw it was RoShawn. He was standing there in the center of her living room looking at her.

"Why in the fuck are you here RoShawn?"

"I miss you, I need you back!"

"Man, get the fuck out of here!"

Going back to RoShawn was not about to happen at all, she didn't have shit to say to him at all, she stood there and said nothing to him, she was just standing there looking good as always in her tight jeans. Sharee would have liked to know how in the hell he got in, but then to ask that question she would have to entertain a conversation about what she was not about to do. If she would have known walking up in her house was not going to be safe, she would have had Bobby walk her to her door until she got in all the way, and having the flower and rose petals all around the house the way that he did was not going to make her go back either.

"Sharee, I can't continue on with life without you."

She still stood there not saying anything at all.

"Sharee, I need you to tell me that you will take me back!"

She still wasn't responding.

"You're just going to stand there and not say anything?"

Her mind was telling her to say something so he could leave and get the hell out. Moments later she decided to say something.

"You want me to say something?"

"Yes, babe."

"I'm going to continue living my life without you in it."

"So you saying it can't be us again?" he asked her.

"No, not at all!"

"I think if we try we can make it work again."

"RoShawn, leave out my house right now and don't come back."

The feeling of him knowing she was probably going to take him back just went out the door. He walked up closer to her.

"Can I have a hug?"

"No, I want you to leave!" she said in a loud voice.

"Can I at least have a hug, damn?"

"No!"

"Baby, but I miss you, I need you and I can't do it without you," he told her as he cried.

"So you should have thought of that when we were together."

The look he had as he stared at her with tears rolling down his face was heartbreaking, it looked like he was very unhappy with what she was saying and very hurt, but she had to do this for herself, she was tired of being the one suffering and unhappy.

"Get out my house RoShawn, you have to go!"

He ran over to her like he was about to do something, she didn't know what he had going on or what he was thinking. "RoShawn, if you don't leave right now and I mean exactly right now, I'm calling the police!"

"Well since you don't want me here I'll guess I'll leave."

RoShawn then left through her front door.

CHAPTER
11

Asia and Gary

Asia called Katrina to see if she could stop by. Of course, Katrina said yes, she felt, by all means, this woman is also always around *my* daughter, she wanted to know what was going on, she cared about what she had to say.

Once Asia made it, Katrina went down to let her in the gate and she got in the car with Asia and rode with her back up to the house. Getting inside Katrina first offered her a bottle of water, then the two sat in the living room to chat.

"So what's going on?" Katrina asked.

"Well, it's about Gary."

"Gary?"

"Yeah," Asia sounded.

Katrina chuckled, she couldn't even hold in her chuckle, and then she had a smirk on her face. Asia looked at her with her smirk but she didn't see anything funny. Katrina sat back to listen. She nodded her head upward saying *what's up* as she looked at Asia.

"Okay, what's going on?" she said again just seconds later.

"I've been having problems with him in his lying, I think he has been cheating. I mean, he shows good intentions in being a good husband, but like damn, I shouldn't be having these thoughts."

Katrina sat there staring at Asia like she was looking in a mirror at herself. She too *has* been in those same shoes with Gary's ass.

"Do you want me to respond or just listen?" Katrina asked her.

"Of course respond, I didn't drive way over here for you to just listen," Although Asia didn't go over there to pour out every single detail of this Paula woman, and the son. Asia kept it short and simple just to get a piece of advice on how she dealt with it.

"Okay for starters, you to hooked up too fast, got married way too fast, it didn't bother you that he was just with someone else like a month before you?"

"It did, but when I asked about it, he said it was mainly about sex, he really didn't love her."

Katrina shook her head, "Yeah, and he might have used you as a rebound to get over the last chick or just so he doesn't have to be by himself."

"Huh, yeah you may be right."

"I know I'm right."

"I don't think he is actually cheating right now but I feel he has since we've been together, I been trying to pay attention to watch for signs, I just don't want to be back happy again thinking everything is cool and it's not."

"But shit, I should have known something was up when he stopped asking for sex like he was when we were married, shit he wasn't asking because he was getting it from my sister."

"So, how did you handle that and then still ended up back with him?" Asia asks.

"You know I was hurt, I didn't handle it well at first, but I prayed about it and I kept myself busy with work and kept my focus on our daughter but when I got back with him that was my idea, and then when we divorced, that was also my idea as well. I just thought my heart would love and trust him again, but it didn't, I just couldn't keep giving him me, he didn't deserve me anymore. What he and my sister did was the only thing that kept popping up in my mind every single day that I looked at him, I just couldn't do it. I'm sorry I couldn't even do it for my daughter. It was best that I left him. I prayed about it and eventually just moved on for good. Now I'm not telling you to leave him, or divorce him. By all means, you love him and think he'll change for you, shit I don't know, he just might. His ass should be tired by now of getting in and out of relationships and marriages."

"The fact that we are married, we should not be going through some of the stuff we go through, and I definitely shouldn't be feeling how I feel sometimes already."

"My advice to you is to pray about it and hang in there, but don't be afraid to talk to him about anything you're not feeling, who cares if he gets mad or feels like something, at the end of the day, that's your heart."

"Thank you, Katrina, so much for this talk."

"You're welcome Asia, so have you guys talked?"

"Well, we talked, but our last argument was just a few days ago."

"Oh, ok, well don't settle for his arguments, make him talk to you like he has some damn sense, you are a beautiful woman and it will not be hard for you to find you a man."

Asia chuckled. Asia stood up from off the couch, "Thanks again Katrina for this."

"Girl, no worries." Katrina walked her to her front door. Asia left.

She went back home not in the best mood at all. She had a lot to consider, the fact that he had cheated, kept it a secret, and then lied about it, and then told the truth after finding out. Having a new business she needed to be focused without any drama going on in her personal life, then her losing the baby behind stressing over him. Although he seems to be good now, she just hopes he really is, because for whatever the reason, she kept thinking about Paula. She went in looking for Duke; she walked all around the house looking for Duke, but still, couldn't find him.

"Gary, where is Duke!" she yelled asking him

"I let him go outside and run around in the backyard," he told her.

Asia went and sat on the couch in thought, as she sat there thinking, just thinking back, she was beginning to think he really didn't care or love her for real, she was starting to wish she would have never married him, or at least so quickly.

After Gary was done being on the computer, which he had been for the past hour, he went to the livingroom to sit next to Asia.

"Hey baby," he rubbed his hand on her thigh looking into her eyes.

"Hey babe, can I ask you a question?" she talked in a light sweet tone.

His head tilted back leaning on her arm, "Yeah what's up?"

"If you loved your wife, why did you sleep with her sister, like you say you love me, but you already had sex with someone else, your ex."

"Asia, why are you bringing this shit up?" he asked.

"Well, that's where I just came from; I had wanted to ask her some questions about you."

He sat up, "Why were you over there anyway asking her questions about me, if you want to know anything about me, just ask me, not my ex-wife. If you want the true facts, she's going to tell you only what she wants you to know."

They were sitting there going back and forth. But then she yelled out of nowhere. Gary's eyes widened, damn he wondered where in the hell did this just come from when she was just talking mad but regular as hell at first. She was still yelling out stuff. He continued to look at her. Her tone was not fake at all. She brought that out deep from within, but that was her way to get him to say what she wanted him to say. She got upset from his comment, like what she was mad or concerned about really didn't matter.

Gary didn't even want to talk anymore while she was yelling, he shook his head from side to side, and then he stood up and walked to the room and closed the door.

"Gary, are you going to go outside and look for Duke or what, he would have come in the house by now!" she shouted.

Gary came back out the room, left out the door to go and look for Duke. He went out there looking everywhere and he still didn't see him. He got in his car to see if maybe he could find him. He ended up driving out to the main street to see if his little ass was wondering the streets or something. Gary made it half way up the street and noticed Duke laid out in the street dead. He immediately pulled over and called Asia. Asia cried instantly, she was so hurt behind the news of her dog. Gary pulled off and busted an u-turn and went back home pissed.

"So you want to get another dog?" he asked her.

"That's not going to bring Duke back Gary."

"I was thinking that our next dog should be a blue nose pit, my boy has five of them right now."

"Gary!"

"I know baby, but I know how you love dogs and I was just thinking of getting another one for you."

"Goodnight," she lay down early, they went to bed mad.

The next morning Asia went to work. Leaving home Asia was still upset about Duke. After work, she didn't make any stops, she went straight home.

"How was business today?"

"It was good."

"Just good," he paused.

"Yeah, just good," she replied.

"Shit, normally Asia you have way more to say than that, don't tell me you're still mad."

"Yes, I am!"

An hour after getting home and her sisters called. "Hello," she answered.

"Sis, you okay, how are you doing, we were calling to check on you."

"Even from out of state you guys know just when to call, but I'm alright, I could be better though."

"He still is doing stupid shit?"

"I really don't want to talk about it right now."

"Asia!" Myisha said loudly through the phone.

"Duke got ran over."

"Oh sis, nooo, I'm so sorry to hear, what happened?"

"Gary let him outside in the back yard, and his ass got out to the front and he went on that main street and got hit."

"Awww Asia, I'm so sorry."

"I'll be okay sis."

"Well, make sure you call us if you need us, and we will be right there in a heartbeat."

"Okay,, I love you guys."

"Love you more Asia."

"Okay, bye."

"Bye," They hung up with each other.

When she settled down from work is when he went to go talk to her.

"Baby, sit down." They both sat in the kitchen at the dining room table.

"Baby, check it out, it was easy for me to get right back into another relationship because I wasn't in love with her."

"How were you in a full blown relationship with someone, tell them you love them *probably,* but really don't, it just doesn't make any sense to me?"

"I don't know, but I was and I did not love her."

"How do I know the shit you were telling me was some real shit or some bullshit?"

"Because it was some real shit," he told her.

"Man, I'm not about to be tolerating this lying and shit!"

"Babe, I'm not and I promise you that you don't have to worry about that no more and whatever I have to do to keep proving to you I will and thank you for not making things easy for me when I fucked up, and me proving to you that I am worth you staying with me has been worth every bit. It has made me grow up for real, it made me think about my actions before just doing and most importantly it made me think about how I don't want to lose the best thing God brought to me. I love you, baby."

He didn't have a choice but to deal with it when he did; she had to give him tough love for a minute.

"I love you too."

If only she knew if he's telling the truth, but if the shoe was on the other foot she would at least want a second chance too. Since Gary has been proving to her she is going to continue to let him. Her feelings were still up and down and she was still mad about it, but he was happy. She finally agreed to put it behind them, for the most part, they were trying to hold on to their marriage.

The next day Gary showed up to the boutique with flowers for Asia. They were so lovely she was receiving a lot of compliments. He sat around until she closed, then they left and followed each other home.

The next day he showed up in the middle of the day, he didn't have any clients, he had a light day, so he stopped by the Boutique wanting to buy

Asia and her staff lunch. Asia was busy with customers so he waited for her by the counter until she was done. From across the store, she looked back at him, raised her eye brow, and waved at him. After she was done helping her customer find some clothes she walked her customer to the counter and charged the customer for her items. Asia's customer left. Asia smiled and walked from behind the counter to Gary.

"Hey, baby."

"Hey," they kissed on the lips.

"How was your morning?"

"Steady."

"That's right."

"What's going on with you, you're here early today?"

"Yeah, I had a light day. I didn't have any clients this afternoon, so I decided to stop by here and I wanted to see if y'all have had lunch, I wanted to buy you and your staff lunch."

"Aww, look at you treating everybody today."

Gary smiled looking into her eyes.

"What are you buying?"

"What is it that you all have a taste for?"

Asia told her staff that her husband is about to buy lunch for everyone. After seeing what they had a taste for, it was decided that they all wanted barbecue. He then took everyones orders, then Gary left to buy the food.

Shortly Gary came back in with two plastic bags with the barbecue.

"Thank you, Gary, for lunch," Mellissa shouted out.

"You're welcome Mellissa," he shouted back out to her and smiled.

"Awww, thank you so much for lunch Gary," Pamela said.

"I know right, this is so sweet of you," Yolanda said.

"Thanks, Gary," Star and Jadah smiled as they both looked at the food. Even though Asia knew why every day he was doing something different, to try and prove himself to her, it was the fact he was willing to work at it for her and that's what she appreciates. Gary had ordered himself something too and sat there with the ladies and ate his food too. After he was done he took all the trash and put it in the trash.

"Do y'all need anything else?" he asked.

"Oh no, that was bomb," they all told him.

Gary stepped to Asia giving her a hug and a kiss.

"Babe, I'm about to walk through the mall, I'll be back."

"Alright," she told him.

Every day since a few days ago Gary began to spend his evenings after work up at the Boutique. It was unusual for her to have her husband sitting up at her store every day, but it was cool. As weeks passed she was becoming better and so was her heart. It was good he came up there because this is what they both needed.

After a long week of just work, he decided just him and Asia needed to go out on a date. He thought *what they haven't done so far* and *Bowling* popped up in his head. That Saturday Gary and Asia went to the Bowling Alley, as soon as they got there they ordered a pitcher of beer, then they looked at the menu board to see what food they're about to order. Their eyes scanned everything real quick. Asia pointed at the double cheese burger. Gary looked at her.

"You want that?" he asked her.

"Yes," she shook her head up and down. Then Gary had ordered two double cheese burgers and some fries that they were about to share. Their order didn't take long to make, it was done in three minutes, they expected it to take longer. They sat down, and she moved her chair closer to his and they talked. They ate and drank their beer first, before even starting their first game. Gary expressed to her how after being up at her store these past few weeks he was so proud of her, how she is running things, and how this being her first business she is doing a great job. She smiled at his comments to her.

"Thank you, Gary, I really appreciate that."

"Also, for you mister I see you've been doing a lot of proving yourself these last few weeks and I appreciate it, that shows me you really do care because you had me thinking that you didn't at first."

"I'm so sorry babe."

"I know it now."

They kissed. When they kissed they both felt the passion and they both stared into each other's eyes.

"I love you, Asia!"

"I love you too Gary!"

Then they finished up there food. After taking their last bite they were about ready to play. They took off their shoes and put on the other shoes.

"Now, that was delicious," Asia said.

"I know, it was huh, that hit the spot." Once the game started they started competing against each other trying to see who was going to have the highest score. Gary ordered them another pitcher of beer. Asia wasn't really a drinker like that to take down another pitcher of beer with him, but hey, what the hell. The waiter brought over their beer and the two poured their glasses full. Asia shortly began to feel herself acting a little crazy, but she didn't care, she was enjoying herself with her husband. They were really enjoying themselves. Although Gary was winning because he had the highest score towards the end he began to play around with the ball getting gutter balls so that his wife could win. She was drunk and didn't even notice, but when she found out she won against him she was happy and that's all he wanted anyway.

Even though she's been hurt really bad by his past actions, his sweetness is why she had fallen in love with him in the first place. She misses the fun they use to have and enjoy the fun they're have now. Although in all her old relationships before him, she used to run them, for whatever the reason was for him to be in control now that she thought about or even wanted to, she just wanted to try something different this time, since whatever she had been doing really wasn't working.

After they were done playing, they left and went home. It didn't take them long getting home and walking inside Asia walked in taking off her shoes. She walked straight to their room. Gary walked to the kitchen and grabbed the both of them a bottle of water from out the refrigerator. He then walked to the room and passed Asia a bottle of water.

"Thanks, babe."

"You're welcome babe."

It's been a while since she has wanted to be intimate with him. The feeling of wanting it now has returned. Telling him what she was feeling and what she wanted he began smiling showing all his teeth, then he took a sip of his water. She couldn't do anything but laugh. Asia got up from off the bed and connected her cell phone to the speakers that were sitting on their dresser, she turned on her Pandora to the R & B station, then she got back in bed. He grabbed her by her arms pulling her close to him; they both hugged each other as they looked into each other's eyes. They undressed and Asia got on top of him, she was making sure she gets hers first tonight. How she was kind of feeling, she only cared about her tonight. As she's on top riding him going up and down on him, he began sucking her nipples as he massages her breast. Then next he moved his hands down to her butt and began massaging her butt inward in a circular motion. She leaned down forward giving him a kiss, but then he pushed his tongue into her mouth giving her a tongue kiss. After thirty minutes into it, she felt herself about to climax. Asia began moaning.

"Ahh, Ahh, Ahh."

She began riding him faster he held on to her waist helping her with her speed, making his dick go up in her even deeper. They switched positions, she turned over and he went in from behind. His speed was fast and continuous up until he had cum. He wished they could have sex all night long, but unfortunately they both have work in the morning. Afterward, they both took big gulps of their water until it was all gone, then they both made their way to the shower. They took a shower together scrubbing each other's body. Then after they were done they got out the shower, dried off. Asia put on one of his gray t-shirts and he threw on some pajama pants," his blue and black plaid ones. Asia went and unplugged her cell phone from the speaker and walked towards the bed sitting her phone closer to her on the little dresser on her side of the bed, then they went to sleep. Waking up the next morning Gary and Asia were getting ready to start their day.

"I love you, Asia!"

"I Love you too Gary!"

They hugged each other tightly. Asia felt good she glad she stopped letting the bullshit and drama consume her mind, she had a business to run and a new marriage to be happy in.

"See you later babe, you have a good day today at work," she told him.

"You too sweetie," they kissed on their way out leaving for work.

They left the house and were headed for work.

***

Charlie walked in Asia's store for the first time; he couldn't help but see her beauty and all those curves. Asia noticed a guy walking around her store that kept glancing up at her smiling; she was trying to figure out if she knew him for him to keep looking at her smiling. Asia was just trying to stay focused on all the customers walking around in her store which was her only focus. Once the gentleman was done shopping he walked up to her counter, he held out his hand as he introduced himself to her as Charlie as he smiled.

Asia shook the nice gentleman's hand and introduces herself as Asia, the store owner as she smiled back into Charlie's eyes.

"You are so beautiful!"

"Thank you so much," she told him with a smile.

"What's your nationality, are you Dominican Republican?"

"No, I do get that a lot, but I'm actually mixed with Black and Jew."

"Oh, okay, that's a pretty mix."

"Thank you so much." She stood there smiling, but wondering did he need anything else, but she didn't want to be rude at all.

"I see you're married," he said.

"Yes I am," she said with a smile.

"But are you happily married," he asked her.

"I'm married."

Charlie chuckled.

"Are you married?" she asks him the question now.

"No, I'm not married and I don't have a woman I could take care of."

"Take care of."

"Yes, I love taking care of my woman, well when I had one."

"That's what you're supposed to do when you have one!"

"Are you going to let me take care of you?" he asked her.

"I'm married I told you," she smiles.

"How about we could take care of each other," he said. "Let me have some of that receipt paper."

Asia ripped Charlie a piece of receipt paper and handed it to him.

"Thanks, let me see that pen."

She passed him the pen.

Charlie wrote down his number and gave it to Asia. Asia didn't take this guy seriously, she was not about to keep his number, she was about to throw it away into the trash, once he turns around to head for the door. Charlie left the store without her number, just the bags in his hand with the clothes he just bought, that didn't bother him, him not getting her number; he felt their small conversation was interesting enough to make her interested. He felt like she just may use the number soon. A few days later Charlie showed up at Asia's business to talk to her, but she wasn't there, so he asked one of her staff for her number. It was Pamela who had helped him and gave him her cell number. He thanked her and asked her, her name. Pamela, she told him, and then Charlie thanked her again, but this time saying her name. After him leaving her job he walked to his car. After getting inside his car he began to dial her number, but then he ended the call after only pressing five numbers he wanted to give her at least one more day to see if she was going to use his number and call him. The next day came and she still had not called him. So he decided to contact her.

"Hello," she said slowly to an unrecognized number.

"Hello beautiful, how are you doing today."

"Hello who is this?" she asked.

"Wow, you already forgot about me I see!"

"What, who is this!" she asked again.

"It's me, Charlie," the guy you met at your store a few days ago.

"So, how did you even get my number?"

"Oh, your employee with the teal colored hair gave it to me."

"Oh yeah, she did huh."

"I'm sorry did I call you at a bad time."

"Yes, you did!"

"Oh, well I can call you back at a different time."

"Yes, you do that."

Asia immediately hung up with him and immediately dialed her store number. She was hot as hell.

"Hey Asia," Pamela answered. Looking at the caller ID she saw it was her boss.

"Pamela, why did you give a customer my number," Asia asked.

"Oh, because he stated he needed to talk to you."

"But Pamela, you don't give anyone my personal number, you could have given him the store number."

"My bad Asia, I'm so sorry, he made it seem like he knew you."

"How is that?"

"Because when he came in he said your name."

"Because he said my name, but that doesn't mean he knows me just because he said my name, I can't believe this. Just don't let that happen again, Pamela!"

"Alright Boss, I won't, I'm sorry once again!"

"Asia hung up."

"Pamela, what happened, why was Asia tripping on you like that?" Jadah asked.

"Oh, because I gave a customer that came in here yesterday her number," she told them.

Yolanda looked over at her, "What, her cell phone?" Yolanda asked.

"Yes, I know I probably shouldn't have done that, that was my bad."

"Yeah, it was." Yolanda shook her head from side to side.

A week later Charlie visited her unannounced at the boutique, her employees were standing where they were looking at him as he came in with flowers for her.

He looked around at everyone smiling.

"Hey ladies," Charlie sounded loudly.

"Hello," they all said back to him smiling.

Twenty minutes later Brandy walked in Asia's Boutique with Paige. She saw a guy that looked like Charlie from the back there at the counter chatting with Asia. She wondered was it him, as she got closer she sees that it was him, and she wanted to know what in the hell is he even doing there.

"Charlie?" he turned around at the sound of Brandy calling out his name. *"Aww shit,"* he mumbled under his breath, he shook his head from side to side. He knew she was about to start tripping out on him in this store, he just looked at her.

"Hey Asia," then she glanced back at Charlie as she was approaching the counter, then her eyes went back to Asia.

"Hey Brandy, Hey Ms. Paige!"

"Umm Asia, how you know Charlie?" she pointed in his direction.

Paige walked up to her step mother and gave her a hug. "Hey sweetie," Asia said to Paige as she hugged her. Then her conversation was back with Brandy.

"Oh, you two know each other?" looking at the both of them, the last thing Brandy felt like being was friendly, especially to his ass, but she wanted to give Asia some respect at her store. If she would have followed her instincts she would have been going off on his ass. Thank God she thought about it first.

Charlie stood there in a hell of a shock. Brandy is who he would have never thought he would run into up there. He stood there contemplating if he should say anything to her since it has been three months now since he last heard from her. But it would be his luck that her boyfriend would walk in next. He thought he'd just leave now while it's still safe, he didn't need any more problems with her, because that last situation she put him in wasn't cool at all.

"What the fuck are you doing here?" Brandy's voice rose loudly to Charlie.

"Wait, hold up, this is my store and it's customers up in here," Asia whispered, trying not to be loud and make a scene as they are.

"Asia, you know him?" Brandy said with her firm voice.

Charlie just walked away before anything escalated.

After work, Asia went home. Going in through the kitchen she sees all this food Gary had cooked and candles lit on the kitchen table with two plates and champagne glasses, she looked around the kitchen to see if she saw anything else but that was it.

"Gary, I'm home!" she yelled out to him.

"Come upstairs!" he yelled out.

Asia shook her head and smiled. She walked upstairs. There were rose petals leading down the hallway to their room, as she continued smiling she continued walking. Asia walked in the room and Gary was sitting on the edge of the bed naked. She immediately stopped and smiled and shook her head. He smiled. He was teasing to her eyes which made her instantly moist down there.

"Hey baby," he smiles.

"Hey," she says soft and seductive.

"Take your clothes off."

Asia walked up to him and kissed him. He began to unbutton and pull off her clothes. He grabbed her hands pulling her closer to him, he wanted to suck on her breast. He wiggled her breast with both his hands in his face as he pecked her nipples with his mouth and tongue, after a few minutes he slid his arm around her waist pulling her down onto the bed next to him. He kissed inside her mouth with urgency with his tongue, like she liked it suddenly they went back slowly until the both were flat on the bed, after their long and passionate kiss he pulled himself up and went down in between her thighs.

"Let me scoot back some more," she sounded softly.

Gary sucked her until he tasted her cum in his mouth. Then he went in her strong and steady. As he's going in he began sucking her breast into his mouth as his hip area moves fast inside her and out her. She held on to his back as she took in all of him. No words, just moans were coming out her mouth. On top of her his speed kept going faster, then the position was switched she rode him. He held a grip onto her butt massaging it inward as he grinded with her. The warmth he felt up in her had him speechless no talking, no moans, just full on concentration as she's giving him the best of her. Asia was pleasing him with her body, for a long while she was on top, then the position was switched back, he felt her hips moving up and down towards him keeping up to his pace. Then suddenly his body began shaking, he exploded inside her, once his body stopped, he felt hers, he thought it was only his body shaking for a moment. They just laid there for a moment, then they walked downstairs and ate the food he cooked. Talking telling each other about their day, eating, sipping on some champagne. It was very romantic what he did.

CHAPTER
12

Mike and Katrina

Katrina woke up while Mike was still asleep. The kids were still asleep, she wanted to get her six o' clock walk on at the park. Katrina put on her leggings and her t-shirt, left out the room, locked her front door, and then drove to the park. The park was empty, it was just her. She got out the car and walked the trail. Getting back home Katrina was leaving out again, but this time to go get her hair done. After getting her hair done and returning home she came back with some food.

"You look good."

"Thanks, babe."

"Yeah, she did a good job."

Katrina smiled as she looked in the mirror at herself.

"What's that in the bag?"

"I bought some Chinese food!"

They ate, then they both had laid back on the bed watching TV. They just chilled the remainder of the day.

It's two in the morning. "Babe, it's time to wake up, our flight is leaving in three hours," all he wanted to do was sleep at least for one more hour.

"Baby get up, you can sleep on the plane!"

Mike grabbed his pillow and placed it over his head. Katrina stood over him laughing, but she wasn't moving. She grabbed his pillow off his head.

"Baby, get up!"

"Okay."

Mike got out the bed and began getting his self together. Both their suit cases and their bags were packed. Katrina was already ready. An hour later she glanced down at her phone looking at the time.

"Okay baby, we need to leave!"

"Alright," Mike said.

"You sure you got everything?"

"Yeah," Mike said.

"Okay, let's head out."

"Let's head out."

Katrina and the kids went and got in the car, their Uber driver was out front waiting already. As Mike checked the house making sure everything was locked, closed and all the lights were off. He left setting their house alarm. They left heading to the airport. They talked to their Uber driver the whole drive to their airport.

Landing in Atlanta Katrina was already grinning, she loved it there. They went and got their things. Leaving the Airport they went and checked into their hotel and as soon as they got there, the first thing they all did was quickly walk around their suite glancing around checking things out, it was really nice as always. Moments later after checking out their suite and putting their luggage into the closet, Katrina had called their friend Andrea, Mike Jr.'s god-mother.

"Hey, girl I'm out here!"

"Hey!"

"Righttt, what are you doing?"

"Nothing," Andrea replied.

"Well, can you meet me in an hour at the Restaurant, we need to catch up, talk, and have a drink?"

"I can't wait to see you!"

"Me neither, well I'll see you in an hour!"

"Okay, see you in an hour."

"Alright, bye," she said.

"Bye." They hung up the phone.

"Babe, what if our Uber driver left, you think he's still down there waiting?"

"He should be, I told him to give us twenty minutes."

"Oh, ok, well I hope he's still down there."

They were all ready now, they hadn't been in Atlanta yet for a full hour and they were already about to hit the streets. Mike heads to the door and opens the door, Katrina walked out first followed by Simone and Mike Jr. They were back down there in fifteen minutes. Getting to the restaurant Andrea was already there waiting to see them.

Katrina smiled. "Mike Jr, go and give your godmommy Andrea a hug,"

Andrea smiled. "Katrina, look at him, he has gotten so big." Mike Jr. ran up to Andrea and jumped in her arms to give her a hug.

"So, how is everything Katrina?"

"Everything has been going good, work is good, and family is good."

"How about you boo, how is Atlanta treating you and the new job? It's been a little minute since I last seen you, I miss you boo."

"Awww, I miss you too boo!"

"Yeah, I love it here, Atlanta has been treating me good, the new job is great, but you know I have also been thinking about starting a little business," she told Katrina.

"Oh yeah, that's right, what type of business because I was just thinking about the same thing?"

"I'm not really sure."

"I was thinking about the same thing lately, that's crazy, but what type of business?" Katrina asked her.

"Mmmmm, I was thinking about starting my own waist trainer business. What do you think about waist trainers, you think I'll do good in that type of business?"

"I think you will do good Andrea, everybody wants to get their waist smaller."

"You're right."

Katrina began to notice it was looking like one of the employees had eyes for her husband. She sat back and peeped things out before she gets up to address it. Listening to Andrea, but watching her husband and the employee over there.

"I'll be back," she told Andrea.

Katrina went up to the employee and pulled her to the side.

Angela felt bad, she didn't notice her staring at Mike was noticeable, she couldn't believe his wife caught that. Katrina began telling the girl off, but she kept it professional. Andrea's eyes grew bigger with her surprised expression on her face, she wondered did she know. Andrea was sitting back at the table looking at Katrina's head move from side to side with her long hair swinging as well, wondering what the hell happened so fast. Afterward Katrina had walked back over to her table. Angela couldn't believe she was just approached by the head boss's wife, she hopes this doesn't cost her, her job.

"Girl, what the fuck happened?" Andrea asked as Katrina was sitting back down.

Katrina laughed. Then Andrea laughed. "When I looked over there and saw your head moving from side to side I was wondering what done happened now, shit it was no need for me going over there, I was like my girl got whatever it was shit, it didn't look like the girl was saying too much back."

"No, she wasn't."

As Andrea sat there listening to Katrina it was obvious she didn't know yet, *but I'm going to keep my mouth closed. I want to say something, but then Mike would be so mad.* They continued their lunch, then they hung out for a little while. Katrina took the kids with her. They stayed gone for two hours. After returning back to the restaurant Andrea hugged them all.

"Girl, let's go shopping tomorrow," Andrea said.

"Hell yeah, we can."

"Oh, did that new store open yet in the Mall?" Katrina asked.

"Oh yes, girl it did."

"Yeah, I need some new boots."

"Yeah me too," Andrea said.

"Hell yeah," Katrina sounded again just thinking about her boots.

"Okay, we can hit them up first, then we have to hit up this other store up in there, they just got a new shipment in yesterday and I need to see what new dresses they have."

"You, me too," Katrina said with much excitement.

Knowing the shipment dates to certain stores was what they did. The next day they went shopping, as they were shopping they had many conversations and during their conversation, it was good to hear that her girl Andrea found her a good man, because the last time she was down there she acted like it was hard to find a man.

The next day Katrina woke up early to iron Mikes, hers, Simone's and Mike Jr's, clothes while they were all still asleep. He had a few meetings to attend too, but afterward, they all planned to hang out to do some family things. Afterward, they did some family things together they had a blast.

The next morning Katrina woke up and dialed Andrea.

"Hello!"

"Hey lady, you up, you getting ready?" Katrina asked Andrea.

"Yeah, I'm up, about to take a shower and get dressed."

"Alright, see you in a minute."

"Alright," Andrea said. Then they hung up.

That morning Andrea got out of bed to Katrina's call, she stepped out of bed and looked at the clock, it had barely turned ten thirty. She went and showered. After she was done and out the shower, she walked out the bathroom with only her bra and panties on. Andrea went to her closet to see what she was about to wear. She was about to hook up with Katrina soon. Phillip, Andrea's man was waking up himself. She turned around to look at him.

"Good morning Babe!"

"Good morning babe, you're leaving," Phillip asked.

"Yeah, in a little while, remember babe I told you my girl and godson's mom is out here, who I had lunch with a few days ago. The same one I went shopping with the other day and who was out here from Cali and that we were going shopping again today," she then turned back around facing her closet.

"Oh yeah, my bad, I forgot, you did tell me that."

"Yeah, and my godson has got so big he's running now, I miss him."

"Babe, so what, are you going to be gone all day again today? he asked.

"No, we're just going shopping. We're only going to two stores, then we're going to go for lunch, then I'll be right back home."

"Okay."

"Baby, come here!"

"Alright, give me a minute babe, let me find something to wear really quick."

He got up from the bed and walked up to her from behind. He wrapped his arms around her waist standing really close to her from behind making his chest rub against her back as he kisses the back of her earlobe. He began stumbling backward with her in his arms all the way to the bed. She began laughing. It was clear to her he wanted some of her love making.

"Babe," Andrea sounded.

"Yeah, baby."

He turned her around and the two began kissing each other on the lips. Then he went down and began sucking her center, shortly she began to feel like she couldn't take it anymore. He didn't even look up to come up for air. Andrea seeing only the top of his forehead, she was trying to hang, but then she felt herself trying to close her legs close with his head still in between her thighs. He felt a little pressure on his head with her thighs. He began to laugh.

"It's not funny," she chuckled then a moan sound came out her mouth. He came back up and began sucking on her nipples. Then the two began having sex. The breathing was heavy and the moaning was loud. The two were bobbing their heads up and down to the movement of him going in and out of her fast like he was, she was very moist, it was clingy, it was warm and it was wet. It was slippery, it kept coming out; with her hand, she guided it back inside her.

"Mmmmm," Was the long moaning sounds as they continued.

Twenty minutes after getting her some she went back to her closet to try it again. Shortly after staring at her clothes she finally decided on what she was about to wear. She ended up pulling out her white dress with the purple flowers and her purple heels. Seconds later Phillip watched her slip into her dress and then grabbed her shoes off the floor and walked over to the bed. She sat on the edge of the bed and began putting on her shoes. She walked to her dresser and picked up her eyeliner. She began putting on her eye liner. Then next she picked up her lipstick. She was only going shopping and hanging out with her girl, she had no need for more make up than that. Andrea left her apartment to go pick up Katrina from the hotel. She dialed Katrina's cell holding the cell up to her ear.

"Hey, hey girl," Katrina answered.

"Hey love, I'm here!" Andrea says.

"Ok, I'm coming down now."

"Okay."

They both hugged as Katrina got into the car.

"It took you long, what were you doing?"

Andrea's face turned towards her and smiled.

"What, your boyfriend was trying to get him some?" Katrina smiled.

"Trying, he did." Andrea chuckled.

"What, he off on the weekends?"

"Un. Yeah," then her eyes looked back to the road. Her expression and her response just told Katrina something different, that he didn't have a job. But that's not her business to respond, so she's not going to respond to that. Andrea kept her eyes on the road as she changed the conversation hoping that Katrina doesn't start asking her questions like where Phillip works.

"Girl, remember that time we bought that pizza and we couldn't wait to get home and eat, and we started eating in the car, and soon as we took our first bit, we burnt the shit out our mouths."

"Girl my shit was hurting for three days!"

"Girl, that shit turned my gums white instantly," Andrea chuckled.

"Mines too, I will never forget about that shit!" Katrina had no idea she was going to take her memory back that far. Those sure were the good times.

"Yeah, what made me bring that up is because I have a taste for pizza today for our lunch later!" Andrea said.

"Well, let's get pizza then."

They reached their first store. Then afterward they made it to their second store. They think they're done shopping after that second store, they almost bought the whole store. Andrea and Katrina ate pizza for lunch today.

Phillip was then left there in the apartment by himself. He watched T.V and chilled, he had no plans. Waiting for her to get back he decided to clean up the house. He folded the clothes that were left on the couch, washed dishes and mopped. By the time he was done she still had not made it back. Two hours later is when Andrea decided to bring herself home. Andrea walked in smiling and looking around from where she stood from the living room and was surprised he cleaned up everything. *She thought to herself, he must want something.*

Katrina never went straight up to the hotel after being dropped off, she went to two more stores that were right next to the hotel. Later coming back to the hotel she walked in grinning. She knew Mike was going to be like baby, you bought the whole store.

"Katrina, how much did you spend?"

"Too much," Katrina replied.

"Who card did you use for all that stuff, yours or mines?"

She sat down and just looked at him. She was looking at him like he was asking a ridiculous question. *Of course, she used his.*

Day five in Atlanta Katrina was having a ball with the kids at the Zoo. Later that day when Mike came back to the Hotel she chilled with him inside the hotel. Simone was downstairs in the Jacuzzi. They were chatting as they took sips of champagne.

"Babe, have the kids been enjoying themselves?" he asked.

"Yes, they sure have."

"That's right, I been seeing y'all having more fun than me," he chuckled.

"It's all business, no play for you buddy," she grinned. "You had fun the other day on our little outing."

"I sure did. Oh yeah and babe, Angela told me about you having a talk with her the other day."

"Yeah, I did."

"Yeah, because she came up to me apologizing, and I didn't know what the hell she was apologizing for."

"Oh."

"Yeah, I asked her what she was apologizing for then she had told me."

"Yeah, because I felt that is was inappropriate how she was staring and shit, I didn't come at her crazy or anything."

"Baby, you don't ever have to worry about me like that or ever disrespecting you in any type of way, she's nothing to worry about, I will never mess up what I have for anyone."

She still didn't like to see what she had seen sitting at the table the other day. Days later Mike is realizing that *they haven't talked much these past two days ever since they had a talked about how Katrina felt uncomfortable with the waitress she saw him talking too.*

Mike approached her. "Baby, now that I put two and two together I feel like things have been a little different by you these two days, staying gone longer, still shopping and hanging with Andrea, so have you been upset from the other day baby?"

"No," she paused. "No, I'm lying; yes I'm still upset, especially after I had to pull her to the side from how she was looking at you, Mike."

Their conversation was being interrupted by Katrina's cell. Deborah was calling.

"Hey mom," Katrina answered.

"Hey Katrina, I was calling to see if you guys will be back for Christmas?"

"Of course mom, we will be back tomorrow."

"Okay baby," her mother said and then they hung up.

Mike and Katrina continued chatting. "So babe, Andrea said she was going to come by the hotel in the morning to tell all of us bye!"

"Okay," he mumbled.

The next morning Andrea finally made her way up to the hotel. Simone let her in and gave her a hug. Mike Jr. ran over to her jumping up in her arms.

Andrea's smile grew. "Hey godson, I wish I had your energy all the time," she chuckled.

Katrina saw the bags with gifts inside her hand. "Aww, thanks, Andrea." Andrea passed Katrina the bags.

"You're welcome, I have to keep my godson fresh."

Andrea looked at Simone. "This is for you Simone," she handed Simone over a gift too.

"Aw, thank you, Andrea!"

"Since your birthday was a week before y'all came down, that's like your birthday and Christmas gift all in one," she grins.

"Thank you," Simone said again as she takes her gift out the bag.

Katrina, Mike, and Andrea sat there on the couch and chatted for thirty minutes, then Andrea left and they began to get their things back into their suitcases. They were leaving that afternoon.

Katrina wouldn't dare miss Christmas with her family, all the holidays with her family and her husband's family were very important to her with all the fun, food, and laughter with the family was always priceless.

Christmas this year for them was going to be at her Aunt Ann's house since they spent Christmas at her cousin Michelle's house last year.

December 23rd, they arrived back in California just like they said. Getting to the house they were just going to drop off Simone and Mike Jr, but they were both tired and wanted to take at least an hour nap before going shopping. Mike went and checked their mailbox for mail, and Katrina checked their answering machine for messages; afterward the two took a nap. After an hour long nap that actually turned into a three-hour nap that was way needed they left. They drove to Wal-Mart Shopping Center and getting their Katrina went and grabbed the shopping cart and she and Mike began hitting every aisle. Coming out the store the sun had gone down already, they were in there longer than what they both needed to be.

"Babe, that's this Christmas weather, it's cold as hell, I don't know what I was thinking and didn't bring my jacket."

"I know, me too, with this cold weather we're all going to be sick!"

"Naw, we just need to wear our jackets!"

"Right, which we didn't do," he chuckled. He was looking at Katrina shiver.

"Are you laughing at me?"

"Yeah," Mike kept laughing.

"It's not funny, shoot I'm cold" she chuckled. As soon as they both got into the car, the first thing she did was cut on the heater.

Getting back home it was almost night time, it was very cold, the fireplace was needed tonight. Mike turned the fire place on and he and Katrina sat on the couch snuggled up watching a movie.

Waking up the next morning it was Christmas Eve, Katrina and Mike wrapped up all the gifts. The next morning it was Christmas and Simone couldn't wait to get to their Aunt's house to help her Aunt and her grandmother bake cakes. Everybody woke up that morning getting dressed and left the house by eleven. Getting there Mike got their son out the car seat and then closed the back door. Simone and Katrina were both getting out the car too.

"Baby, his pull up sagging," Mike said.

"Aww, see if his pants wet?" Katrina asks.

Mike felt his son's pants. "Baby, it's just mushy," Mike says.

"Ok good, soon as we get inside I'll change his pull-up."

Mike looked at Katrina, "I'll change him, babe."

"Okay babe."

"I'm putting you down little fella," Mike held his hands and helped him walk.

Going inside Simone went straight into the kitchen, Mike went to the family room to change his son, and Katrina saw her grandmother and her sister. She was glad she was there already, she needed to tell her about herself. But not before saying hi to her grandmother and giving her a hug. Then she looked at Brandy.

"Brandy come here!"

"Alright," she said regular, but, *"oh lord,"* is what she mumbled. Brandy went to go see what her sister wanted.

"What is your problem girl, you don't want to get a job? One week you're working then the next week you're not, sis you need to find something steady and something you actually like, so you can actually enjoy what you do. Yeah, I found out you stopped working. Why are you using your vagina to get the cash" We weren't raised like this, I don't know what the hell your problem is. You can't be that lazy!"

"First off, I don't talk to anyone anymore, but Terrell. The guys who used to give me money I didn't have to fuck them to get anything, they just did it because they wanted to. Call it what you want, but all my bills and all my shit is paid, don't worry about how I'm getting mines, but since you that concerned, Terrell is working now."

Katrina just looked at her.

"What, you mad?" Brandy asked her.

"Mad at you," she chuckled. "Yeah," Karina told Brandy as she shook her head.

"Well, don't be Katrina," she replied.

"Well, I can't help it. You have my niece around this shit, she sees everything you do, whether you try and hide it or not, trust me, she still sees it and that's not cool at all Brandy."

"Don't try and tell me how to be a mother to my daughter, Sister I got this, and like I said, I don't deal with anyone anymore besides Terrell!"

"Where is Terrell?"

"He isn't coming, he's at his family's house in Bellflower!"

"Oh, okay," Katrina nodded her head.

"Well, sis just to make it clear, don't try and figure me out!"

Deep down Katrina had the feeling of wanting to slap her just one good time to slap some sense into her head. But she knew it would be pointless until she's tired of what she is doing, her concern really was her niece Paige.

Paige was already in the kitchen helping their Aunt and her mother cook. She and Simone were in there baking cakes. The two began baking cakes once Simone got there. Simone was making her special lemon cake and Paige was making her strawberry cake. Every Christmas they hooked it up. After placing their cakes into the oven they both went straight to their bowls to eat the left over cake mix. The cake mix was the best part of baking their cakes. No matter how old they got, that never changed for them. They waited for 30 minutes and their cakes were done.

"Girls, you got them cakes looking good as always!"

"Thanks, grandma!" they both said as they whipped on the frosting. After they were done they covered their cakes with the glass tops, then they both went to the living room with the rest of the family. Simone and Paige came walking out the kitchen holding the cakes they just baked. They both sat the cakes down onto the table.

"Ooooh, I want some of both of y'all cakes," Katrina said.

"And I want a slice too," Mike says.

"Momma got to have the biggest slice, Paige!" Brandy shouted.

Paige and Simone were both smiling, they all said just what they thought they would all say.

"Simone and Paige y'all did that!" Mike shouted.

"Thank you!" they both said at the same exact time.

Everybody was sitting around the table talking, laughing, taking pictures, recording videos of them, and posting it up on YouTube and Facebook and enjoying themselves as always. Once everyone came out the kitchen they were ready to open up their gifts. Robert was about to play Santa Claus.

Robert grabbed the first box; he looked at the name on it. "Ok, to Robert, oh shit to me from Marie. He opened his gift. He looked at Marie, "Thanks, sis!"

"You are welcome," she smiles.

"Just a shirt, where are the pants?" he continued looking in his box taking out the tissue paper. Everyone started laughing.

"Thanks, sis," he told her again. She nodded her head at him and smiled.

He reached under the tree and grabbed another gift. "To Brandy from Katrina," he passed Brandy hers.

Brandy opened her gift from Katrina, ripping off the Christmas wrapping her eyes widen. "Aww, thanks sister for my Michael Kors purse!"

"You're welcome, that's the one you wanted huh?"

"Yes boo!" Brandy smiled.

"Thank you, Katrina!" Brandy thanked her again.

Robert grabbed another gift. "This one is to Katrina from your Aunt Ann!"

Ann looked over at Katrina. "Hey Katrina, when we found out you guys were going to make it back in time, I gone back and got it at the last minute."

Katrina opened her gift from her Auntie and it was a pair of gray suede boots. Katrina smiled, she loved them, and then she looked up holding her boots. "Thank you so much, Auntie I love them!"

"You are welcome baby, I didn't have time to order the olive green pair from off their website, I'm sorry, I know olive green is your favorite color right now. Those are the only color besides black they had in the store."

"Oh, no worries Auntie, these are perfect, I love them. I already have an outfit to go with these too, Thank you so much!"

"I like those boots K, those are bad. I wanted some of those too that go all the way to my knees," Brandy blurted.

"Thank you," she replied.

Robert grabbed the little gold bag from on the side of the tree, he reads: "To Deborah, from your oldest child and your son in-law!"

Deborah grabbed her bag from Robert. "Thank you Katrina and Mike!" she blurted as she smiled. She looked inside and took her card out the bag, she opened her card and it had a gift card inside. "I'm going to Nordstrom, I'm going to Nordstrom," she sings.

"She's happy about her gift card," Robert said out loud smiling.

"Yes I am," she smiled.

Robert grabbed another present. "To Mike from Aunt Ann!"

Mike opened his box and it had a button down shirt and a pair of nice jeans, he started dancing.

"Do your dance, do your dance!" Simone shouted in a singing tone.

"Mike, you're going to sweat your shirt out," Deborah chuckled.

"I don't care, it's mines," he laughed as he continued dancing. Then after he was done dancing he stood up from the table to go give Aunt Ann a hug. "Thanks for my gift!"

"Oh, you're welcome baby," Ann told him.

Robert picked up the envelope that was on the floor underneath the tree. "This envelope is to Aunt Marie from Mike and Katrina!"

"Let me give it to her!"

"Alright," Robert sounded. He handed Katrina the envelope.

"Here Aunt Marie, Merry Christmas!" Katrina said loudly.

Katrina handed her Aunt an envelope, she wanted to surprise her Aunt with some money. After her mother was just telling her a few days ago how her Aunt is having a hard time paying her bills and that her utilities keeps getting cut off. Everyone watched the envelope being passed, no one knew but Mike. Mike had a smile on his face, he couldn't wait to see her smile once she finds out what's inside and how much.

"Thanks, Katrina and Mike," she held it as she looked at them both.

"You are welcome," they both sounded.

"Auntie open it!" Katrina burst out.

Marie opened her envelope with a smile, now that her niece told her to open it, now she knows it must have money in it. Marie opened it and slid out her card, it was really thick inside. By the thickness of it, she knew it had a lot of money or a lot of ones in it. She opened it and it was two thousand dollars. All Marie could do was cry. Tears started rolling down her face thinking it was no one but God. She had been praying and praying that some money would come from somewhere. She couldn't stop crying tears of joy, she stood up and gave Katrina and Mike the biggest hug.

"Thank you guys so much for this money!"

"You're welcome," they said as she continued to hug the both of them. That was one hell of a gift and Katrina and Mike was blessed they were able to bless her Aunt with that. Her Auntie couldn't stop crying, she was so grateful for her gift; her crying made everyone else cry too. Robert grabbed another gift.

"This gift says to Katrina from your husband," Katrina's gift was handed to her.

"Thanks, babe," she told him. Mike nodded his head and smiled. She was about to open her red Victoria Secret Box.

"Babe, you might not want to take that all the way out," he smiled.

"Baby," she smiled peeking inside with half the box opened. Looking inside she sees it's a red lace lingerie piece with the nipples out. Yeah, after seeing part of that she had to leave that inside the box. She looked up at Mike and smiled. He was already looking at her smiling, giving her that look like he wants her to wear that tonight.

Robert grabbed another gift from up under the tree. "This one says to Mike from Simone!" As Mike's gift was being passed to him, Simone stood up and smiled. "Dad, you're going to like the gift I gotcha!"

Mike tore off the wrapping paper, as he opened the box he started pulling out a sweat suit. He smiled, "I knew it!"

Simone laughed.

"See, somebody caught onto my hint, that's why you were asking me about the different sweat suits I like and my size, I knew you were up to something," he chuckled.

"To Mike from your sexy wife!" His gift was passed to him he wondered what did she get him. He opened his gift and it was another Rolex chain, but bigger with diamonds. That right there he was not expecting her to get, but he was glad she did, he really loved his gift. He leaned over and kissed her.

"Thanks, baby!"

"You are so welcome hunny!" she told him.

Robert grabbed another one. "To Uncle Robert!" he looked at them, "That would be me, from Katrina." He looked at Katrina, "Thanks, K," he told her.

"You're welcome!"

Robert stood there and ripped his gift open.

It was a pair of shoes; he looked up at Katrina, "These are tight, thank you so much," he smiled. Then he sat his box of shoes on the couch behind him.

Robert picked up another gift. "To Katrina from Mike!" her Uncle Robert handed her gift to her.

Katrina reached for her gift as she looks at her husband. "Aww babe, what's this?"

"Don't tell me it's going to be another gift we can't see Mike," Katrina's grandmother had sounded, then she laughed.

"Naw, y'all can see this one," he said smiling.

Katrina took off the wrapping paper and opened her gift; it was a diamond necklace, a diamond ring, and a diamond bracelet. Katrina loved her gift. She had Mike put her necklace on her neck, she slid her diamond ring onto her finger, then she snapped her bracelet on her wrist.

"Oooh baby, look at that wrist," her mother said.

Katrina looked over at Mike. "Baby I love it, I love it, and I love it!"

He smiled. "Thanks, babe!" she said.

Brandy glanced at her sister's diamonds from her wrist to her neck. "Shit, I wish Terrell's ass would have gotten me something like that, I love that sis!"

"Thank you, Brandy," Katrina said.

Everybody loved Katrina's gift.

Then Robert grabbed another gift. "To Brandy from Mom," he passed Brandy her gift.

Brandy opened her gift and it was a box of perfume.

"Thanks, Mom!" she smiled.

"You are welcome baby."

Robert grabbed another one. "To Paige from Katrina!" Paige's gift was passed to her.

"Thank you, Auntie Katrina!"

"You're welcome sweetie."

Paige opened up her gift. She was happy because this is what she wanted too.

Robert grabbed the big box leaning up against the wall. It reads: "To Simone from Mommy and Daddy Mike!" Robert laughed.

"That's right," Robert sounded. Then he passed Simone her gift.

Simone opened her gift and it was a pink electric scooter.

Robert grabbed another gift, it was to his mom. "To Mom, from your kids Me, Deborah, Marie, and Ann!"

Robert walked over and passed his mother a gift from him and his sisters. Then Robert went into his back pocket and grabbed all the gift cards he had in his back pocket and gave all the kids a gift card for two hundred and fifty dollars. This is what he did every year for them so they all knew they had it coming. They gave him a hug and told him thank you.

Suddenly, knocks sounded at the door.

"Brandy, please go and see who's that knocking at the front door," her Aunt Ann told her. Brandy got up from the table to see who it was at the door, looking through the peep hole it was her cousin Edward. A big smile was on her face, she had not seen her cousin in almost six years. Brandy swung open the front door.

"Cousin!!" she smiled with much excitement.

Edward has the biggest smile on his face too. "Hey cousin!" he sounded.

The two of them hugged each other so tight.

"Where's everybody at?" he whispered.

"In the dining room at the table," she whispered back to him.

"Nobody knew I was coming back home for Christmas, I wanted it to be a surprise."

"Oh yeah, they are going to be very surprised alright, especially your mother." Going inside Edward was eyeing his mother from behind Brandy, he could see her looking across the room. His mother was looking to see who was walking behind Brandy. Edward threw his hands up in the air, "Hey family!" he shouted.

"Edward!!" Ann shouted. "Hey, baby I didn't even know you were going to make Christmas this year."

Edward walked over to his mother first and gave her a kiss and a big long hug, Ann was so happy that he was there she was still in shock.

"When I found out I was stoked and I wanted to surprise you all is why I didn't call beforehand."

"Yes, this is sure a wonderful surprise!" everyone stood up giving Edward a hug. It's been six long years since they all had seen him last. This was already the best Christmas. Really, every Christmas with family was, but this was special. One thing was for sure, Edward loved putting a smile on his mother's face and the fact he could still do that at age sixty-two was a wonderful feeling.

"Cousin, you want me to go make your plate!"

"Yeah sure!" he told her.

"Alright," Brandy began walking straight to the kitchen.

"Edward, come here!"

Katrina called her cousin Edward for a picture.

"Brandy, can you come take our picture right quick!"

"Ok."

Brandy began snapping pictures, and then she went to the kitchen.

This was Edward's first time meeting Mike, he had heard about him, but this was his first time meeting him. Edward was observing him on the slide. He seemed like a nice dude, but he knew that he would be because his cousin Katrina does not play that shit.

"There's no woman in your life right now baby?"

"Well, not really ma, I do have a friend though, her name is Kayla, but we're just friends. I haven't known her long enough to make her my lady yet!"

"Oh, okay!"

Christmas with family was always fun: eating, kids playing around with their cousins and their gifts while the adults drink and chat about things they use to do back in the days, or just catching up on what everybody's doing right now. Oh, and can't forget about pictures, something they like to take a lot of. After everyone ate seconds and thirds is when Katrina and Brandy both went into their Aunt's kitchen and washed all the dishes for her. Katrina washed and Brandy rinsed and put them all in the drainer and then stacked the rest that couldn't fit in the drainer.

Days later after Christmas Mike, Charles, and Keveyon met up with their Uncle Charlie. It was the end of the year and their Uncle wanted to see what ideas they had in mind to bring in more money and more customers to the restaurant. They all sat at the table elaborating on the ideas each of them came up with.

Katrina sat at the table and dialed her mother. "Hello," her mother answered.

"Hey, mom, what's going on?"

"On my way to see your grandmother," she said.

"What's up with my granny?"

"Nothing, she's just been saying that her head has been hurting her all week, and she's not feeling too well."

"What, you about to take her to the hospital?"

"You know your grandmother ain't going to nobody's hospital."

"I know, granny hates going to the hospital."

"Yeah, she does. Where are you?"

"Up here at the restaurant with Mike, he's in a meeting with his brothers and their Uncle."

"Oh ok, well baby I'm driving, I'll call you when I get back home."

"Ok mom, tell granny I love her. I love you, mom!"

"I will baby and I Love you too!"

Later getting home Katrina was deciding on shrimp tacos or fish taco tonight for their Taco Tuesday night. She chose shrimp tacos. Mike sat in the kitchen with her as she cooked dinner. He talked to her as he watched her chop onions, cilantro, and tomatoes.

Katrina went and ran her some bath water. It's been a long day for sure. "Babe, we don't have any more Epsom Salt?"

"No babe, I used the last of it!"

"You mean you used all of it!"

"You used it too babe," he chuckled.

"Yeah, one time I did," she chuckles.

"Babe, you getting in without your husband," he grins.

"Babe, I'm about to sit in a hot bath and relax."

"How about when you get out the bath, I give you a full body massage!"

"Yes, I need that!"

"Ok well, you will get that once you get out!"

"Thank you, baby," she smiled.

"Un huh," he sounded.

As soon as she stepped out the bath he was ready to give her, her full body massage. She lay down on the bed. He poured oil all over her body, but just enough to not get it all on their sheets, and then he began her massage. His firm hands sliding up her body massaging every inch, every muscle, and every pain she feels. His massages always made her feel some type of sexual sensation and she always wanted to do something once he's done. He massaged her for about an hour long. He leaned down to her ear. "Baby, you want it?" he whispered in her ear as her eyes closed from that very relaxing massage he just gave her.

"You know I want it, baby," she sounded back softly. He turned her over slowly onto her back as he was kissing on her breast first because he knew that's what she liked. He started at the side of her breast but then once she was flat on her back is when he began to push her breast into his mouth as he sucked on it even more. He went from kissing all over her breast to sucking on her nipples, then to massaging her breast in a circular motion as he licked and sucked on her breast, not just one, but both of them. Afterward, he lifted his head a little, he watched her face as he grabbed on to it and slid it inside of her. He went all the way in moving his hips around in a circular motion. After several minutes he stopped with the circular motion and began going in and out of her. As he continued going in and out of her, with each thrust she kept sounding a moan as her eyes were still closed. Suddenly she slid both her hands under her butt and spread her butt cheeks apart and as he went back she pulled them apart and when he went in deep she pushed her cheeks closed.

They both were breathing heavy, she was warm inside, he continued going in and out of her. Once he felt that sensation going through his body, he knew he was about to cum, even she knew he was about to cum. She wrapped her legs around his legs, with one arm he placed it around her waist area just to hold on tighter as he goes down in her, even more, deeper than he began faster. She held onto him as she too was going the same speed as he and then in minutes they both had cum. After all that they were tired, left with no energy to keep going they went to sleep.

The next morning they realized in two days it's New Years, tomorrow is the last day of the year and still, they haven't really decided what they were all going to do yet. But now they only had two more days to think. They just knew whatever it was it was going to be big. They had to end twenty fifteen and start twenty sixteen off right. The next day they decided to all go over to Sharee's house for New Years.

They all celebrated New Years at Sharee's home; they all got off work, got dressed, and went straight there.

The New Years' weekend started off right, Katrina invited her sister to church that Sunday; she accepted the invite and rolled with her sister to church. That Sunday and leaving from her house they got there on time. Church started off with three songs from the choir, afterward the pastor stood up and walked up to the podium and began preaching. Sitting in church that morning seemed like the preacher was talking to her. Brandy felt no matter how long it's been since the last time she went to church, she feels like every time she goes, it seems like the message is for her.

After church Karina dropped her sister back off at home and went home herself. Getting home she went up to the bedroom and sat on the bed. She began to look around and vision their room to be a different color, it was a new year and she wanted to change up their color scheme in their room. Katrina's phone starts ringing. "Hey lady," Katrina answers her cell, it was Sharee.

"What you doing?"

"Sitting on my bed looking at this room, over here thinking what color I want to change this color scheme to."

"What color do you have in mind?" Sharee asks.

"I don't know yet, I just started to think about it right now."

"You should do like an olive green, white and brown or a brown, tan and turquoise. I keep throwing brown in there because I like brown."

"Ok me too because right now it's brown, white and like a dark orange, like the orange color, looks like burnt orange," Katrina told her.

"Yeah, just keep it neutral, not too feminine, not too masculine."

CHAPTER

13

Hospital Visit

Even though Katrina and Mike both were good and well off financially, she didn't want to start paying for day care, but it was time to get back to work. Ten months in the house. Yes, she enjoyed her time with her baby, but she was ready to get back to work already.

Katrina had finally gone back to work, the morning returning to the office, Suzy was so happy to have her girl back along with everyone was there welcoming her back with flowers and balloons. Following the welcome, they were about to have a staff meeting as always before going out into the field. Right before the meeting started she saw Crystal.

"Hey lady, I missed you," Katrina told her.

"Hey, I missed you too, today is my first day back too!"

"Oh yeah, that's right, from where?" Katrina asked.

Carolyn interrupted, "Ms. Thing over here just came back from vacation."

"Oh really, how cool. I heard that, where did you go?"

"The hubby and I went to New Orleans!"

"That's right," Katrina says.

"You know Jeremy loves the Raiders, we went to the Raider game out there."

"Okay, that's right," she smiled.

"When I say hot, yes it was hot," Crystal said.

"New Orleans, I need to do a trip out there; Mike and the kids, we do Atlanta a few times a year to go check on his business, but I do want to go to New Orleans."

"Yeah, we had fun, now it's back to work, we spent so much money down there."

"I can imagine but I know it was worth it," Katrina told her and chuckled.

"Yeah it was, we had fun, I know you probably hated you had to come back huh, enjoying your time off."

"Oh no honey, it feels good to be back around people, girl I spent most of my time at home alone during the day, just me and my baby, you know at least until my husband got home from work."

"Yeah, that's true," the ladies walked into the meeting and they all sat down at the round table for the meeting. After the meeting Katrina went to her office, she needed to look over her listing first and make a few calls.

Sergio came and knocked on her office door.

"Come on in!" she sounded loudly. Sergio came in with a suspicious smile.

"Hey, what's up Katrina, I need a huge favor!" he nodded his head up at her smiling as he walks over to her desk. He grabbed and held her hand.

"Yeah, what's up Sergio?" she wondered what it was that he was about to say how he come in, grabbing onto her hand.

"I need you to take a client off my hands."

"Ok, no problem, I got you!"

Sergio had this annoying client that he didn't want to deal with anymore, so he passed his client onto Katrina. Katrina took Irvin Gomez, the annoying client, he was extremely picky and what he said he wanted she plans to find for him. Off to show him the first two properties, she found she thought it would be what he likes, but he still didn't like either of the properties. She was getting frustrated dealing with him already, but she plans to hang in there until she gets him what he wants. He had a whole lot of money and he was ready to buy, no way is she about to let him go. The following week she got in a new listing. She called up her client Mr. Gomez and told him that she saw a few good ones she believes he just might have an interest in. She's thinking he more than likely will pick one of these homes. Walking into the first house she let him walk in first before her, she wanted to hear his first reactions to it.

"This is perfect."

She smiled, *whew, finally she thought to herself.*

"So you like this one," she smiles.

"This is it!" he said as he began walking to the living room, then through the kitchen as she followed him.

"You sure now, you know we have more on the list for today, you want to go check those out first before making your final decision?"

"No, I like this!" he told her again as they were still looking around the place.

"Okay sounds good to me," Katrina wanted to show him the upstairs; they walked upstairs. They walked from room to room, looked inside the closets and both bathrooms. As she's showing and talking, he's imagining him and his family inside there. After walking down the hallway it was the last room, the master bedroom.

"Okay, Mr. Gomez, let's go back downstairs so I can show you the back yard."

"Really I don't even need to see the backyard, I love this, I want this," he stood and looked around from at the top of the stairs. Katrina laughed, her laugh echoed through the empty house.

"Okay then, well that's it for the tour if you feel no need to look at the backyard."

They walked back downstairs.

"So Mr. Gomez, when will Mrs. Gomez be available to come see it?"

"If not tomorrow, then for sure on Thursday," he told Katrina.

Katrina stood there not saying anything, she was thinking about her schedule for tomorrow and Thursday.

"Let me call my wife to see what days she can come."

"Yeah, it would be better if you found out."

He made the call to his wife and said she was available tomorrow at one in the afternoon. He hung up the phone with his wife.

"Ms. Katrina, she said tomorrow at one is fine."

"Perfect, I will see you both tomorrow at one then," they shook hands and smiled. Katrina locked up and closed the door. Then they both began to leave the property. Mr. Gomez turned around and looked back at her to thank her again.

"Oh, you're welcome Mr. Gomez, it was my pleasure," they both got in their cars.

This was definitely the place he could see himself living in. Katrina closed a deal on a fifteen million dollar house. She was happy to come back to work already closing a big deal. She was happy that she could find a home finally that her client liked. Katrina's work day ended early since she didn't have to show him the other three houses, and since he was her only client for that day. She was able to get to her babies sooner than what she'd planned. She left the property happy and so was her client.

The next day Katrina went to lunch with three of her colleagues Jackie, Veronica, and Sonia to celebrate her deal she closed upon her recent return back to work, they also closed deals this week too.

Katrina looked at Sonia and smiled. "So what's been going on lately Sonia?" Katrina asked. Katrina felt like she had to play catch up with them too since she had been off work for a long while.

"Girl, just work and more work."

"No new boo or nothing?"

"Well, yeah. You know the relationships to me be about sex and money, I don't be putting my feelings in shit, because I'm not about to get hurt, so the fact we getting serious I'm getting super nervous. It's still early so I don't want to make a big deal about it and bragging about him, then shit go left field."

"Girl, I hear you on that big time!"

"What about you Veronica, anything new or a new boo in your life?"

"Girl, same here, just work, work, and more work for me, I'm not even trying to meet anyone really."

"Veronica, I hear you on that because they can be a big distraction," Jackie chuckled.

"Jackie. Jackie girl, I want to say thank you again for being willing to help me out with my clients when I was on leave."

"Oh, girl no worries because that was money in both of our pockets, that was TEAMWORK," Jackie sounded out.

Afterward, they went back to work feeling all good and full. They didn't have much to do but check emails and messages. They stayed until it was time for them to get off, then they left. Getting home Katrina took off her shoes was the first thing she did, and then she went to go kiss and hug her husband, he was home already. She went and sat with him on the couch.

"How was your day?" he said.

"It was good and long."

"How was yours babe?"

"Good, good!"

"Babe, I'm about to go to the gym and work out, you want to come?"

"Yeah, sure babe, I'll come work out with you!"

"Alright, I'm going to put on dinner first before we leave."

"What's for dinner?"

"I was making boiled chicken breast, some homemade fettuccine pasta with shrimp and cheese, and a salad."

"Ummm, sounds good babe!"

"Yes, and It's going to be. So since it will take two in a half hours to boil, we just have to make sure we are back way before then."

"Alright, that's cool; we can get an hour workout in."

"Yeah, that sounds good!"

"Alright, sounds cool to me," Katrina made the salad and started the chicken, then the two left for the gym. Getting to the gym they both started on the treadmill. They did that for thirty minutes, then he moved to the weights and she got on the bicycle. Then they reached their hour and they left. Once they made it to the car he grabbed them both a water bottle from out the trunk. He passed her a bottle of water.

"Thanks, babe," she told him, then they pulled out the parking stall and drove back home.

"Did you enjoy your workout?"

"Yes I did, it just my foot hurt."

"When we get home I will massage them."

"Thanks babe."

Getting back the chicken had another hour to cook, Katrina then started the pasta and shrimp, the salad was already done. After the chicken was done she made their plates. Passing him his plate, he glanced over at hers.

"That's all you're going to eat?"

"Yeah, just this salad," she said.

"You are going to still be hungry!"

"I know, but I need to get back to my diet and eating salads."

He knew he couldn't argue with her about that because that's all she's been trying to do these past few months is get back to her size and lose that baby fat. After he was done eating they went up to the room. He grabbed both her legs and slid his hand down on her right leg. As she talked he grabbed her feet and began massaging them. They stayed up all night long watching movies. They both were acting like they didn't have anywhere to go in the morning. The next morning Deborah, Katrina's mother was coming over. That morning Katrina's mother pulled up. Katrina was just about to leave, she thought she would go to the store and make it back to the house before her mother gets there, but that didn't happen her mother arrived early this morning.

"Hey mom, come ride with me to the store."

"You driving or am I'm driving?

"I'll drive, but let me go tell Simone something real quick, the car door is open mom." Her mother went and sat in Katrina's car and Katrina went back inside.

"Simone!" she yelled. Simone came out her room to see what her mother wanted. Katrina told her the chores she wanted her to do while she was gone to the store. It was just the regular chores she did anyway, except she just wanted them done now instead of later. Then Katrina left and got in her car.

Deborah noticed Katrina's weight gain, and also a little in her face too.

"Katrina, are you pregnant?"

"Why you ask that?" she smiles.

"You are, aren't you, because I thought you were working out to lose the baby weight you gained, but it just looks like your gaining instead of losing."

"Mom, why it can't be just me gaining weight because I still eat up everything, although I am trying to stop, why does it have to be Katrina are you pregnant?"

"Well, are you?"

"I hope not!"

"Well, the only way we will know is if we go take a pregnancy test," Deborah told her.

"A test right now?" Katrina asked her mother.

"Yeah, what else were you doing besides going to the store this morning."

Katrina looked at her, and then she sat quietly. Instead of them going straight to the store they passed the store and was heading over to the clinic where they did a free and fast pregnancy test, she wanted this done quick. Approaching the clinic she heard her mother in her ear saying, "Well, are you going to stop?" They were there.

"Are they even open?" she asked Katrina.

"Yeah, they are, but Sundays they close early, at noon." Katrina pulled into the clinic. "Alright, mom I guess we about to find out if you're about to have another grandchild."

"I guess we are."

Katrina got out the car and closed her door and went inside. Her mother stayed in the car and waited for her. Taking the test was an in and out thing. Katrina found out that yes, she was pregnant again. Walking back towards the car her mother looked her straight in her eyes and Katrina nodded her head up and down. Katrina got in the car, her mother's eyes were still on her.

"Yes mom, I am," is what Katrina sounded. Then Katrina turned her head looking at her mother, she caught her mother smiling, while she's thinking *Am I ready for another child this soon*?

"See, I was right, you take me through all of that, and you are pregnant!" she smiles.

"Well, I didn't think I was."

"Why not, you weren't feeling a little different, did your cycle stop?"

"I have been feeling the same, my menstrual cycle really has not been irregular and the pains I have, I thought were because of me working out at the gym."

"Oh, well now you know that you're pregnant, it will be things you have to stop now, like working out at the gym."

"I can still work out, just not a strenuous workout!"

"Alright baby, just take it easy, remember you have my grandchild up in there!"

"Mom, you already know how I am about talking about it, in the beginning. I like to pass my first trimester before I start telling people, so please keep this quiet for me."

"Awww Katrina, you're about to give me another grandbaby," Deborah said happily.

"See, that's what I don't want," Katrina smiled.

"I'm not going to say anything, but look at you, my baby about to have another baby," Deborah couldn't stop smiling.

"Okay, I will stop, can I at least say congratulations?"

"Yes mom."

"Congratulations baby," she smiled.

"Thank you, mom, now no more talking about it for another month, then I will announce it, okay," Katrina told her.

"Okay baby," she smiles.

"Mom," Katrina sounded.

"What, I can't smile."

"Crazy part is I only been back to work six months now and in another seven to eight months I'm going to have to take another leave."

"Yes, you are."

"So much for me trying to get my six pack back, I swear this wasn't planned, it just happened out of nowhere."

"Don't even worry about that right now, just worry about eating right and having a healthy baby."

Katrina nodded her head up and down.

They made it to the store, Katrina parked and they got out the car. Katrina and her mother walked into the store.

"Good morning!" Katrina told the lady behind the counter.

"Good morning!" she said back.

Katrina told the worker what she was looking for, but then the worker advised her they don't carry it in the color she wanted and unfortunately, she couldn't find the size she needed in the color they did have. Simone wanted a specific color dress, so she had to find something else. Katrina found something else but with the color, Simone wanted. Than her and her mother left the store and drove back to Katrina's house.

Mike's in the Kitchen seasoning his meat.

"Babe, are you cooking that now?"

"No, I'm just going to marinate them until we get back from the church, then I'll throw it on the grill."

They began getting ready for church.

"Baby, you ready!"

"Yeah, babe in like five more minutes!"

"Okay!" she spoke out loudly.

"Simone!" she yelled out her name from downstairs.

"Yes mom!" she responded.

"Here, I have the dress for you!"

Simone came running down the stairs to get her clothes. "Hey granny!" Deborah was sitting down there on the couch, they were all going to ride to church together. Simone gave her grandmother a hug. Then Simone went back upstairs.

Looking at the time ten minutes later Katrina yelled out to Simone, "Are you almost ready, we're leaving in five minutes!"

"Ok, I will be down!" Simone sounded.

"Babe, here I come!" Mike said loudly.

"Alright, I will be in the car!" she yelled out to them.

Katrina, her mother, and the baby went and got in Mikes truck, he was driving today. Shortly after Mike and Simone came walking out the house. Then they left driving to the church house to hear the word of the Lord. During the service, Katrina heard a voice. She twisted around to look back to see it was her sister Brandy, Katrina didn't even have to guess or wonder, she knew her sister's voice. Brandy began catching the Holy Ghost. Her niece Paige was sitting right beside her, Katrina tapped her mother and Mike, then she, her mother and Mike turned back around smiling nodding their heads, then their eyes were back on the preacher. After church Katrina, her mom, Simone, and her husband hugged Brandy and Paige. Then Katrina invited her sister and her niece over to their house to eat.

That evening getting back home Mike threw some steaks, salmon, shrimp kabobs, and asparagus on the grill. After everything was done it was time to make plates.

"Babe, which one you want, steak or salmon, or both?" he yelled out.

"No babe, I'm just going to eat some salad!"

"That's it babe!" he yelled out.

Deborah looked at Katrina, then her eyes looked down at her stomach, then back up to her.

"Okay babe, you can give me everything!" she shouted.

"Alrighttt!" he sounded.

Mike made plates for everyone. They all sat together as a family at the dining room table and enjoyed their Sunday dinner. Afterward, Deborah, Brandy, and Paige left. Katrina walked up to Mike and kissed him. "I love you, Baby."

"I love you too babe," he said back to her.

"We're having another one."

"Another one," he looked into her eyes. "Another baby?" he asked.

"Yes," she smiles.

He picked her up he was happy that she is pregnant.

"Mom knows, but I told her don't tell anyone, you know how I am with the first trimester."

"Yeah, so baby you make sure you take it easy."

"I am babe."

"Congratulations to us," he said, then kissed her again.

The next morning waking up Katrina looked at Mike. "Babe, why you dressed like you about to go to the gym or something?" she wondered why he doesn't have on his work attire.

"Because I was baby, I was going to call Charles to see if he wants to get a game in this morning before we start working."

"The gym is open this early on a Monday?" she asked him.

"Yeah, they open seven days a week at seven." Mike just felt like getting in an early morning game of basketball.

Mike called Charles to see what he has going on this morning and asked if he wanted to shoot some hoops before work. Charles was down, he and his brother hasn't played ball together in a minute. Mike and Charles were headed to go hang out and play some basketball at the gym, on the way there they chatted about him and Shante. Mike noticed when he mentioned Shante's name, he smiled. Mike told him that he sees Shante is the perfect lady for him, she brings the best out of him and he's been even happier than before since he's been with her.

Mike's cell went off. He looked down and it was Jamal. "Hello, hey what's up man, I was just thinking about you the other day!"

"What you doing?" Jamal asked.

"Man, Charles and I about to head up to the gym and play some ball for a minute, you should come up there!"

"Y'all going up to the one on the corner, that's five blocks from your house across the street from that hamburger stand?"

"Yes, sirrrr!" Mike sounded.

"Alright bet, see y'all in a minute."

"Alright gone," they hung up.

The fellas made it up to the park, and Jamal had just pulled up there at the same time too. Jamal walked over towards them. Mike already had a smile on his face, he was happy to see his boy. They approached each other giving each other some dap.

"Man, where you been, Katrina and I was just thinking about you and Sherell the other day!"

"Oh yeah," he replied.

"How y'all been man, you ain't hit me up in a minute, that's why when you just called not too long ago I was surprised, man you been good?"

"Naw man, I haven't even heard from Sherell in a month."

"Isn't she still pregnant?"

"Yeah, but shit, she letting her other baby daddy run shit. She's talking about this baby she's pregnant with just might be his and he doesn't want me around until they find out."

Mike hearing this from his boy was crazy as hell. He began to think in his head how he was glad he doesn't have to worry about any baby daddy problems; He and Gary have an okay relationship *now* and the fact he only has a kid with Katrina, she doesn't have to worry about any baby momma's, her being his only baby momma, they were good.

Charles stopped dribbling the ball.

"Man, that's fucked up my man," Charles told him.

"Tell me about it, I been fucked up!"

"Shit, I would be too," Mike added.

"Man, when she told me that shit I just wanted to go over there and hurt her ass real bad!"

"Naw man, because your ass would end up in jail and we can't have that shit, now on the other hand ole boy, where in the hell is he?"

"Shit, I think he's over there, I'm not really sure, but shit, if she doesn't want me there then that dude has got to be there."

"Yeah, we should pay somebody a little visit," Mike looked at Jamal. Jamal nodded his head. "Man, that's what's up, but first let's do what we came here to do!"

Charles started back bouncing the ball, and the three played ball.

"Man, I need to go to a chiropractor," Mike sounded.

"For what?" Charles asked.

"Man, my back and my arm have been killing me!"

"Man, if you don't have Katrina just give your ass a massage!" Charles laughed.

"Mike, y'all ready to head up over there?" Jamal asked.

"I'm ready," Mike sounded.

"Me too," Charles replied.

Mike and Charles followed Jamal over to Sherell's house. Half way there Katrina called.

"Hey baby," he answered.

"Hey, babe you still at the gym?"

"Naw, me and Charles following Jamal over to Sherell's house, where are you?"

"Just making it to the office, oh, how are they doing, we were just talking about them the other day."

"I know, that's what I told him, but baby, they ain't doing good, she put him out for some other guy."

"What another guy?"

"Yeah, her other baby daddy," he told her.

"Isn't she pregnant with his baby?"

"Shit, that's what I thought and apparently so did Jamal, but something about her other baby daddy saying he doesn't want Jamal around because the baby might be his."

"Oooh, so she was cheating on Jamal!"

"Yep, you hit it right on the nose."

"Baby, do not be over there getting caught up in their drama."

"I know babe, we just going to show moral support. Well we're just now pulling up in front of her house, we're going to sit here I think, to see if he's going to come out soon because if he does then Jamal is going to holler at him."

"Baby, don't be fighting!"

"Babe, I'm going to call you back in a little while, Jamal just got in the car, we need to talk business."

"Alright, babe but you heard what I said."

"Hey Katrina," Jamal yelled out so she could hear him.

"Tell him I said hi babe, but you heard me right."

"Man, she said hi," Mike told him.

"Yeah, babe I heard you love you."

"Love you too," they hung up.

Jamal sat in the car with Mike and Charles. They sat in the car, and waited for an hour out there, but nothing ever even happened and no one came outside. Then the three just left.

That afternoon Katrina received a text from Mike telling her he is taking her out to dinner tonight.

Katrina was having a very busy day, but was glad that she was done early enough to still make it home, shower, and be ready for date night with her hubby. How things were looking earlier she thought she was going to be late.

The next morning getting into work Katrina saw Suzy reading. "Hey boo, what are you reading?"

"Girl, I am reading this Secret Love Series. It's really good and the juicy drama just has me laughing, these characters are funny and it's a steamy hot read; you should read her books!"

"Who is the book by?"

"Her name is Author LaShane Moore!"

"Alright, one of these days I will go check her out."

Katrina went to her office checking emails and looking at her listing. Then she went and checked on a few houses. After she checked on four houses Katrina reached in her purse to dial Kim; she wanted to see if she had time to see her right now to do her nails. After talking to Kim she then began to head there. On her way there Katrina called Shante and Sharee to see if they wanted to join her and then go have brunch afterward. Of course is what they both said. Her girls met up with her at the nail shop. The three got their nails done, but Shante got her eye brows done too. Afterward, they followed each other to BJ's Restaurant, they were going for their shrimp tacos.

They didn't need to look at the menu, they already knew what they wanted to order, they were sitting there waiting for the waitress to come over to their table. Katrina's cell starts ringing. It was her mother, "Hey mom," she answers.

"Hey Katrina," her mother replied.

"What's wrong Mom, why are you sounding so sad!"

"Where you at?" her mother asked.

"At BJ's Restaurant with the girls, we just got here."

Deborah was silent.

"Mom, what's going on tell me is everything okay?"

"Katrina, Your grandmother is in the hospital, she is in a coma."

Katrina instantly broke out crying at the restaurant. Her girls wondered what the hell is going on, they were both concerned.

"Mom, what hospital is she at?" tears filled her eyes; tears were rolling down her face.

Her mother told her what hospital.

"Where are you at mom?" Katrina asked her.

"I just made it here now; the rest of the family is on their way now."

Katrina, Shante, and Sharee left the table they didn't even bother ordering, they just left and were now headed to the hospital.

On the way to the car, Katrina dialed Mike's cell phone. "Hey baby," he answers.

"My mom just called and said my grandmother was sent to the hospital, she is in a coma!" she was so loud he heard her loud and clear, then she began crying.

"Where are you?" he asked her.

"I'm headed up to the hospital now."

"Which one?" he asked.

Katrina then told him which hospital her grandmother was at.

"Okay, me too," he said.

"Okay."

"Baby, calm down, take a deep breath please baby, but I'm going to need you to focus while you're driving, please drive safe, please!"

"I will," she says as she's still crying.

Once Katrina got stopped by the red light she dialed her sister to see if mom had called her already. Katrina put her phone on speaker, then sat the phone on her lap as she drives.

"Hello," Brandy answered crying.

"Brandy, momma just told you?"

"Yeah," she cries. "I'm about to go up to the hospital in a minute, I can't focus, I can't stop crying K!"

"I know sis, me neither. We got to try and be strong, you know Granny would want us to be strong for her."

"I know, but it's hard."

"I know, it's hard for me too," as they both continue to cry.

Paige called Chris from her cell phone to tell him about her great grandmother being in a coma. Chris was silent for a moment, he couldn't believe what Paige just said to him.

"What!"

"Yep, my great grandma is in a coma."

In the short time he knew her for those four years she was the sweetest old lady with no problem of telling it how it is, and that's what he always loved about her.

"Paige, how are you holding up?" Chris asked her.

"Not too good."

"How about your mother?" he asks.

"She's not doing too good, she just keeps on crying."

"So what's going on now?"

"Everybody's about to go up to the hospital, my grandma is already up there though," Paige replied.

"What hospital is she at?"

After Paige told him he wrote down the information. "Ok, got it, I will meet you guys up there okay!"

"Okay."

Paige and Chris hung up the phone. Paige walked into the living room and saw her mother crying on the couch, she went and sat next to her rubbing her back, "It's going to be okay mom."

Brandy nodded her head up and down, but she couldn't stop crying. "Mom, when are we leaving to go to the hospital?" Paige asked.

"I was trying to see if Terrell was going to ride up there with us," she says crying.

"Did you call him?"

Brandy shook her head yeah, "But he didn't answer."

"Mom, where is your phone?"

Brandy handed Paige her cell phone, she felt like she was losing it. Paige dialed Terrell's cell from her mother's phone, his phone just rung and rung, so the ringing let Paige know his phone was not dead. Paige left him a message telling him what happened and what hospital they're about to go to. After leaving a voicemail, Paige text him everything she'd just said on his voicemail. Then she passed the phone back to her mother.

"Mom, let's go."

"Okay," Brandy responded. Paige went and got her car keys. She helped her mother off the couch, locked the door behind them, then they left and were headed up to the hospital.

Chris grabbed his keys out his pocket, locked up his house, and headed up to the hospital. Chris made it to the hospital to be there for the family for Mrs. Estella. Chris made it up there before Brandy and Paige. The family was kind of surprised he was up there, but they appreciated the fact he was there in support. Chris stayed out in the hallway with the family that has not gone in to see her yet, and the ones who already came out from seeing her.

Shortly after Brandy and Paige made it. Chris saw Brandy and walked up to her giving her a hug. "You ok?"

Brandy shook her head in silence, her heart was in pain. Katrina walked up to her and so did her mother and father and they all walked in at the same time. Paige hugged him, "Thank you for coming."

"No sweetheart, thank you for calling me."

They sat down with the rest of the family. The waiting area and the hallway were all filled with just their family. Coming out Brandy went to go stand by the window and cried even more after seeing her grandmother in a coma lying in the bed, and the way that she looked, it looked like she's already dead. Chris walked over to her to hold her hand as the tears continued rolling down her face. "Hey, you okay?" he whispered.

She nodded her head yeah even though he knew that she wasn't. He wrapped his arms around her. "It's going to be okay Brandy," he tells her. Chris was just trying to be there for her in her time of need. He wiped her tears every time a tear drop rolled down her face. Paige walked up to them.

"Chris, can you and mom go in there with me?" Chris looked at Brandy.

"Baby, go in there with Chris, I can't go right back in there right now, I will in a little while," she says as she was still crying, but even harder.

Chris looked at Paige. "Yeah sweetheart, let's go," Paige and Chris walked towards her great grandmother's room. Chris swung open the door and let Paige walk in first, but then Paige took a few steps back and got behind Chris. Chris kept walking towards her bed a tear began to roll down his face. Paige stood behind him on the side of her face pressed up against his back as she held on to his left arm staring at her great grandmother crying. They stayed in there just staring at her. An hour later the family all left.

A week later the plug was finally pulled and the charge nurse contacted the family. Once the call was made to Katrina she stopped from what she was doing to head to the hospital, she dialed Mike.

"Hey baby," he answered.

"Babe, they just announced my grandmother is dead!" she screamed through the phone. She was crying so hard. It was hard for her to cry and drive, she could barely see the road for her tears.

"Damn babe, you serious!"

"Babe, just meet me at the hospital!"

"Do you want to drop the car off at home and we ride up there together so you don't have to drive?"

"No babe, I think I can handle it."

"Okay, where are the kids?"

"School and daycare still."

"Do you want me to grab Simone?"

"Ummm, yeah, you can."

"Ok, I'm not that far from her now."

"Okay well, I will see you in a minute."

"Okay, babe I love you!"

"Love you too!"

On Katrina's way there to the hospital, her Aunt Marie called her asking if she could pick her up. Katrina went and picked her Aunt up, then they rushed to the hospital. The two cried the whole way driving there. Katrina's cell began ringing.

"Hey babe," she answered, it was her husband,

"Hurry up!" they're about to get ready to take her body to the morgue."

"Babe, tell her to hold on, let the nurse know your wife is on her way."

"Alright babe," they hung up.

Katrina was pissed that she was catching every damn red light. Can't get on the freeway it's too packed.

Katrina's cell rung again, it was Mike.

"Hello," she answers.

"Babe, where are you, are you here yet?"

"No babe, I had to drive the streets, the freeway was too packed, and it's like I'm catching every red light."

"Well, this nurse said if you're not here in the next five minutes that she has to take her body down to the morgue."

"I will be there in a minute."

Finally getting to the hospital and up to her grandmother's room she wasn't in there anymore and she didn't even see any of their family, it looked like they had all gone already. By the time they made it to the hospital her grandmother was already taken to the morgue. Katrina asked the nurse that was at the nurse's station closest to where her grandmother's room was at *where her grandmother was.*

"Oh, ma'am I'm sorry, it's too late already."

"No, I want to see my grandmother right now, that was me that my husband was trying to tell you I was on my way, take me to see her now!" She became exceedingly frustrated at this nurse behind her grandmother.

"Ma'am, I'm sorry, but I can't."

"No, let me speak to your supervisor!" Katrina took her chances asking her supervisor, and if she didn't cooperate she still was not about to take no for an answer. Once the supervisor came she asked if she and her Aunt could see their grandmother and mother for the last time. The Supervisor said to them both, *"Follow me."* They followed her to the elevator. Going down the elevator to the basement is where the Morgue was. Katrina couldn't wait to see her grandmother. As the three got off the elevator they followed the arrows; they read morgue. Walking down the halls leading to the morgue it was getting colder and colder. As they approached a double door the charge nurse pushed the doors open leading to the outside. This is not what Katrina was expecting, but then again, this was her and her Aunt's first time going to a morgue. Then they approached another door, the charge nurse grabbed onto the door knob to open the door as she looked back at Katrina and her Aunt.

"Are you both ready?"

Katrina and her Aunt both became nervous, but yes, the two were ready to see her.

"Yes," they both replied back at the same time slowly. The nurse opened the door all the way and the three went inside. She then opened the refrigerator like door to the right at the bottom and pulled out her grandmother. Her grandmother was inside a black body bag. As the nurse unzipped the bag she took a step back and let them say their last good byes. They stood there talking to her for five minutes, then they thanked the nurse. The nurse then zipped her back up and pushed her back inside and locked the door. They left out. Katrina and her Aunt Marie began crying, they were holding onto each other as they walked down the hallway back to the elevator. Getting off the elevator Katrina dialed her husband.

"Babe, y'all left?"

"No, we're down in the lobby in the front of the hospital."

"Ok, I'm about to come around there."

"Alright," Mike said.

Katrina and her Aunt Marie hugged Mike and Simone. "Did y'all go up there?"

"Yeah we did," Katrina sounded softly.

"She didn't let y'all see her huh?"

"Babe, I was not taking no for an answer. I talked to her supervisor and I had her take us down to the morgue, I was not playing."

"I'm glad you guys saw her."

"Me too.", "Me too," Katina and her Aunt sounded back to back.

The family planned the arrangements for the funeral. The funeral was set for a week later. Days later Katrina had found a really cute dress for the funeral on Wednesday. She wasn't about to wear black, she wanted to wear mint green like her grandmother. They all did: her husband, daughter, her Aunts and her Uncle. Upon arriving and walking in with the family they were all handed a funeral program before getting to a seat. She began looking over the pictures that were inside, everyone that was in the sanctuary crying. Chris even showed up. Once Terrell saw him he felt awkward seeing his girl's ex there, but he wasn't about to even take it there, this is a funeral. Chris walked in and an obituary was handed to him, he looked down and sees she looks just like the obituary. They used an updated photo. He sat down and began reading the obituary. After reading the obituary he closed it to look back at her picture. Then he looked up at the preacher as he begun preaching. Once the service started the church was packed from downstairs to upstairs. There were so many people there besides family to pay their respects. Chris sat on the family side; he was just six seats behind Brandy. Brandy turned around looking at all the family behind her and saw Chris from the corner of her eyes, she nodded her head at him, then she turned back around. Terrell turned around too after her and noticed Chris was sitting on their side, he turned around reaching his arm around her shoulders.

During the service, tissue kept being passed to her and other members of the family for their crying. Everyone that was there at the funeral was crying, it was very sad; she was surely a woman who was loved by all. It became time to view her, Brandy and Katrina took a deep breath. They both walked up to the stainless steel casket together and just stood there shedding more tears, they hesitated to move, they both stood there rubbing on their grandmother's hands as they silently talked to her. The line to view her body became backed up. They walked back around to their seat and sat back in the pews. After everyone viewed her body they closed her casket, it was over. After the funeral, Chris hugged everyone in the family and then told them bye. He was beginning to leave when he heard his name called.

"Chris, thank you so much for coming and being here for my grandmother," Brandy said to him.

Chris looked into Brandy's eyes "Your more than welcome, take care."

She nodded her head. Chris left.

Everyone that showed up to the church had followed each other to the cemetery. After the cemetery, everyone drove to the repast. Katrina sat most of the time talking to the family, she was overwhelmed with her continued crying. Some others were standing around crying too still.

A WEEK LATER

Katrina was running late, just ten minutes late, she pulled up and parked, she walked in and went straight to the conference room. Walking in they hadn't even started the meeting yet, she was hoping they would have started the meeting already. She wondered what was taking them so long to start the meeting, she needed to check her emails and voicemails. Her work gave her a basket of flowers, balloons, and a card that they signed for her losing her grandmother. She began shedding tears, Katrina thought this was so sweet of them to do this for her. She was looking forward to a busy day today with her back to back clients, she did not expect this at all. After the meeting, everyone parted. Katrina went to her office to begin checking her appointments, her emails, and voicemails.

Katrina was sitting at her desk in her office. As she was in the middle of reading her emails Suzy showed up knocking on her door. She looked over at her.

"Hey lady, what's up?"

"Girl, I just finished reading chapter three and now I'm on chapter four in part two and oh my God," she smiled.

Katrina grinned, "I still haven't got the book yet, I have to get those books. What was that author's name again?"

"Girl, her name is LaShane Moore, you have to get all three, I swear her books will leave you on the edge of your seat!"

Katrina laughed, "I've been so busy, but I love me a good juicy book to read, I will get her books."

Suzy's eye brow raised, "Soon girl, because this part I'm on kind of sound like you and what you went through with Gary."

Katrina's eyes got big, "For real."

"Yes," Suzy shook her head.

"Read it to me."

"Okay," she said happily. Suzy went back to her receptionist desk to get her Secret Love 2 Book. She couldn't wait to read this scene to Katrina. This scene sounded so much like what she went through with her ex-husband. Suzy came back with her book and began to read.

Separating her family for good was not going to be easy at all, but with that image that kept popping up in her head with him having an affair with her sister, she knew it could never be the same, so why waste her time anymore.

Glancing down at her wedding ring, she slowly slid it off. She looked down and then back up at him; she felt it was over. She was giving up on trying; she felt she couldn't go on with him anymore.

Suzy stopped reading and looked up at her. Katrina almost wanted to tell her to read more, it amazed her how much what she just went through and is doing is so relatable to her, yes she definitely has to get these books.

The house was quiet, Mike took Mike Jr. to the park and Simone was out with her friends, she was enjoying her evening of no noise, just quiet with her and her new book. Two hours later her man returned. Mike couldn't wait to bother her, he thought about it all the way home from the park. The moment he walked in Mike began messing around with her.

"Babe, leave me alone while I'm trying to read." He kept messing with her, she began laughing.

"Baby," she chuckled as her eyes are still looking down at her book.

"Is that book way more important," he chuckled.

"Of course not babe," she says as her eyes are glued to the pages.

"Let me see the name of that book?"

As she still reads she faces the front cover of the book his way.

"Secret Love -In the Beginning," he read. "I hope that book is not going to tell you how to find you a Secret Love."

She pushed his shoulder, "Be quiet silly of course not, but this Secret Love Series, it's very good. She has three books in this series, so I bought all three. You know the receptionist Suzy?" she asked.

"Yeah!" he sounded.

"Yeah, she got me hooked on this author!"

"Who is the author?"

"LaShane Moore, she's a very good writer. Her books are so easy to read, she tells the juiciest stories, she talks about some real stuff, and it's been keeping me on the edge of my seat. Suzy told me she has a new book that just came out called Having It His Way, I have to make sure I get that one next when I'm done reading her Secret Love Series, Suzy has been telling me about her books, but I just started reading them last week. I wish I would have been reading her books," she says.

"Oh, ok," he sounded.

"Yeah, so far I just read nine chapters, so I'm almost done. I have one more chapter to go, which I will be done by tonight, then I'm going to start with her Secret Love part two tomorrow after work. Then I'm reading her part three after that!"

"Oh, Ok, then let me leave you alone, yeah you get back to your reading sweetheart," he grins.

"Thanks, babe I love you!!!" she shouted as he was walking out the room.

"Love you too!" he walked back to the living room.

The next day once Katrina got off work she drove straight home. The sun had barely set and she was just arriving home. She's ready to go lay down underneath her cover and get back to reading The Secret Love Series. She couldn't wait to see what's about to happen in part two. Arriving home she approached her husband with a hug.

"Hey honey!" he kissed her.

"How was your day babe?"

"Very long, just seeing a lot of different clients showing them houses," Katrina says.

"How was your day?" she asked him.

"It was good," then he took a sip of his beer. "Babe, dinner is on the stove. Mike Jr. has already been changed, he ate his food, and he barely went to sleep ten minutes ago."

"Oh, okay. Simone is not home yet?"

"No, but she called."

"What did she say?"

"She said she was at Lauren's house watching a movie and when it's over she'll be home, she said Lauren's mother is going to drop her off."

Mike sat back down on the couch. "Babe, you wouldn't guess what I'm over here reading."

"What," she looked at him.

He grabbed the book and raised it up so she could see. "Secret Love In the Beginning."

"Aww shit, look at you babe!" she shouted out loudly with a smile.

"Yeah, this book is good so far, I had to see what you were reading that had you ignoring me," he laughed.

"Babe, don't say it like that," she chuckled.

"Well it's the truth," he chuckled. "This Brandy is something crazy."

"Yeah, she's wrong!"

"How far have you gotten?"

"I'm just on the part when the sister comes home early to question her sister about her husband, but she denies it."

"Oh, ok," she smiled.

"Shit, you already doing what I was just telling myself in the car what I wanted to do once I get here because I'm about to start on part two now,"

"Yeah, I see why you were so into the book the other day and yesterday, it's entertaining for sure," he took a sip of his beer, then sat it back down on the floor next to him.

"See, I told you," she said. "Babe, you already ate?"

"No, I was waiting on you," he said.

"You want me to go make your plate?"

"No, not yet, I'm going to finish this chapter first, then I'll be ready to eat"

"Okay."

Katrina went to go change, then she went and got her book and sat beside Mike as they both read their books together silently. They cuddle up and watched a movie.

Later that night Mike wanted to see if Katrina was going to notice him doing some positions from that Secret Love book they are reading. Katrina had taken a shower. Katrina stepped out the bathroom and stood to lean her hand up against the wall with just her purple lace lingerie on. He walked up to her and pulled her to the bed. He slid off her lingerie and laid her down on the bed. He getting on top as she takes in all of him. Katrina sounded a laugh and that's when he laughed, he had a feeling she had caught on. They continued.

The breathing was heavy, the moaning was loud. The two were very wet, it was slippery and it kept coming out. "Babe let me get a towel so I could wipe it off, it's way too wet."

"Babe it's no such thing as it's too wet." She smiled. "I know I feel it but what are you getting a towel for, just lick it."

Mike licked her up and down. She laughed. "I was kidding." She said smiling looking down at him.

Mike got up to get a towel. He wiped them both and afterward she grabbed onto his balls gently caressing them with her fingers then she began sucking them. Then she grabbed him placing her hand on the bottom and her other hand at the top. She firmly began stroking him in opposite direction with her hands up, down and twisting it at the same time. Massaging him. Slowly, her face moved to his penis to use her mouth to get him harder, she began sucking it. Katrina took over for a minute. She had Mike feeling just as she wanted him too. She took his penis from out her mouth once she began to feel it stretch out. He jerked from the feeling of her mouth passing the tip of his penis.

He put it back in her vagina and sped up into a fast paste. Katrina held on to him, he began mumbling words she couldn't even understand. He felt her hips moving up and down towards him.

"Babe get up," she whispered.

Mike got up and so did she. "Sit on the edge of the bed," she told him.

Katrina bent down right in front of him placing her hands on the floor. "Babe now grab my legs up on the bed and put it in." Katrina began moving her body up and down on it. She was also doing some moves on him from that Secret Love Series, then suddenly his body began shaking, he exploded inside her.

"Baby, that's from the book," she moaned.

CHAPTER
14

Charles and Shante

Seems like Shante will be the first woman Charles could see himself marrying, and the only one for that matter. Shante still can't believe she is about to get married soon, she has been waiting for this day for a very long time now.

That morning they got up at seven to get ready to go hiking up the mountain with his brother, his sister, and their friends. Once Sharee, Katrina, Mike, and Michelle made it to their house they were ready to leave. Katrina's cell rang and it was a client that needed to see a house before his flight left, this was the only time he had. Katrina did not like to miss out on potential clients. She apologized to her hubby and her friends, but they understood. Katrina left Shante's house to meet up with her client. Mike stayed and was about to roll in the car with his brother since Mike and his sister had rolled in the car with Katrina. Michelle left her car at Katrina's and Mike's house. Michelle began walking towards Shante's car to ride with them too.

"Michelle, come ride with me so I don't have to roll up there by myself!" Sharee shouted.

Michelle stopped and looked back, "Ok," she sounded, then she turned around and walked to Sharee's car. They took two cars up to the mountain.

Charles's boy Levell was meeting him there. Getting there seeing everyone he had his eyes on Sharee, from a distance getting out the car he saw every reason to want to get to know her. She had a killer body and he wants all of it, she's curvaceous is what she is and all in the right places. Considering he's there for his boy, he didn't want to push all up on her in front of his fiancé and her homegirls not knowing her relationship status, but he sure can't wait until after this walk and ask Charles.

"Sharee, this is Charles's boy Levell," Shante introduces Levell to her girl. Shante figured he's single she's single, just might be a match, who knows.

Sharee looked him up and down as she smiles.

He reached for her hand as she brought her hand to his and they shook hands. "Nice to meet you Levell," she replied smiling.

"Nice to meet you Sharee," Levell replied.

Sharee looked up at the mountain, "Shante, I hope you don't expect us to walk way up there to the top of that mountain?"

Shante laughed. "Naw, of course not girl, we just walk the trail."

"Oh, okay, cool, I was about to say," Sharee chuckled.

They all began walking the trail. Everyone was all engaging in conversation as they walked. After forty-five minutes Michelle's feet were hurting, she began to slow down her pace.

"I feel like it's taking forever," Michelle sounded.

Charles turned around looking at his sister, "Come on sis, catch up!"

"I'm trying brother!" she shouted.

Charles laughed.

"Girl, March fifth will be here sooner than you know, then you're going to be like where did the time go," Sharee told Shante.

"Girl I know right, rushing still trying to do stuff at the last minute." Sharee was getting nervous for her girl as they approached closer to their wedding date.

Once they all made it back to their cars, Charles had a case of water in his trunk; he threw everybody a bottle of water.

"Hey Mike, I can drop off you and Michelle at the house on my way home," Sharee sounded.

"Oh fa sho, please," he said.

"Oh yeah, no problem," Sharee sounded. Mike ended up hopping in the car with Sharee and his sister. Everybody was about to get ready to leave, then Shante and Charles said their good byes to their friends and his sister and brother, then they went straight home and just chilled out. Later that evening Shante had gone over everything with Charles about their wedding rehearsal days, who will carry the rings down the aisle for them, the reception, and the DJ. He was fine with everything she had mentioned.

Shante was happy her aunts are coming down for her wedding, she was glad she could give them a reason to come down. She has not seen her aunts and her cousins since they all moved to Florida. After another thirty minutes of looking over her guest list, she just went and got in bed. Shante slid underneath the covers with Charles.

"Don't worry baby, everything is going to turn out perfect baby," he told her.

Charles noticed her nervousness; he had to reassure her everything would be okay.

"I know baby, I just want our special day to be perfect."

"It will be," he told her and then she nodded her head as she looked into his eyes and then the two kissed. After they kissed he was still looking at her.

She nodded her head. He shook his head from side to side in silence. As she still stared into his eyes she slid down underneath their cover on her knees in front of him slowly. She let him slide it slowly down into her mouth. She began stroking her hands that were wrapped around his penis slowly in a twisting and turning motion as she continues to go up and down with it. He pulled the covers back from off her as she was sucking on it.

After a long while he had her lay down, he went up to her lips for a kiss then finally he made his way down to her other lips for a kiss. He began kissing them so passionately, then he slid his tongue up into her center, then he started flicking his tongue back and forth inside it.

Her face had an expression that he couldn't see right then, she was glad for that. He loves how her insides taste. As always it was feeling so good. After he was done down there, their lips came together and kissed a strong firm peck. That still didn't stop the feeling she felt down there as if his tongue was still up in it. They made love sliding up and down on the bed.

Afterward, their mouths were dry as hell. She was already expecting that is why she already had some bottled waters in the refrigerator for them that she had put up in there earlier.

She went and got both waters. They sat there in bed and drunk their whole bottles as they were still catching their breath. They got underneath the covers; he pulled her back by her waist and then they cuddled close against each other and went to sleep.

The next morning waking up, she went to the kitchen and made them both breakfast. Afterward, Shante made a few phone calls.

Shante has been touching base with everyone that's going to take part in the ceremony. She and Charles had discussed dinner for everyone tonight and a toast. Shante also called down to the restaurant and made reservations. They couldn't wait for later tonight, they have a special dinner planned for them tonight.

As the day went on, later he walked in the house surprising her with flowers. He walked up on her while she was putting on her makeup.

"Hey, baby!"

"Hey!"

She turned around to give him a hug and kiss, as she was turning around, he brought the flowers from behind him and passed them to her.

"Awww baby, they are beautiful!"

"Not as beautiful as you!" he told her.

They kissed and then they hugged.

"You ready to head to the restaurant?"

"Yes!"

"What time are your girls meeting us there?"

"I told them all six o' clock."

"Okay cool, I told the boys the same time."

"Alright, babe I'll be ready in five minutes."

Getting closer and closer to the date things were becoming hectic, they wanted to show some love and appreciation to their bridesmaids and their best men is why they invited everyone out to dinner, their treat.

Shante couldn't wait to see her four beautiful bridesmaids to eat: Katrina, Sharee, her cousin Joy, and her sister in-law Michelle. Charles was having his four best men: Mike, Levell, Keveyon, and his cousin Malik meet there too. Shante and Charles wanted to thank them for being willing to be a part of something so special to them.

Sharee smiled, she sees Charles's homeboy from the walk at the mountain a few weeks ago about to walk in.

Levell stepped up to her. "Hey, beautiful you remember me!"

"Yes of course," he was very hard to forget with his handsome looking ass, his sexy ass brown eyes, and his curly hair.

Katrina walked up to them, "Is this the guy you were telling me about?"

"Yeah," Sharee smiled.

"Katrina, this is Levell, Levell, this is my girl Katina, Mike's wife."

Katrina looked him up and down as she smiles.

"Nice to finally meet you Katrina, I've heard a lot about you from my boy Charles and your husband, it seems like I already know you."

"Yeah, I know right, I'm surprised I'm just now meeting you, I've heard about you too, you and Charles use to play ball together back in college."

"Yeah, we did. I just moved back down from New York."

"Oh wow really, that's not where you are from right?"

"No, I was out there for work, but I'm from Toronto. I have family down here but then the rest are back in Toronto," he smiled.

"That's right!"

After that everyone began to find them a seat at the table.

Once the waiter poured the Champagne in everyone's glasses Charles had everyone lift their glasses up, he wanted to say something. Then all drinks were raised and everyone stood up. Shante and Charles stood at the head of the table, Shante started off the toast. "I would like to thank my wonderful best friends and my new brother in-law Mike, and my cousin Joy, you guys have been an extremely big help in making our soon to be special day special!"

"Katrina and Sharee, you ladies have always meant the world to me. You bring me joy and happiness even when I don't feel like it, you two know how to bring it out of me. You both hold special places in my life and in my heart, I love the both of you with all my heart, you're the best, you two!"

"Awww, we love you too!" Katrina and Sharee both said at the same time.

"To my cousin Joy," Shante held her hands balled up to her chest, as she looked her cousin straight in her eyes. "Cousin, I don't know how you did it girl, but you did. You managed to go to work, handle your household, and still helped me with everything, not one time did you tell me no, you kept making sure I had everything covered. Girl, you are the best!"

Joy's smile grew on her face, "You're welcome cousin and I love you too!" she shouted.

"My turn," Charles said.

"Wait, wait, and wait!" Shante chuckled, "To my new brother in-law, all I have to say is that you are the best brother in-law a person could have!"

"Thanks, sis!" Mike smiled.

Charles turned his head and looked at his fiancé. "I'm done baby," she smiled.

Charles' eyes looked straight at his brother and Katrina first, "To Mike and Katrina, I just want to say to you that I love you both so much, because you two are the main reason on why we are here tonight. If it wasn't for Katrina telling my beautiful fiancé about me and if it wasn't for my brother Mike giving the message that was passed down, this day wouldn't be and speaking for me and Shante we just want to say thank you to you guys and we truly love you both!"

"And we love you guys too!" Mike and Katrina shouted out at the same time. Mike and Katrina stood there with their glasses up smiling at them. They were just happy to put two lovebirds together.

"Joy, I want to thank you for being their helping Shante out with everything, we appreciated it so much!"

"You're welcome!" she shouted out smiling.

"To my sister and to my boy Levell, thank you guys for being a part of our journey, we love y'all and we thank y'all!"

They both shouted. "We love y'all too!"

"Last but not least, I had to save the special one for last!" he chuckled, looking at Shante. Charles said a special speech to Shante, his fiancé after his speech they all drank their drinks up, then Shante and Charles sat their glass down and kissed. They gave each other a big kiss on the lips.

"That's right y'all, I wish you both nothing but love and happiness forever!" Mike shouted.

Two weeks later during rehearsal all the bridesmaids and best men were there.

Levell went up to Sharee to say hello.

"Hey, Levell so you're one of the best men now?"

"How'd you know?" he smiled.

"I figured there are only bridesmaids and best men here tonight, then not to mention you were also at the dinner a few weeks ago!"

"Okay, Okay, even though I could have been just hanging out with y'all," they laughed together.

"I'm sorry, it was Sha--- what again?" he asked her.

"It's Sharee!" she smiled.

"How you forget mines and I remembered yours!"

"My bad," he told her.

"So Levell what made you come over here to me?"

"I have been wanting to talk to you since the mountain, plus you look like someone I want to get to know."

"Oh really, do you?"

"Yes, and you have nice, beautiful brown eyes."

"Thank you."

"They're sexy," he told her.

"Thank you."

"You're welcome."

"You happy for your boy getting married!" she smiled.

"Yeah, I am my man straight about to be getting married in the next month."

"Right, it's coming fast!" she grinned.

"Oh yeah, sure is," he grinned too.

"Is it okay that I ask you for your number?"

"Sure!" Sharee gave him her number as he punched it in his phone.

"I'm calling you now so you can have mines too."

"Okay," just as she was saying okay her cell was already sounding off.

"Got it," Sharee said.

"Alright, cool."

They gave each other a friendly hug. Sharee enjoyed his hug, his arms wrapped around her were delicate to her body and not all aggressive like how RoShawn's hugs used to be. After the rehearsal, everybody left the building at the same time.

"Hey, what are you about to do?" he asked.

"Ummm, go home."

"You want to go have a drink at the bar with me?"

She stood there looking at him smiling.

"Just one drink," she sounded.

"Okay."

The two followed each other to the bar. Driving there she thought about how interesting this was about to be because she hadn't been out drinking with a man in a while, but come to think about it, she had not been out drinking with a man at all, just her girls. They soon made it to the bar and getting there they found them a table. He pulled out her chair for him to show his true gentleman side. She sat down and crossed her legs and he sat across from her.

"For a Tuesday night, this bar is crowded!"

"Yeah, I know huh," she said.

The waitress came over and Levell was ready to order them drinks. "Hello, what can I get for you two tonight?"

"Hello, how are you, I will let the beautiful lady order first," then his eyes glanced at Sharee.

Sharee smiled, and then looked at the waitress, "Yes, I would like to order a margarita please!"

"Ok, one margarita coming up and then for you sir?" the waitress looked at Levell.

"Yes, for me I'll take a Margarita too!"

"Ok, so two Margaritas; can I get you anything else tonight? We have fifty cent tacos going on all night for Taco Tuesday."

Levell looked at Sharee, "That explains why it's so crowded on a Tuesday, I forgot about Taco Tuesday."

"I know, me too," she said.

"So Ms. Lady, would you like a few tacos?"

"Sure, I'll have two."

Levell looked up at the waitress, "Ok, we'll take six tacos along with our drinks."

"Ok, coming right up," The waitress walked off.

Sharee's eyes turned to Levell. "So you drink Margaritas, I can see you as a straight Hennessey type of man."

"Yeah, I drink that too."

"Oh ok," she smiled.

"Yeah, I just wanted something that wasn't that hard tonight."

"I hear you on that," then shortly their drinks came.

"Let's toast to a new friendship," they raised their drinks up in the air. She had a big smile on her face and so did he. Their glasses clinked and they both said cheers to a new friendship, they took a sip at the same time and then sat their glasses on the table. Sitting across from each other talking and sipping on their drinks they couldn't help the eye contact they were giving each other.

"Oh I'm sorry, would you like anything else to go with your tacos?"

"No just the tacos are good."

"Ok."

Shortly their order arrived at their table, the waitress placed Sharee's plate in front of her and then she placed Levell's order in front of him. The two began to eat.

"So, are you single?" he asked.

"Yes, and are you?"

"Yes, I am too."

She pulled her glass up to her lips and took another sip.

"I know you've been seeing someone, you are too beautiful to be single."

Sharee took in a deep long breath. "Well, actually I just got out of a relationship a few months ago."

"Wow, that bad huh."

"Yeah, he was something else but I'm glad that's over, that's a conversation for another night."

"Oh, no worries, so what have you been doing to fulfill your sexual needs, you haven't been seeing any one?"

"I haven't," she laughed. "I haven't had any interest in sex, and I don't just go around sexing some random just because, no, I believe I can wait," she grinned.

They both began to talk about their personal lives and about life, the conversation was very interesting. They finished their drink.

"Would you like another drink?"

"Yes."

Levell called over the waitress. "Can we get another round please?"

"Of the same thing?" the waitress asked him.

"Yes please, a margarita for her and this time I'll take a Cadillac Margarita."

"Ok, coming right up." The waitress took their empty glasses and walked over to the bar. Moments later she came with another round for them. The waitress came sitting their glasses down on the table right in front of them.

He wanted her to sit closer; she stood up as Levell slid her chair over closer to him.

"Are you enjoying yourself?"

"Yes I am, and I'm enjoying you and our conversation."

"I'm enjoying you and our conversation too," he replied. He wrapped his arm around her shoulder talking with her as he continues his drink. Normally she wouldn't be so open, but with him she was, since it was something about him she liked she thought it to be important to get to the point in the beginning of what she's not going to go through again, so there wouldn't be any surprises later. This was a first he thought, a beautiful woman such as her being straight forward.

"How old are you?" he asked.

"I'm thirty-four, and you."

"Thirty-six," he said.

"When is your birthday?" he asked.

"January seventeenth," she replied.

"Mines is July eighth."

"Oh, ok," she sounded with a smile.

"So tell me why you are single, you are very attractive?"

"Okay, so here's the thing, I haven't met anyone serious that wasn't with the games. Then it's like if they were serious, they came with too much drama, like baby daddy problems, I wasn't really with all that."

"So, what do you do for a living?"

"I work at a school district."

"School District," he repeated.

"Yeah, I work in the payroll department. I file papers, do data entry, process checks, calculate employees work hours and type up checks."

"Oh wow," he nodded his head.

"Yes, it's cool I have been with them for years."

"That's real cool Sharee," he sounded.

Talking with her he was still surprised how open she was and he liked that about her, the only thing she hasn't mentioned is why her and her ex-broke up, only saying he wasn't treating her right. Levell was just glad that she got herself from out that situation, he didn't deserve her anyway. It's been two hours chilling with her at the bar; he didn't want to leave, but it was getting late and they both have to work tomorrow.

Just being a gentleman he had to ask, "Do you want another drink?" he asked.

"Oh no, no more for me. I'm already tipsy enough, I can still drive home, but another one would just make me drunk," she smiles.

Levell couldn't stop his gaze into her eyes. "I want to kiss you," he sounded.

"Huh!"

"I want to kiss you," he mumbled again.

She turned her head and pointed her finger to her cheek and Levell leaned towards her giving her a peck on her cheek. Twenty minutes later he looked down at his watch. "It's getting late, you almost ready to leave?"

"Yeah." she said. It had already been a long day with work, then the wedding rehearsal, and now sitting two hours at this bar. She was ready to call it a night too, but she was really enjoying herself right now.

Leaving the bar he walked her out to her car. Reaching her car he gave her a tight hug, wrapping both his arms around her waist.

"Well let me tell you, I have enjoyed myself with you tonight Ms. Lady and I pray we continue to see each other and go out on many more dates."

She looked into his eyes, "Of course," she said flirtatiously as she brushed her hair back behind her left ear with her fingers. He smiled and shook his head up and down, and then she hugged him back as his arms were still wrapped around her.

"Thank you, I had a good time as well," she told him.

That night after getting home she began getting text messages from him saying he made it home and how he really enjoyed their date. Once the text messages stopped Sharee had a hard time going to sleep. Sharee tossed and turned, she couldn't get her and Levell's date and the good time they had out her head. Of course, Sharee didn't want to, but she was tired and wanted to get more than five hours of sleep.

***

That night getting home Charles got into the shower first while Shante stood in front of their bedroom mirror wrapping her hair and wrapping a scarf around her hair. Once he got out he hopped in the bed, then she got in. She took a quick shower and did a quick shave down there as well. She came out the shower talking. He rolled over from off his stomach onto his back once he heard her voice entering the room.

She flopped on the bed next to him. The two talked holding a conversation, the conversation led them to sex. They kissed holding each other by the cheeks, their clothes came off. He slid down and licked in between her, afterward he got on top. He moaned. Shortly switching positions Shante got on top of Charles. Suddenly *Oh God*, she moaned; with each thrust the moans sounded.

"Baby, it feels like I'm getting a cramp."

"Then let's stop for a minute."

"No baby, I can't stop, I have to keep going, it just feels too good." He kept it in with his firm grip to her butt massaging it as she kept gliding him up and down, he was so deep in.

"Baby," she sounded; she laughed as she kept gliding.

"Ooooh!" he said with strong emotion.

"You ok baby?"

"No, I'm getting a Charlie horse and this shit is hurting like hell," he said. But the stronger his pain, the firmer he would hold her, he kept his grip, and Shante kept going as he was plunging into her moaning loudly with his eyes closed. He didn't want to stop, he couldn't, he felt his orgasm it was coming. He began holding her even tighter going faster, she was going faster with him, once the screaming and moaning stopped they both had cum.

"Whew!" he sounded. She got up and sat on the side of him. He immediately tried to massage out the pain in his leg, but the pain was still getting stronger. Shortly he got the pain to stop.

"Whew, that shit hurt bad as hell!"

"Well, I told you to stop."

"Baby, what you do to me?" he laughed.

"Babe, don't blame that on me, I tried to tell you to stop," she chuckled.

"Well I couldn't, it was just feeling too good, I had to say to myself fuck that pain."

All she did was sit and look at him and smile. Then they both called it a night and cuddled under the covers.

That next morning waking up they realize they have less than thirty days before their big day. That morning Shante's phone began to ring, it was six in the morning. Her mother was like her alarm clock, she called about the same time every morning. "Good morning mother," she answers.

"Hey, Shante I was calling to tell you to have a good day at work baby."

"Thank you mom, you have a good day too."

"Tell my son in-law I said have a good day too."

"He's still asleep but I will tell him."

"Okay baby," then they hung up.

She glanced down at him, he was sleeping so peacefully. She didn't want to wake him, but she had too. She leaned down kissing his face, "Baby wake up," she sounded in his face. Her low voice, she was surprised he heard her, but he did. He got up and the two took a shower together. They both got out the shower naked and began to get dressed. After they were ready they went to the kitchen. He sat down at the table and she got the pan from out the cabinet. She took some eggs out the refrigerator and scrambled them. Shante grabbed the loaf of bread out the cabinet and made them an egg sandwich, something fast and quick. Then they left. He went to the restaurant and the law office was her second home. Mountains of file folders to file from different attorneys cases, cases to look over, court dates to schedule for them, and during the process she got to talk throughout the day with her girls. She loves her coworkers. They always kept each other alive at work, always having something to talk about and laugh at. In addition to having her girls to eat lunch with and they enjoyed treating.

That evening getting off work Shante couldn't think about anything but relaxing, she didn't want to see no mail, no papers, or anything; she didn't want to read anything, just her, her couch, and her TV is all she wanted.

Getting home Shante walked in and sees she needs to clean up, she has let a few days go by. It wasn't that bad, but there were a few things that were on the floor and around the house that she could clean, the bathrooms and vacuum the carpet and clean the kitchen. Although that is not what she wanted to come home and do first, she knew if she didn't get that out the way now she's not going to feel like doing it later. An hour later she was done with everything, then her cell phone rang, Shante walked to the table and grabbed her phone, "Hello," she answered.

"Hey baby, I was calling to ask you about the wedding rehearsal yesterday, so how did it go, did everybody show up?"

"It went very good, and yes, everyone showed up, we had fun."

"That's good baby."

"It's coming fast."

"Yes, it is baby you guys have a month to go."

"Yeah."

Shante's Mom could hear her daughter's tone getting nervous. "Are you sounding a little nervous over there?"

"I just hope everything goes right, that's all."

"It will baby."

"But what if our wedding gets ruined, what if it decides it wants to rain that day, it has been raining all week."

"Well, you can't speak that into existence."

"I know, but it's been raining all week non-stop, what if it's raining then too?"

"Well, you're getting married next month Shante!"

"I know mom, but this is spring." she paused. "It's not supposed to be raining right now just cold. It is Charles birthday month, he wanted us to get married the day of his birthday, but his birthday falls on a Wednesday the second and I didn't want to have our wedding on a weekday so we decided to have it the Saturday after."

"Oh ok, that makes sense."

"Well baby, I'm going to pray that it doesn't and that you guys's day be just how you planned it to be, I'm surprised that it's even raining now."

"I know and thank you mom, we need the prayers."

"You're welcome sweetie."

"I am glad everything is done already."

"I know, me too."

Shante was just glad she can now say she is done with all the arrangements and details for the wedding and reception, she can now relax. Shante's cell line was clicking.

"Mom, hold on, my other line is ringing," she pulled the phone away from her ear to see who it was before clicking over. It was Sharee.

"Oh, this Sharee," she mumbled.

"Alright baby, just call me back or just call me tomorrow, I'm about to lay down."

"Mom, you and your seven o' clock bedtime," she laughed. "Alright, mom, good night, I love you."

"Good night baby, love you too Shante."

Shante hung up the call with her mother and clicked over.

"Hey lady," she answered.

"Hey Shante!"

"What's going on with you lady?" Shante asked.

"Girl at home doing nothing, just relaxing and got some food in the oven," Sharee replied.

"Oh, that's right," Shante responded.

"Lady, what were you doing?

"Nothing, just getting off the phone with momma, she was asking about the wedding rehearsal and how it went."

"Oh, ok."

"Girl after my long day I couldn't wait to get home and relax, but when I got here I remembered I needed to clean up," Shante said.

"Yeah, I did that earlier when I made it home from work too. Sooo speaking of your wedding rehearsal, I'm not sure if you paid any attention to me and Levell the other night."

"Un Un, why what happened?' Shante asked.

"We exchanged numbers and have been talking ever since."

"I'm not dating anybody no more," she chuckled.

"Be quiet," Sharee laughed.

"Hey, that's what you told us, I'm just saying," Shante laughed out loud. "I knew that shit wasn't going to last long. Naw, but he's cool, he has a good job, very respectful, no kids, a very humble dude."

"Does he have a woman?" Sharee asked her.

"No, I don't know why he doesn't, but yeah he's a good guy."

"Well that's good to know, he seems like it. I just wanted to make sure. He asked me for my number at the wedding rehearsal."

"Okay, that's right, did you give it to him?"

"Yeah I did, I've talked to him twice so far, just wanted to make sure he was cool."

"Oh, ok, yeah he is."

"Oh, ok, thanks boo, alright talk to you later."

"You're welcome. Alright bye!" they hung up.

Sharee began to think about *what he was doing*. She looked over at the time, it was seven twenty-nine. *Ummm, should I call him or wait until eight to call she asked herself; she decided to wait until eight to call.* Sharee got out the bed to check on the food, it was ready. She couldn't get enough of steak; Sharee had made herself one steak and homemade mash potatoes. She was so hungry she was done in ten minutes. She took her plate back to the kitchen and returned to her room. She then went to the bathroom. After she used the bathroom, she got back into her bed, then suddenly her cell began to ring. She looked at the screen of her phone and grinned, it was Levell.

"Hello," she smiled as she answered the phone.

"Hey sweetie," Levell said to her.

"Hey, Levell your ears must have been ringing."

"Oh, you were talking about me?" he asked.

"I was just thinking about calling you, I was thinking should I call him right now or should I wait until eight to call him, then ten minutes later you call. Good to see we were both on each other's mind at the same time."

CHAPTER

15

Finally Someone Special

Sharee went into work the next morning a little sluggish, she was tired.

"So how was your weekend, somebody had a late night," her co-workers said.

"It was good," she smiles.

"It must have been very good; you smiling give us all the details."

"Well, I met a guy a few weeks ago, wait actually a month ago when I was first introduced, but then weeks later he actually step to me himself and asked for my number. He called last night and we stayed up all night talking on the phone"

"Ooooh, for real?"

"It was cute because neither of us wanted to get off the phone, it had reminded me of our high school days; you stay up all night talking to y'all fall asleep together on the phone or until your mother get on the other phone and tell you to hang up the phone."

"Ok, I remember those days," Jennifer said. "Me too," Catherine said as she laughed softly.

"Tell us about this new man girl," Jennifer said. This was the normal talk for them in the payroll department, this was how their days fly right on by.

"Well, I met him a few weekends ago. We were at a wedding rehearsal when he actually asked me for my number."

"Did you give him some already?"

"Girl naw, we just met."

"I'm just saying you ain't had any in a minute since RoShawn."

"Girl you're so crazy, I'm not desperate for the D like that Jen," Sharee chuckled.

"Ok, so yesterday was y'all first phone conversation?"

"No, he's already been calling and then he also called last night," Sharee told them.

"That's right, so how does he look?" Catherine asked with her raised eye brow.

"He looks good."

"And," Catherine sounded.

"He's tall."

"And," Catherine sounded again.

"He's very charming and talkative and wants to talk to me," she smiles.

"You should invite him over for dinner and let him taste your yams!"

Sharee couldn't help but laugh at Catherine's comment. "Girl, you're still talking about those yams," Sharee said.

"Umm. Yeah, your yams are the best!"

"You're so crazy," Sharee chuckled.

"For real, I can't wait until we have another potluck because I'm going to make sure when we do, we put you down on the list for yams."

"I might have to make a larger pot next time."

"Yeah, I think so," Catherine and Jennifer said.

"The one I bought was big too; I didn't know everyone in the office was going to get seconds and thirds."

"See," Catherine sounded.

Later after work Sharee contacted Levell and invited him over for dinner. After getting home and preparing a very nice dinner for them two Sharee showered and got ready. She put on something nice and she was ready to have dinner with Levell. She put on her black strapless bra, it hugged her breast very well. She stood in the mirror looking at herself and she liked what she sees. Since she wore her black short dress, the thin fabric one, she wasn't wearing any panties. She wanted to tease him with her dress.

He was so happy to be invited over. He arrived at Sharee's house at six forty-five, he was fifteen minutes early. He rang the doorbell.

"Who is it!" her voice sounded. She had no other company coming over but him, she just felt like saying it anyway.

"It's me, Levell!" in his deep toned handsome voice.

When she opened her front door he was standing there holding a bottle of wine and roses for her.

"Thank you, you're so sweet," she smiled.

"You're welcome beautiful," as his eyes roamed her body up and down; she was like the woman he dreamed of in his dreams. He didn't see why her ex couldn't or didn't appreciate this beauty.

She took the flowers smiling and then went to put her beautiful flowers in a vase.

"It smells so good up in here."

"Oh thank you, dinner is almost done." She is surprised it's not done already, as long as she has been in this kitchen cooking over this hot stove preparing their meal.

"Ok, cool."

"You look very nice by the way."

He looked down at his outfit all the way down to his shoes. Then he looked up at her, "Thank you," he said. Levell had on a pair of black slacks, a button down royal blue dress shirt, and some black shoes. He already knew he was looking clean, but thrilled to hear it coming from her. He had a fresh line up and a fresh cut.

"So do you beautiful."

"Well thank you," she said with a smile.

"You have a really nice home."

"Thank you so very much."

"Is this a condo?"

"It's a townhouse."

"What's the difference?"

"This is a house that's just next door to another one and condos are like individual apartments."

"Oh, okay, that's crazy, I never knew the difference. I thought it was the same."

She laughed.

He took a seat on her couch. "You need some help up in there?"

"Some help," she repeated.

"Yeah, I'm not a stranger in the kitchen; I do know how to cook too."

"Oh really, okay well that's good to know," she replied happily.

"So, tell me more about you?" she sounded from the kitchen.

"Well, I am an only child. I grew up in a two parent household and I was one of those nerdy type cool kids."

She laughed walking back into the living room with him. He grinned.

"Nerdy, no way," she grinned. The look of him does not show nerdy.

"Well, I grew up in a two parent household, but I didn't have it as good as you. Both of my parents had good jobs, but there were ten of us. I have five sisters plus me and four brothers."

"Wow."

"Yeah, your daddy was getting it in."

"Yeah, he sure was," she chuckled. "Three of them I never met."

"Oh wow, why?"

"Back in the days my dad cheated on my mother and had three kids on her by three different ladies."

"Oh damn."

"Right, and then my mother was not trying to be cool with no other woman."

His gaze was deep into her eyes as he listened. "So, have you tried to reach out to them as an adult?"

"Well yeah, I tried but they are not messing with me."

"Why not?" he asked.

"My dad used to tell me that when he did try and get them to come around they told him that they were not fucking with him since he acted like he couldn't be a part of their lives because he was only worried about me and my brothers and sisters by my mom when he had other kids."

"Well, I'm so sorry to hear that."

"I know, and one of my sisters has two kids and won't even bring my nieces over here to meet their Aunt."

"Dang," he sounded.

"That's crazy huh?"

"Yep," he shook his head.

They chatted for only twenty minutes and she already wanted to dive down his throat. She didn't want to at first until now, my God, his stares and his lips she had to kiss him. Seconds later she thought to FUCK IT. She leaned over, puckered up her lips, and pecked his lips and boy o boy they were soft; she kind of wanted to do it again.

"Damn!" Levell said as he nods his head with a gaze into her eyes.

Levell's gazes into Sharee's eyes was now stronger.

"Okay, let me go make these plates," she sounded. She went to go make their plates. He looked behind his shoulders watching her walk to the kitchen. They sat and ate dinner together enjoying their time.

After he took his last bite he looked up at her and smiled. "Thank you for that great meal, I have been enjoying our evening."

"Oh, you're welcome."

She took their plates to the kitchen and came back out the kitchen with a bottle of wine and two wine glasses.

"You know, since the bar I couldn't stop thinking about our conversation and all I could think about is you and being here for you."

"Awww," she sounded.

"So you still haven't told me about why you and your ex-broke up," *shit* he just wanted to make sure he doesn't make the same mistake and lose her. After asking her, by the look on her face he could tell she really didn't want to speak on it.

Sharee took a breath, she blew out her mouth. "Well, the reason why my ex and I broke up is that he was abusive. He was abusing me mentally and physically. Like he had anger issues and after a while, I just couldn't deal with it anymore."

"So you got out the relationship, I'm so glad you did. I can't believe he was like that with you, I would have never done that to you," Levell sat there shaking his head.

After Sharee told Levell all about the pain she endured with her ex, he really felt bad for her and what she'd been through. "Well, you can trust me."

"Oh, I can huh," she stared him deeply into his eyes smiling.

"Yes, I'm nothing like him."

"That's what he said too when we first got together, he said a lot of things he wouldn't do to, but everything he said he wouldn't do, he did."

"When you let me become yours I'm going to love, and not just say I love you I'm going to show it daily. I'm not going to use you, I will help you in any way I can and the way you want me too. I would make you my wife after three years, not just have you as a girlfriend then move on to the next. I'm here to stay and I'm not just talking, I really mean what I say and I'm a man of my word."

As their gaze continued it was steady, neither of them blinked. "I know I can trust you, Levell," by the look in his eyes she could tell that he was serious.

"And you can," he said.

"Oh, so that's what you plan to do, marry me in three years?" she smiled.

"Well, I said three years because it sounded like that has been your longest relationship time, three years."

"Oh," she sounded as she kept a grin on her face. The look she's giving him, he feels he might have to do a little proving, but he had no problems doing so. He wanted her to know he's not just talking, he is actually serious. And if he has to prove everything he is saying, then so be it. Sharee has been hurt and treated badly when she shouldn't have and she deserved some proving.

"All I want to do is protect your heart from any pain; I'm different from any of those other men you have come across, I will show you."

She gave him that look of I will believe it when I see it. She began to be a little flirtatious rubbing her fingers across her chest. Twirling her hair as she gazes into his eyes. They pecked again, slowly and firmly as their lips pressed against each other.

"I like kissing you."

"I like kissing you too."

He slid his hand behind her back and down her dress unsnapping her bra with only his fingers, like he was a pro at this. Seeing her big breast drop down after he had slid off her bra he was mesmerized. He couldn't stop looking down at them and her nipples were poking through her dress, through the fabric he could see them just too damn good, it made him get hard instantly. He slowly slid down her dress half-way, just enough to massage and suck on her breast. As his hands simultaneously wondered her body, a tingle flowed through her body; feeling the warmth of his hands on her body felt so damn good, she was enjoying this. He continues to gently suck on her nipples, the passion had rose. He then began to pull more into his mouth with his hands as he was now massaging them in a stroking position. They taste so good he slowly began to suck a little faster as he takes in more than just her nipples. After he sucked them both Levell slid her dress back up, her eyes slowly opened. He didn't want to go too far which he almost did, although he did notice that she wasn't trying to stop him either. Whoa, he thought to himself, *I could have almost gone all the way.*

His gaze returned back to her eyes. "Wow, I have been having such an amazing time with you tonight, I almost don't want this night to end, but it is getting late so I'm about to head out."

"Ok, and yeah I agree I don't want this night to end neither as you can probably tell," she smiled, "I have been really enjoying our time tonight too."

Levell stood from sitting on her couch and she stood to her feet too. Their look of passion in their eyes they have as they stared into each other's eyes they couldn't stop. His hands began rubbing down her arms as they stood there, "I want you to have a good night tonight and think about me while I'm gone."

"My night has been wonderful thanks to you, and I will think about you while you're gone," she smiled. Then they both hugged each other. Levell grabbed his jacket from off the arm of the couch.

"I will call you a little later," he told her.

"Alright, bye."

He left and she went to bed to lie down. The next morning waking up she was still thinking about Levell. It was Monday morning, Sharee wished it was still the weekend and still spending all day with Levell. While getting ready for work Levell called her.

"Good morning Levell," she answers.

"Hey, good morning, I was calling to tell you I had a great time with you last night and I wanted to make sure I didn't go too far if I did. I'm so sorry, I will try and control myself next time. I couldn't help myself, you tasted so good."

She chuckled, "No, you were just fine, I really enjoyed myself too."

"Oh, ok, I just wanted to make sure."

"Oh no, you were fine."

"What you doing?"

"Getting ready for work," she told him.

"Ok, sweetie well you have a good day."

"You too, thank you."

Today she went to work happily walking through the office smiling just because. Sharee's coworkers all had something positive to say about her smiling. She finally had something good that was making her smile the way she was besides just being at work. As the week is going by she continues to talk to him daily. They were not going a day without talking to each other. Wednesday he took her lunch. Once she was called to the front, it was shocking because he didn't tell her he was coming up there to her work. Boy, did that place a smile on her face. That was him, *spontaneous and full of surprises, and would do anything just to see his lady smile.*

"Hey, Levell!"

"Hey, I brought you lunch."

"You are so sweet, thank you," she smiled. He passed her the bag with her lunch inside he'd just bought along with her drink.

"So what are you doing this weekend, I would love to take you out?"

"That sounds good because I don't have any plans besides to be with you."

"Sounds good to me," he smiled. They hugged and then he left.

Days later Levell paid her another visit. Levell came in, Sharee hugged him and kissed his lips. "Hey, Levell thank you for coming over."

"Anytime, Anytime," he said and grinned. Levell came in having a seat on her couch. "So, how was your day?"

"My day, my day, mmm, it was good," she said.

"What about your day, how was your day handsome?"

"My day was great, every day is great."

"I know that's right."

"Can I have some water?"

"You want water or do you want a beer or something?"

"I'll take a beer."

Sharee brought him out a beer from her refrigerator. She passed him the beer and sat next to him on the couch, as he drank his beer she ran her fingers through his curly Mohawk. They talked and watched TV at the same time. After a few shows, he thought she may want a massage.

"You want a massage?"

"Yeah sure."

She lie down on the couch on her stomach to be more comfortable as he gives her a massage. He started with her shoulders, to her neck, then down her back. After massaging every part of her back he went past her butt and began massaging the back of her legs. Then he moved down to her ankles, then her feet. Then he started trying to crack her toes. Then he moved over to her other leg repeating what he had just done.

"Levell, if you want you can spend the night," she sounded.

He started laughing. *Ok,* he thought. Levell really liked Sharee a whole lot and he was not going to go ahead of her pace. It was getting late, he didn't intend on spending the night when he came over, he was just going to also come back over tomorrow and again on Sunday, but once she asked if he wanted too it didn't take long to answer.

"Yeah, sure that'll be cool."

He wasn't about to tell her, no, of course, he wasn't going to tell this beautiful woman no. After her most needed massage, the two went to sleep. The two enjoyed their weekend just being underneath each other. Then it was back to reality, it was Monday, why can't the weekend be more than just two days. The work week went by fast and the weekend was approaching again.

Sharee received a call from Levell. He wanted to let her know that tomorrow he wanted to take her out to dinner to a nice restaurant. The next morning all she could think about was *thank God it is Friday.* That day all day at work she wondered what she was going to wear out to dinner tonight with Levell. Once the evening approached and at seven o clock, Levell was headed to Sharee's house.

Sharee cell phone rang. "Hey," she answered.

"I'm here," he told her as he parked in the parking stall.

"Ok."

Levell then walked up to her place. Ringing the door bell, Sharee had let him in. He walked in handing her a dozen roses. She didn't remember getting roses this much during her and RoShawn whole relationship. "Awww, thank you, Levell," she smiled at him, she smelled her roses. "I just love the smell of fresh roses," she says. Sharee walked to her kitchen and sat her roses in a vase, then she read the card, it said: *I love the time we spend together.* "Awww," she sounded then looked at him, "I love the time we spend together too. Levell took Sharee out to a nice restaurant that they both got all dressed up for.

Having another great time Levell had dropped her off back at home. That weekend he was scheduled for some extra and double time hours at work, so this weekend his fun with her was short.

Monday in the payroll department was full of juicy bedroom talk with her coworkers, "So, did you give Mr. Mohawk some this weekend?" Jennifer asks.

Sharee smiled "I want to give it some time before I give him some, I want to take the time to get to know him. Even more, we've only went out on two dates, this weekend was only our second date."

"Oh, okay, where did you go?"

"We just went out to a very nice restaurant, he picked me up, gave me a dozen red roses, then he taken me to dinner at a nice restaurant. We were both dressed up at dinner. He was very pleasant. I enjoyed myself and the food was really good too!"

"That's right, so where did you two go on your first date?"

"Well, our first date was at my place remember. I cooked for him and he came over dressed very nicely. He brought over flowers and a bottle of wine and we talked and had a good time!"

"Oh yeah, that's right!" Then they all continued working. They loved hearing Sharee stories now. They were not this interesting before.

The weekend approached and Levell wanted to take Sharee out to dinner, but she was on her monthly cycle, something she was too embarrassed to let him know so she made up a whole lot of excuses about why she couldn't go. She almost gave in and just told him, he wanted to take her out bad the way he kept asking her and how many times he said please. She felt bad not letting him know the truth about why she couldn't go. Not only was she going to feel uncomfortable bleeding while out with him, but she was cramping really bad. He couldn't believe she was saying no, he thought she would want to go out since they didn't get the chance to last weekend. Sharee and Levell both had busy work schedules, with weekends off which worked out great, it just last week his boss asked him to work and he wasn't going to turn down the extra money and hours, he really hoped she was not mad at that. They have been spending a lot of time getting to know each other is why it didn't make sense to him why she didn't want to go out tonight.

Just how she was as a person really grabbed him by his heart, and when a woman could do that like his momma always told him, she's a keeper and don't do nothing to mess it up. Not only was she doing something to his heart, but he was surely doing something to hers as well by being in tuned to only her, he was giving her something she had not received from a man in a long time and she loved and appreciated every bit of it.

The next day was a struggle for her at work. Mondays were always a busy day, the beginning of the work week. By noon she looked down at her cell and wished it was five o' clock already, she was ready to go, cramping and in pain, she just wanted to go home and lie down and drink on her green tea. After two days passed and off her cycle, Sharee and Levell had made plans to go out together. Later that evening she looked down at her cell and saw it wasn't five o' clock yet; she was ready to go out to dinner with Levell. After work, she called him and he met her at her house to pick her up. He arrived and when they both seen each other they both grinned. They were happy to see each other. They left and headed straight to the restaurant. They ate and had a good conversation for nearly two hours, then they left and went back to her place. He dropped her off. They gave their good night kisses and hugs bye then he left. They were both a bit tired from their long day. As soon as Sharee walked into her bedroom her cell rang, letting her cell only ring once she answered. It was Shante.

"Hey boo," she answered.

"I knew you were up," she chuckled.

"Yeah, I just got in."

"Oh yeah, at this time of night from where, work this late?"

"No, from dinner with Levell."

"That's what's up, how was dinner?"

"Great as always."

"Oooh look at you, *great as always*. That's right, I'm glad you two have been enjoying each other."

"Yeah, I know."

"Shante, I'm about to put you on speaker while I undress." Sharee placed the phone down and put the phone on speaker. "Okay, so why are you up?"

"Girl, I can't sleep."

"Where is Charles, he has not made it home yet?"

"No."

"Oh, ok."

"He on his way, I just talked to him not long ago," Shante replied.

"Oh, okay, that's right, so how was your day?"

"It was good," she paused. "And yours besides your dinner?"

"It was amazing," she says.

"Amazing huh," Shante said.

Sharee chuckled, "Leave me alone Shante," Sharee continues to chuckle.

"Okay, since when has work been amazing Sharee?" Shante asked.

Sharee was still chuckling, "He's really great, he even makes my days better, I can see us together right now."

"Are you ready to be in another relationship right now, how are you feeling since the RoShawn break up?"

"You know what, I have never felt better."

Shante laughed, "Enough said."

"Yeah, actually I felt this way since the day I broke up with him," Sharee was getting an incoming call, it was Levell. "Shante, speaking of him, this is Levell calling now."

"Alright, lady well I'll talk to you later."

"Alright, love you."

"Love you too lady," they hung up and Sharee clicked over.

"Hey Levell," she answers.

"Hey babe," he called her as she answered.

"Hey," she says again, still blushing from the fact he just called her babe.

"My cousin is throwing a skate party tomorrow night, you want to come?"

"A skating party that sounds like fun, I haven't been skating in years!"

"Me neither."

Sharee chuckled, "I hope I don't fall out there and embarrass the both of us."

"Shit, we're going to be holding on to each other," he said.

"And we're going to be falling together too," they both laughed.

"Sharee, you should see if your girls Katrina and Shante want to come and tell them to bring my boys too."

"Okay, cool, I will call them up right now."

"Alright, cool babe, well call me after you talk to them."

"Alright, will do," she said.

Sharee called Shante back and told her and she said yeah she's down to go and she will tell Charles. Then she called Katrina next.

Katrina wanted to know what type of night it's going to be. "Yeah, of course, we'll come, do you know what type of night it's going to be tomorrow night, is it hip hop, R & B or oldies?"

"Let me call him and I'll call you right back."

"Alright," Katrina told her.

Sharee dialed Levell.

"Hey babe," he answered.

"Babe, Katrina wanted to know what type of night is it."

"You know what, honestly I didn't even ask her, but I'm sure my cousin taste in the music night is going to be good."

"Oh, no worries, she had just wanted to know, so I was like let me call and ask, but we're all going to do our thing and have fun anyway, I was just asking because she wanted me to ask you, that's all."

"Oh, no worries, but yeah it will be fun."

"I know I can't wait. Well babe, I'll call you back I'm about to call her back."

"Ok."

Sharee called her back and told her just what he had said. Katrina was still excited to go out skating something she hasn't done in a long time, something she used to enjoy doing as well.

The next day they headed out to the skating ring for Levell's cousin's skate party. Once they got there the party had already started an hour earlier and they were already drinking. They went in ordering them drinks too, afterward they all went out and began skating. They were having a great time. After the party they all hugged Levell's cousin, then she gave them all a hug back and thanked them all for coming out that on a week night to celebrate her birthday with her. Then they all left.

Days later the weekend approached. Sharee called Levell.

"Hey babe, I was just thinking about you," he answered before she could even say hello.

"Yeah, what you doing?" she asked.

"Nothing," he replied.

"You have any plans for this weekend yet, I was just going to ask you the same thing."

"Oh yeah," he laughed.

"Yeah, I wanted us to go out."

"So, where would you like to go?" he asked her.

Sharee was very surprised by his question, she wasn't at all used to her man asking her where she wanted to go because with her ex RoShawn it was always where he wanted to go and she just had to be down with it. Her face showed it. He smiled because he could tell it. "Whale Watching," Sharee spoke.

"Ok great," how long is it going to take you to get ready?"

"I can get ready right now; it won't take me long at all."

"Ok, cool."

He picked her up and then they left. Getting there he paid with cash to rent the life jackets.

"This is different."

"Yeah, it is."

They were having a good time on the boat, and then out of nowhere he suddenly became sick. Their outing started off really good, but ended crazy as hell.

Getting off work Sharee couldn't wait to call her girl. Sharee called Katrina. "Hello," she said once she didn't hear the phone ring anymore.

"Hello."

"Girl, guess what!"

"Aww shit, what happened!"

"So Levell and I went whale watching yesterday and girl his ass got so fucking sick his ass started throwing up and shit."

Katrina busted out laughing as she held the phone to her ear. "Girl shut up, for real, his ass was throwing up on the boat."

"Girl yes, embarrassing," Sharee said.

"There were a lot of people on the boat?"

"Only like sixteen people on there, but still."

"Damn, that's crazy as hell," she laughed out again.

"Girl, he was like baby and then I was like huh, then girl he just started throwing up."

Sharee couldn't help but laugh with Katrina.

"So besides all that, how did you like whale watching?"

"I liked it, we had a good time up until all that happened."

"Aye, I remember the dating stories you used to have for me after you and RoShawn broke up."

"Girl Ugh, don't remind me."

"Remember that date you had and he didn't have any damn teeth?"

"Girl, un un un. Girl that shit was all bad," Sharee laughed. "Girl his shit was all spaced out and shit."

Katrina chuckled, "Girl I couldn't have done that, I like to tongue kiss and I wouldn't be able to focus on shit with his ass but his damn teeth, girl what was his name again?"

"Sam," Sharee replies.

"Girl, you're better than me, the first moment he would have opened his mouth it would have been over. Girl, you used to have me dying laughing when you used to tell me stories about his ass."

Sharee laughed. "Yeah, but Levell he is sweet, I enjoy every single time we have spent together so far, he's a good guy just like Shante said. So far he's way better than the last one, the dates, and the boyfriends!"

"Well that's good and he's got all his damn teeth!"

"Yeah," she laughed.

Katrina laughed again too. "Where are you?"

"In the car driving home," Sharee says.

"Oh, but yeah, I'm happy for you," Katrina told her. "You went to work today?"

"Yeah, I did."

"How was work?"

"Girl it was cool, minus my coworker always telling me about her damn girlfriend, I don't want to hear that shit every day."

Katrina laughed, "Girl what has she been saying!"

"Just the shit they talk about, or the places they were going together. But today she was like one of her other homegirls was chilling at the house with her and her girlfriend and the homegirl had sex with her girlfriend when she left to go to the store."

"Why in the hell was her girlfriend left at the house by herself with the friend anyway."

"Girl, I don't know, I didn't even ask her, I was like hell fucking naw. I told her my homegirls and I don't have the same taste in men, and we damn sure haven't fucked each other's men."

"Girl for real, we have our own different taste in men, that shit is crazy."

"Exactly, that's what I told her."

A call was coming through on Sharee's other line. She pulled the phone away from her ear to look at her phone to see who it was that was calling. It was Levell. "Oh K, this Levell, let me call you right back."

"Okay, his ears must have been ringing right now."

"Right," Sharee laughed.

"Alright bye," Katrina said.

"Bye, I will call you right back," they hung up.

"Hey Levell," she answered.

"Hey beautiful," he said.

"Hey, I'm sorry."

"About what?" he asked her.

"Yesterday," Sharee replied.

"Oh, don't trip, you didn't know."

"Are you feeling a little better?" she asked him.

"Oh yeah, I feel a lot better, I was just fucked up yesterday."

"Yeah I know, that came out of nowhere because at first, everything was fine, then when you first told me you were feeling sick, I knew you weren't lying because even your face was looking like something was really wrong with you."

"I'm sorry if I messed up our little outing."

"No, it's fine, I didn't know being on the boat was going to get to you like that."

"Yeah, I don't fuck with the water like that."

"Why you didn't tell me then?" she chuckled.

"Well, because you said you wanted to go and wherever you said you wanted to go, I had to make sure that happened."

"Awww, how sweet of you, but next time if I pick a place that's going to get you all sick, please, by all means, let me know, I'm not trying to have a part two," she chuckled. He laughed too, right along with her.

"How was work?"

"It was good."

"That's right what are you doing right now?"

"Just getting home, about to walk in the door right now as we speak. I want to see you."

"Alright, I'll come through there; I want to see you too."

"So, how was work for you?" Sharee asked him.

"It was good, just glad to be off."

"I know that's right."

Sharee's cell started clicking, an incoming call was coming in, looking down at it in disgust Sharee is wondering why RoShawn is calling her. A long time had passed and RoShawn decided to call Sharee. He thought since months had passed she would finally give them another chance now, since he has been out the picture for a while.

"Hold on baby, let me see what the hell this fool wants."

"Who babe?" Levell asked her.

"My ex," she told him.

"Oh."

Sharee had clicked over to answer her other line. "What the hell do you want; why are you calling me RoShawn!" she answered.

By the way, she answered he already knew whatever he thought or was thinking he was wrong. "Umm, I guess nothing; I thought I was calling you to see if you were willing to give us another chance."

"Man, you must be crazy out your mind, you fucked that all the way up a long time ago, and I'm not going backward, Bye!" She hung up on him, left him with a dial tone in his ear and clicked back over to Levell.

RoShawn called her right back. RoShawn refused to stop calling her, he was determined to get his woman back is why he kept calling her. Sharee sees him calling back again, she pressed the decline button. He called again and she did it again. He sees that maybe them getting back together is not going to happen the way she keeps hanging up in his face. He called her again.

"Babe hold on," she clicked over.

"Whatttt!" she screamed.

RoShawn pulled the phone away from his ear quickly, "Sharee what did you do with my photo book and my tent I had in your garage?"

"If you didn't take it, then I can't tell you, I haven't seen it."

"No, for real, it was in your garage."

"That's why I told your ass to take all your shit when you left if you left anything I threw away whatever you left behind."

"Damn, for real!"

"Yep, I told you to take your stuff; I didn't see any purpose of holding on to any of your things if you're no longer here and we're not together."

"Damn, that's fucked up you throwing away my shit like that!"

"Bye RoShawn," she hangs up on him again, she didn't have the time to entertain this phone call anymore and clicked back over.

"Sorry about that."

"Oh nah, that's cool, what did he want?"

"Talking about he thought maybe we can get back together, and then after I went off on him, he started asking about some pictures and a tent he left here."

"Oh, his stuff is still there?" Levell asked.

"I threw it away."

"Oh."

"Yeah, after I told him I threw it away because I am not a storage he got mad and he started yelling, I starting yelling back, but then I decided it wasn't necessary to entertain him so I hung up on him."

"He's probably going to call you right back again."

"He bet not, if he does I'm not answering it."

"So, what are you about to do right now?"

"I'm about to go get in the bath and wait for you."

"Alright, well I will be there in a minute, just wait for me so I can wash your body."

She blushed, "Okay," she told him.

"Okay, be there in a minute," they hung up.

Once Levell made it there they kissed a passionate kiss. Sharee turned around and then walked to the bathroom, he followed behind her. Sharee began taking off her clothes, he stood behind her and watched. She stepped in her bath water one leg at a time and sat down.

"You just lay back, let me do all the work."

Sharee did just what he asked her to do. As she's relaxing laying back her eyes are gazing into his.

Levell kneeled down on his knees rubbing his fingers over the front of her nipples back and forth, then he began tracing around her nipple with his fingertips. He leaned in closer kissing her lips. He proceeded bathing her, he put soap onto her face towel and began with her chest, then down both her arms. Her gaze followed his hands. He leaned his body to her and kissed her. Then Levell began dragging the towel to her back and her neck. Afterward, he reached down into the water and pulled out one of her legs to scrub, then he scrub her other leg.

"Alright stand-up," he told her.

Sharee smiled. She couldn't believe he was actually cleaning every part of her body. She stood up and he cleaned her vagina and then her butt. Levell cleaned her whole entire body. Her body was making him horny as hell. She sat back down.

"Babe, I still can't believe my ex-had the nerves to call me tonight."

"I know, some nerves."

"I don't know what made him think in his right mind that I would take his ass back."

Levell continued looking down at her body as he washed it. "Well babe, let's not talk about him anymore, he's old news now," they changed their conversation.

He leaned towards her and kissed her giving her a peck on her soft lips and then he kissed her again sliding his tongue inside her mouth this time. Sharee raised both her hands out her bath water and wrapped her wet hands around his neck. The deeper his tongue was going inside her mouth the more he would rise from off the floor. Shortly his lips released from hers. Their gaze stayed.

"You want it?" she said in a low toned voice.

"Yes," he nodded his head.

He wanted her right now. She wanted him too and not to just fuck him, but to make love too him, she wanted to feel his body warm her insides. Their gaze was strong, he stood up to his feet and he pulled Sharee up, he helped her step out the water and he kissed her. He began drying her off and after he was done she put on lotion and perfume as he stood there and watched, looking at her body up and down. She grabbed onto his hand and made him rub across her breast over and over again, touching her breast and her nipples with one of his hand and with his other free hand she had him rubbing her thighs then around to her butt, up and down to the curve of it, feeling his warm hand against her skin. She let her body tease him tonight. Fresh out the bath, smelling good she knew just what she was doing. It's been a while and she thinks she's ready for him tonight. They started back kissing so passionately. Then Sharee led him over to her bed, they sat on top of her covers. She suddenly became nervous, she didn't know where this was coming from, she wasn't even nervous at first.

"You look like you are all nerves."

"I'm not," she says as she stared him in his eyes although she was, she wasn't about to tell him that.

"Good, because I was about to say don't be," he whispered. She leaned in forward kissing him gently on his lips. Then she leaned back how she was. He then leaned in towards her and started kissing on her neck. Her eyes closed. Minutes into it, he went to the other side of her neck and continued seductively kissing her. He moved to her lips and he held her cheeks between both his hands. The kiss is all they heard besides the moans from their mouths.

Levell began taking off his boxer shorts. Looking down at his penis she didn't see him as the type of man that shaved down there or maybe because the thought of him naked had never crossed her mind either. They went back to kissing, as the two kissed his hands rubbed the backside of her body again, he couldn't help it, she felt so good. Her hands were placed behind him on his back. Their lips then released from each other's, but the gaze into each other's eyes remained.

"Lay back, just relax."

Sharee liked how he'd like making her feel so relaxed; she could get used to this. She leaned back on her back. He trailed his tongue down her chest, Levell pulled her legs open wide, as he went down slowly tongue first.

"Tell me how it feels when it feels good to you."

"Okay," she said softly.

The first lick she moaned.

"Mmm," she moaned again with that second lick. She felt the whole width of his whole tongue. Levell had his tongue flat down on her as he licked her up and down.

"It feels good," she says in a low tone. He went down and licked up.

"Un, it feels good," again she said. He went down and licked up. All she saw was the top of his forehead, and then she felt herself slowly closing her eyes.

"Ooo," she moans again. He kept up at what he was doing. In that same spot he started from the bottom and licked up with the whole width of his tongue making her feel just how he wants her to feel.

"It feels good," she got it out her mouth barely once, again and again, he went down and licked up. She held up her legs in the air while he licked it over and over again, then he began flickering the tip of his tongue on her lips. Only minutes into him flickering his tongue down in between her center Levell hands slid under her butt and moved her hips even closer to his face as he went in deeper. She began moaning nonstop, he's just loved how her moans sound, he began shaking his head all up in it. Her eyes were closed as she began licking her lips. After a while he was done, he was ready to put it in now. Sharee lifted up.

"Let me do you," she said in a low tone. He sat down and she began to stroke it, the more she stroked he jerked. The control was all in her hands and it was funny to her because he couldn't do anything about it, it felt too good to stop it or to tell her to wait a minute. She kept on, he was shivering and jerking away. She watched his face, his eyes were rolled in the back of his head. She then eased the tip of her tongue on the tip of his penis and gave it a lick. The way she licked it, all he could think about is how great sex with her is about to be. He was certain it was going to be great. She kept licking, with each lick she felt him move, then in seconds she slightly opened her mouth more to take in the rest of him until it touched her throat. She grabbed on to it and continued to stroke it as it was inside her mouth. His body kept moving up and down as she continued.

Shortly after his body began shaking, he got up and aimed his penis for the opening of her lips down there with the tip of his head. In seconds he felt it slide in her. They both released a moan. He settled inside her as he went in and sliding it back half way out, then he slid it in again all the way, then he pulled it back out half way. He continued doing the same thing for a long while, going in and coming out slowly. She felt him deep inside her, with every thrust Levell made Sharee sounded an *"Ummm"*. Sharee held onto his back as he continued in the same position, the warmth inside her made him go in her deeper and deeper. He couldn't pull back anymore, he stayed deep in it. Then her moans became louder. She couldn't help herself, but neither could he. He began moaning and talking asking her *how does it feel* and asked if *she wants it deeper*. He had her feeling so much in another world she couldn't get her words together to answer the things he was saying, all she managed to say was *"Un huh"* and barely got that out. He began moving it inside her in circles. She was becoming so wet by the seconds. She opened her eyes, she felt something, he was hitting her spot. He looked down at her with a straight serious look on his face. Levell rolled over as he was still inside of her so she could ride him.

She held on the sides of his arms as she rode him, feeling her pussy lips go over his hard dick she had him in silence. Looking at him his eyes were closed, her speed picked up a little. She was moving on it back and forth, but then the deeper she felt it, made her begin to go slower; with the grip of his hands she feels on her waist pushing her down harder on him as her eyes were closed. Levell had a tight grip, but then with the movement of Levell's hips pushing up into her helped, Sharee starts going faster. Gliding back and forth continuing in that same position they didn't want to change, it was so memorizing. Then after a while, they both began to feel it. Their moaning had escalated at the same time.

"Oh," she sounded.

"Un," he sounded after her. His hands slid from her back down to underneath her butt helping her rhythm. Sharee rode on top of him for a long while, she had a lot of energy. Suddenly a feeling came about, they both were having at the same exact time. He held onto her tighter, she clenched him tighter, they were both feeling it come. She was sitting on top of him going faster and faster; they felt it coming, the speed went even faster, like she was riding a horse in a horse race at the track, they feel it coming. The moans got even louder and then in seconds they both had cum, his cum burst up inside her as they kept going in and out each other. She slowly opens her eyes as she is seeing him already looking at her. They held it inside, the two kept their bodies pressed hard up against each other they didn't want it sliding out right now. No talking just hard breathing they were both out of breath. Once it had slid out of her she eased off him and lay beside him still out of breath, hot, wet and sweaty. They both were out of energy breathing hard. They eventually caught their breath and once they did he held her close to him.

"You okay?" he asked.

"Yeah," she smiled.

"You feel so good."

"You do too."

They felt the feeling, the warmth of each other, every inch of him and the way he made her body shiver felt so damn good. Afterward, they cuddle and watch TV.

"You can stay the night."

"Thanks because I didn't want to leave."

"I don't want you to ever leave."

"I want to make us official, I want you."

She looked back at him and kissed him. "Then we're official," she whispered and then kissed his lips again. After watching TV for only an hour they were very tired, they couldn't stay up any longer.

"Goodnight."

"Goodnight," he replied back to her.

The two closed their eyes and slept in each other's arms the whole night until the morning. The next morning they showered together and left for work. Throughout the day Sharee kept having moments where she was thinking about Levell and their night. Last night she had an amazing time with him and every other time as well and just the way he makes her feel was just overall amazing. Sharee was happy to have a man now and one that made her happy.

In the short time they had known each other they have learned a lot about each other and she wanted to be with him not because the sex was just great, it was more than just a physical attraction and he felt the same as her. She's glad she doesn't have to spend her nights alone anymore. He bought clothes over, he wasn't going anywhere.

After a long work week, she was excited for this weekend, her honey had something planned for them. That weekend Sharee and Levell spent it at his house just to be doing something different, he had called her and told her he had dinner ready for her. Getting over there he had everything set up, it was very nice, with the wine, food, candles, and flowers. After dinner they talked and then they talked until it was time for them to head out to the drive in. Their conversations were always interesting. Getting there she didn't have to spend anything, not even to help him pay for anything, he spent his own money. He paid for everything with his credit card. He bought drinks and snacks for the both of them. There was no need to buy food because they were both still pretty full from that big dinner he had cooked.

As they got back into the car from getting stuff to drink and snack on they got into the back seat to watch the movie. As they were eating their snacks, he glances at her and caught her already looking at him.

They began to watch the movie. It really had their attention, it was good. Half way through the movie she took her right hand and began rubbing on his penis and his balls through his pants. She was having a hard time keeping her hands to herself with the sex scenes that kept on popping up. Sharee wanted to feel it, so then he lifted up a little to unzip his pants, then she put her hand inside his pants. Sharee simply pulled his penis from out his pants, squeezed it as she began stroking it up and down.

Knowing they were at the movies, in a minute he was not about to care. "Alright babe, you're about to start something at this drive in."

"Ok babe, sorry, I couldn't help it," she grins.

Sharee placed it back inside his pants and zipped him back up. Levell kissed her lips with his, it was nice and slow then his tongue began going in deeper and deeper. Once the movie was over he started up his car and they left. The two drove back to Levell's house for the night.

It didn't take long before his body reacted to the touch of her soft hand stroking his penis up and down the way that she did at the drive in, he got on top of her and started kissing her even more. In minutes it went from kissing to now wanting sex.

Shortly the two got up from off the bed still kissing each other, she raised both arms up in the air as they both stared each other in the eye. His hands rested on her waist.

"Oh, your hands are warm."

"They're always warm to your cold body."

"I know right," she laughed.

He slid his warm hands up her skin sliding off her shirt and over her head carefully. As he stood in front of her, he reached his arms around her snapping off her bra. His eyes looked down at her breast, his mouth went straight to her nipples. He stuck out his tongue rolling his tongue around her nipple in circles. Then he pulled one of her tits into his mouth, he began sucking her breast. Minutes later he began sucking on her other breast.

"Ummm," she sounded a moan.

He released his mouth from her breast and began unzipping her pants. She slightly opened her eyes and watched him slide her pants off. They made it back to the bed. He slid down slowly as he stared her into her eyes, his hand slid underneath her, he slightly lifted her up just a little as his tongue slid in it all the way inside. He let her get a few moans in before he stuck it in. He was on top for a long while, then he wanted to switch the position.

"You want to get on top."

"Yeah, I don't care," they switched.

Shortly he started moaning as he clenched tighter on her butt.

"You about to cum?" she asked him.

"No, not yet," he replied

Sharee kept rocking her hips back and forth on his dick. In seconds she could feel him going up inside her deeper as she goes forward. She began moaning loudly. They enjoyed themselves all the way to the end. After they were done she laid on him and wrapped her arm around his chest and they both started snoring.

The next day waking up they woke up smiling and well rested. By noon they were back at her house, she had clothes to wash for their work week. Levell received a call from his dad telling him he needs him to come over. Sharee kept washing their clothes and Levell left to go check on his pops. After getting to his pop's house they chatted for a minute, then he found out the real reason he called him over. Then Levell dialed Sharee.

"Hey baby," she answers.

"Babe, I have something for you."

"Oh, okay what is it?" she smiled.

"I'll be back through there in a minute, I'm still at my pops house."

"Okay babe," they hung up. Once his pop was ready to head out he made a stop back by Sharee's house. Levell handed her some money. Her smile grew bigger. Sharee looked down at the money then looked back up at him.

"What's this for baby?" she asked him as she reached for it.

"For whatever you may need it for."

"Awww, thank you, I so appreciate it," she smiled.

Sharee took the money then gave him a hug.

"Thank you."

"You're very welcome."

"Well, I was just stopping back by to give you that."

"Oh, you're leaving?"

"Oh, I have to go to the airport."

"Oh, ok."

"Yeah, I have to take my dad to the airport."

"Where's he going?" she asked.

"To Toronto to see my Aunt," he replied back.

"Oh, okay."

"If I'm done early I will call you to see if you're up and I'll come back."

"Okay," they kissed and then he left.

After she was done with the laundry she was about to start folding the clothes, but then her cell rang. She smiled, she knew it was Levell, but looking down at her cell it wasn't, it was Stephanie. "Hey Steph," she answered.

"Hey girl," Sharee was on the phone with Stephanie as she had started folding up the laundry.

"What you doing?"

"Just got through washing clothes and just barely started folding them now."

"Okay, get it out the way."

"Girl me, I would have that stuff in the laundry basket almost a whole week before I put it away, by that time it's time to wash all over again."

Sharee laughed, "I know what you're saying, that's why I have to get it out the way now because if I wait until later I'm not going to feel like doing it."

"Okay, so have you talked to your honey?"

"Yeah, he just left."

"Oh really, I heard that, what were y'all two love birds doing?"

"Nothing really, he came over to see me, we talked then he gave me some money."

"For what?" she asked Sharee.

"I don't know, just because."

"Oh, that was nice of him."

"I know right."

"Wish somebody give me some damn money."

Sharee laughed.

"Girl, I'm for real."

"Well, I'm so happy for your happiness with him Sharee, for real girl."

"Well, I had prayed for a good man for a while now. I'm like thank you God for sending him to me."

"Yes, that's what he does honey, he answers prayers."

"Amen to that."

Shortly after Sharee and Stephanie hung up. A few hours passed since Levell was there and yet she looked at her clock on her nightstand, it was getting later and later and still no call from Levell yet. She went and pulled out her night gown from out her drawer and slipped it on and sat back down on her bed watching more TV; twenty minutes passed, she was beginning to get sleepy. *Ok, I'm going to wait another ten minutes.* Once the ten minutes passed she turned off her TV and her night lamp and became comfortable on her pillow. Another ten minutes passed and Sharee's phone rang. It was Levell calling.

"Hello," she answered.

"Aww, you sleep?"

"I barely closed my eyes."

"I'm sorry."

"Oh no, it's fine."

"Well call me as soon as you wake up."

"You're not coming?" she asked.

"You still want me to come and you're already going to sleep?"

"Well you might as well, you already have me up."

"Alright, I'm on my way."

"Alright," they hung up.

Sharee was planning on taking her shower early in the morning once she woke up if he wasn't coming over, but now that he's on his way she decided to get up and take a quick shower before he got there. Once he made it there he rung her doorbell and she walked down the stairs to open the door for him. As soon as Sharee opened her door, they both smiled, they were both happy to see each other even though it's late in the night. Levell had a bowl of banana pudding in his hand. He handed it to her.

"This is from my mother, it's the best you'll ever have."

"Oh yeah," she replied.

"Yes."

"I will take it to work tomorrow."

"I had a bowl too, as you see I already ate it," he laughed.

"Tell your mom I said thank you," Sharee put her bowl in the fridge. It was late, they kissed each other and walked straight up stairs and went to sleep. They both had a long day and they had to both get up early. They both left out at the same time that morning, they hugged and then got into their cars. Sharee looked back and waved bye to Levell as she was pulling off. He waved back to her and then he pulled off.

In a few days it will be Valentine's Day, he was excited he had so much planned and she didn't even know it. Once Tuesday approached it was Valentine's Day, he stopped by her job to take her, her gifts. He gave her a big red heart box of chocolates, a dozen roses, and a bottle of wine. This was special, but this is what he did for her all the time so this was nothing new, every weekend or every other weekend was Valentine's Day with him.

He plans a big surprise for Sharee, it was another part of her Valentine's Day gift. She thinks he went back to work, but he had already requested this day off weeks back. She was at work, so he had enough time to go to the store to get everything he needs. He bought two life adult size bears that were holding a red heart that says *I Love You* and then he blew up eighty red and eighty pink balloons by mouth. He wanted to fill the whole entire room up with balloons. Several hours later it was almost time for her to get off by the time he was about done blowing up all those balloons. He was trying to hurry up. Levell's cell started going off. It was her.

"Hey babe," he answered.

"Hey babe how is work going?"

He hesitated to try to think of something fast to say without spoiling the surprise. "Umm, it was good I guess, the good part is that I got off early."

"I hear you on that," she sounded.

"How about you babe, How is work going for you?" he asked her.

"I just got off early too, I was trying to beat you home and surprise you with a nice dinner, but it looks like you just might beat me home."

"A-a-ha," he laughed. "Aww, how sweet. Babe, just because I might beat you home that doesn't mean you can't still hook something up."

"I was any way, it's Valentine's Day, I have too," she told him.

As she's talking, he's quickly preparing their plates on the table making it all fancy with pink and red Valentine's decorations on the table, the food was still hot. He lit the candles. The balloons were almost done now. Now he just wanted everything to go like he'd planned.

"Babe, I love you," he said.

"I love you too, I can't wait to get home to you and cook you up something good," she said.

"Well, alright babe, I guess I'll see you at the house. Aye babe, let me call you right back, this is my job calling."

"Alright," she sounded. "I hope they're not going to tell you to come right back to work."

"I hope they don't babe!"

Levell had only a little time to hurry up with these damn balloons, he had just a few more, this is why he's glad he took today off and he's glad that he had cooked dinner first. The plates are already made sitting on the table, candles on the table along with her gift and a bucket of ice with her favorite bottle of champagne. Rose petals were spread all over the bed with a box of chocolate covered strawberries in the center of the bed. Doing all this was a first for him with the balloons and rose petals. But he had to make it extra special for his special lady. When Sharee pulled up Levell was already there out front in front of the house wiping down his car. He was trying to play it off like he'd just gotten there. He threw his towel down on his car and walked over to Sharee.

"Hey babe," she laughed.

"Hey, baby."

"So, you beat me home I see," she sounded.

"I just pulled up too, I haven't even been inside yet."

"Why not?" she asked him.

"Oh, I just pulled up and started wiping down my car, it was looking a little dusty."

She glanced over at his car.

"It's looking good to me babe."

"Yeah now," he chuckled. Then she laughed. They kissed and hugged. Then they both were headed to the front door together, him leading the way.

"Is the door open?"

"No, I told you I haven't even been in yet."

Since Levell didn't use the spare keys she keeps under the door mat, he stepped to the side so she could unlock the front door. Sharee unlocked the front door and his eyes were already looking at her from the side smiling, he wanted to see her expression.

"Ahhh!" her mouth fell open, she laughed and looked at him. He was looking at her smiling.

"Babe, you did all this!"

"Yes," he smiled.

"Oh my God babe, you are crazy!"

He stood there smiling excitedly over seeing her happy.

"Look at all these balloons; you blew up all these balloons? She looked at him. "You're crazy, this is a lot of balloons babe," she kissed and hugged him.

"That's not all," he said. Levell grabbed her hand walking her to the dining room table looking at the dinner he cooked for them too and her gift. She began to cry tears of joy and happiness. She kissed him again on his lips.

"Babe, that's not it either," he said.

"Babe," she said as tears were still rolling down her face. He walked her to the room as she looks down at the rose petals leading their way.

"Aw, babe this is so beautiful." She was in love with her life size bear and the red and pink chocolate covered strawberries in the middle of the bed.

CHAPTER

16

The Special Day

Shante and Charles went away for the weekend to Sacramento.

"Wow, it has been a long time since I've been here, a lot has changed."

"Oh yeah, how long has it been since you've last been down here?"

"Ooh, it's been like seven years now."

Shante grinned. They made it to his family's house. They walked up the porch and he rang the doorbell.

His cousin Sandra answered the door. "Wow, what a surprise cousin, it's been seven long years since you last came to visit me," Charles hugged her.

"I know, yeah it has been a long time," Charles walked in holding Shante's hand. Everyone looked at the two saying hi.

"You still look the same, Charles."

"Family, I want you all to meet my fiancé Shante," Charles introduce her to all his family, even the little cousins. She spoke and hugged everyone. This was a surprise, but they were all happy to meet her. His family didn't know he was coming and then bringing Shante, he wanted it all to be a surprise. The only thing they knew about her is that he really liked her and that she was beautiful and has her stuff together, that's all they knew, it was a pleasant surprise to finally meet her in person. After their first thirty minutes of talking with her they already liked her, by that night they all had fallen in love with her. Shante was sweet and they all showed her so much love.

Shante and Charles were both having a good time with the family he had that lived out there. His cousin, Leona called their other cousin Denise, then the rest of his cousins were all on their way to see him and his fiancé too. Some were already there, but now they were waiting on everyone else to come over to the house. That night they gave a big dinner, enough for everyone. During the dinner, Charles felt it was a perfect time since everyone was there to tell everyone at the same time about his and Shante's wedding in three weeks.

"In three weeks you guys getting married!" Leona and Sandra shouted.

Charles and Shante both shook their heads yes.

They were all surprised, but very happy for the both of them, they all told them congratulations. Their Friday night dinner turned into a celebration. They only stayed down there for one night. The next morning waking up his cousin cooked a big breakfast they continued sharing old memories with Shante. By noon Charles and Shante were back on the road.

Getting back Shante's mother had called. "Hey mom," she answered.

"Hey, Shante you sleep already, baby?"

"I'm tired, we just got back home driving from Sacramento seeing Charles's family down there, what's going on mom?"

"Oh, okay, nothing baby. I was just calling to check on you, so time is coming really fast I can't wait to see my daughter in her beautiful dress."

"I can't wait until you see it too."

"How was Sacramento?"

"It was nice, I enjoyed myself. I met a lot of his family down there, they cooked up a lot of food, they were really nice," Shante told her.

"That's right."

"Yeah, I'm glad we decided to take that drive because at first, he wanted to just tell them over the phone about the wedding, but then we decided to just take the drive down there."

"So they're coming to the wedding?"

"Yeah, they are really excited too."

"That's right."

The two talked a while longer, then they hung up. Shante was still tired from the driving so she lay back down and closed her eyes. Lying down with her eyes closed, an hour passed and she realized she is still awake, she didn't know why she couldn't fall back to sleep as tired she was. So Shante got up from out the bed and walked to the living room where Charles was still sitting at watching the game that he had pre-recorded.

"What's the score?" she asked.

"Twenty-one and thirteen," he responded as his eyes didn't leave the TV screen.

"And this is the second quarter?"

"Yes, and that means my team has a chance of winning."

Charles turned his head and looked at Shante. "Oh, babe the caterer called."

"Oh, what did she say?"

"She said she wanted to go over some food dishes and appetizers with us."

"Ok, cool, so which one is this one?" she asked him.

"The one with the husband, wife, and their two sons," he told her.

"Ok, did that other caterer company ever call your phone?"

"Yeah, they said they were booked for around that time."

"Oh, okay, well, I'm not tripping."

Shante went and sat at the dining room table and dialed Katrina. She put her cell to her ear as the line was ringing.

"Hello," Katrina answered.

"Hey lady, what'cha doing."

"Girl nothing, watching TV," Katrina replied.

"What you doing, what's going on Ms. Soon to be a married woman?" Katrina asked.

"I know right, girl nothing, over here tired and can't sleep. Look, I was thinking about strippers, I need some strippers."

"My sister knows some I'm sure, hold on let me call her on three-way."

"Okay," Shante held the phone. It was silent. Katrina had called her sister on three-way. "Hello Shante," Katrina sounded making sure she was still there.

"Yeah," Shante sounded. Then Brandy answered.

"Brandy."

"Yeah," she said.

"Brandy, Shante is on the line too, she needs some strippers for her Bachelorette party."

"Hey Shante," Brandy spoke.

"Hey Brandy. Please tell me you know of some good ones. Some fine ones."

Brandy was quiet for a few seconds while she thinks, and then she remembered she still had that card in her purse. "You know what, I do and they are brothers, they look good and they have been stripping for a long time. I don't know them, but I met one of the brothers one day when I was at the sex store. He was out promoting him and his brother business and he was saying they just barely turned it into a business, like doing parties; they were only doing it for a club before. But let me check my purse to see if I still

416

have their card," she searched her purse for that business card from that guy from the sex store. She found it and gave it to Shante. Shante called the Hamilton Brothers to book them for her bachelorette party February twenty seventh which was coming up in two weeks. This was going to be their first event so they told her they were not charging her. They planned to use her Bachelorette party as their promotion party. They didn't have the experience of a private party, but they both had the body and the experience dancing in strip clubs for years. They resembled each other, they looked like twins but they were five years apart with the looks that the ladies were going to love for sure.

FEBRUARY 27TH

It was the night of the Bachelorette party. The Hamilton Brothers were already there and ready, the ladies were already ready. They were ready to give a good show. This was their way to get their name out there. They wanted to make this out to be the best show these ladies ever seen.

Lorenzo looked at his brother, "Dre, you ready!"

"Yeah, I'm ready to give these ladies the best show they've ever seen."

Andre started off first coming in slowly taking off his shirt. He had a black basketball hat on, blue jeans and a six pack. The way he was moving his hips in circles had the ladies grabbing their dollars out their purses. Then he began grinding, moving that six pack of his up and down, had them all yelling out screams. His body was dancing to the playing music made Michelle's friend Cynthia be the first to put one of her dollars inside the back of his pants in his butt area. The way it was hanging off his oily butt, showing part of his butt, the crack and all almost made her want to pull it down. Andre began walking the floor walking around to the beat of the music gazing at all the women. As he saw the lady he was about to dance on first he began to do a dance in the center of the living room moving his shoulders and his arms in a pop locking motion as he moved his hips at the sound of the beat. Before he could even make it to the woman he was about to dance with first, he noticed four ladies Michelle, Sharee, and two of Shante's homegirls get up from their seats smiling and was coming his way. He then turned around and began dancing holding onto the wall and those four ladies began dancing all on him from behind. That lasted five minutes. Once they sat back down he turned around and two more ladies were coming his way putting money all over his oily chest. He began dropping it down to the floor and popping back up still dancing had the ladies going, more ladies came up to him still placing money into his loose jeans. Their tongues hanging out their mouths, the screaming had him giving them a good show.

Lorenzo came out and went straight for the woman of the night, Shante. The ladies loved the Hamilton Brothers. This free promotional party brought them, clients, the same night, the ladies were already booking them for parties; they had the ladies damn near coming out their clothes. This was their mood all around the room. Just as Lorenzo suspected the ladies were going to love them.

Charles and the boys were out. His brothers and his boys threw him a Bachelor party. They were having a good time

Wednesday, March 2, was Charles's birthday. Shante took her fiancé out to dinner and a movie, just the two of them for his birthday. They were all partied out. They didn't plan on partying until their reception.

Later that night they came back and went to sleep. The next morning Shante continued lying down until it was actually time to start her morning. She had a long night a few nights ago and then the other night she stayed up until the next morning until Charles made it home. Then taking him out last night she was still trying to recuperate, and still was tired and needed just thirty more minutes before getting out this bed.

***

Morning of March 5, 2016

Shante nervously went over her speech for the fortieth time.

"Why are you so nervous?" her dad asked her.

"I don't know, I guess the closer we're getting to walking down the aisle, the more nervous I'm becoming."

"Hey, Shante!"

Shante's head quickly turned around, "Hey Auntie, you made it!"

"Girl, you know I wasn't going to miss this for nothing in the world."

"Awww, thank you so much, this means a lot to me!"

"Shante, you look amazing in that dress."

"Awww, thank you cousin," Shante gave her Aunt and her cousin a hug."

Shante's nervousness went away when she saw her Florida family. Her new Sacramento family just showed up, even her San Diego family is now there too, she was so happy to see them all, especially her Florida family; the fact they flew in from so far meant everything to her. Seeing everyone that came from afar made her wedding day even more special.

The music began to sound, that was everyone's cue to go in. They walked in as rehearsed. Once Shante made it down the aisle to Charles she looked at him and they both smiled at each other, then they both faced the minister. The minister talked, they listened as he united them together in marriage amongst everyone in the church, they exchanged rings and then they kissed. They were now married. Following the ceremony was their reception. Shante was ready to toss her bouquet, after she tossed it she quickly turned around laughing; she wanted to see which one was going to catch it out of her girl Sharee or her sister in-law Michelle. Turning around she knew at least Sharee or Michelle was going to catch it, but it was Toni, a friend of the family and she has been married three times, hopefully, that bouquet gives her some luck.

The DJ began playing music, some were walking around mingling with others and some were dancing.

Shellie, Shante's cousin was walking towards her, "Congratulation cousin, I'm so happy for you, you're married now!"

"Thank you cousin, and I want to thank you again for not missing my wedding."

"Girl, you knew I wasn't going to miss this, but aye cousin, who is that buff dude with the dreads, he's looking good."

Shante turns around and looks in the direction her cousin is pointing at.

"Oh, that's Mike, that's my best friend Katrina's, husband."

"Oooh, he looks good."

"Girl, don't start, don't even look his way."

"Girl, he bet not look my way."

Shante's eyes narrowed in at her cousin with her serious face. "Shellie for real, there's plenty of other men here to look at!"

"Yeah, Yeah ok cousin."

"Thank you," Shante said.

"Man, I would fuck the shit out his ass!"

Shante quickly turned around looking at her cousin and nudged her with her arm, "Shellie!" she said.

"I'm sorry, I'm sorry, I just had to get that out my system," she laughed.

"Yes, please do, my girl Katrina will shut this shit down for her husband."

"I guess, if that was my husband I would too," Shellie couldn't stop staring at Mike.

"Yes, and I would do the same for mines."

She smiled. Shante walked off mingling with others, but still kept Shellie in her eye sight to make sure her eyes are from Mike.

Shante slid off and went to talk to her crew.

"Hey, boos!"

"Hey boo," Katrina, Sharee, and Michelle said back.

"Hey, come here Katrina," Katrina got up from the table with her drink in her hand smiling.

"Hey!" Katrina sounded.

"Girl, why not too long ago my cousin was like *cousin, who is that buff dude with the dreads*, I looked and I was like *that's my best friend's husband.*"

"Un Un," Katrina sounded with a smile.

"She was all losing her mind over him girl. I was like *girl, you bet not look his way, my girl will shut this whole wedding reception down*," she chuckled.

Katrina bust out laughing, she thought it was funny. "That's right boo, thanks for letting her know."

"Girl yeah, I had too before her ass become another Brandy in this motherfucker and get her ass beat in front of everybody," they both laughed.

***

Weeks later Michelle thought about them Hamilton Brothers. She wanted to throw a naughty girl party and have them there. She called Katrina so they could get the girls rounded up and ready once again.

"Hey sis," Katrina answered.

"Hey sis, so what do you think about me throwing a naughty girl party?"

"Ooh girl, you nasty," Katrina told her and smiled.

"If I throw a naughty girl party you're coming right?"

"You know I'm there sis!"

"Now who's nasty," Michelle laughed.

"You should call the ones who did Shante's Bachelorette party."

"Yes, girl you know I am."

"Oh wait, hold up, I still have their flyers in my purse," Katrina went through her purse looking for the flyers, as soon as she saw the flyers she pulled out one of them to read out the number to her. Michelle was ready to write down the number, then Katrina began reading it.

To Reserve call the Hamilton Brothers the exotic dancers call 323-892-1043 now.

"Un huh girl, yes please call them brothers. But they don't have anything on your brother."

"Hell yeah, I'm calling them now to reserve them. Yeah, my brother wish he had their moves," she chuckled.

"Leave my baby alone," Katrina chuckles.

"Are they really brothers?"

"Yes girl!"

"Oh, ok."

"Speaking of brothers, I hope your brother doesn't get made that I'm about to see them again."

"Yeah, you and Shante's ass all married and shit, Sharee almost married."

"Almost married," Katrina chuckled. "Girl, you a fool!"

"For real, the way they are they acting like it and shit," she chuckled. "I can't believe I'm still single," Michelle muttered. Her mind began to wonder; *Clearly my standards were way too high and I don't care, I know one day, I don't know when, but I know just one day God is going to send the type of man I want*, she thought to herself.

"Sis, won't you come over and have a glass of wine with me," Michelle says.

"Alright, be there shortly."

Katrina thought she should go over to her house since she always comes to hers, she made it over and Michelle already had their glasses ready.

The two chatted and sipped their wine. After finishing their glass of wine, Michelle poured them more. After five glasses they both had enough.

"Alright sis, it's been real, I enjoyed myself once again."

"I enjoyed you too sis," the two hugged.

"I'm about to get home and cook up some dinner for your brother."

"That's right, what are you going to cook?"

"You know what, that's a good question, I'm not even sure yet, I'm about to go see what's in that freezer that's not going to take all night to cook."

"I heard that."

They gave each other another hug, then Katrina left. Michelle closed her front door after Katrina left out

Later in the day Michelle called and booked the Hamilton Brothers for her naughty girl party. The party was a month away, but Michelle and all her girls were ready for them brothers.

The day of the party getting things together up until the start of the party was hectic, but Michelle made sure everything was handled and got it all done. Michelle even had a nice big banner made that said: "Naughty Girl Party Pleasure Me." The Hamiltons came to show out and to bless her party with great body and good eye candy they all were going to enjoy.

The brothers had arrived and tonight the Hamilton Brothers were coming to give these ladies a show. They had their black leather pants on, no shirts, black leather vest, and red scarves wrapped around half their faces only showing their eyes and up. They both walked in dancing, these ladies were ready for them tonight. As soon as they began to walk pass the ladies dancing they were already putting money down their pants. These brothers had a routine tonight, they both began grinding their hips right in front of the ladies, they had them reaching out at their crouch area and smiling.

These ladies loved them and they had only been there for three minutes. They were dancing with two women at a time. These ladies were dropping money on their chest, Lorenzo began to do his solo dance. They took it back old school, grinding to the songs had them screaming and dancing with him. He was in the middle of the floor grinding, acting like he had a woman in front of him. Then the song to an oldie which was a Luther Vandross song, that's when his pants came off, it had everyone up out of their seats. Lorenzo was doing more than dancing, he was lip singing to the song as well.

Michelle's friend Keisha got right in front of him with a stack of money and with every movement he was making she was slapping money down gently onto his chest, her girl was throwing money down right at him on the floor like she was passing cards in a card game. But then the next song changed to R. Kelly, he walked the floor to see who he was about to grab. Michelle screamed out and pointed down to her girl Tamika.

"It's her birthday. It's her birthday!" she screamed out.

424

Secret Love 3: *The Saga Don't Stop*

Lorenzo stepped to the birthday girl *"Tamika,"* as he was still dancing he pulled her to the middle of the floor; she stood there and let his fingers do all the work. He began teasing and touching on her breast then to her vagina with the tip of his fingers to the sound of the music. Her vagina is where his fingers stayed rubbing all on it. Then after a few seconds he licked his fingers then placed both hands onto her hands raising them up in the air where she kept them while his hands were placed on her breast moving his hands around on them in a circular motion as he sings R. Kelly's *"Imagine That"* song. Then his hands instantly went down to her waist grabbing her and flipping her upside down as he held her tight in his arms. Their stomachs were touching as she was upside down holding on to his calves. Then he lifted her up in the air onto his shoulders with his hands on her waist, her knees on his shoulders, his face was inside her dress in between her legs, and her hands were on his six pack. Then he slid her back down where both their stomachs are back against each other, her hands were gripped on his butt holding on. He then laid her down easily onto the floor right next to the can of whip cream and the bottle of chocolate he had. He picked up his whip cream and his bottle of chocolate and began shaking his can of whip cream as he walked around her staring down at her. All the ladies were screaming, feeling all hot and horny watching what he was about to do next to Tamika.

His brother Andre passed him a big brown towel that he used to place over and in-between her legs, then he spread her legs wide open leaving them up in the air as he placed whip cream on her center area as he's still singing that same R. Kelly song. He sprayed the whipped cream in circles followed by the chocolate he added. Then he hopped up and then slid down onto the floor and underneath the towel, he began licking off the whip cream and chocolate from off her center. After licking off all the whip cream he sprayed, it was his brother Andre's turn to do his solo.

Andre came out walking up dancing and rotating his hips up on Michelle's Latino home girl Melissa, he hadn't done anything to her yet and she was already putting money down the front of his pants. He grabbed her hair that hung down her back, then he got on top of her seating on her lap grinding on top of her. As he slowly took off his vest she began rubbing all over his oily chest. He began flexing his chest, that made her put dollars all over his chest.

He got up and began dancing in the center of the floor. He was working that body of his and had everyone up screaming and throwing money. He jumped down on the floor, he was all over the floor humping the floor. He went from humping the floor, shaking his butt, and then hitting the floor and spinning around on the floor with his tongue sticking out his mouth flicking it up and down.

Michelle's girl Jessica walked closer to him throwing money right on top of him. Her coworker Beatrice was waving her money in the air smiling, he noticed her and raised his finger telling her to come here. He stood up from off the floor and made her lick all over his chest. Then he turned her around and brought her down to the floor as he squatted down and began humping on her butt. Beatrice couldn't do anything but smile and laugh while she takes it. Some of Michelle's and Beatrice's other coworkers came over to them and began throwing money down on them.

He saved his last dance for the host of the party. Andre leaned his head down towards Michelle putting his head down at her crouch; he began to eat her out through her pants as she sat on the chair. After the dance, his brother came out to the center of the floor and gave each other a high five and then everyone began clapping for them.

Then after all the claps Andre went and talked to Michelle, thanking her for having them for her party. Lorenzo went back to go talk to Tamika.

Michelle had made both of them a plate. She made it to go, but Andre took the foil off his and ate his right then. As Lorenzo was still with the birthday girl, the music came back on. Andre had started back dancing, a lady he was dancing on, now he had her bent over while he danced on her from behind. Lorenzo saw his brother and start dancing along with him. The look on the other ladies face was the look of them trying to wait their turn; they were truly turned on by all of this. Lorenzo and Andre recalled seeing most of their faces at the promotional party for the bachelorette party two months ago. After the party was now finally over Lorenzo walked over to Tamika the birthday girl, giving her a hug.

"You enjoy your birthday tomorrow," he told her.

"I already did thanks to you."

"I'm glad you did," he handed her some of his business cards and asked her if she could give them out to her friends.

"Of course I can," she replied.

"Thank you," then he began to walk away.

"Hey," she said quickly. Lorenzo turned around to her.

"Bye, I really enjoyed myself, you and your brother did y'all thing tonight baby," she walked up to him to give him another hug. Hugging him back again, this time his teeth grazed her left earlobe then he whispered in her ear.

"Come with me," he whispered.

"Huh," she replied with a smile.

"Come with me."

"Come with you," she repeated back to him as she looks at him strange, her smile continued.

"I'm Lorenzo and yours?"

"Tamika," she told him.

"Put my number in your phone."Tamika already had her phone in her hand. *"What is it?" Tamika asked, he gave it to her then asked if she can call it.* She called it.

"Alright, cool, now I have yours to see you in a minute."

Minutes later Lorenzo looked around and didn't see Tamika anywhere. Lorenzo texts her it reads, *"Where you at?"*

She replied, *"Oh, I left, where you at?"*

He replied back to her, *"I'm still at the house, I was waiting for you."*

Tamika texted back, *"Oh, my bad, didn't know you meant right now."*

Lorenzo had texted her, *"yes."*

"Oh, okay, I'm turning back around now," Tamika replied.

Lorenzo text Tamika back, *"Alright."*

Tamika wasn't far at all, she pulls back up on Michelle's street. Her phone rings, it was Lorenzo.

"That's you that just turned on the block?"

"Yeah," she sounded.

"I'm in the black Audi with the headlights flashing."

She pulls up right beside him, he starts smiling. "Hey," he said to her, he couldn't stop smiling. Then a smile abroad her face, as she shakes her head.

"Are you coming with me?"

"Sure, I guess I can come." She followed him. She began following him to what seemed to be a hotel coming up. Getting to the hotel they both got out of their cars. After he paid for their room, they walked to it as he began talking making conversation.

"So Tamika, do you have a man? I mean not that it matters because we already here," he grins.

"Actually I don't."

"Why is that, what you just don't want one?"

"I do, just haven't met anyone who really wants something serious, which is very crazy."

"Yeah, I hear you on that, the ones I run into act like I can't be trusted just because I'm a dancer."

As she sat in the chair next to him, he sat on the edge of the bed. She couldn't help herself after just a few minutes. "I just want a kiss," she said to him, they kissed as her left hand slid down his chest on to his penis. She rubbed it from the top to the bottom down to his balls area, then she came back up slowly. They began kissing again. One thing, of course, was leading on to another. She got on top of him and he suddenly slid it in, letting her feel all of him. She was riding him and clenching herself tight. He was going in and out of her continuously, the more pleasure he felt the deeper he went inside her, pulling her closer to him with each thrust. He felt himself wanting to cum.

"You want me to cum," he asked her, but she shook her head no.

"Damn baby, you going to make me cum doing it like that."

"I know the person who was getting this mad they aren't getting this anymore."

She looked at him and grinned as she continued. His hands curved her butt tighter. "Damn," he sounded. They began to go faster, both their eyes were closed as their moaning became louder, bed squeaking noises even became louder. Once they were done they stayed still, neither one wanted to move from out their position. Moments after is when he slid it out.

"Tamika, you make me just want to say fuck everything and say I'm coming with you."

Afterward, she lay on his chest looking up at him as he rubbed her back and her arms with both his hands. Looking back at her into her eyes, he's thinking he has found his woman.

Later that night, Lorenzo refused leaving her without making her his, he was already falling for her, but she had no emotions yet, due to the fact she was horny she wanted some of him and once the question was asked to her, *could you be my girl*, she grinned. Tamika didn't answer his question, but her gaze became deeper into his eyes and she leaned to him giving him a kiss on his lips.

Epilogue

Michelle invited her brothers and their wives and Sharee and Levell out with her to one of her girlfriends party. She was the only single one. It was a launch party at the club celebrating her getting her own radio station. They all met up at Michelle's house and she rode with Mike, Katrina, Brandy, and Terrell and then Sharee and Levell rode with Charles and Shante. There was no need in taking five different cars. They were all dressed sharply, everyone was looking good. Arriving at the club they all walked in, everyone sat at the first table they saw that had many chairs to fit them all. Michelle stepped away for a moment to try and find her girl to let her know that she'd made it. As she walked around she was seeing so many fine men, but of course, they were with their women. *Wait,* not all of them, but most as she continued to walk around towards the back there was a gentleman who stopped her. She stopped, he was damn good looking, fine as hell, and dressed very well.

"What's your name beautiful?" he held his hand out to shake hers being a gentleman. As she quickly scanned his hand for a wedding band she looked back up and smiled, making eye contact she shook his hand.

"Hello, my name is Michelle!"

"You are so beautiful, I had to stop you!"

"Well thank you," she smiled.

"I would like to know if it would be possible that I take you out sometime?" he asked.

"Sure." They both exchanged numbers, then she went back to searching for her girl. Once she found her they hugged, chatted, took a selfie, then Michelle went back to her table. Getting to the table the fellas had already ordered everyone some hot wings and fries. They all were talking as they waited for their food. Michelle was so happy she met a man tonight, like one she could finally see herself dating.

Acknowledgments

My acknowledgments go first to God for it is He who is still blessing me to do what I love to do, which is put out page turners that readers love to read. I am grateful and I am blessed.

My children Bryant Jr., Brandon, Derrick Jr. and Daijah, I appreciate all four of your patience through the long days, nights and months of writing until I was finished. Also for your understanding of the "quiet", I needed during my editing time of my book, and for the excitement, you all had for my characters through the process up until I was done, all the way down to my book cover. Thank you for believing in your mom as an Author and touring with me to different cities, bookstores and book events to take pictures and to pass out my flyers. I love you four, you are my motivation.

To all my relatives who in one way or another shared their support by either verbally telling others about me and my books or by buying my book when they come out, I truly appreciate it, thank you and I love you.

To everyone who prays for my success and my books, your prayers and kind and encouraging words mean the world to me. God bless you and I'm truly thankful for you all. I can't say thank you enough for being in my life some type of way through my book journey.

During this project I'd also want to thank Tyra Shaw who also enjoys this Secret Love Series just as much as I, with your help and time you offered to read my book being my second eye, I needed that. You are awesome and I thank you.

Another special acknowledgment goes to my Market Manager Darrell Frye, for always taking my vision with all my projects and giving me just what

I'm looking for each and every time. You are awesome and I truly appreciate you and I truly love my book cover you designed.

Also to Johnny Frost, I want to say a special thank you for all the help you gave me, I have known you for two years now and you are a wonderful friend and a great person inside and out. It is a great pleasure every time we are in the presence of each other and you have truly been a great help to me and to my company in this project and I want to say thank you.

Last but not least I want to say a very special thank you to the people reading this right now, my readers. I want to truly thank you for your endless support and for choosing to keep my book as your reading option.
I look forward to reading your book reviews. Please leave all reviews on Amazon. Also visit my website www.moorehousebooks.com for all my latest releases, products and upcoming events and book signings. Also, leave me your email on my contact page to be added to my email list.

I Have More

My Point of View
Message
Reading Group Questions
Other books by Author

My Point Of View

My intentions with this book was to continue spreading the love because everyone needs it. Remember, it's the small things that matter, like saying I love you, giving kisses, being romantic and cutting out all that unnecessary arguing. Oh, and not to mention, building each other up. But for reading and entertainment purposes I still had to bring you the juicy drama because it's entertaining, especially when you are reading it and it's not involving you. This Secret Love Series touch basis on all different aspects that take place in relationships, marriages, friendships, workplaces, churches, etc. Sometimes it could be just the smallest thing or something that could have gone differently that could have saved the relationship or marriage when something's not going like it should because the relationship/ marriage tend to change when the couple changes. This Novel will help save relationships and marriages to repair and strengthen, it will help not end in a breakup or divorce if we could focus on the main thing which is love, communication, consistency, happiness, loyalty, the family, building each other up, the relationship and the marriage. This series is a great read for both women and men.

This was and is a series that can continue. This series reads just like a movie, I truly love this Secret Love Series not because I wrote it, but because I really do, and because the feedback I get from this series is nothing but awesome. So to the reader reading this right now, help me save some people right now, for that person or friend who think they have to use their body as a tool to get things they want, or for that friend who is stuck in an abusive relationship and you as their friend don't know how to tell them, let me tell them for you through my character's actions, help me save some relationships and marriages right now by spreading the word about my Secret Love Series, or even for that friend who thinks the intimacy is gone in their relationship, let me help them gain that back through my characters. Let them know where they can go to purchase. Thank you.

Message

Learn to know the person inside to know who you are really dealing with, it could all be just an illusion or it could just be the real deal. Just remember to make things clear in the beginning. Find yourself a life partner, one you can marry and stay married too, not just anyone to sleep a night or two with.

Book Discussion Topics for Book Clubs

1. After reading this novel why is communicating honestly important?

2. Have you ever kept secrets from your husband or wife that they found out about anyway? Why did you keep the secret?

3. So what do you think about Brandy's and her daughter Paige's relationship?

4. Reading this book do you think this is how love is supposed to go and/or start off? Everyone shows love in their own different way. How much of your own relationship can you compare to the different couples in this book?

5. What part in the book was your favorite scene, is either your favorite or that it reminds you of yourself?

6. Should Asia have given Gary a chance to do better after finding out he and Paula had relations knowing his past? Although he didn't do that again he proved to her he is worth staying with. What are your thoughts on that?

7. How would you have handled the news coming from the other woman about a child you knew nothing about that your husband has with her? Would you have handled it like Asia if it was you? How would you have handled it?

8. Although any and all children need to stay in a child's place and be respectful to all adults, was Paige wrong for expressing her feelings finally after all this time about her mother's behavior?

9. Should Asia had done what she did to Paula's car after finding out her husband started back sleeping with her? After all, she knew the

type of man she married and still stayed with him and she was the one to reach out to her first asking the questions she asked.

10. Once Paula asked Gary the question, "Can we sleep together?" Why didn't he just leave right then? Yes, he said the right thing in response "I don't want to jeopardize my marriage again," but his statement didn't stand. Why do most men give in so easy forgetting about what they have at home?

11. How do you like Shante's and Charles's relationship in this Secret Love part 3 Novel: The love, respect and consistency they have for each other in their relationship? Is this something you wish you had or do you already have this now in your relationship?

12. Do you think Sharee should have waited longer than what she did before getting involved in another relationship?

13. Was Asia's sisters wrong for getting involved in her and Gary's marriage with all the questioning and spying on him?

14. How did you enjoy the Hamilton Brothers, did they entertain you good enough? Would you like more of them in this series? Which one did you enjoy more? Which one turned you on and got you moist down there?

15. In this Secret Love Part 3 novel, what does Mike's Sister Michelle bring to the book? What type of character does she play?

16. Based on Mike's character in this series as a husband, stepfather and father do you think it's hard to find a man like him in real life? Do you already have a man like him? What's the difference from Mike in this series compared to your real life man?

17. What do Mike's and Katrina's relationship and marriage bring to this series and what could people/readers take from it to use in their own relationships?

18. If you could name at least three things, what would you name that could bring strength, growth, and romance into your relationship or marriage from this book?

19. Should Asia have been in shock after finding out her husband slept with an ex?

Please don't forget to have each person leave reviews

on Amazon.com

type in lashane moore

Other Books By Author LaShane Moore

Secret Love 1

You can purchase book from

my website www.moorehousebooks.com

Secret Love 2

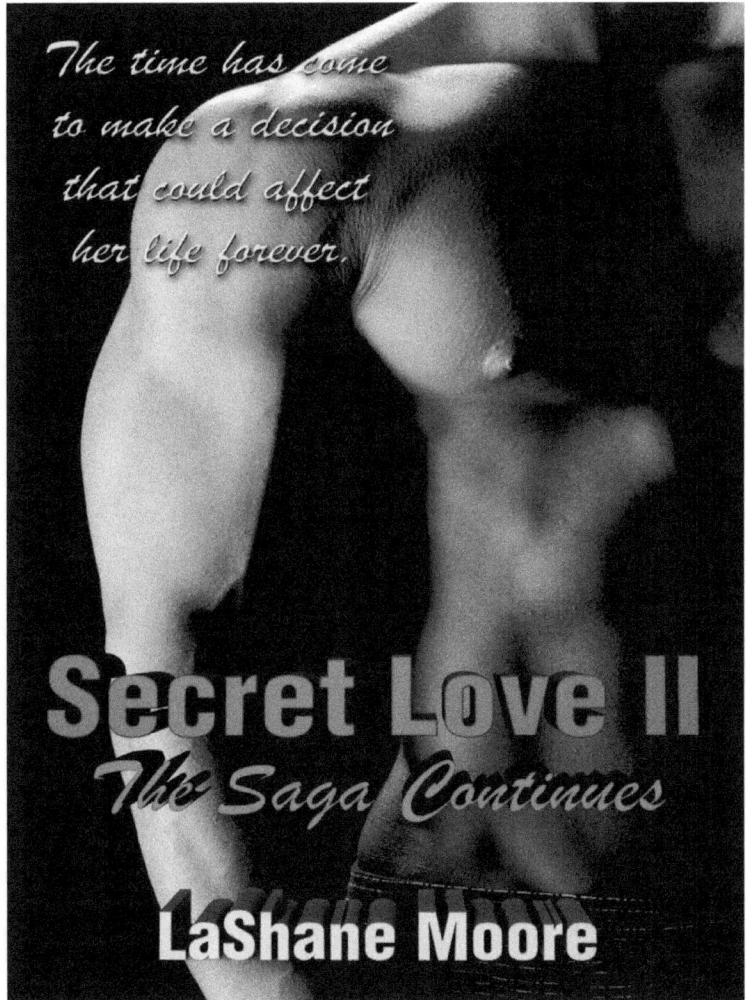

You can purchase book from

Having It His way

You can purchase book from

my website www.moorehousebooks.com